MW00576063

WHAT WE'LL BURN LAST

Also by Heather Chavez

Blood Will Tell

No Bad Deed

Before She Finds Me

WHAT WE'LL BURN LAST

HEATHER CHAVEZ

Little, Brown and Company
New York Boston London

Mulholland Books / Little, Brown and Company
Hachette Book Group
1290 Avenue of the Americas, New York, NY 10104
mulhollandbooks.com

First Edition: July 2024

Mulholland Books is an imprint of Little, Brown and Company, a division of Hachette Book Group, Inc. The Mulholland Books name and logo are trademarks of Hachette Book Group, Inc.

The publisher is not responsible for websites (or their content) that are not owned by the publisher.

The Hachette Speakers Bureau provides a wide range of authors for speaking events. To find out more, go to hachettespeakersbureau.com or email hachettespeakers@hbgusa.com.

Little, Brown and Company books may be purchased in bulk for business, educational, or promotional use. For information, please contact your local bookseller or the Hachette Book Group Special Markets Department at special.markets@hbgusa.com.

ISBN 9780316531658
LCCN 2024932900

Printing 1, 2024

LSC-C

Printed in the United States of America

For the Chavezes,
my chosen family. I know I can count on you
for love, support, and future alibis.

WHAT WE'LL BURN LAST

CHAPTER 1
LEYNA

Ten days earlier

In profile, the young woman seated in Leyna Clarke's section looked so much like her sister that she nearly dropped a plate of chorizo and eggs. Then the young woman shifted in her chair, and her nose was a little too long, her mouth a little too wide.

Not Grace.

It will never be Grace.

After sixteen years, Leyna understood that. Most days, anyway. Still, it didn't stop her from looking for her sister in every woman who was the right height or had the right shade of strawberry-blond hair or from wanting the stranger to be Grace so intensely that the scar on her forearm began to itch. Hands full, she couldn't scratch, and the itch flared, hot and insistent.

The past hated to be ignored.

Apparently, so did the two men at table thirty-four. One of them cleared his throat loudly enough that Leyna at first worried he might be choking. She pulled her attention away from the strawberry blonde to focus on the man with the phlegmy throat, but she felt the other woman's presence like a pulse beneath her scar.

The man, shaved head a deep coral with the heat, cleared his throat again and waved aggressively at the plate she carried. "Think we can get that while it's still warm?"

"Oh. Yeah. Sorry."

She set the plate between the bald man and his companion, forcing a wide smile. Although it was early in her shift, her cheeks already throbbed, but she really needed the tips to make rent. Leyna had worked at the café since moving to Reno at eighteen, and with the run of triple-digit temperatures, it was the deadest she'd ever seen it in the ten years since. Especially her section on the patio. Despite the spray misters, overlapping umbrellas, and tiny fans they handed out to the customers, the outdoor seating remained mostly empty. Even the potted trees that lined the stamped concrete looked like they were headed for the door, leaves drooping slightly as if flagging for the check.

"Can I get you anything else?" she asked, casting a sideways glance toward the back of the patio. Why had the young woman been seated there? With a choice of two- and four-tops, the host should've put her inside, or at least closer to the other tables.

The bald man shook his head as he shoveled eggs onto the toast plate, the spicy scent of the chorizo heavy on the feeble breeze. One breakfast special to share, along with the two waters she'd delivered earlier.

Definitely won't make rent off table thirty-four.

Excusing herself, Leyna wiped her palms on her jeans. Her former manager had let the servers wear Bermuda shorts when the weather grew unbearable, but Stefan was far more rigid. Black or dark blue jeans only, no rips. White collared shirts, no more than one button undone. When Leyna pointed out that he managed a café and not the French Laundry, Stefan had scheduled her for Tuesday-afternoon shifts on the patio. Even now, she caught him glaring at her from inside the restaurant. Waiting for her to make another mistake.

Ignoring Stefan, Leyna hurried toward the back of the patio where the strawberry blonde waited, gaze fixed on her phone. As Leyna drew closer, she saw the woman was even younger than she'd thought. Eighteen or nineteen, she guessed. Only a couple of years older than Grace had been when she'd disappeared. In her classic plaid skirt and green cap-sleeved blouse, she dressed a lot like Grace had too.

Fingertips brushing the smooth skin of her scar, Leyna made note of the two sets of silverware on the table. "Are you waiting on someone?"

"A friend."

The young woman seemed nervous as she stared at her phone, an older model with a cheap plastic case, and her nose wrinkled at whatever she saw on the screen. Her nails were short, the manicure fresh enough that lavender polish filled the grooves on both of her pinkies. On her wrist she wore a hinged, open gold cuff with a scarlet rose capping each end. The bits of red glass in the petals glinted in the harsh sunlight.

Finally, the girl set her phone on the table and looked up, and Leyna's breath caught mid-exhale. Though not the icy blue of Grace's eyes, the color was close enough that she felt a stirring in her chest. The young woman squinted, and Leyna took a step to the side, throwing the table in partial shade. Deprived of the sun, the stranger's hair darkened, no longer the golden-streaked red of Grace's. At her part, a quarter inch of roots grew a dark brown.

Leyna fought a surge of vertigo. *This isn't Grace,* she reminded herself. *The version of Grace she reminds me of no longer exists.*

Her sister would've been about to turn thirty-three. If she'd been alive, she might've started to develop faint lines at her mouth or eyes. Grace had laughed often—loudly and open-mouthed, more dare than invitation. At least until those last few weeks. The Grace who would've existed now might've cut her hair or even shaved her head. She'd talked once about doing that. She might've traded pastels for black or bold colors, both of which would've suited her better than the faded hues of delicate flowers easily crushed. Grace might've married, had kids, moved to Kyoto, started a band, been a banker. Leyna would never know which version of Grace she would've become, because she had been reduced to a cautionary tale. *Be careful who you love.*

When the young woman frowned slightly, Leyna realized she'd been staring. She tried to soften her gaze but she could feel the intensity in it. In reaction, the girl's eyes flashed too—worry? Surely not fear—before her expression faded again to bland sweetness. The kind of girl born to wear pastels.

Pull it together, Leyna. Stefan would fire her if he had to comp another meal.

Leyna used her shoulder to wipe sweat from her neck. "I'm sorry, it's just—you remind me a little of my sister."

The young woman offered a tentative smile—finally, a reason her server was behaving so oddly. "Are you close?"

We were, for a while. "You know sisters."

"I wish. I only have a younger brother, so it's not like I can even borrow his clothes. You from here?"

"Plumas County originally, but I've lived here since I graduated high school." Leyna shifted her weight on the balls of her feet, abruptly uncomfortable. "Would you like to get started with something to drink?"

"No, thank you. I'll wait."

The girl picked up her napkin and blotted her temples. The cheekbones that had looked as sharp as Grace's from across the patio now seemed more a trick of liberally applied contour, lightly smeared by the quick swipe of cotton.

"Sure you don't want me to move you inside where it's cooler?" She'd lose the tip, but the girl looked to be on the verge of heatstroke.

On the table, the young woman's phone buzzed once. Probably a text. She picked it up again, folded her fingers around it like it was a talisman. "My friend doesn't like crowds." She brought the phone to her chest, a gesture of protection—whatever message had flashed on its screen, she wanted to keep it private.

Leyna glanced at the makeup-smudged napkin. "There really aren't many people inside. I think there's even a spot open in the corner."

"I'm fine here." She tapped her phone with the pads of her fingers. "I'm Ellie, by the way. Actually, Elisa, but no one calls me that."

Leyna pointed to her name tag. "Leyna." She glanced at the guys on the other side of the patio, her only other table at the moment. Their water glasses were full, and they were lingering over their shared meal. She turned back to Ellie. "So who's the friend you're out here melting for?"

Though Leyna's tone was light, the young woman winced, then covered by sitting straighter in her chair.

"No one special," she said with a small smile that suggested the opposite. "How long have you worked here?"

"A while." Leyna was evasive too, but after what happened to Grace, she'd always been slower to trust. What was Ellie's reason?

With forced cheer, Ellie said, "Actually, I'll take you up on that drink."

"Sure. What'll you have?"

Ellie fidgeted, breaking eye contact. Tentative. In that way, she wasn't like Grace at all.

"I would love a mimosa," she said, gaze still averted.

Nice try. "Can I take a quick look at your ID?"

The young woman's cheeks flushed beneath her heavy makeup, and she made a show of checking her small purse. After a few seconds of fumbling, she looked up. "I must've forgotten it in the car."

Or several years in the future. "Would you like me to wait while you get it, or do you want something else for now? Maybe a lemonade or a soda?"

Hands clutching her small purse on her lap, Ellie nodded once. "A lemonade would be great."

"Coming up." She glanced toward the restaurant. "Let me know if you change your mind about sitting inside. The air-conditioning is mostly working today."

Ellie shook her head and twisted her hair in a knot. "That's okay. My friend's really private."

The flag that popped up in Leyna's brain wasn't just red, it was an electric flashing red. Though her *friend* might really be an introvert, he might also be married—or maybe he didn't want to be seen with a girl too young to order a mimosa.

Just how old was Ellie?

Ellie raised her napkin to her face again. The cotton came away smudged with more makeup. Her lips parted as if she were about to say more before curving into a slight smile.

"Can I please get that lemonade?"

"Of course."

Leyna hesitated, but the silence grew quickly awkward. Leyna moved away, slowly at first, stealing glimpses of Ellie as she made her way across the patio. The young woman bowed her head, fingers dancing across the screen of her phone. Texting her creepy and possibly married boyfriend? With her hair knotted at her nape, there was an awkward vulnerability to her. How many times had Leyna seen Grace in the same pose, bent over a textbook or curating the Polaroids she strung along her bedroom wall?

She blinked hard. *Stop it, Leyna.*

When she could no longer see the young woman, Leyna moved with renewed purpose to the bar; she grabbed a glass from the closest shelf, filled it first with ice and then with lemonade from a jug in the minifridge. The woman wasn't Grace, and the urge to be back in her company wasn't reasonable—but it was compelling. On her way back to the table, Leyna walked quickly, in such a hurry that the toe of her sneaker caught a dog bowl, sloshing water onto the concrete.

Leyna estimated she was gone about ninety seconds—no longer than two minutes, certainly—yet when she caught sight of Ellie again, the young woman was standing, gathering her purse. When Leyna got within a few feet of the table, Ellie's eyebrows quirked upward in apology.

"Um, sorry, but my friend's been held up." Her voice hitched. As her finger brushed the phone's screen, it illuminated, and Leyna caught a glimpse of it.

Adam.

Leyna set the lemonade down on the table before it could slip from her hands.

The name wasn't uncommon. Likely thousands of men named Adam lived in Reno alone.

Still, the only Adam she'd known well had a type—strawberry blondes with blue eyes. Girls who looked like Grace.

Ellie misread the silence, pulled a wallet from her purse. "I can pay you for the lemonade."

Leyna shook her head and forced the words off a sandpaper tongue: "Your friend's name is Adam?"

There was a shuttering of Ellie's eyes as she moved to leave. Leyna blocked her path. It was an aggressive gesture, but she didn't care, even when she sensed Stefan approaching from behind.

She pinned Ellie with her gaze. She heard someone calling her name—Stefan? The bald man at table thirty-four?—the voice warped by the blood roaring in her ears.

"What's Adam's last name?"

She took a step forward, and Ellie tried to retreat, but the table was at her back. There was nowhere for her to go. When Leyna grabbed her wrist, the girl flinched. The sharp edges of the roses on the girl's bracelet cut into Leyna's palm.

Ellie shook her head too hard to be convincing. "I don't know anyone named Adam."

Her eyes were bright. Curious, but maybe also afraid? She pulled away, leaving Leyna holding the bracelet. She held it out, an offering, but the young woman looked at it suspiciously, as if it were a snare waiting to be sprung. Her gaze drifted from Leyna to a spot over Leyna's shoulder. A spot now occupied by Stefan, who spoke Leyna's name, his voice firm but not so sharp as to offend the customer. "You're doing it again."

When Stefan put a warning hand on her arm, Leyna shook it off, focused only on the stranger who looked like her missing sister.

Leyna said, more forcefully, "I know it's Adam. I saw it on your phone. Is his last name Duran?"

Ellie's eyes widened, and Leyna knew she was right.

Ellie looked away quickly, gaze darting along the tree-lined path that Leyna blocked as if looking for a weakness in Leyna's barricade. The air seemed thicker than it had a moment before. Leyna's heart flailed in her chest like a trapped animal. She was suddenly sure that the *friend* Ellie had intended to meet was Adam Duran.

Then Ellie held up her phone. She covered the text with her hand, but the contact showed clearly:

Amaya.

For a moment, Leyna froze, stunned, which gave Ellie an opening. The other woman grabbed her bracelet and brushed past.

No. Don't go. I'm sorry.

But Leyna knew this girl wasn't the one she really wanted here or the one who deserved her apology. Or not her alone.

Leyna managed only a single step before Stefan grabbed her arm again, more tightly but still not as hard as she had grabbed Ellie's, and it took several seconds for her to wriggle free. By then, the girl who looked vaguely like Grace was gone. At least this time, it was only a lemonade Stefan would need to comp.

Scar tingling, Leyna bit her tongue so she wouldn't be sick.

CHAPTER 2

LEYNA

Friday, 6:25 p.m.

Ten days after meeting her sister's lookalike and losing her job, Leyna had established a new routine.

She would wake at six a.m. and check her phone, DMs, and email. Log onto her laptop. Pretend to look for a job before being distracted by Google News and the message boards.

These searches had always been as much about proving Adam's guilt as about finding Grace. For too many years, Leyna had alternated between those two competing beliefs in her head: Grace was alive; Adam had killed her. Most days, she believed—*needed* to believe—that her sister was out there, and Leyna just had to execute the perfect Google search to bring her home. But meeting that girl had started a familiar spiral. The darker theory insisted.

She would interrupt these daily searches with frequent snacks. Ramen, toast, bananas, black tea brewed in the fridge. Off-brand peanut-butter-cup ice cream she'd found on sale. Didn't matter what she ate. It all tasted like dust anyway.

Midday, she'd shower and change into her cleanest sweats. Or not. Then she'd update the poster-size sheets of white paper that covered her apartment walls as if she were a private investigator in some universally panned limited series. It was always like this when she was reminded of her sister in some major way. For weeks, she would replay her memories of that long-ago day, picking at the scabs to see if she could raise fresh blood.

Sometimes, if a new detail needed clarifying, she would place phone calls, or she'd submit a couple of job applications to maintain the illusion she might still make rent. Then it was back to the computer until sometime after midnight, brain and laptop battery exhausted, when she'd fall asleep with the lights on in a series of long blinks, staring at that day's updates scribbled in purple and brown ink on white paper, looking for connections that didn't exist and following clues that led nowhere. Her sister remained as much a ghost as she had been in the sixteen years since she'd disappeared.

That Friday, Leyna was standing inches from one of the sheets trying to determine if a late-night scrawl read *after* or *alter* when her cell phone vibrated on the coffee table. A prospective employer calling to schedule an interview? A friend asking if she wanted to hang out?

She walked to the table and leaned over to check the screen.

Private caller.

If it was a hiring manager calling about her application, the person would leave a message.

She returned her attention to the flip-chart sheets on the walls where she tracked Grace's case and other cases like hers. In spots, she'd taped photos printed on cheap copy paper. The only thing missing from her reconstruction were the four Polaroids Grace had removed from her bedroom wall the week she'd disappeared. Back then, Grace and her instant camera had been inseparable. Her sister had strung lengths of twine on the wall to clip her favorite photos to. When one string filled, she'd start another. String number six had been half empty the night Grace went missing. A twelve-year-old Leyna had pointed to that half-finished string as proof that Grace planned to come back. A twenty-eight-year-old Leyna wasn't as optimistic.

Before she left home for good, Leyna had spent hours in front of the photos in Grace's room. Leyna could still picture those four blank spots on the wall as clearly as she could the Polaroids that had surrounded them. So many times over the past decade, she'd considered going back for the remaining photos. Staring at her own wall now, she regretted not taking them when she left. But she'd been understandably distracted.

Her phone buzzed on the table. Again, she ignored it.

As she studied the photos of her sister and other women who'd gone missing in the ensuing years, Leyna sucked in a lungful of thick air. The apartment had grown stale and too warm, but she couldn't risk cracking a window in the living room and alerting others she was home. Her unit faced the courtyard, and she'd skipped her last couple of showers. She wasn't exactly visitor-ready.

She briefly considered breaking her routine and grabbing a quick shower now. Maybe doing some laundry and a light cleaning of the kitchen. That would at least improve the air quality in the apartment. Instead, she picked up her laptop, sank onto the couch, and started typing.

The search for Grace and Adam yielded frustratingly familiar results: Random names and details about people who were not her sister. Who cared if a Grace Clarke in Iowa had been awarded her real estate license or a Grace Clarke in Michigan had posted photos on social media of her new puppy? Leyna jumped down each rabbit hole anyway.

The terms *Plumas County* and *missing girl* were only slightly more fruitful. *Two Quincy teens are believed to have run away together*, the first news story read. Then a few days later: *Missing teens found in Portola area.*

The next hit was for a sixteen-year-old girl who'd been reported missing after attending a party. A day later, the post had been updated with the news she'd been found. Another runaway.

In Chester, a fifteen-year-old boy had been missing since spring. On this page, there was no bold update header. Sometimes, families never got closure.

Next, she typed Adam Duran. That got twenty-five million results. Adam Duran Plumas County—two hundred fifty thousand. Adam Duran dating profile—four million. She checked birth and wedding announcements too and cross-referenced his name with hobbies he might still enjoy. Adam Duran archery. Adam Duran physics. Adam Duran killer. She even did an image search using an old photo.

Leyna knew there was little chance of her searches bearing fruit. The photo was too ancient to be useful, and killers in hiding tended to change their names.

Finally, for the second time that day, Leyna clicked on one of the many pages she'd bookmarked and scrolled through a bare-bones website that maintained information on missing persons in the area. She studied the columns of grainy photos provided by family or pulled from social media and read descriptions she'd long ago memorized before she stopped on the only one that mattered.

> Grace Clarke. Missing age: 16. Current age: 32. Last seen: North Fork River Campground, Plumas County.

Bullshit.

She stabbed the Back arrow. She'd done it so often, the key had started to stick.

After taking a breath, Leyna moved on to neighboring counties: Lassen. Shasta. Tehama. Yuba. Butte.

She usually searched as far east as Washoe and as far south as Placer, though sometimes she went farther. At one point or another, she'd searched all the counties between the Pacific and Atlantic Oceans.

That day, she got only as far as Sierra County.

Missing Sacramento teen's car found near Truckee.

Leyna guessed she'd clicked more than a hundred links that day, thousands that month, and her tap on the mousepad was muscle memory, her eyes half glazed when the page loaded.

> A search is underway for a missing Sacramento teen who vanished Thursday night after texting a friend she was on her way home. The car she was driving was found abandoned this evening at a campground in Sierraville, about twelve miles north of Truckee.

Leyna skimmed the opening paragraph, trying to remember if she'd used the last of her eye drops, nearly dismissing the article as irrelevant. That was the problem with routine: sometimes it muted instinct. Her finger hovered over the mousepad, a moment away from clicking to the next link—Teen disappears from electronics store in Carson City—when every muscle in her body contracted, her lungs freezing mid-breath.

Campground. The last lead on Grace had also ended at a campground.

But that wasn't what made Leyna abruptly dizzy. It was the photo.

For an instant, eyes bleary, Leyna hadn't recognized the girl. Her brown hair was tied back in a ponytail. She wore a purple-and-white soccer shirt. No makeup. In the photo, she didn't look at all like Grace.

The name underneath the photo was Elisa Byrd.

She was sixteen. The same age Grace had been when she'd disappeared. Not a woman at all.

Leyna read the rest of the article quickly.

> The blue Honda Fit, borrowed from a friend, was discovered earlier today at the Upper Little Truckee Campground by a Sierra County sheriff's deputy.
>
> At 3:15 p.m. Thursday, Elisa, who goes by Ellie, texted a friend that she was stopping to use the restroom and might head into Truckee for dinner. She said she expected to be back in Sacramento by 10 p.m. She has not been seen or heard from since, according to the Sacramento County

Sheriff's Office. Elisa was reported missing late Thursday night by her parents, Paul and Sarah Byrd.

The car was found unlocked. The keys and Elisa's phone have not been located.

Anyone who might have seen Elisa or knows of her whereabouts is asked to call . . .

Leyna heard the girl's voice in her head: *I'm Ellie, by the way. Actually, Elisa, but no one calls me that.*

Ellie's visit to the restaurant had been the excuse Leyna needed to jump back down the rabbit hole. Without a job, Leyna certainly had time for obsession. But though the girl was the catalyst, she wasn't the *reason* Leyna had spent most of the past ten days staring at a screen. The reason would always be Grace. Ellie had merely given Leyna new data to populate the search field. But reading about the missing girl now, Leyna felt an unexpected pressure in her chest. What had happened to Ellie Byrd? Had she fallen or had an accident? Car trouble? What if the person who'd stopped under the pretense of offering help had exploited the isolation and darkness to shove Ellie in his trunk, intending to bring her somewhere even more remote? In the forest, it was easy to disappear. Even easier if someone meant you harm.

And then the question that always clawed its way into Leyna's consciousness: How might this be connected to Grace?

After reading the story about Ellie several more times, Leyna navigated to the message boards on her favorite true-crime site. She'd bookmarked dozens of websites—some dedicated to cold cases or missing persons, others to photography or Grace's favorite bands—but she logged the most hours on the true-crime boards. With its use of Comic Sans and its antiquated layout, this site had a retro aesthetic that offered comfort. Leyna imagined it looked the same as it had the last night she'd seen Grace.

Leyna scanned the boards for mention of Ellie, but the conversation was focused on a murder trial in Los Angeles. After two decades buried in a Los Angeles backyard, a woman's remains had been unearthed—bones and scraps of the polyester dress the woman was wearing when she disappeared. The dead woman's ex-boyfriend, a former tenant, had been arrested.

Leyna typed: What is everyone hearing about Ellie Byrd?

She didn't need to add details—the people on that particular forum would be familiar with the case; if not, they'd immediately start googling the name.

She didn't have to wait long. A frequent visitor who went by Boston Betty chimed in: Just what they're saying on the news. Texted her friend that she was using the bathroom and then disappeared.

Leyna: Weird that she'd use a portable toilet at the campground when there's a market not far up the road.

Boston Betty: Maybe she didn't have to go then? You sound like you're familiar with the area?

Leyna hesitated. Most of the people there knew her story. The parts she was willing to share, anyway. Some, she typed before quickly changing the subject. The friend had to be getting worried long before Ellie didn't show. They had to be sharing locations, with her friend so far away.

Boston Betty: Driving her car too. Maybe her phone died?

Leyna: Convenient.

Boston Betty: Agree. And stupid to be all the way out there without a portable charger.

Leyna felt herself tense. Maybe Ellie had a charger and it or her phone was taken from her. Leyna typed: Anyone know if she had car trouble?

Boston Betty: ??? Is that what you heard?

Leyna: Just wondering.

A new name popped up: SouthernBella. Leyna tried to remember if she was from Chattanooga or Charleston.

SouthernBella: Also strange that she would be so far from home. Why would a 16-year-old from Sacramento be out in the middle of nowhere anyway?

Boston Betty: And by herself. That's asking for trouble.

Leyna knew trouble found you even if you weren't asking for it. But

Boston Betty had a point. What had Ellie been doing on Highway 89 that night?

Someone named Kyle's Mom tagged Boston Betty in a reply: Victim-shame much?

Being sixteen and newly licensed, Ellie would've been prohibited from driving another minor, but Leyna had no time for the conversation to turn ugly. She quickly typed: What about a boyfriend?

A flurry of responses flashed: Why was she asking? What had she heard? And, from Kyle's Mom: Don't think she had a boyfriend.

Leyna was trying to make sense of this latest piece of information when Kyle's Mom, who Leyna suspected had connections in law enforcement, shared the rest of what she knew. Ellie's best friend, Amaya Dutton, had loaned Ellie her car, and she woke up her parents when Ellie failed to return as promised. Amaya's mom called Ellie's, who reported her missing Thursday night. When the car was found the next day, the navigation history had been cleared, and the bumper dented.

CrimeChaser2000 joined then. Ellie's young and pretty. At least she'll get coverage.

Ferret Girl: My Black father-in-law vanished on a road trip to Vegas a year ago. Ellie's already gotten more news stories. This was followed by a link to a foundation dedicated to searching for missing people of color.

CrimeChaser2000: Remember the obsession with Gabby Petito? I predict it will be like that.

Ferret Girl typed a list of other names, familiar to all of them. Leyna flashed to the missing boy she'd read about earlier, the one whose case remained open. He'd been Cuban American. Then there were the missing indigenous women the group had discussed on the boards only the week before.

There was a minute when no one posted—a moment of communal silence.

Then SouthernBella typed: Goes back to Virginia Dare, doesn't it?

She didn't elaborate, but everyone in the chat likely knew who she meant. The first English baby born at Roanoke. An ill-fated child, born at an ill-fated colony.

Boston Betty: Everyone loves a good true-crime story, especially when the victim is blond.

Kyle's Mom: I'm guessing the families don't love the stories.

Boston Betty: Unless the attention helps them find someone they love.

CrimeChaser2000: Speaking of, has anyone looked at the parents? People do some sick shit to their kids. She might've even made it back to Sacramento.

SouthernBella: They would've gotten an emergency order to ping her phone by now. There's no mention that she ever made it to Truckee.

Boston Betty: Her phone could've died, or she could've turned it off.

SouthernBella: Come on. We all know how it went down. Ellie got out of her car. She took her keys and her phone with her. And somewhere between that portable toilet and her car, she disappeared.

Boston Betty: Agree. There's no second location. Someone took her from that campground.

CHAPTER 3

MEREDITH

Friday, 6:46 p.m.

On the patio behind her house, Meredith tried to pay attention to what Serena Silvestri was saying, but the screaming made it difficult to concentrate.

Damn the Durans. Their house was at least three thousand square feet. With all that space, Meredith would've thought their daughter and her friends could spend at least a few summer evenings inside. It almost made her long for an early winter.

The neighborhood would've been quiet enough to hear the wind if not for the pack of wildlings in the street. Ridgepoint Ranch had been built around a golf course that had eventually failed, and the nature preserve planned on the abandoned greens had been stuck in legal limbo for as long as Meredith had lived there. Phase two of home construction had stalled too when the developer, Rocky Hamlin, went bankrupt—the double hit of a recession and an inability to stay faithful to his attorney wife. Meredith understood the cheating—Rocky's now ex-wife was one of those city types drawn to the area for its nature who then complained that the shopping sucked—but he should've been smarter about his investments.

The subdivision had once been envisioned as a self-sustaining golf community with a market, clubhouse, community pool, and rows of glass-and-stone homes with backyards that butted up against forestland. But Rocky had caught the tail end of the golfing boom, and only five homes had been built. Four were occupied year-round.

Unfortunately, one of those homes was occupied by the Durans—Rocky's cousin Richard, Richard's wife, Olivia, and one of the wildlings currently threatening to make Meredith's eardrums bleed.

Serena motioned to the bottle of cabernet next to Meredith and held out her glass.

So she plans on staying longer.

Meredith gave her half a pour.

Serena smoothed the front of her tank top, a buttery yellow like the wide-legged lounge pants she also wore. She might've given the impression of having just been roused from a nap if not for the large gold hoops and chunky bracelet she wore. That, and the full face of makeup. Serena didn't step outside without, at a minimum, bronzer, mascara, and Chanel lipstick. Illusion was her preferred shade, though she cycled through half a dozen others. She'd given Meredith a tube for her last birthday, claiming it might *do something* for her pallor. Meredith had considered tossing it but instead stuck it in a drawer. It would save her shopping for Serena's next birthday.

The opportunities to socialize were limited on the street, which was part of why Meredith had moved there.

Serena took a sip of her wine. "You really aren't worried about the forecast?"

Her neighbor had come to Plumas County less than a year before the Dixie Fire. She tracked the weather the way women trying to conceive tracked their menstrual cycles. The potential for dry thunderstorms had Serena nervous.

"Not really," Meredith said. She preferred vigilance to worry. Far more productive.

She'd already pointed out that while about three-quarters of Plumas County had burned at one time or another, Ridgepoint Ranch had always been spared, even by Dixie. But everyone needed a hobby, and Serena's was drama.

"You've at least got a bag packed?"

Meredith nodded. She always had a bag packed. Part of being vigilant. "I even packed my Taser." That, a change of clothes, her best bottles of wine, and her paintings were all she planned on taking.

Her paintings. Meredith had been introduced to her broker, Brian, through the man she'd made the mistake of marrying, John Clarke, whose confidence as an artist was eclipsed only by his mediocrity. After failing to sell his own paintings—*Genius is often misunderstood,* he was fond of saying—John decided to try his hand at forging the Impressionists. How hard could it be? he'd reasoned. He'd brought Meredith along to a cocktail meeting with Brian, where John showed him photos of some fourth-rate fake Monets.

"I've heard a good forgery can fetch thousands," John had said.

To which Brian had responded: "A *good* forgery can fetch many times that."

The three bourbons had dulled John more than usual, so he'd misinterpreted Brian's meaning. When, flush with hope, John excused himself to use the restroom, Brian leaned in and whispered to Meredith, "I only took this meeting to talk with you. John's paintings are crap."

She'd left with Brian's card secreted away in her pocket, and John had left with another name on his list of people who didn't yet recognize his talent.

Meredith and John had divorced soon after, and he'd never known of her partnership with Brian. He likely thought she still worked in insurance. It wouldn't have occurred to him that she might succeed where he had failed.

Serena's eyes widened. "You have a Taser?"

"I'm a woman living alone in the middle of nowhere. Of course I have a Taser." She sipped her wine, hoping it would dull her anxiety and the squeals of the children. The pack should've been two houses down, but they'd migrated closer to her home. "It's currently in a locked box in my overnight bag. It fires barbed probes up to fifteen feet and can twist a man's testicles."

Serena grimaced. "Sounds unpleasant."

"Why do you think I keep it locked up?" While testicular trauma wasn't common, she certainly wasn't about to leave herself vulnerable to a lawsuit.

Serena finished her wine and held out her glass.

Meredith's gaze dipped to her neighbor's outstretched arm. "Won't Frank be home soon?"

"He won't be back for a couple of hours." She smirked. "You've got me a while longer."

Meredith poured Serena a few more sips of cabernet. The rest went into her own glass. Headache blooming, she didn't plan on finishing it, but if it got Serena to leave soon, the wine wouldn't be wasted.

The screaming of the children stopped abruptly as Olivia Duran called them inside, and Meredith exhaled in relief.

Finally.

"It's got to remind you of Grace."

Meredith's hand jerked and cabernet sloshed on the flagstone.

"What are you talking about?"

"The girl."

Thoughts still on the pack of girls now silenced, Meredith said, "Thea Duran?"

Serena weaponized a sigh. "Really, do you listen to anything I say?"

Some of it. "Of course I do."

Serena bit the inside of her lip, which Meredith knew signaled irritation.

Meredith set her wine on the flagstone and shook a couple of stray droplets from her hand. "You were saying?"

"The missing girl from Sacramento. Ellie Byrd," Serena said. "Sixteen, and her car was found in Sierraville. You really haven't heard about her?"

At Meredith's quick shake of the head, Serena said, "Probably another runaway. Like your daughter."

A chill burrowed into Meredith's breastbone, and she channeled it into the look she gave Serena. If the other woman noticed, she gave no indication.

"I know Grace left earlier than you would've liked, but can you really say she would have been happy if she'd stayed?" Serena asked. "There's not much here for girls that age."

Meredith appreciated that her neighbor talked about Grace as if she were still alive. Everyone else in the neighborhood had given up that pretense long ago.

CHAPTER 4

LEYNA

Friday, 7:01 p.m.

Grace had left 466 days too soon.

From her first day of high school, Grace kept a calendar on her desk counting down to graduation. Every few weeks, she would tear out one of the pages and leave it on Leyna's pillow.

1,300 days

1,115 days

895 days

Below the number, she would draw a silly face, tape a leaf she'd found in the woods, or share a song lyric or a quote from one of Leyna's favorite books. That was her way of softening the blow to come—*750 days until I'm gone.*

Leyna should've had 466 more days with her sister at home. Instead, she'd been without Grace for nearly 6,000.

She was thinking about that, stress-eating a pint of peanut-butter-cup ice cream in front of her laptop, when her phone started buzzing again.

Private caller.

What if it really was a job? She'd already blown through a third of the money in her checking account to buy office supplies and groceries. But it wasn't thoughts of replenishing those funds that compelled her to set down the ice cream and pick up the phone. It was thoughts of the missing girl and what it might mean for Grace.

Leyna stabbed the screen to connect. She heard breathing first, and then a familiar voice, low and deeper than she remembered.

"Hey, Leyna."

Not a potential employer or someone calling about the missing girl.

Dominic Duran.

In the pause that followed, she tried to picture Dominic's face, but the only image she could conjure belonged to the past. It had been a decade since they'd spoken, and she wondered if the call meant he'd finally forgiven her.

"Hi, Dom." She said it as if talking to him were the most natural thing in the world and there weren't a walnut-size lump in her throat.

It had been Grace, Adam, and Dominic for years, until Grace settled on Adam, and Dominic left for college. Leyna was the stray that always trailed them, years younger but tolerated. And sometimes when it was just her and Grace, they would hike the forest, off the trails, while Grace shared dreams of being a wildlife photographer or traveling to the Bamboo Grove in Kyoto. The woods near home had been theirs for a while. Until Grace turned sixteen, and her moods had darkened, her breath started smelling of mints or stolen alcohol, and she began spending more time alone with Adam. In the last year Grace was home, with Dominic away at the University of Nevada, Leyna was tolerated less, and when she followed, she was usually relegated to the Durans' kitchen to help Aunt Olivia assemble charcuterie boards or brew sun tea.

Looking back, Leyna couldn't pinpoint the precise moment her sister stopped having time for her, but it had closely followed Adam's transformation from cocky jerk to full-blown asshole. Not that anyone but Leyna seemed to have noticed the transformation. And even Leyna hadn't realized how dangerous assholes could be.

Later, after Grace and Adam disappeared, having moms who hated each other made it difficult for Leyna and Dominic to maintain a friendship, but it was Leyna herself who struck the killing blow, shortly before her nineteenth birthday. She only wished she'd had the foresight to ruin everything before they'd started what could have been something great.

The sound of Dominic's voice immediately brought back the scent of cedar and a warmth to her cheeks. Leyna sat on the coffee table and knocked over an empty ice cream carton. The spoon inside slipped out and rattled on the fake wood.

"What's up?" The lump in her throat hardened, threatening to choke her.

He seemed unaware of her inability to breathe.

"How've you been?" he asked.

I've been fired, she thought but didn't say. *And I still can't let Grace go.*

In the two months they'd been together as a couple, they could spend an hour debating which was the best superpower—time travel, obviously—or dissecting a passage in a book. How was she expected to distill a decade of life into a couple of sentences?

"I'm fine." Though he couldn't see her, Leyna smoothed her hair and took stock of the pajamas she still wore. What would she have done if he'd shown up at her door instead of calling?

But no, Dominic would never do that. Not after how things had ended.

"And how're you, Dom?" She said his name again just to feel it on her tongue, as if she could force a connection that had long ago been severed.

His response came back equally awkward. "I'm good." Even with all the years lost between them, she recognized the lie, but she had no place asking about it. "Assume you heard about the missing girl?"

So it's someone calling about Ellie after all.

"Yeah, I've heard," she said. Or tried to say. The words came out garbled. *Damn lump.* Leyna went to the kitchen and got a glass from the cupboard. She filled it with water from the tap and drank until her throat cleared.

"I've been working at this nonprofit in Quincy that focuses on underserved youth and their families. Counseling, classes, tutoring. Connecting them to other resources if needed."

That sounded like a career he'd have chosen. Dominic's grief had always been more productive than hers. Leyna set the glass in the sink and returned to perch on the coffee table. She was grateful he didn't ask what she was doing with her life.

When the silence grew too heavy, he said, "Any chance I could convince you to come home?"

She leaned back, surprised. *Never. Not even for you.* "It's not home."

"Okay, then, back to Ridgepoint."

"They wouldn't want me there." *Why do* you *want me there?* She'd learned that you didn't make many friends vilifying a golden child, especially one still missing.

On the other end of the connection, Dominic exhaled, his weariness as thick as the air in her apartment. "The missing girl was here."

"Plumas County?"

"The neighborhood."

She braced herself on the edge of the coffee table, her hand bumping the discarded ice cream spoon. She might've gone to the freezer for another pint to self-medicate if she'd thought her legs could carry her.

"When?"

"Midday Thursday, right before she showed up at the youth center where I work."

"What time was that?"

"A little after one p.m."

Leyna did some quick math. The campground was just over an hour away. So what had Ellie been doing in the hours between her visit to Quincy and her disappearance?

"I met Ellie," Leyna said. "She came to the restaurant."

"I know."

Her grip on the coffee table tightened, and the fake wood bit into her palm. It reminded her of the glass-petaled roses from Ellie's bracelet. "How do you know?"

Dominic didn't answer that, and when he spoke, his voice was low in his throat. "It's a lot to ask, but it would be better if we talked face to face."

If it had been anyone else, she would've disconnected at that moment. But because it was Dominic, she hesitated.

This won't go well, she thought. But if Adam *was* involved, she needed to know. Leyna couldn't fail her sister a second time.

"If you've heard about her, you know she disappeared from a campground. Like Grace."

"That's what people say, anyway."

He sighed, but there was little fight in it. "Not this again."

Several weeks after Grace and Adam disappeared, a caller to the hotline Dominic and Adam's mom set up had claimed they'd seen the teens in a car along the North Fork Feather River at a campground on Caribou Road. According to the witness, a boy who looked like Adam had been driving, a girl in the seat beside him. A girl with a strawberry-blond ponytail who was wearing a blue blouse, the same blouse Grace had been wearing the night she disappeared. The theory was, the teens had been camping in the area. By the time the police arrived—somewhat reluctantly, since runaways weren't a priority—the teens were gone. If they'd ever been there. Leyna had her reasons to doubt her sister and Adam had ever camped along the Feather River.

Over the years, there were a few more sightings of Adam, but none of them panned out, and no callers ever again mentioned Grace. After the reports about the teens on Caribou Road, Grace wasn't seen again—except by her sister in the faces of strangers.

In the face of Ellie, a sixteen-year-old girl now missing.

Finally, Leyna said, "I'll come."

She agreed as if it were a decision she'd just reached, but it had been made the moment Dominic mentioned Ellie's visit to Plumas County. At the least, she could gather Grace's Polaroids. New photos might spur new ideas.

Then there was the question that nagged, always nagged—what if Adam was back?

Leyna's gaze landed again on the sheet of white paper stuck to her wall with the reference to Caribou Road. She'd never heard the recording of the anonymous call that had driven attention to the campground eighty minutes to the northwest, but she'd memorized the details from the transcript.

Pretty girl. Reddish-blond ponytail. Light blue blouse.

Leyna would've put more stock in the tip if she hadn't known that Grace wasn't wearing the blue blouse when she left. She'd changed into a black one because of the blood on one sleeve.

THE FIRE

As the giant pine dies, sunshine bleaches the sky, and a dry but gentle wind blows in the Plumas National Forest. If there'd been more rain that winter, the pine might've been able to fend off the attack. But stressed by drought, it had little sap to defend itself when the beetles launched their offensive that spring. Now the giant is scarred by tunnels and shedding bark, slowly being killed by a pest the size of a grain of rice.

Beside the pine, other trees sway, some still healthy but many infested too. Leaves whisper. Dead branches, brown needles, and hard, crisp leaves carpet the forest floor. Here, plains roll into vast expanses of timberland. Incense cedar. Douglas fir. Ponderosa pine. Trunks sticky with resin nearly as flammable as gasoline. Other trees have downed beneath the dense canopy, among the millions killed by drought and disease.

A single spark could ignite this parched hillside in minutes.

In Northern California, the month of July has sweltered. Historically, July is always hottest, but this year, heat-related records have been set in many towns.

It isn't the heat alone that worries the residents near the Plumas National Forest. Here, along the northern edge of the Sierra Nevada mountain range, a fire-weather watch issued Friday morning surprises few.

The humidity is low, and it's been a long while since the region got any rain. A high-pressure system is brewing.

There's also the wind. An anemometer measures it at ten miles per hour. Not too bad yet. But it unnerves some residents, especially those who lived through the Dixie Fire, which burned nearly a million acres and stopped just short of the town of Quincy's border. Residents reassure their neighbors and themselves. *At least it's not a red-flag warning,* they say. Then, remembering Dixie, *At least the wind isn't howling like it did that morning.*

Still, some pack bags and locate pet carriers. Just in case. And they listen to the wind.

As the arid morning passes, the trees continue to sway, and the leaves continue to whisper.

Friday evening, though, the wind picks up. It blows at fifteen miles per hour, with gusts double that. Humidity plummets too, settling below 10 percent.

And then there are the dry thunderstorms. As the sky shakes, rain evaporates before it hits the ground. There's no moisture to dampen the earth when lightning strikes. These bolts, several times hotter than the sun's surface, can cause steel to melt. Trees to explode. Flesh to cook.

Given these changes, the weather service elevates the alert. It's now a red-flag warning.

But not everyone gets the notification.

To reduce wildfire risk, the local electric utility cuts power for a remote area southeast of the capital, which disrupts cell phone service there. An inconvenience, to be sure, but one deemed necessary to keep the towns safe. Besides, utility executives reason, the outage affects only a few hundred people, and service is predicted to be restored quickly.

One of those areas left without service is the Ridgepoint Ranch subdivision.

Thirteen miles to the north, lightning strikes the giant pine. Now marked for a quicker death, the pine starts to smolder.

CHAPTER 5
LEYNA

Saturday, 8:00 a.m.

Leyna stopped at the campground where the car owned by Ellie's friend was found, but the car and police were gone, and the patches of gravel and weeds had nothing to tell her. The same was true of the message boards and local news, both of which she checked again from the shoulder along Highway 89. The Sacramento County Sheriff's Office planned a press conference with the parents at 10:30 a.m.—she'd set a reminder on her phone—and both Sierra and Plumas Counties had added news of Ellie's disappearance to their social media sites. But the news was the same as it had been when Leyna went to sleep sometime after two a.m.

No sign of Sacramento girl missing since Thursday night.

In Sacramento, word of Ellie Byrd's disappearance was starting to spread; Ferret Girl appeared to be right. But to the north in Plumas County, where residents didn't have a deeper connection to the story, the bigger news was the weather. A red-flag warning was still in effect, and the winds were expected to pick up again later that morning.

Leyna stowed her phone—a quarter of a mile or so up the road, it would be useless, and it would stay useless until she got closer to Sierraville—and pulled back onto the highway.

Only a few hundred people lived in the town of Sierraville, which served as a place for travelers to get their bearings, pick up some snacks, and use the restroom before they headed north to Quincy, west to Downieville, or south to Truckee. Not many made a life here in the most rural areas of Northern California. The ones who stuck around cited the small-town feel, the close-knit community, everyone knowing everyone, as their reasons for staying. The ones who left cited the same reasons for going.

Word would've spread if Ellie had stopped here Thursday.

The market on the main strip was as Leyna remembered it. Wood buildings set against a backdrop of mountains and blue sky. Picnic tables out front. Cows out back. Asphalt stretching in every direction, making it easy to turn around if you got lost.

Though it was early in the day, the market was already several degrees cooler than the air outside. Bags of brightly colored snacks were displayed in tidy rows. Signs on the refrigerated cases advertised MILK EGGS JUICE BACON and COLD BEER. A man Leyna estimated to be in his forties stood behind the counter, bottle-brush hair in mid-retreat exposing a broad forehead. When he smiled in greeting, he showed large white teeth planted in perfect rows.

Leyna returned the smile as she tried to picture him as he might've been sixteen years before. The last time she'd been there. Had a younger version of this man helped her that day?

She'd come into the market with Adam and Grace three weeks before they'd disappeared. Grace had just returned from a few months with their father. She'd gone to stay with him midway through the fall semester, with plans to stay permanently. *If it works out for me, Ley, you'll come too. We can both be free of her.* But it turned out a few months was all their father could handle. Apparently, his third wife hadn't liked the reminder of his more attractive first wife sleeping on their couch.

That morning in February, Leyna caught Grace palming their mom's car keys, and she'd bargained her way into a spot in the back seat. On the drive, she'd studied the backs of their heads as if they held hints of her own future. The sun that streamed through the glass cast only a passing glow on Adam, but it set Grace's hair ablaze, seeming to anoint her. Leyna's breath had caught on a sudden swell of love and envy.

I want to be her. Then, a moment later: *I'll never be her.*

As Adam cut the engine in front of the market, he cracked a joke about atoms splitting—nerd humor, Grace called it—and her sister had laughed and turned toward him. That was the last time Leyna could remember Grace smiling—in profile, staring at the boyfriend who'd never been worthy of her.

Before they got out of the car, Adam took off his flannel and handed it to Grace.

"You look cold."

"I'm not."

"Please." A smile. "I don't like thinking you might be cold."

Grace rolled her eyes but put on the flannel.

Inside the market, Adam trolled the aisles while Grace snatched the first items that caught her eye: a bag of toffee-covered peanuts and a bottle of blue punch. Grace's impatience was legendary, and Leyna recognized the simmer that always began in her face. Mouth pinched, she said, "We're going to be late."

Late for what, she didn't say.

Adam's gaze remained on the rows of chips and nuts, so he didn't notice the tic at the corner of Grace's mouth. "They'll wait."

He selected a bag of spicy cheese puffs and two packages of plastic-wrapped snack cakes. He handed one of the packages to Leyna. "Why don't you go and ask the guy at the register how much this is."

The price was labeled on the display, but when Leyna pointed that out, he'd smirked. "It might be on sale." Then he'd picked up a bag of sunflower seeds. "These too. And maybe ask the best way to Truckee."

There was only one way to Truckee—even at twelve, Leyna could've done the navigating—but she took the snack cakes and sunflower seeds to the register while Adam headed to the refrigerated cases in the back.

At the register, Leyna did as she'd been told—"How much are these? Can you tell me how to get to Truckee?" She spoke a little louder than she needed to, trying to mask her sister's voice, which had risen too.

"You've got to be kidding."

That was followed by hushed conversation and then a sound, quick and sharp. Something thrown? Something broken?

A moment later, Grace and Adam joined Leyna at the register, Grace wrapped in the oversize flannel. Adam paid for the cheese puffs, probably because the bag was too large and the crinkle of the plastic too loud to easily hide.

Back in the car, Grace stripped off the shirt and threw it at Adam, then followed it with a series of projectiles she yanked from her pockets and waistband: Sunflower seeds. Toffee-covered peanuts. Snack cakes. Two bottles of beer, one of which grazed his cheek. The cap left a scratch. Grace kept only the blue punch. Staring ahead out the window, Grace took a sip and screwed the lid back on. "Take me home."

Adam glanced over his shoulder at Leyna before returning his attention to Grace. "We have to—"

"Now."

Leyna wasn't sure how Adam had convinced Grace to stuff the beer and snacks in her waistband—maybe it had been her impatience to be back on the road, or maybe he'd softened her with another of his nerd jokes—but in her mind, Leyna still heard the sound that had followed Adam's whispering.

Now Leyna closed her eyes and gently slapped her arm, still unsure if that's what she'd heard that day. The cashier's smile had grown strained. How long had he been holding it while she sank into the past?

"Something I can help you with?" The cashier had a deep voice, the kind perfect for insurance commercials. His gaze landed on her arm where she'd slapped it. She realized it was her scar that had drawn his attention.

She introduced herself, but he seemed reluctant to do the same. She nudged. "Hi—I'm sorry. I didn't catch your name."

"Ronny."

"Hi, Ronny. Have you heard about that missing girl?"

The cashier nodded, but his smile faded. "Police were in here asking about her yesterday."

"What did you tell them?"

Ronny looked suddenly nervous, rubbing a hand over the dark bristles that started in the middle of his head. "Not sure I'm supposed to say."

She considered offering him the cash she had on her, but she doubted three dollars would get her much information. "I'm sure it's okay. They're probably going to release it to the public at the press conference anyway."

"Come back then."

"Please. She's my sister."

The man squinted as he studied her face. "Don't see a resemblance. And I don't remember the police mentioning a sister."

"Stepsister."

Ronny continued to stare, mouth settling into a tense line. "You do look familiar."

She thought again of Grace's pockets bulging with stolen beer, and the sound that might've been a slap.

She asked, "How long have you worked here?"

"About a year. You come in here before?"

"Not for a really long time." She remembered her story. As Ellie's stepsister, should she live in Sacramento too? She decided to stick close to the truth in case this man could recognize deceit as easily as she could.

"I grew up in Plumas County," she said. "I haven't been back this way since I graduated high school."

"I hear that a lot. You still have family in the area?"

"No." Also close to the truth. Though they still exchanged the obligatory holiday phone calls—Christmas, birthdays mainly—she and her mom hadn't felt like a family since long before she'd left home.

"Then I can see why you wouldn't be back. Not everyone appreciates the quiet."

"So was Ellie Byrd in here?"

The cashier's face went stony; whatever rapport she'd thought they'd been building was gone. "I shouldn't say." His tone was friendly but firm.

Again, Leyna wished she had more than three crumpled dollar bills to offer him. Then she realized she had a different type of currency to trade—information.

"If it makes you more comfortable, how about I tell you what I know too?"

His expression relaxed slightly, the door not all the way open but ajar. "What do you know?"

"She has a boyfriend." *I think.*

The tension returned, etching lines at the corners of his mouth. "She doesn't have a boyfriend."

"When I—" Leyna stopped herself; she'd been about to say *When I met her.* "Last time I spoke to her, she said she had a boyfriend"—*Only a small lie*—"but he was a really private person. He didn't like her talking about their relationship. Maybe she just didn't want to say anything about him?"

He smirked. "She was definitely single."

"How can you be sure?"

"The other guy who works here, Cal, is only a couple of years older than her. When she stopped by Thursday morning, he asked if she was seeing anyone. She said she wasn't."

"So she was here Thursday morning?"

"Around ten thirty."

"Not later in the day?"

"If you're asking if she stopped in on her way to that campground, no."

"Could she have come when you weren't here?"

The shake of his head was decisive. "We close at seven, and I was here about thirty minutes after that."

So the missing hours between Plumas County and the campground remained a mystery. She tried to hide her disappointment, but she was sure he saw it. "Was Cal here until seven thirty too?"

Ronny pressed his lips together tightly. Leyna could guess what he wasn't saying: Cal hadn't been there, but Ronny was reluctant to betray his friend.

Leyna let it go. "Is he here today?"

"He's off." His deep voice rose an octave. "But he was here when the police came in. He confirmed with them that was the *only* time he'd seen the girl." He paused on the emphasis, letting it sink in. "Ellie Byrd gave him her number, but he never had a chance to reach out."

"Can I get that number?"

The tightening of his jaw told Leyna she wasn't going to like his answer. "I can ask," he said, but he folded his arms across his chest, sending the same clear message: *I'll talk to you, but only as far as loyalty to my friend allows.* His body language told her that particular request was a dead end.

"Did Ellie say what she was doing in the area?"

"Just fueling up." He looked away for an instant, enough for her to wonder if he was hiding something to protect his friend. Or himself.

"Did she tell you where she was going?"

"She asked if either of us was familiar with Plumas County—we told her we weren't. I assume that's where she was headed, but I don't know for sure," he said. "She was here, then she was gone." The words raised the hairs on Leyna's exposed arms, and he blanched. "I'm sorry. I didn't mean it like that."

Leyna pictured Ellie standing where she was now, paying for her gas, and it hit her—wouldn't she have paid at the pump?

"You said she stopped here to refuel." At his nod, she said, "Why'd she come inside?"

"She paid cash."

So she hadn't used a card. If the car Ellie was driving hadn't been found fifteen minutes down the road, the police would never have known Ellie stopped at the market.

"Plus she bought snacks," he said. "Some Hostess Cupcakes and a ginger ale."

The temperature in the market seemed to spike, making sweat bead along Leyna's hairline. Those had been Adam's favorite too.

"Did she mention someone named Adam Duran?"

He leaned forward, overtly curious. "Is that the guy she was supposed to be seeing?"

Damn it. Rookie mistake. She shouldn't have planted the name. Leyna forced her face still and waited for him to confirm her suspicions even as she hoped Adam was living on another continent or dead. She didn't trust herself to speak for fear she'd lead him to the answer she wanted instead of the truth she needed.

When Leyna didn't respond, he shook his head. "No Adam. I've already told you everything." He paused, rubbing his head. "Except..."

"Except?"

He shrugged. "It's nothing. Just a feeling."

"What kind of feeling?"

"I really shouldn't start rumors."

"It's only a rumor if I spread it to other people, and I promise I won't."

He scowled and stared, as if trying to decide if he could trust her with whatever bothered him—because he was definitely bothered. She could tell by the tension in his jaw and the way his eyes narrowed as he studied her.

Finally, he let out a long breath. "She was nice. Like I mentioned, she and Cal were friendly," he said. "But she seemed anxious too."

Leyna swiped the sweat from her forehead with the back of her hand. "Why would she be anxious?"

He shrugged. "It was just a feeling. I probably shouldn't have said anything."

Ronny turned and made a production of straightening a display of snacks on the far side of the counter. For several seconds, only the air conditioner's murmur interrupted the silence. Then, his back still to her, he said, "If Adam Duran's the guy she was going to see, she certainly wasn't happy about it."

CHAPTER 6
OLIVIA

Saturday, 8:50 a.m.

During the earliest years at Ridgepoint Ranch, Olivia Duran had believed giving birth to her first son, Dominic, would be her life's greatest pain. She was nearly a child herself—only nineteen—and she'd had no idea what to expect. Labor lasted nearly two days, and toward the end, he got stuck. By the time he was wrenched free, Olivia felt as if she'd run a marathon while being pelted with rocks. Every inch of her ached.

But that wasn't the pain that laid claim to the worst-ever spot. That came in the silence that followed when she waited for a cry that didn't come and she looked over to see his newborn body limp, his skin with a bluish cast. It was hours before she was told Dominic would be okay and weeks before she believed it.

A couple of years later, when Olivia found out she was having another boy, although the pregnancy was planned, the fear hit first. *Not again.* Other mothers reassured her: *The second birth is easier.* And it was. After only half a day of labor, Adam emerged pink and screaming. She'd survived the worst of it.

How stupid she'd been.

Olivia released the arrow, but the tremor in her hand sent it several inches below the bull's-eye.

Keep it together, Olivia.

Richard had built the simple archery range with his cousin Rocky's help as a gift for their younger son's sixteenth birthday: A couple of flat targets flanking a large foam goblin. Green netting to catch stray arrows. All of it circled by trees. It wasn't much, but Adam, a huge Green Arrow fan, had greeted the gift with the enthusiasm of a boy half his age.

No way. Beaming. *This is so cool.*

He'd had only a couple of months to use the range.

Olivia's gaze wandered to the trees, and she thought of the safety she'd once believed they offered—a buffer against the worst parts of the world. When they'd first moved to Plumas County, Richard suggested they install security fencing. Olivia had brushed off the idea. *Who's a threat to us here?*

The idea had occurred to him because of his dad, of course. His father had been born in Quito. His parents met when Richard's Santa Cruz–raised mom visited Ecuador's capital with some university classmates. She'd extended her stay, and eventually they'd traded his home for hers—but according to Richard, Santa Cruz had never truly felt like home to his father.

When they inevitably divorced, his dad moved back to his family's Quito home, then occupied by three generations of Durans. It was hidden behind a concrete wall topped with broken soda bottles. A young Richard had visited Ecuador only a few times before his dad died, but years later, he still remembered that wall topped with glass. The image stuck with him as surely as the memories of his great-aunt's cooking, the long and sunny days, and the altitude sickness that had leveled him on his first trip. When he was a boy, that wall and being surrounded by family had made him feel safe. Loved.

Richard approached from behind and handed her a glass of water. "It's already warming up."

To mollify him, she took a drink, then set it down on a flat patch of earth, then looked around to make sure Goose hadn't followed him out. She couldn't have the dog wandering into her shooting line.

Seeing no sign of Goose, Olivia adjusted her bow and studied the target. She tried to still her hand and her body, wait for her shot between the gusts.

"Got a call from the mechanic," Richard said. "The part for your car is in."

Her hand tightened on the bow. *Steady.* She tried not to think about how that cracked radiator had ruined her life.

He said, "We should have it back the beginning of the week."

"That's great." Olivia backed up a step and nocked the arrow on the bowstring. She pictured Richard's face on the target and drew back the string.

"Who're you picturing on that target?"

Startled, she released the string too soon. It snapped her arm, and the arrow fluttered to the ground several feet short. Even with the armguard she wore, the bowstring burned her wrist.

She took a step away from him and knocked over the glass of water. "Who says I was thinking of anyone?"

"The way you were staring at that bull's-eye so intently. It was Meredith, wasn't it?"

"You know me so well."

He picked up the glass—always so helpful, her husband—and gestured to the bow. "You were too tight in your shoulders. May I?"

She handed him the bow and an arrow from her quiver.

Richard placed one finger above the arrow and two below. He stared down the target as intently as she had. He pulled the string back in a straight line, his hand cupped around it next to his cheek.

"You need a consistent anchor," he said. "On the string and near your face."

She'd taught him this, but she nodded as if he were reminding her of something she'd forgotten. She noticed a slight bend of his spine, and his elbow was pointed a little low. She predicted the arrow would go high and to the right.

He narrowed his eyes at the target. "Rocky loves that you spend so much time out here."

Olivia's jaw tensed. She tried for a casual tone. "Have you talked to Rocky lately?"

"Last night. Why?"

She placed a palm to her chest, reassured by her heartbeat. Most days, she felt as if her chest were filled with dust and ash. "Just wondering how he's doing."

Richard released the arrow but moved the bow away from his face a fraction of a second too quickly, obviously eager to see where the arrow landed. It lodged on the line between the blue and red circles. High and to the right, as she'd predicted.

"Damn." He held out the bow. "He's as good as he ever is."

She took the bow from him and an arrow from her quiver. As she positioned it on the string, Richard said, "Nearly done out here?"

Olivia kept her focus on the paper target ten yards ahead. The thought of going inside turned her stomach. Out here, with her arrows and surrounded by trees, she could be invisible.

"Ten minutes."

The wind calmed, and Olivia stretched her spine—she'd always had perfect posture. Elbow cocked, her fingers curled around the pressure point, index finger sitting gently on the front of the bow. She pulled the string back in one smooth movement, feeling the tension in it even as she forced her shoulders to relax. When she let go, her elbow continued backward, completing the motion.

The arrow landed in the middle of the center yellow.

As he smiled, the skin at the corners of his eyes crinkled. "Guess you didn't need my help after all."

She smiled. "Lucky shot."

Olivia walked toward the target. His stare was heavy on her back. She knew he watched. He always watched.

He called to her. "You're stunning, you know."

The slight catch in his voice brought heat to her cheeks. Now that she was in her early fifties, the compliments she received had asterisks. *You're in such great shape for your age.* And *I would've guessed you were ten years younger.* Richard never qualified his compliments. He'd always accepted her exactly as she was.

In her life, he'd been the only one who hadn't sought to change her. Even her parents had tried. Especially her parents. Her father had attempted to force her into a career in science, although she had no aptitude or interest in it, but her mother was worse. For Olivia's twelfth birthday, her mother had given her a blue taffeta dress with Swarovski crystals sewn onto the bodice. "Isn't it the most beautiful dress you've ever seen?" her mother had asked.

Though it was too loose and a couple of inches too short, Olivia nodded, because agreement was what her mother expected. Her mom's need for control probably had roots in her own chaotic marriage. She couldn't stop her husband's transgressions, but she could force her daughter to wear taffeta and learn to play the violin.

Olivia had always taken pride in parenting better than they had. Until Adam disappeared.

She sometimes wondered if she should've let Richard install that fence. But it wouldn't have protected Adam—not when the danger came from someone he would've gladly given the security code to.

When Olivia returned from gathering her arrows, Richard smiled and moved to leave. "I'll tell Dominic you're out here."

Though they'd invited their son for brunch, he was more than an hour early. "Dominic's already here?"

"I assumed you heard him arrive."

Why hadn't she? The archery range wasn't far from the house. But she'd been distracted for days. She needed to pull it together, quickly, or Richard might suspect she knew his secret. "Where is he?"

Richard's pause lasted several beats too long, and Olivia's hand froze around the bow.

"Richard?"

"He's in your office."

Why would it matter that Dominic was in her office? It wasn't even really her office anymore. Now that she was semiretired from her career in corporate communications, Richard and their daughter, Thea, used it more than Olivia did. "Doing what?"

"He's on a call."

She sighed in exasperation. "With who?"

"With Leyna Clarke."

Her body grew as taut as a drawn bowstring. "Why's he talking to Leyna?"

It was Richard's turn to be exasperated. "How should I know?"

"You heard them talking."

"I heard her name when I went in the kitchen to grab some pretzels."

"You must've heard something more than that."

"I was more focused on finding pretzels—which it turns out we're out of—than on eavesdropping on our adult son."

She couldn't keep the pinch of irritation from her face. *Wonder how stunning he thinks I am now?*

"It's Leyna," she said. "Of course I want to know what they're talking about."

"I didn't realize I'd been recruited as a spy." He strained to keep his tone light, but she could tell he was annoyed. "And you're missing the important part—we're out of pretzels."

Olivia blew out a long breath. "I'm sorry. You're right."

"It's okay. We can pick some pretzels up at the store." He grinned, but he studied her face as intently as she had the paper target. "What do you think about inviting Rocky over for brunch too?"

Olivia kept her eyes pinned to his. "Sure. We have more than enough." She forced a smile. "Would you mind checking if we have asparagus for the frittata?"

They had several bunches in the crisper, but she needed the time alone to compose herself before going back into the house. In there, she could hide nothing.

"Of course," Richard said. He added playfully, "Should I spy on our son too?"

Yes. And if you could record the conversation, that'd be great.

"No. It's fine."

Richard leaned in and placed a hand on the small of her back; his thumb made small circles there.

"Is everything okay, Liv?" he asked. "You seem distant today."

"It's the heat, I think. This weather always puts me on edge."

She didn't blame Leyna for what happened to Adam. She'd been only twelve at the time, and there were greater shares of blame for the other Clarke women—Grace and, especially, Meredith. But it was Leyna who'd tried to ruin her son's memory, and Olivia could never forgive her for that.

She comforted herself with the thought that at least Leyna was in Reno, closer than Olivia would've liked but still an hour's drive from her home and her son.

Richard's thumb traced a last lazy circle on her back before he dropped his hand. "You'd tell me if something was wrong?"

"Of course," she lied.

Olivia shifted away from him, but her skin still prickled where he'd touched her.

CHAPTER 7
LEYNA

Saturday, 8:50 a.m.

Before she'd left Sierraville, Leyna called Dominic to let him know she was twenty minutes away. A few minutes into their conversation, the call dropped. Strange that she couldn't get a signal on that stretch of highway. Dominic had mentioned the power was out at Ridgepoint Ranch—a preemptive measure, he'd said—but she wouldn't have thought it would affect service that far south.

Leyna couldn't help but take it as a warning. With the exception of Dominic, no one in the old neighborhood would want her there. And, truthfully, she wasn't even sure how Dominic would react. A phone call was one thing, being face to face for the first time in a decade another.

Their relationship had started slow. Too slow. The problem was, Dominic knew her too well. A version of her, anyway. Growing up, Leyna was the girl who'd sulked when she got a B in English—she could handle failing math, but that less-than-perfect grade on a midterm paper had been a minor devastation. She was the girl who'd eaten a whole jar of maraschino cherries and gotten sick—Grace had called her Pinkie for a month for the color of the vomit she'd left on the bathroom floor only a couple of feet from the toilet.

That's you, Pinkie. Always falling just short. Back then, Grace had said such things with a teasing smile.

But that's who Leyna was at Ridgepoint Ranch. A girl to be teased for vomiting cherry juice, for disappearing into the forest with a tattered copy of *And Then There Were None.* A girl who could climb trees effortlessly but sometimes tripped while walking on asphalt.

A child.

That summer before her nineteenth birthday, Leyna hadn't wanted to be a child in Dominic's eyes. So they'd spent a long weekend in San Francisco, ostensibly to attend a music festival, but most of the time they'd been in their hotel, talking over plates of crispy-skinned chicken and watching movies on the TV in their room, everything from romantic comedies to *The Purge.*

The five hours that separated them from home had done the trick. They'd left a couple.

Recently, Leyna had come across *The Purge* on TV, and she'd instantly heard his voice in her head.

If there was a Purge here, I would build a shelter where no one could get to you.

I assume you'd be there too?

It's only fair, since I built it.

We'd need to stay put, though. We couldn't fall for their tricks to flush us out.

His voice had rasped when he'd said, *If we were there together, what reason would I have to leave?*

Later, Leyna gave him plenty of reasons to change his mind about that.

The closer Leyna got to the old neighborhood, the lighter her foot got on the gas pedal. Though she was in no hurry to return to it, the Ridgepoint Ranch of Leyna's childhood had been a place of wonder. Homes like scaled-down castles. Azure skies, cloudless until evening, when puffs of white would appear as if conjured by a child's wish. Pine- and ozone-scented air that felt heavy in her lungs. The scent of woodsmoke, but only in the winter, when night started early and fire wasn't a threat.

But mostly, the lure for Leyna had been the forest. The pines and firs and cedars that marched shoulder to shoulder from her backyard and up the mountainside.

That glossier, brochure-ready version had stopped existing long before Grace went missing. As Leyna pulled up, she saw that the street that dead-ended at the Clarke home was well maintained—weeds trimmed, asphalt intact. The Miller house, now operated as a short-term rental, was starting to show signs of wear, but the other houses had been kept up. Glass still gleamed, front doors were freshly painted, and cars were kept in the driveways.

But Leyna knew that a quarter mile down the main road, slabs intended for houses had cracked. A few houses from the second phase of construction had been framed, but most of the wood had been scavenged. The last time she'd been home, only a few pieces, warped and water-stained, had littered the ground. Now, after ten years, those were probably gone too.

Another few hundred feet up the road, no slabs had been poured; the street was gravel and dirt. Beyond that, the golf course and its empty pool. As they were the only children on the street back then, the grounds had belonged to the four of them—the Duran brothers, the Clarke sisters. They would sneak onto the fairway and toss rocks into the water traps, climb the trees with branches closest to the ground. They broke into the half-built clubhouse and claimed it as their own until Grace found a dead possum next to a roll of discarded insulation.

Leyna had no intention of staying long enough to see what had become of their former playground. An hour, two max, and she'd be back on the road to Reno. She climbed out of the car and held up her phone, tapping the top of the screen. No bars. Not even the SOS showing she could summon emergency services.

She scanned the neighborhood but saw no sign of Dominic. She wondered again what he might look like now and if he still used the same cologne—the one with notes of cedar and fir that smelled as much like home in her memory as the surrounding forest.

It was dangerous, being here.

Leyna started to punch in a text, then remembered she had no service. She wasn't about to knock on the Durans' door. She glanced reluctantly at her mom's house. Only one step better than going to the Durans'.

But this she had to do, if for no other reason than to get Grace's old photos. Leyna told herself they might hold some connection to Ellie, but she didn't really believe that. She wanted the Polaroids because they wouldn't fade as much as her memories would. Leyna worried that eventually, she'd forget all the moments that once brought Grace joy, and the last of her sister would disappear.

And then there were the questions she could ask only her mom. About Adam.

Despite Leyna's resolve, her stomach twisted as she climbed the steps to the front porch of her childhood home. She brushed her fingers across the scar in the middle of her left forearm. A couple of inches long, the scar had once been ropy and pink, and it had itched like crazy. Her skin had produced too much collagen during healing, the doctor said. But injections and time had softened it until all that remained was a small strip of discolored skin and a phantom itch during times of stress. Like now. She fought the urge to pick at it.

She imagined her mom's drawl and the judgment that always masqueraded as concern: *You need to move on, Leyna. Stop seeing your sister in the faces of strangers.* Wind whistled through the pines that lined the driveway, sounding a lot like one of her mom's disappointed sighs.

That sigh of wind worried her, but she focused on more immediate concerns.

She tapped on the door, then peered through one of the sidelights that flanked it. Behind the house, the generator hummed, but candles flickered on the entryway table, as if her mom were inside channeling the dead. Maybe she'd finally accepted that Grace wasn't coming home.

A gust rattled the pines again, scattering needles on the ground.

As Leyna balled her fist and prepared to knock with more authority, the door swung open, revealing her mom in a red painter's smock, blond hair pulled back into an artfully messy bun, a small ruby pendant nestling in the hollow of her throat.

Despite the strategically curated elegance, there was nothing delicate about Meredith Clarke. Her spine seemed a rod anchored in the ground, her arms muscle and bone, as if anything unnecessary had been stripped away.

When she saw Leyna, her forehead puckered, and her jaw went slack. She managed a quick "Oh."

After ten years, that was what Leyna got: A startled exhalation followed by an awkward silence. More than she'd expected.

Her mom had four inches on her, five if you took into account Leyna's slouch. Only Grace had had the height to look their mom in the eye. Leyna pulled her shoulders back, her gaze falling to a plastic bag in her mom's hand. *Was that—*

"Is that a bag of dog crap?" Her mom wasn't a dog person. She was even less a dog-*crap* person.

"It is indeed a bag of dog crap." Her eyes glittered like the ruby at her neck. "It belongs to the Durans. I was on my way to return it."

Leyna couldn't imagine her mom talking to Dominic's mom, even to prove a point.

As if she'd read her daughter's skepticism, she sighed heavily.

"I'm not lighting it on fire and ringing the doorbell, if that's what that look is about. And I'm certainly not talking to that woman." She frowned, nose crinkling, her default expression when mentioning the neighbor. "I'm merely going to leave it on their porch to remind her to keep her dog out of my garden."

This wasn't how Leyna had envisioned their first face-to-face conversation in a decade, though she guessed the bag of crap was symbolic enough. Leyna tilted her head toward the side of the house, where the garbage bins were kept. "Don't you think it's better just to throw it away?"

Meredith's cool blue eyes held her daughter's. "Let's not argue today," she said, as if the arguments were always Leyna's doing and as if they could be so easily avoided. She stalked over to the bin and tossed in the bag with exaggerated reluctance. Back on the steps, she gestured to the door. "I suppose you want to come inside."

Not really. "If you're not busy."

Her mom looked down at her paint-splattered smock, then up again. "It's fine." She pushed open the door.

Leyna was only a couple of steps across the threshold before her chest constricted. Her mom had a way of filling a space so that it became hard for her to breathe, but that wasn't why she now planted a steadying palm against the wall. It was the smell, thick and sickly sweet. Another scent from the past.

Spiced vanilla.

The scent of the candles on the entryway table burned her nostrils. She fought a wave of vertigo, pressing her palm more firmly against the wall. Too many memories had intruded lately.

Her back to Leyna, her mom missed the reaction. She walked to the kitchen sink to wash her hands, calling over her shoulder, "Why are you here?"

The scent of spiced vanilla grew stronger. Leyna hadn't experienced the scent of those particular candles since she was a child. An image of Grace flashed, as bright as the row of dancing flames. She switched to breathing through her mouth, then pushed away from the wall.

Her mom returned to the entryway and picked up the candle snuffer on the table. She lowered the metal cup over each flame in turn. Leyna worked to mask her gratitude, which her mom would've read as weakness.

"I've come to talk to Dominic about that missing girl," she said. "And I was hoping to get Grace's photos."

Her mom's eyes narrowed at Dominic's name, and she harrumphed. "Everyone wants to talk about that girl," she said. "As far as the photos, I could've mailed them to you."

"I'd hate to put you out." Her mom would've thrown them in a box with little care. Leyna wanted to preserve the memory of all of it—the order in which they'd been hung, the blank wall left by those that were missing, even the way the twine had been coiled by her sister's hand.

Her mom cocked her head, gaze predatory. "Shouldn't you be at work?"

"I'm off today." *And tomorrow, and the day after that...*

Her mom set the snuffer down and looked at Leyna for the first time since they'd entered the house.

"I don't know why everyone's so interested in that girl. She's not even from here, and that car she was driving was found in Sierra County."

"Heard she was in the neighborhood that day."

Her mom's eyes narrowed to slits. "I didn't know you and Dominic were still talking."

"We aren't."

Leyna moved into the living room, away from her mom and the lingering scent of the candles. She'd always heard that childhood homes shrank with the passage of time, no longer exaggerated by a child's perception. To her, though, this room seemed to have grown larger, even stuffed as it was—there were four tufted armchairs, a gray velvet sofa, and a cherry leather ottoman the size of a twin bed. All new. Her mom got bored with furniture quickly. Even though she rarely entertained, ten guests could've lounged comfortably here. On cooler autumn nights, when a fire blazed in the fireplace, the living room could feel almost cozy. But that afternoon, the stacked granite that stretched to the ceiling overwhelmed the space, and the blackened fireplace served as a reminder of the threat posed by the current weather.

"Grab your photos and go home, Leyna."

"Soon." No one was more eager for Leyna to leave than she herself was. "Did you talk to her that day? See her in the neighborhood?"

"If that girl was here, she didn't knock on my door."

Her mom was the queen of loopholes, so Leyna tried again. "Then you didn't see her?"

"That's what I said."

"Actually, it isn't."

Her mom's face pinched with weariness. "Why must you be difficult?"

That's right. I'm supposed to be the good *daughter.* Leyna had been shoehorned into that role at birth for no other reason than that she'd arrived last in her small family. By then, there hadn't been room for another big personality. Now, even with the Clarke family pruned to just the two of them, it felt like there wasn't enough room for her, and Leyna had stopped being the good daughter ten years ago.

Leyna walked to the dining room, which had a better view of the forest and of the Duran home. In contrast to the living room, the dining area was empty except for the easel near the window with a canvas propped on it, a table holding painting supplies, and the large tarp covering the floor. Her mom used the dining area for her painting since, she said, it got the best light. Though the canvas faced mostly away from her, Leyna caught a sliver of green and gray. She could guess what her mom had been painting. What she always painted. Her mom's artwork had paid for the house and allowed them to keep it after her father left.

When her mom noticed Leyna looking, she shifted the easel so the sliver of canvas disappeared. In the kitchen, a phone started ringing. The landline. Her mom made no move to answer.

"You're not getting that?"

"There aren't many people I want to talk to." Her expression indicated that she counted Leyna among the people she preferred to avoid.

"What if it's important?"

"Then they'll call back."

When the phone trilled into silence, Leyna turned to the window. Though the houses sat on large lots, she had a decent view of the Miller house and, just beyond that, the Durans'. The house where Adam once lived.

"If Ellie was in the neighborhood Thursday, you would've heard something."

"So maybe she wasn't here."

"She was."

"You've always been so certain of your convictions." Her tone made it clear this was an insult.

"That's why they're convictions," Leyna said. "Who else was in the neighborhood Thursday?"

"I don't know. The Silvestris. The Durans. Not sure about the Kims." She inhaled sharply, as if a conversation with her younger daughter exhausted her. "The Miller house has been empty all week."

"How about Adam?"

In the window's reflection, Leyna caught her mom's flinch.

"Why would you ask about Adam?"

"Could he be back too?"

Leyna studied her mom's reflection, but she'd recovered from her surprise. Or whatever the hell it was that had made her draw back at the mention of Adam's name.

"Why would you think Adam might have returned?" Meredith crossed her arms. "I know we don't speak often, but I definitely would've called you about that."

"Ellie bears a resemblance to Grace."

Even in the window, Leyna saw her mom roll her eyes.

"Really, Leyna."

Leyna started to turn away from the window, but a flash of movement at the door of the Miller house caught her mid-pivot. At first she thought it might be Dominic. But then tension snaked between her shoulders.

Wasn't the Miller house supposed to be empty?

Leyna stepped closer to the window, her forehead an inch from the glass. The door of the house between the Clarkes' and the Durans' was open, but no one stood in the doorway. If someone had been there, whoever it was had retreated into the house's dim interior. Leyna told herself she was seeing things again. Just as she had at the café when she'd imagined Ellie might be Grace. But if the house was unoccupied, why was the door open at all?

Leyna worried the scar on her arm. "Are you sure no one's staying next door?"

"There shouldn't be."

"The door's open."

"Probably the cleaner preparing for the next guest."

An odd time to clean, given the heat and the power outage.

Leyna squinted at the house. She was sure now. Someone had definitely gone in. Because the houses on the street sat close to the forest, most were in partial shadow, yet the lights inside remained off. The power was out, but like most people out there, the Millers probably owned a generator.

She took a step to the side so she was no longer framed in the window and checked her watch. Where the hell was Dominic?

Leyna remembered a story she'd heard in childhood about a hiker who had been mauled by a mother bear protecting her cubs. The bear had torn the skin from the woman's face and dislocated her jaw.

Beyond the Miller house, she saw golden shafts of sunlight cutting through the trees. Moss-covered trunks. The yellow-green leaves of dying ferns. It all felt oddly peaceful.

Still, Leyna's ears roared as if they contained the gathering wind. She couldn't help wondering if the hiker had felt something similar the moment before the bear mauled her.

CHAPTER 8

MEREDITH

Saturday, 9:18 a.m.

Meredith watched Leyna stare out the window, expression resigned. She touched her scar—for the fourth time since entering the house, Meredith noted. She could always tell when Leyna was thinking about her sister.

"Someone is definitely inside the Miller house," Leyna said.

"I told you, it's probably someone from the cleaning service." A lie. The cleaner had been at the house earlier that morning, but Leyna had always been annoyingly curious, and Meredith wanted her gone.

Leyna shook her head. "Not with the lights out." But her expression seemed less certain. That had long been Meredith's superpower: making her younger daughter doubt herself.

With Leyna distracted, Meredith took full stock of her daughter's appearance. Her blond hair was constrained in a tight ponytail, the layers grown out. She obviously hadn't been to a stylist in a while. At least she'd tamed her eyebrows. When Leyna was eighteen, they'd given the impression of a pair of warring woolly bear caterpillars.

Then there was her face—round since birth, it seemed puffier than usual, her natural pallor turned positively pasty. Her twill joggers and T-shirt were worn loose. Leyna was definitely stress-eating again. As a child, she could finish half a box of ginger cookies before a big test or after a heartbreak. She'd gained twenty pounds in the months following Grace's disappearance. So why was she bingeing now?

Asking that question might take the conversation in an unwelcome direction, so Meredith remained silent. She shifted to better block her half-painted canvas.

Seemingly unaware of her mother's scrutiny, Leyna gestured toward the neighbors' house. "Think the Millers booked it last minute?"

"With the power out and the red-flag alert, that seems unlikely."

Growing up, Leyna had lived mostly in her head and in books. It'd made for a much quieter house, but now Meredith regretted having enabled her daughter's Agatha Christie habit.

"Why does it matter who's inside the Miller place?"

If anybody even was. Meredith squinted at the house on the adjacent lot. Leyna had mentioned the door was open, but it was closed now. The house appeared empty.

"It doesn't matter," Leyna said, but she continued to stare. The wind had started to pick up again, and a gust shook loose a flurry of pine needles. "You sure there's enough gas in your generator?"

"I topped it off earlier this week when the weather started to turn."

"New batteries in the flashlights?" When Meredith scowled in response, Leyna mirrored the expression. "If the generator fails, it'll be hard to find batteries in the dark."

"I know how night works, Leyna. And if the flashlights run out of juice, I have candles."

Leyna looked over her shoulder toward the entryway. Her eyes clouded. "Not those candles?"

"Those candles, and others," Meredith said.

Her daughter's hand landed on her arm again. That made the fifth touch. This time, her fingers lingered on the discolored skin.

That damn scar.

Leyna had gotten it on the day they'd lost Grace. It had been a wet March, and with a five-day storm fizzling out that morning, neighbors had emerged from forced hibernation to rake leaves, clear debris from driveways, and unclog rain gutters. Meredith spent the day in her garden, but even after night fell, she'd vibrated with unspent energy. She tried painting and two shots of bourbon. Neither helped. After a huge fight with Grace—par for the course in their house but unusual in that the bloodshed that night had been more than figurative—Meredith felt an unexpected urge to check on her younger daughter.

Meredith found her asleep in bed, lamp casting shadowed light across her face, a copy of *Murder on the Orient Express* cutting into her cheek. Likely sensing Meredith watching, Leyna shifted in her sleep, exposing her arm—and a two-inch cut, jagged and raw. The wound hadn't been there earlier.

It seemed an omen—as if the ugliness of the day had manifested in the bloody mark on her daughter's arm and foretold worse things to come.

Meredith had shaken Leyna, more violently than she intended. Leyna startled from sleep, and Meredith pointed at the wound.

"You need to get a bandage on that."

Leyna blinked slowly, coming fully awake. "I didn't know where to find the Neosporin."

Meredith noticed a balled-up tissue spotted with blood on the nightstand.

"You should've asked," she snapped before realizing they'd used the last of it the month before on Leyna's tree-scraped knee and how unfortunate it would've been had Leyna actually gone looking. Better she'd been asleep.

Leyna started to sit up, but Meredith placed a firm hand on her shoulder. "Tomorrow." She reminded herself to be gentler with this daughter and leaned in to take a closer look at the cut. "What the hell happened?"

"It was an accident," Leyna said, rubbing her eyes.

Those words chilled Meredith still. *It was an accident.* In those days, an even more popular excuse than *Grace didn't mean to do it.*

She'd tucked Leyna back into bed and paused in the doorway until her daughter closed her eyes. If only it had been as easy for Meredith to do the same that night.

The memory had teeth, and it took several shakes to loosen its grip. Meredith crossed her arms, a comfort as much as a blockade.

"Think I'll check on what's going on next door," Leyna said. "If they've just come from town, maybe they have an update on the weather."

It's hot and windy. There's your update.

But Meredith knew what really drew Leyna to the house next door. She'd been chasing Grace's ghost for sixteen years. For just as long, Meredith had been praying she'd never catch it.

"Fabulous idea," Meredith said dryly.

"I won't be long. Thanks for your help with Ellie." Her delivery was deadpan, but Meredith recognized the sarcasm.

With that, Leyna glanced one final time out the window, then left in search of whatever ghosts she imagined waited for her on the other side of the glass.

CHAPTER 9

LEYNA

Saturday, 9:29 a.m.

Though the house next door was built of the same stone and wood as the neighboring properties, it hinted at its status as a vacation rental. No cars were parked outside. The landscaping was low maintenance, without grass to mow or flowers that might need careful attention. Sensors were wired into the sconces flanking the front doors so the lights could blink on at dusk, off at dawn. The generator was silent, unlike those at the other homes on the street.

Leyna noticed all of this but knocked anyway. She gave it a minute before ringing the bell. Another minute before trying the knob. It twisted freely, so she pushed open the door and shouted a greeting, loud enough to carry to the rear of the large house.

Someone had been here moments ago. She was sure of it. Staring out her mom's window, she'd felt as if someone stared back. It shouldn't have mattered—she was the outsider in the neighborhood now, and for all she knew, the person belonged in that house. Leyna didn't. But she was drawn forward just the same.

Her mom's voice trilled in her head: *Leave it alone.*

As if she'd ever been the type to do that.

Leyna crossed the threshold into the open living space and shouted again. "Hello?"

The word echoed. When no response came, Leyna risked several more steps. Like in the Clarke house, the living room featured a grand fireplace and skylights cut into wood beams. It offered the same floor-to-ceiling windows and panoramic views, the same glimpse of forested hillside and white-blue sky.

The similarities ended there. In the vacation rental, the light oak furniture was catalog-chic—shades of beige and brown with the occasional throw pillow's pop of color. All the pieces intended to be inoffensive and interchangeable, easily swapped out in case of unexpected breakage.

Empty but close to the other homes, the vacation rental made the perfect hiding place. She imagined Adam in one of the bedrooms that faced his childhood home, watching, alone or with Ellie. Even if the young woman had come willingly, Leyna knew how deeply Adam could hurt the ones he claimed to love.

Leyna moved farther into the house, pausing before each door, searching for a sign she'd been right, that she hadn't imagined the movement in the doorway. Each time she entered a new room, her pulse quickened as she wondered if this would be where she found Adam or Ellie.

In the kitchen, she found a welcome note addressed to the Hahns stuck to the refrigerator; it included rules, a list of contact numbers, and the Wi-Fi password. The check-in date was two days in the future. On the counter, a pen and notepad and artfully fanned brochures of local attractions were arranged.

In the bathroom, a stack of brown towels was folded on a rack next to a soaking tub large enough to float a kayak. No scent of pine or bleach lingered. Whoever had watched her, it hadn't been the house cleaner.

Leyna should've felt more at ease the deeper in the house she searched, but instead she felt like she was engaged in some warped version of Russian roulette, where each vacant room represented the click of an empty chamber. While she hoped to find Ellie, a perverse part of her also hoped Adam was with her—to prove to everyone that Leyna had always been right about him.

She imagined another of her mom's disappointed sighs.

They ran away, Leyna. Let it go.

He's dangerous, Mom. He's always been dangerous.

She'd been back less than an hour, and she was already having imagined arguments with her mom. As if the real ones weren't enough.

Leyna stepped back into the hall and moved toward what she assumed was the master bedroom. She had just stepped inside when she heard it—a distinct *thump.*

She tensed. Somewhere in the back of the house.

Spine rigid, she pricked her ears, waiting for the sound to repeat. Under the assault of the wind, the house creaked. Had that been what she'd heard?

She listened for several long seconds but heard only the wind's whine and the groan of the walls.

After checking around the bedroom, she began to think maybe the thump had come from outside. Had a patio chair upended? Had a limb fallen onto the hot tub's cover?

Leaving the master bedroom, she hurried to a side window that looked out over the patio. She saw a pair of Adirondack chairs and a small round table, all upright. The only debris on the hot tub was a dusting of pine needles.

Strange. She could've sworn she'd heard something.

Thump.

No way she had imagined it that time. Leyna hurried to a room in the back of the house. Unlike the master bedroom's, this door was closed. She tried the knob, but it wouldn't budge.

She returned to the kitchen and grabbed the ballpoint pen from the counter.

Back at the door to the locked room, Leyna knocked loudly, then called a warning: "Coming in."

She waited thirty seconds, and when no rifle shots or additional thumps came, she removed the ink cartridge from the pen.

It was Grace who taught Leyna how to pick a lock. Leyna could still picture the way Grace's face scrunched in concentration as she replayed the video dozens of times, her fingers nimble as she finessed the lock on her bedroom door. She'd insisted Leyna try too. When she'd asked why, Grace shot her a look of bewilderment.

People lock up the things they want to hide. As if she had the right to other people's secrets.

In Leyna's initial attempts, her fingers had been thick and clumsy, and she'd practiced for hours on her own to earn her sister's approval. She was rewarded with one of Grace's smiles, rare in those final weeks. But the smile quickly faded, and when Grace leaned into the shadows, her pupils swelled so that her eyes appeared black.

Protect yourself, Ley. Her tone hushed, insistent. *You never know who you can trust.*

Sixteen years later, Leyna shivered still.

On her knees in front of the locked door, Leyna rolled the ink cartridge between her fingers. It seemed sturdy enough, and the diameter was right. She pushed the cartridge in the hole, wiggling and twisting, first in one direction and then the other. It wouldn't budge. She applied more pressure.

Finally, the lock clicked. In high school, Grace could've unlocked the door in less than a minute. It had taken Leyna at least five.

Leyna opened the door to the cloying scent of lavender potpourri. Like the vanilla candles her mom had been burning, the scent conjured the sting of loss. She supposed everything there would feel like loss to her, but it wasn't like she could hold her breath or wander around the neighborhood with her eyes closed. At Ridgepoint, there had already been far too much of that.

She stepped into the room, which was as simply furnished as the rest of the house. Matching bedroom set—queen bed, dresser, nightstand—built from the same pale wood used in the other rooms. Though the blinds were closed, the red stripes on the comforter had faded slightly where the sun would've reached through the window. She touched that spot, imagining the warmth that had bleached the color from it. The dresser next to it had signs of wear on the corner, the polished edge showing less of the grain.

Leyna moved to the closet and opened the door. She bit the inside of her cheek hard enough to draw blood.

There, in the closet, a girl stared back at her with warm brown eyes set in a face that was even paler than her own except for twin spots of coral. Her long brown hair hung loose, and she tugged at the hem of a lavender T-shirt.

"I don't think you're supposed to be here," the girl said.

Leyna took a step back. "Are *you* supposed to be here?"

"Of course not. Why do you think I locked the door and then hid in the closet?" She brushed past Leyna, hopped onto the bed, and sat cross-legged. "Did I scare you?"

"A little bit," Leyna admitted. "Did I scare you?"

She shook her head. "I could see out of the closet, and you didn't look scary."

"Not everyone who's scary looks it."

"My mom says that too." She rolled her eyes. "I thought you might be Rocky."

At the mention of Rocky, Leyna could see him as he'd been that day ten years earlier when she'd finally confronted the Durans: in a henley shirt and jeans, at least six inches taller than anyone else in the neighborhood, his light brown hair starting to silver. He was the only one who'd looked at her with any compassion. True, there was anger mixed in with it. It had probably been mostly anger. But there was a hint of compassion too. Maybe.

Though Rocky's dream of building out Ridgepoint Ranch had stalled, he still owned the land and lived alone in a cottage a short walk into the woods. Leyna guessed the pending lawsuit over permits made the land unsellable. But with no family in the state except the Durans, where else would Rocky go anyway?

The day Grace and Adam had gone missing, the deputy had taken a report from Olivia Duran before telling her there was little they could do about runaways. Though Olivia had protested—*My son wouldn't have left without saying goodbye*—the neighbors had quietly supported Meredith's claim that the kids had been planning to leave. Adam was obsessed with the Museum of Science and Industry in Chicago, also home to Grace's favorite band. Even Richard admitted Adam had talked about moving east with Grace. The former owner of what was now the Miller house went so far as to say she thought she'd seen the couple headed toward the road that night, carrying bulging backpacks and holding hands.

But though the neighbors agreed with Meredith, their support went to the grieving Olivia, who drew more sympathy and less blame. What kind of woman must Meredith be to allow two teens to run away from her home and then keep that information from the other teen's mom until morning?

Leyna had been excluded from the search—Olivia wouldn't allow it—but she'd heard every word, and she'd trailed behind them even though she knew they would find nothing. She wanted to shout at their backs: *You're going the wrong way!* She wanted to point them in the right direction, but then she would've had to tell them everything. She would've had to admit what she'd done, and she hadn't been ready to confess her role in that night.

Sixteen years later, she still wasn't ready.

"Why would you think I was Rocky?" Leyna asked.

The girl's grin drooped, replaced by a slight reserve. She shrugged.

"He sometimes fixes things for the Millers when the house is empty." She started bouncing on the bed. "Before I hid, I was looking for our dog. His name's Goose. He's part French bulldog and part something else."

Leyna tamped down her curiosity and the tension that always came with it. Her smile made her cheeks feel unnaturally tight. "Goose. That's an unusual name."

"Mom wanted a dog, and Dad said she should get a bird instead. So she compromised and got a dog named Goose."

Olivia had just given birth when Leyna left that last time. That baby had to be this girl. "So where are your parents?" Leyna had no interest in seeing Olivia Duran again.

The girl wrinkled her nose, her eyes closing to slits. "My mom told me I shouldn't talk to strangers."

For someone who'd been told not to talk to strangers, the girl certainly had a lot to say.

"Your mom's right." Leyna sank onto the bed, on the edge, far from the girl.

The girl pulled a granola bar out of her pocket and offered it to Leyna, who shook her head but smiled. "My mom told me not to take food from strangers."

The girl unwrapped the granola bar and took a bite.

"How'd you get into the house?" Leyna asked.

"My mom has a key for emergencies," she said, chewing around her words. "How'd you get in?"

"The front door was unlocked."

She wrinkled her nose, obviously irritated by her own mistake. "So how'd you get in the bedroom?"

"I picked the lock."

The girl's eyes widened. "With what?"

"Part of a ballpoint pen."

The girl tossed the half-eaten granola bar on the nightstand, and when she spoke, she was nearly breathless. "Can you teach me how to do that?"

"I thought you weren't supposed to talk to strangers."

She bounced on the bed. "I'm Thea. Now will you teach me?"

Imagining the look on Olivia's face if she learned that Leyna had taught her daughter how to pick locks, she laughed. *Sorry, kid. Never going to happen.* "Have you seen anyone else around besides your dad's cousin?"

The girl studied Leyna through narrowed eyes. "If I tell you, will you teach me how to pick a lock?"

"Thea."

The voice came from behind Leyna, and it raised the hair on the back of her neck. She'd once thought it the kindest voice she'd ever heard. How wrong she'd been.

Leyna turned and locked eyes with Olivia Duran, who stood in the doorway looking as tall and stunning as she'd been back when she was still Meredith's friend and Leyna had called her Aunt Olivia. At twelve, Leyna had gone to the Durans' house expecting comfort. Instead, she'd been told to go home with words that haunted her still and had devastated her as a child:

You can't be here, Leyna. Not today. Not anymore.

And then Aunt Olivia had shut the door with enough force that the frame vibrated.

The feud sparked by that slammed door might've cooled over time if not for the incident with the flyers. The summer Grace would've turned twenty-three, Olivia hung new MISSING posters all over Quincy and Portola. Below the banner, in bold: **Help bring Adam home.**

No mention of Grace.

That in itself wasn't new. Every year, Olivia headed into town to replace the old, tattered flyers with updated ones, always with a new photo. Sometimes multiple photos. But somehow, there was never room for her to mention Leyna's sister, even in the section that gave the details of Adam's disappearance. It said only that Adam never returned home after visiting a neighbor's house. Though simply stated, there always seemed to be an accusation hidden in those words, and everyone knew which neighbor to blame.

In years past, Leyna had put up her own flyers, of course, but when she'd checked on them later, they were gone. A random act? Maybe. But more likely, they'd been torn down by Olivia or Richard or even her own mom, who always insisted Leyna leave it, as if she were a dog being encouraged to drop a stolen sandal.

Olivia usually replaced the flyers in March to coincide with the anniversary, but with a new baby at home, she'd been several months late getting to it. That Olivia had hung the damn posters so close to Grace's birthday had irritated Leyna, but that she'd chosen that photo of Adam for the new poster enraged her. Leyna recognized the photo immediately because the original had included Grace.

Olivia had eliminated Leyna's sister from the photo. One quick crop, and Grace no longer existed.

Leyna had just ripped one of the flyers off a utility post when she'd heard a voice from behind her.

"I'm sorry."

When Leyna turned, her gut clenched, and she almost said her sister's name.

"I didn't know Grace well, but I was a year behind her in school. She seemed sweet."

The woman had to be telling the truth about not knowing Grace well. No one who'd known Grace well would've described her as *sweet. Passionate,* definitely. *Mercurial. Charismatic.* Maybe *kind.* But *sweet*? Never that.

The resemblance between this woman and her sister was disconcerting. The reddish-blond hair. Blue eyes. The slope of her jaw, and the contour of her cheeks. This woman was a few inches shorter and, of course, years older than Grace was when she disappeared. About the age Grace would've been if it had been her standing on Portola's main street.

The woman shifted, filling Leyna's awkward pause with a smile. She introduced herself as Dawn, and Leyna finally found her voice.

"If you knew Grace, did you know Adam too?"

The smile faded. "I did." She hesitated, and Leyna waited for her to say more about Adam. Instead, the woman's expression grew guarded. "I hope you find out what happened to your sister."

Leyna noted the word choice—*what happened to your sister,* as if information were all she could possibly find. She also noticed that although the woman apparently knew Adam too, she offered no sympathy or hopes for him.

Dawn made a move to leave but it appeared half-hearted, and she stopped when Leyna took a step toward her. There seemed to be more this stranger wanted to tell her.

Leyna gave her an opening. "How did you know Adam?"

But Leyna guessed before the other woman answered.

"We used to date. Before Grace." The smile returned, though it broke at the corners. "Adam had a type."

"It didn't end well?"

Dawn's sigh was weary. "Do high-school relationships ever end well?"

"What happened? If you don't mind my asking."

"Adam had a temper, especially when he was jealous. And he was jealous a lot."

"What did he do to you?"

Dawn laughed harshly. "He wasn't jealous with me. Just with her. Your sister. It kind of kills a relationship when the guy you're dating gets jealous because guys are paying attention to another girl." She shrugged. "It's okay. We didn't date long, and even in the beginning, I figured I was a substitute for Grace. Not great for my ego, but I suppose I dodged a bullet." She looked sheepish. "Sorry."

Leyna ignored the apology, entirely focused on what she'd said before it.

"Dodged a bullet how? Do you know something about what happened to them?"

Dawn's eyes went wide, the shake of her head emphatic. "Oh. No. I only meant he broke a guy's arm." She wrinkled her nose in obvious repulsion. "Adam claimed it was an accident. The guy tripped. But the day before, he'd asked Grace to Homecoming, so..."

Leyna knew all about Adam's type of accident.

Dawn offered one last sympathetic glance. "Hope you get closure. Six years is a long time to wait for answers."

Then she'd hurried away, leaving Leyna clutching the flyer she'd torn from the pole.

In the Durans' driveway later that day, Leyna had confronted Olivia and Richard, holding the now wrinkled paper inches from Olivia's face, hand trembling but gaze steady.

"Say her name," Leyna said quietly.

Olivia took a step back but stayed silent.

"Come on, Aunt Olivia. It's the least you can do, since your son is the one who killed her."

Leyna didn't raise her voice, even when she told Dawn's story of Adam breaking a guy's arm. Even when she started sharing the ugliest memories:

Adam told Grace she was lucky to have him, since she had nothing but her looks to offer, and those wouldn't last long.

He'd called her fat. Stupid.

When Grace stopped having sex with him, Adam hooked up with Grace's friend and then convinced her she was to blame for not loving him enough.

Adam slapped Grace hard enough that she'd needed to ice her cheek.

The last one hadn't been a lie, exactly—Leyna knew how violent Adam could be—but it had been close enough to one that everyone could see it. That cast doubt on everything else she'd said, even though it was true. All of it.

So Leyna kept at it, nearly pleading for them to believe her—"Why can't you see that Adam is a monster?"—even after Olivia blanched, and Richard said, icily, "That's enough, Leyna."

When she'd finished her tirade, she noticed Dominic and her mom were among the spectators. She knew she'd gone too far when she saw even they looked horrified.

Olivia wore the same horrified expression now.

So, not happy to see me then.

CHAPTER 10

OLIVIA

Saturday, 9:43 a.m.

Until Leyna's public attack on Adam, Olivia had cared for Leyna more than she should have.

The elder Clarke girl had been the one most people noticed first. She was bolder, louder, quicker with a witty remark. Nearly four years older than Leyna, she'd gotten the icy-blue eyes, the waves of strawberry-blond hair, the growth spurt at fourteen. Leyna never could catch up. It hadn't surprised Olivia that Grace had mesmerized both her sons—especially Adam.

Leyna, in contrast, was quiet. Earnest. Olivia had loved the girl from the moment she'd shown up at age five with a bucket of mud and worms, asking Olivia if she'd like to play.

One of the hardest things Olivia had ever done was turn Leyna away when she'd come to her door at twelve seeking solace. In that way, Leyna had broken Olivia's heart too. But Meredith and Grace were black holes, the pull of their gravity so strong that even light couldn't escape. What hope had there been for sweet, gentle Adam? Olivia wouldn't have anyone else in her family pulled into that cold, lightless emptiness. After Leyna's tirade in front of their home, Olivia knew she'd been right to cut off the girl.

"Thea," she repeated now, still standing in the bedroom doorway. "Time to go home."

Thea hopped off the bed and moved toward the door but didn't leave. "I didn't find Goose."

"Goose will come back. He always does."

Thea made a face and Olivia expected an argument from her, but instead Thea waved at Leyna and whispered to her as she left, "Don't forget about the lock."

Olivia meant to follow her daughter from the room, but she found herself unable to move. Leyna had her own gravitational pull.

"Why were you talking to my daughter?"

"I'm looking for Ellie Byrd."

"Oh? I wasn't aware you're a deputy now."

Leyna's expression stayed neutral, but Olivia knew she'd caught the sarcasm. "I'm not."

"Haven't seen you around in a while," Olivia said, trying not to sound prickly but failing.

Leyna pushed herself off the bed and leaned against the wall. "So we're doing this?"

"Doing what?"

"Making small talk. Pretending you don't hate me."

"I've never hated you." *Hate* was too strong a word, though in her darkest moments, she'd come close.

Leyna's face gave away nothing. "How's Richard?"

It was Olivia's turn to slip behind a mask. "Great."

"And Rocky?"

"Good, I think." She instantly cringed—*I think*. Before what happened to Adam, she'd been certain of everything. Favorite food? Ecuadoran dumplings made with mashed plantains and filled with pork and cheese because they made her think of Richard. Favorite season? Spring, because it was a time of renewal. Politics, music, books—she had easy opinions on it all. Always, she chose the movie and booked the vacations, and she never answered a question with *I think* or *I believe*.

Now, she could no longer stomach dumplings because they'd been Adam's favorite too, and spring was the season of fresh grief. And Olivia used qualifying language, because how could she be sure of anything when the world had stopped making sense sixteen years before?

Olivia grew aware of Leyna staring, and she thought that maybe the young woman had asked another question.

Thought. Maybe. Two more.

"Why so curious about my family?" Olivia asked. "You know how that went for you last time."

Leyna flinched, telling Olivia her barb had hit its mark.

"Why did you come back, Leyna?"

Leyna tilted her head, that intense gaze of hers assessing. "Dominic wanted to talk about Ellie Byrd."

Olivia grimaced. Dominic's first weekend at home in months, and he'd brought Leyna in his wake. Her next question fell from her mouth before she could stop it. "Have you heard from Grace?"

Silence stretched between them, and for a moment, Olivia thought Leyna might have news to share. Then she shook her head, and Olivia's chest tightened with disappointment. Leads were hard to come by these days.

Then Leyna said, her voice almost a whisper: "We both know I'll probably never hear from her."

The implication landed like a punch, and Olivia said, nearly in a hiss, "Adam didn't kill your sister."

Angry tears formed, but she kept them from breaching. Progress. Maybe in another sixteen years, her eyes would remain dry when someone mentioned Adam or accused him of murder. Maybe she wouldn't flinch at every trill of the landline or chime of the doorbell.

That terrible day in early March, Olivia had been alone in the house, though she hadn't known it. With Richard away on business and Dominic at college, it had been just her and Adam.

And then just her.

But that morning belonged to another time. She'd spent the first hour outlining a communication strategy for a major client, a beverage company—a woman claimed she'd found a syringe in a bottle of their orange juice—as if that were the most urgent crisis she'd face that day. Then she'd scrambled half a dozen eggs, unaware the boy she scrambled them for wasn't home to eat them.

Eggs done, Olivia had turned off the stove, taken out the container of mixed berries, and popped two slices of bread into the toaster. Grief still smelled to her like overcooked eggs and toasting bread. Then she'd headed to Adam's bedroom, knocked—two quick raps—and called through the door, "Adam."

Not yet worried, world still intact. Still thinking about syringes and orange juice and phrases like *brand reputation*.

When Adam didn't respond to her repeated knocking, she called to him a second time with words guaranteed to pull him from his bed: "Breakfast is ready."

The void on the other side of the door swallowed her voice, giving nothing back.

She knocked again, reluctant to enter. What if he was listening to music on his headphones? Or what if he was sleeping so deeply that even the promise of breakfast didn't wake him? From what Olivia had observed over the past few weeks, he and Grace had been having a hard time. Not that he'd shared any details, but Adam was a sensitive child. She could always tell when he was hurting, even if she didn't always know the cause. It was part of the reason she'd made breakfast. But maybe this morning Adam needed sleep more than eggs and toast.

Still, she stood rooted outside his bedroom, the first seed of worry starting to sprout. The sulfur scent of cooling eggs turned her stomach. From the kitchen, she heard the toast pop up, ready for the apricot jam Adam liked so much.

She leaned her ear against the door, which seemed less intrusive than entering. When she couldn't hear anything, she closed her eyes to better focus. She told herself she was being stupid, but the worry grew more insistent, and her instincts started screaming.

No longer concerned about her son's privacy, Olivia shoved open the door. No Adam. Sheets rumpled, blanket half on the floor. But that meant nothing. He was a teenage boy who seldom remembered to make his bed.

She shouted then. "Adam!"

Checked the bathroom. Every room in the house, his name trailing behind her. She fought to keep the fear out of her voice, even though there was no one to hear.

She called his cell phone. It went straight to voice mail.

She ran to the Clarkes' house. Pounded on the door. Meredith was slow to answer, and when she did, she gave the illusion of having just come from bed, still in her pajamas and robe, hair mussed.

But Meredith always woke early, and the slow blinks and stifled yawn seemed performative.

"Have you seen my son?" Olivia asked, her pitch rising with her panic.

"Which one?" was the reply, though Meredith knew damn well which one Olivia meant.

"Adam." Her throat sore with saying his name. "Have you seen Adam?"

Meredith smoothed her hair and tightened the sash on her robe. "Not since last night."

But the hesitation set Olivia on edge. "Let me talk to Grace."

"You can't."

"Adam isn't home, and the last time I saw him, he was heading over here. To see your daughter." Her fear had morphed into rage.

"She's—"

"I don't care if she's sleeping. Go get your damn daughter."

Meredith winced at the uncharacteristic expletive, and judging from Meredith's expression, Olivia imagined she looked how she felt: feral, every muscle in her body tensed, every nerve raw.

Meredith stared at her for several long seconds, abandoning the pretense of drowsiness, and each silent breath only made Olivia grow more terrified of what she might say.

Finally, Meredith exhaled, sounding as bone-weary as Olivia felt.

"Grace isn't sleeping," Meredith said. "She's gone."

In the hours that followed, the police came. They talked to Olivia and Meredith. They seemed to believe Meredith's story—two runaways in love.

Odd, though, that Meredith hadn't called when she'd first noticed them gone. And if that was her story—that the kids had left voluntarily—then why did her voice break when she spoke of it?

Olivia pulled herself from the memory and instantly felt a presence behind her. Dominic. She hadn't heard him arrive, but she recognized the weight of him without turning her head. He rested a hand on her shoulder, and her breathing steadied.

She thought of all the times she'd invited Leyna to her house over the years. If things had been different, Olivia had some day-old scones she might've offered her now, and she had raspberry tea. When Leyna was twelve, that had been her favorite—raspberry tea with honey and a splash of milk. Did she still like that?

But Olivia would never again invite Leyna into her home.

You can't be here, Leyna. Not today. Not anymore.

"Stay away from my family, Leyna," Olivia said. Then she turned away, just as she had sixteen years before.

CHAPTER 11
LEYNA

Saturday, 9:52 a.m.

Olivia left, but Dominic stayed, assessing Leyna with eyes the brown of a scorched redwood. Since she'd last seen him, a decade of grief had sharpened the planes of his face. Heavy stubble shadowed his jaw, midway between *Forgot to shave for a few days* and *Heading into the woods to harvest timber.*

Though Dominic was only thirty-four, a shallow groove already cut between his brows, and the skin crinkled at the corners of his eyes when they narrowed. Leyna supposed it was inevitable that life had left its mark.

At the echo of the front door closing, his mother gone, he said, "That was a rough one."

"I've had rougher."

The lines near his eyes deepened, but he ignored her reddening face, just as he'd ignored her thoroughly inappropriate crush until that summer she'd been eighteen. He came in the room, leaned against the wall, and crossed his arms.

"Aren't you trespassing?" he asked.

"Aren't you?"

"We have a key. Surprised my mom hasn't already called the police on you."

Though he'd been joking, Leyna felt abruptly awkward, being alone in the bedroom with him. She glanced toward the door.

"We should probably leave," she said.

The entirety of him grew too much for her, so she focused only on his hands, weathered since the last time she'd touched them. Like her, Dominic had always enjoyed the outdoors. Fishing. Hiking. Building birdhouses with the scraps of wood he found at the abandoned homesites. Back then, no matter how often he scraped beneath his nails, there always seemed to be crescents of dirt under them. Now his nails were clipped and clean. Leyna wanted to believe he'd manicured them in anticipation of seeing her, but she thought it more likely he'd just grown more careful about his appearance in the past decade. Since she'd hurt him, he'd probably grown more careful about everything.

She walked across the room and paused on the threshold to wait for him, but he made no move to follow. If anything, he seemed to further relax against the wall. His hands dropped into the pockets of his slacks, causing the fabric to strain against his thighs. Her cheeks grew hotter, and she forced herself to blink.

"So—what did you and my little sister talk about?" he said.

Leyna sighed and walked over to the bed. She smoothed the comforter before she sat. "She wants me to teach her how to pick a lock."

He smiled, and even with all that was going on, she caught her breath. Those damn dimples.

"I'd forgotten you had that particular skill."

"What kind of trespasser would I be if I couldn't pick a lock?" she said. "Actually, I can only do interior doors. I'm not the person you'd call for a heist."

Her eyes burned—she'd obviously forgotten to blink again. She pulled her attention away from Dominic, focused on a distant spot on the floor where a water stain ringed the laminate. But that just made her more aware of his breathing.

"I don't know about that," he said. "I think you'd be great in a heist."

She looked at him again, her gaze a challenge. Proof she was immune. "And why's that?"

"Even though we were all older, you were always the smartest of us."

Yeah, brilliant and unemployed. That's me.

Dominic sat on the bed next to her, and her pulse quickened like she was eighteen again, before she'd ruined everything.

He shifted so he faced her. He looked so damn tired that her heart seized, and she fought the urge to comfort him. She'd forfeited that right long ago. "Thanks for coming." He sounded as exhausted as he looked. "I wish it were under different circumstances."

She inhaled and prepared to launch into the apology she'd practiced in the car. "Me too. I can't believe this is happening again here, of all places. And also—I just—I'm sorry for how it ended between us."

She meant to say more—on the drive, she'd clocked the full version at five minutes—but he waved her off after only a few seconds.

"It's okay."

"You're missing a damn good speech."

"I'm sure I am."

When Dominic's knee grazed hers, her stomach lurched, and she was grateful she hadn't eaten.

"Don't take this the wrong way, Dom, but—why do you care so much about Ellie?" To keep from fidgeting, Leyna folded her hands in her lap, then immediately pulled them apart when she realized she looked like a chastised child. "How do you know her?"

"I don't." He paused, and his gaze on her sharpened. "You sure *you* don't?"

At the intensity of his stare, she thought, *Finally.* This was the reason he'd asked her to come—what he couldn't say in a phone call.

"I met her only that once at the restaurant. I thought you knew her from the youth center where you work?"

"I've never met her."

"But you said..." Her voice trailed off as she realized he hadn't said he knew Ellie. He'd only told her the missing girl had shown up at the center, and Leyna had assumed the rest.

"One of the volunteers called to let me know Ellie had been there asking questions. The next day, when I saw she was reported missing, I started asking around the neighborhood. You know how places like this are—word gets around."

A surge of bitterness flared. Yeah, she knew, though the one time she'd counted on this, she'd been met with silence. Karma, she supposed, since she'd kept her own secrets about that night.

"That's when you found out she'd been here." Though it hadn't been phrased as a question, he nodded. "So this volunteer called you on Thursday?" Another nod, which only deepened her confusion. "But Ellie wasn't in the news until yesterday."

He continued to stare expectantly, as if waiting for something from her. But what? She'd never had enough to offer him.

Finally, he said, "Ellie was asking about me—and Adam."

Dominic said his younger brother's name like a prayer, and she fought an urge to reach out and smooth the worry lines on his forehead.

The Duran brothers had always been close, closer than her and Grace. In one of the first memories she had of them, Dominic had been pushing Adam on a skateboard. Though it was not quite summer yet, Dominic was already tan, and he smelled of the shea butter Olivia insisted he use to keep from peeling. Adam was several shades lighter, his cheeks that day pink from excitement as much as the sun. She thought they'd been nine and seven, though she wasn't sure. Back then, one month dissolved into the next, leaving only bits of memory Leyna strained to remember now.

This day was clearer than most. Adam had been wearing a helmet, but the straps hung limp, unsecured. Each time Dominic gave his brother a tiny shove, Adam coasted a few feet, laughed, and begged him to push harder. After about ten minutes of that—or had it been only seconds?—Dominic placed his palms on Adam's back and shoved hard.

Too hard. Adam wobbled, then toppled off the skateboard. The helmet slipped from his head and rolled across the packed dirt. Stunned, Adam held back tears for several seconds before finally releasing them in chest-shuddering, nearly silent sobs. In her memory, Leyna still saw the horror on Dominic's face when he realized that he'd not only failed to keep his brother safe but caused him pain.

"Ellie had a photo of us—you, me, Adam, Grace."

Leyna rocked back on the bed, stunned. "She had a photo of us?"

"She also mentioned meeting you at the restaurant. And the woman from the youth center sent me this." He took out his phone, and Leyna expected a photo. Instead, he called up a video. "It's from the security cameras there. I've watched this a thousand times, but maybe you'll catch something I didn't."

Leyna squinted at the screen. In the video, Ellie walked through the door and talked to several people, each time holding out her phone. The angle made it impossible to see clearly what was on Ellie's screen, though by the way the others studied it, Leyna guessed it was the photo Dominic had mentioned.

Leyna watched the video several times, zooming in on different parts of the frame, each time sighing in frustration when Ellie pulled up the photo. She guessed which one it was—the photo taken the year Grace and Adam disappeared that had run in many of the newspapers. If only there was a better angle on it so she could be sure.

Before Leyna could ask, Dominic shook his head. "That's all we've got. But at least it confirms the timing. She left by one thirty."

"And the police have this?"

He nodded and shifted on the bed. Sitting that near to him, with a possible lead on Grace so close too, Leyna felt her head buzz as if filled with a thousand honey-drunk bees. "When Ellie was asking around, did she mention my sister?"

He shook his head and stowed his phone. "Just me and Adam."

And now a thousand tiny stings. "What else did she say?"

"I wouldn't have called you if I'd been able to find out more on my own. No one knows this stuff better than you."

I wouldn't have called...

Of course. It had only been about Adam. With Dom, it was always about Adam, just like for her it was always about Grace. It was the reason their relationship would never have lasted.

Her expression must've telegraphed how deeply that admission wounded, because his eyes softened. "I know how much you hate it here. I knew you wouldn't want to come back. There's something else—"

But he'd hurt her, and she lashed out without thinking. "I stopped at the market in Sierraville on the way here. The cashier remembered Ellie. He said she bought the snack cakes that were Adam's favorite."

His jaw tensed; whatever he'd been about to say was forgotten. "And?" He spoke sharply, as if he recognized she'd shared the detail to wound him as he had her.

Leyna already regretted the comment; her cheeks flamed. "Nothing."

But Dominic wasn't letting it go. "Thea loves cupcakes too. Think she's involved?"

"That's ridiculous. She wasn't even born yet."

"So *that's* why it's ridiculous?"

They both fell silent, breathing more heavily than they had been a few minutes before but unwilling to break eye contact.

When Dominic spoke, his voice was chilly. "After I found out she'd been in the neighborhood, I talked to the Kims. Nari took the twins to a water park, and Daniel was at work, so they were all gone until after seven. The Silvestris were home. My dad and Thea too. Rocky was gone until late afternoon, but even if he'd been home, his place is a decent walk from here and not easy to spot. It's unlikely Ellie would've made it that far." His gaze was sharp, as if daring her to say something else about his family. When she didn't bite, he said, "What about at your house?"

She heard her mom's voice, evading as she always did: *If that girl was here, she didn't knock on my door.* "My mom was home, but she didn't see Ellie."

"You're sure?"

Not at all. "Of course I'm sure." Because in the feud between the Durans and the Clarkes, Leyna would always back the Clarke—even when that Clarke was her mom and the Duran was Dominic. "How sure are you that the Kims were gone?"

"Kind of hard to get two six-year-olds to lie convincingly about something like that. Unless you think they're in a crime ring with my little sister?"

Leyna held up her palms in a gesture of surrender. "Come on, Dom. Truce?"

He exhaled, his body releasing its tension. "This disappearance has stirred up . . . a lot of shit." He shifted on the bed, putting a few more inches between them, and she pretended not to notice. "With my mom at a client meeting in Reno until Thursday evening, that leaves the Silvestris and my dad and Thea in the neighborhood when Ellie was here." He paused. "And your mom."

"What are you suggesting?"

"Frank and Richard both admit they saw Ellie that day, and she was flashing that same photo. The one of us. Don't you think it's strange that Ellie visited every house but yours?"

So much for our truce. She folded her arms across her chest. "What did your dad say?"

"Ellie knocked on the door around noon, showed him the photo. He confirmed it was taken in the neighborhood, but he wouldn't tell her more."

"Why not?"

"He didn't know who she was, and you remember that podcaster who showed up here for the ten-year anniversary." She didn't. She'd moved out long before then. Dominic seemed to realize that too, because his jaw tensed again. "Anyway, everyone imagines themselves an investigator these days."

"You mean like what we're doing?"

"That's different."

Is it? "So what happened next?"

"He made Thea a sandwich."

"That's it?"

"Whole conversation took about twenty seconds, he says."

"What about Frank?"

His eyebrows knit, as if her question surprised him. "He won't talk to me."

"That's strange."

"Not really. Serena's close with your mom, and you know how this neighborhood is. Your mom got custody of the Silvestris." He rubbed his forehead until it reddened. "The Silvestris talked to the sheriff's office, at least."

Leyna felt herself slipping into a familiar darkness. In her mind, she saw Ellie walking away from the restaurant, and Grace walking away from the house. The two images blurred together until they became a single movie chronicling her failure. She imagined them both turning and staring at her in reproach for not doing more.

She pulled her gaze away, focused again on the water stain on the floor. A gold ring on fake oak.

The stain flashed.

Not a stain.

Metal.

Leyna jumped up from the bed as if scalded, heart in her throat. She rushed to the dresser, dropped to her knees, and reached for it even though she didn't need to hold it to know what it was. She'd recognized it the instant it glinted in that shaft of sunlight.

An open gold cuff with a glass-petaled rose capping each end.

CHAPTER 12

MEREDITH

Saturday, 10:05 a.m.

Meredith made a very good income replicating artwork.

She'd copied the works of many of the early-twentieth-century masters, but her specialty was the Cubist paintings of Picasso. There was something that appealed to her about how Picasso deconstructed an object and reassembled those fragments into something less literal.

She found it especially exhilarating to break apart people. A copy of Picasso's *Seated Nude,* a figure in nearly monochromatic shapes, almost indistinguishable from the background, hung above Meredith's bed. It was the only one of her replicated paintings she'd ever kept for herself.

In her line of work, the trick was sticking to the rules:

Always use the right materials.

Always pick a painting held in a private collection—although that was important only to her shadier clients, of course, the ones who wanted to pass off her work as the real thing. For them, it made no sense to re-create Picasso's *Accordionist* when a simple online search turned up the original hanging in the Guggenheim.

And always take care with the canvas. Oil paintings could take months to dry, and weeks of work could be destroyed in minutes through careless transport or storage.

Meredith was meticulous, but perfection was impossible. She would never know, for instance, the precise ratio of medium to pigment the artists used or the type of animal hair their brushes were made of.

There were techniques for aging a canvas; the process she used involved bleach, thinner, and brown paint, though she'd also experimented with soaked cigarette butts and tea bags. If the commission was generous enough, she could sometimes find a painting from the same period, strip the canvas, and reproduce a masterpiece in its place. Picasso was a favorite not only of hers but of her buyers—he was prolific and often left his works unsigned. One of her works had convinced an authenticator that a lost Picasso had been found. She'd been proud of that one, even if the client had skirted the law.

What Meredith created was an illusion of sameness, getting as close to the original as the resources and her talent allowed. Fortunately for her bank account, she was damn good at creating that illusion.

If the price was right, Meredith would paint anything. If someone wanted to pay her fifty thousand dollars to paint *Dogs Playing Poker,* she would take the deposit and get straight to work. After all, she wasn't the one taking the risk; she wasn't the one at the mercy of ever-evolving technology that made forgeries easier to detect. She sold her paintings as replicas—she signed the back of most pieces and had contracts acknowledging that fact, though some asked her to forgo this step. Some clients owned the original paintings that she reproduced but hung her replicas and stored the authentic works in free ports to avoid taxation and customs rules or to keep them safe. Some wanted to impress their friends with artwork they couldn't otherwise afford. And some—well, legally, she wasn't responsible for what her buyers did with her work, even if she knew just how important it was to them that she get every brushstroke exactly right.

But the painting she'd hidden from Leyna earlier wasn't for a client.

Meredith knew her daughter believed she'd been working on a commission. She could've corrected the misunderstanding, shown her the canvas, but she didn't feel the need to explain herself—she took great pride in her reputation in the field. And Meredith didn't want to deal with the inevitable questions.

Sometimes she just needed to imagine what Grace might look like.

Over the years, Meredith had painted many such portraits, always in the summer. Grace would've turned thirty-three in a couple of weeks.

Will turn, she corrected herself. The morning Olivia came to the Clarke home demanding to see Adam, Meredith had told her he'd run off with Grace. Meredith liked to believe what she'd said that day was true.

Grace's gone, Meredith had said. *Adam too. You know how impulsive young couples in love can be.*

Meredith liked to pretend it had really ended that way: Her daughter and Olivia's son out there somewhere, together. Happy. Sometimes she considered putting Adam in one of her paintings of Grace, just to see what that might look like. Once, she'd gotten as far as the shadow of his jaw before she'd decided the canvas was ruined and slashed it with a palette knife.

For her Grace series, Meredith always chose a linen canvas. Expensive, but the finer weave produced smoother skin, and Grace's skin had been flawless. Was it still? Or had time and experience marred it? She couldn't imagine that Grace had been leading an easy life.

While waiting for Leyna to return, Meredith tried to find her way back into the painting, but thoughts of the missing Sacramento girl intruded. Ellie Byrd. Her case so much like Grace's.

Meredith picked up a brush, dipped it into a small pot of paint thinner, then dabbed the tip on a towel. She studied the painting, hoping inspiration might strike again. When using oil paint, she built dark to light, fat over lean, with the initial layers containing less oil, the final strokes thick with unadulterated paint. This year, inspiration was slower to come. Usually, she'd be working on the eyes by now—a delicate blending of phthalo blue and titanium white that had taken years to get right—but Meredith was still laying down the first thinner, darker layers. Even then, she was pretty sure the painting was crap.

Lately, it had grown more difficult to paint. Whenever she picked up a brush, her fingers would inevitably tense into rigid claws, her stroke lacking its usual ease. She'd ruined more canvases since April than in the five years before.

Now, with Grace's birthday looming and everyone obsessed with Ellie Byrd's disappearance, she was even more stuck. She was behind schedule on her latest commission, which was likely the reason her broker had already phoned twice that morning.

Movement outside drew her attention. Richard made his way down his driveway. Her spine stiffened.

That dumbass.

Richard held a tool—thin pole, orange handle, black blade. A trimmer. He was headed toward his yard with a damn trimmer.

While the sun baked and the wind howled.

Meredith tore off her painting smock and headed outside to suggest to Richard a better use for his power tool.

THE FIRE

The parched forest northeast of Ridgepoint Ranch faces many threats.

If power equipment fails or a tree falls on it, an arcing conductor might ignite nearby vegetation.

Then there's the human threat. Someone burns trash in the backyard. Tosses a cigarette in the grass. Leaves a campfire unattended. Soaks a hill-side with gasoline and lights a match.

But on that morning in late July, it is the giant pine that has been smoldering overnight that sets McRae Meadow ablaze.

As the morning dew evaporates, what will soon become known as the McRae Fire starts to spread. Smoke unfurls where flames feed on dry brush and oxygen. White wisps uncurl where water steams and evaporates from the trees. Black plumes rise where soot collects.

The wind carries the smoke as a warning, but at first no one is close enough to heed it.

Soon, the fire will flow along bulldozed trails and the folds of the mountainside, pulled toward the former gold-mining town of Johnsville as if following a channel.

A mile away, a man decides to water the patch of grass in front of his cabin. It's a point of pride, that small lawn. When his grandkids visit, that's where they play. They'll be visiting in four days, and he wants them to have a nice place to build their Lego forts.

Five minutes into the man's task, an ember from the McRae Fire lofted by a convection column alights on a leaf near the man's home.

At nearly the same moment, the man catches his first whiff of distant smoke. There's only one main road out of Johnsville, and the man decides it might be time to go. He heads inside to grab his go bag.

To grow, a fire needs three things: oxygen, fuel, and heat.

On his way inside, the man walks past the glowing leaf. An inch to the left and he might've smothered it with his sneaker. But he passes it, oblivious, and the wind blows. There is plenty of oxygen to feed the flames.

Still, the spark is vulnerable and nearly extinguished a second time. It needs fuel, and the grass is now lightly watered. Unfortunately, dried oak leaves have scattered nearby. A gust carries the ember, and more leaves blaze.

Two leaves.

Ten.

Fifty.

Then a patch of dry wild grass explodes.

If the man notices it at this moment, there is still time for him to soak the small fire with his garden hose, abandoned only a few feet away. The fire will cool below its ignition temperature and be denied its third need—heat.

But the man does not see it. He packs his medication as the bonds holding hydrocarbons together break; the newly produced carbon lends a yellow glow to the increasingly insistent flames.

As he looks out his window, the man finally notices the flames of the spot fire.

Too late.

Without cell service and no landline, he's unable to warn his neighbors. Panicked, he can't find the keys to his truck. He leaves on foot.

The father of two and grandfather of three is the first to die in the McRae Fire. He won't be the last.

CHAPTER 13
LEYNA

Saturday, 10:18 a.m.

Leyna rose to her feet and held out the bracelet in her palm. It was a distinctive piece, and she harbored no doubt.

"This is Ellie's," she said, breathless. "She was wearing it the day we met." She tilted her hand so the metal again caught the light.

Dominic plucked the cuff from her palm and held it as if the glass petals were precious gems, as if the cuff weren't some trinket you could order online for twenty bucks. He touched one of the roses with his fingertip.

"You're sure it's hers?" At her nod, he brought the bracelet closer, examined it with the careful attention of a jewelry appraiser. The grim set of his mouth suggested what he searched for—blood or other signs of a struggle.

After he'd gone over it several times, his face relaxed. "How did it get here?" He tested the hinge. "Seems solid."

Leyna remembered how it had come off in her hand when she grabbed Ellie's arm at the restaurant. She suddenly worried they shouldn't have touched it. What if they'd smudged fingerprints or compromised evidence less obvious than blood?

As if reaching the same conclusion, Dominic placed the bracelet carefully in his pocket. It might pick up fibers there, but at least any remaining fingerprints wouldn't be destroyed by the oils on his hands.

"I'll call the police and let them know." His voice rose, obviously excited, and Leyna grew concerned that the bracelet wouldn't give them the answers they so desperately sought. Leyna was accustomed to living with her own disappointment, but the thought that she might give Dominic false hope turned her stomach.

Still, she nodded. "Good idea. Call the police."

Leyna knew how that call would go. They would ask their questions and thank him for calling, but without blood or some other sign the bracelet had been forcibly removed, what did it prove? Only that Ellie had been in the neighborhood at some point. The authorities already knew that. And that was if they took Leyna's word that the bracelet was Ellie's. Leyna was a stranger who'd seen it only once. More decisive proof had already been established in the statements of the Silvestris and Dominic's dad.

"That other thing I was trying to tell you..." His voice trailed off, and when his eyes met hers, they burned. The same intensity found its way into his voice. "What if your mom wasn't lying? What if Adam and Grace really did run away—because she was pregnant?"

The hope in his face made her hesitate, but then she gave a slow shake of her head. "She wasn't."

But his expression remained fevered. Leyna was familiar with wanting something as badly as Dominic wanted this.

"You were twelve," he said. "You might not have noticed."

"You were eighteen. Wouldn't you have?" She said it as gently as she could. "And if that's what happened, why would neither of them get in touch with family? Adam knew what this would do to your mom."

They both knew what it would do to us.

"The math works."

Except it didn't.

Part of her wanted to allow him this lie, because it would mean Grace had lived long enough after she'd left to deliver her baby. It would mean she'd made it out of Ridgepoint and that Leyna might finally find out what happened that night. Her heart hurt with wanting that.

The problem was, it couldn't be true. The Clarke sisters had shared a bathroom. Leyna had seen Grace in her underwear, and those last weeks, she'd lost so much weight that even their mom had grown concerned. She'd pushed enough bananas in Grace's direction to feed a troop of monkeys.

Then there was the incident a week before she disappeared. Grace had forgotten to lock the bathroom door, and when Leyna burst in, her sister had thrown a package of sanitary napkins at her. Her expression dark, accusing. Always so angry at the end. *Shit, Ley, I can't even use the toilet without you stalking me?*

That afternoon, Grace had spent the day on the couch, a heating pad on her stomach, popping ibuprofen every four hours and using her cramps as an excuse to be an asshole to Leyna.

Even had Grace conceived soon after, and even had she delivered weeks early, the baby would've been born in late autumn. Nearly a full year younger than Ellie.

The only explanation that had ever made sense was that Adam had killed Grace or that he'd tried to and Grace managed to escape and start a new life. There was never going to be a happily ever after for Grace and Adam.

Dominic's voice dropped to a whisper, still not willing to let it go: "What if Ellie was looking for Adam because he's her father?"

"Grace had her period, Dom. Right before she disappeared," she said softly, her hand spasming with the urge to grab his. "It doesn't matter if Ellie's not ours. She's someone's. If we can help find her, we will."

His shoulders deflated, and Leyna knew she'd convinced him.

That's me—killer of hope, ruiner of things.

When Leyna's phone vibrated in her pocket, she was grateful for the excuse to look away. She checked her phone, hoping cell service had been restored, but it was only the reminder she'd set for herself earlier that morning: Press conference.

She turned to Dominic to ask if the Millers had Wi-Fi, then remembered the check-in instructions she'd found in the kitchen.

"Press conference is about to start," she said. "Want to watch?"

Dominic shook his head. "I'll watch at home after I call in about the bracelet." He stood. "Catch up with you later?"

He left then, off to make his report and add to the illusion that they were doing something that might actually help Ellie Byrd.

Leyna grabbed her laptop from her car, started the generator—if the Millers complained later, she could always Venmo them a few bucks—went back into the house, and logged in using the Millers' Wi-Fi password. On the screen, the room the press conference would be held in was done in shades of gray, gold, and brown, with a podium at the center. Stretched against the pale wall was the usual lineup of uniformed men—except for the public information officer, they were all men—hands clasped in front of them, at full attention. Holsters at hips and pressed shirts in tan, blue, green, and black were meant to convey that all resources were being deployed in the search for Ellie Byrd. That she mattered.

Leyna had watched enough such conferences to know how this would go: Gratitude for interagency support, appeals for information, the updates never enough to satisfy anyone in the room. She turned up the volume anyway.

As the Sacramento County sheriff stepped up to the podium, Leyna navigated to the message boards on the true-crime website she frequented. She split the screen between the press conference and the boards.

As usual, Boston Betty posted first: I hope they have good news.

A name Leyna didn't recognize popped onto the screen. That tended to happen as cases drew more media attention; casual users joined the fray.

Hal Green: Thirty-six hours she's been gone.

Though Hal Green didn't say it, they all understood his meaning: The more time passed, the less likely the news would be good. Leyna wondered how many people on the boards used these final seconds of silence to study the sheriff's face for a sign they'd found a body.

As the sheriff leaned toward the microphone, his bald head gleamed beneath the overhead lights. "I would like to begin by thanking you all for coming..."

He then recapped the investigation—finding the Honda at the campground, the search of the campground by law enforcement and volunteers, her texts to her friend Amaya, the fact she was spotted in Sierraville and Quincy hours before her disappearance. He shared a description of what she was wearing: brown tank top, high-rise khaki shorts, white hoodie, and white sneakers.

Hal Green: They don't have anything.

Outside the Miller house, people were shouting, Leyna's mom's voice the loudest. Her mom's voice was always the loudest. Though curious, Leyna tuned it out, a skill she'd spent years perfecting, and focused on the screen.

Ellie wasn't her niece. She knew that. But still, she waited for her first glimpse of the parents.

Behind the sheriff, a couple moved into the frame. They leaned toward each other, separated by inches, the man tall and sandy-haired, the woman a brunette nearly the same height. Both wore their grief in downcast eyes and the grim lines of their mouths. Girding themselves for their turn at the microphone.

Neither of them Grace.

Despite what she'd told Dominic, Leyna had hoped to see her sister at that podium.

The sheriff continued his update, but Leyna remained focused on the couple, each of them alone in their grief. She would've expected more intimate gestures of comfort between them. Over the years, she'd cataloged the body language of too many grieving parents: Heads rested against shoulders. Hands clasped in unity. Bodies folded into each other in the battle to remain standing. Maybe it was just because the investigation hadn't yet hit forty-eight hours, or maybe the Byrds disagreed on whether Ellie left voluntarily. Whatever the reason for their distance, if the search ended with a body, Leyna predicted their marriage wouldn't survive it.

The sheriff wound down with the requisite pleas for information, ending with a stoic "Now we're going to hear a statement from the family." He stepped aside.

The woman reached toward her husband, her fingers grazing his hand before pulling away again. Only the man came forward.

"We miss our girl," he said. "We just want her home, safe and well."

The pronoun meant everything. *Her,* not *you*. Whatever Sarah Byrd believed, her husband wasn't talking to a runaway. He was addressing the person who'd taken his daughter. But Leyna had seen enough press conferences to know that a parent who begged for a child's safe return could be arrested days later.

As if reading her mind, Hal Green posted: Think one of them is involved?

SouthernBella: I hope not. They seem like good people. The dad's a teacher.

CrimeChaser2000: The Red Ripper taught literature.

Taryn Is Still Missing: *groan*. Red Ripper? Really?

SouthernBella: Let's focus on Ellie here.

CrimeChaser2000: Just saying. Even Bundy took calls on a suicide hotline.

Boston Betty: You think she ran away?

Ferret Girl: And abandoned her friend's car like that?

Boston Betty: Like a teen can't stage her disappearance.

Boston Betty wasn't wrong. How many times on this forum had Leyna read of a teenager sneaking away to be with her boyfriend or the soulmate twice her age she'd met online?

But CrimeChaser2000 had a point too. How many young women had been lured by a trafficker promising opportunity, a jealous classmate with a knife in her pocket, or a stranger drawn to her hair, her smile, or her proximity?

The dad bowed his head, and when he spoke again, his voice cracked, his hands flitting like wounded birds. "Ellie is . . . she's special. A really special young woman. And smart."

Since Leyna had never met Paul Byrd, she couldn't tell if his awkward gestures and the way he fumbled his words indicated deceit, but she wasn't sure she believed him. Most people didn't lie nearly as well as they thought they did.

"When she was about four, we'd take her with us to do laundry. She loved to watch the bedding spin in the large washing machines. If there was a kid within a hundred feet of the laundromat—the grocery store too—she'd try to invite them over for a playdate. She thought... she didn't see a problem with inviting a stranger to our home. We had to give her a fake address so she wouldn't give out our real one." He stilled and blinked as if surprised to see so many members of the media staring back at him. As if he'd forgotten why he was standing in front of them. "One time when another mother pulled her child away, Ellie tried to bribe her with chocolate chip pancakes." He attempted a smile, but his lips refused to lift. "Ellie's always been like that. She loves everyone. She wants to be everyone's friend. Please be her friend now and help us find her. We'd really..."

Unable to finish the sentence, Paul Byrd stepped back to rejoin his wife. Her hand circled his forearm, and Leyna wondered if even that simple gesture meant there was hope for them.

CrimeChaser2000: Wife's kind of cold, don't you think?

And then Leyna's pulse quickened when Taryn Is Still Missing typed: Her friend Amaya posted a video.

Leyna clicked on the link and hit Play. A young woman's round face filled the screen, her box braids flowing over the collar of her yellow shirt and out of the frame. Her dark eyes appeared swollen. From crying or exhaustion? Likely both. Leyna recognized the look from those early days searching for Grace, back when she'd believed a video like this might make a difference.

"Hey, I'm Amaya. You might've heard, but if you haven't: My best friend, Ellie Byrd, is missing." She paused to take a deep breath and moved closer to the camera. "Ellie texted me Thursday night to let me know she was on her way back to Sacramento. She never made it." Her voice cracked, but she went on without stopping. "She was driving my car, and the police found it at a campground near Truckee. Ellie hates camping." Her lips thinned in an attempt at a smile. "All that dirt, and the bugs. One time, this centipede climbed across her bare foot and she screamed so loud, you'd have thought she was being murdered."

Leyna clocked the instant Amaya realized what she'd said—her eyes went wide and the almost-smile blinked out. But Amaya Dutton was determined. Her jaw tensed, and when she continued, her voice was steady. "Ellie wouldn't've stopped in the middle of nowhere, not even if she needed to pee, because no way would she use one of those disgusting port-a-potties. And she wanted to get home. She'd been texting me all day how much she couldn't wait to be home."

Leyna found herself leaning toward the laptop. She wanted to reassure this sad, strong girl it would be okay, even though she didn't believe it would be.

"Ellie was out in the middle of nowhere for personal reasons, but she wouldn't've stuck around longer than she needed to. She'd be home now if she could be." She reached for something, but whatever it was remained off-screen. "There's not much out there where she disappeared. I'm really hoping someone knows something, because that's what it's going to take to find her."

Amaya held up the item she'd reached for, which turned out to be her phone, and pushed it toward the screen. On it was a photo of Ellie. Not the one of her in her soccer jersey that they'd been showing with news reports. In this photo, Ellie looked more like the girl Leyna had met. Her hair was brown, not yet dyed, but the tilt of her chin and smile were the same.

"This is Ellie. She hates camping and bugs and port-a-potties, but she loves musicals and just about everything else, and everyone loves her. That centipede? She made me take it outside because she didn't want to hurt it. She's just—she's an amazing person, and we all want her home." Her eyes went soft, but she didn't cry. That would probably come once the camera clicked off. "If you saw Ellie, if you talked to her that day, if you know anything—please call the hotline or DM me. Please. I want my friend back."

Leyna found the social media account linked to the video and navigated to private messaging. There, she typed the four words she thought would get the quickest response: I found Ellie's bracelet.

CHAPTER 14
OLIVIA

Saturday, 10:30 a.m.

Meredith hadn't come up for air in five minutes, and the shouting had drawn the attention of all the neighbors. It reminded Olivia of Leyna's performance ten years earlier, when she'd attacked her and Richard with all that bullshit about Adam. The last thing Olivia wanted was another Clarke in her front yard and the neighborhood taking an interest in her family.

The Kims had been the first to notice Meredith screaming at Richard. Nari, Daniel, and their six-year-old twins, June and James, were packing their Honda Pilot when Meredith launched out of her house bellowing that Richard was a moron. For several minutes, the Kims had watched, until Meredith switched to more colorful synonyms for *moron,* at which point Daniel ushered the kids inside for another load, and Nari crossed the street to stand beside Olivia on the porch.

Serena and Frank Silvestri emerged next, Frank shirtless in athletic shorts with his stainless-steel water bottle and Serena in a jersey lounge set with her glass of white wine. It was ten thirty in the morning, but Olivia tried not to judge. Of all the neighbors, Serena Silvestri wore her curiosity most openly, peering over the rim of her glass with something close to delight.

Olivia caught glimpses of Thea at the window, watching too, and Dominic, who stood a safe distance away, as he always did. He didn't seem to notice her watching him, so her gaze lingered. He'd always been such a handsome boy and so much stronger than Adam. Always her rock. Adam's too. Now, years of burying his grief so she wouldn't see it had etched premature lines in his face. Seeing that pain grew quickly uncomfortable and she looked away.

She looked for Rocky. Where was he? Meredith's shouting would've provided the cover for a private conversation. Not that she'd be able to have one now that Nari was standing only a couple of feet from her.

On the edge of the Durans' driveway, Meredith had transitioned from a lecture on the stupidity of using power tools on a red-flag day to one on Goose crapping in her yard.

"My garden is not your dog's toilet," she said, voice rasping from all the shouting. If her throat got sore enough, maybe she'd go back inside and play with her paints, and Olivia could avoid seeing her again for another few months. "If you and your wife can't control your dog, then perhaps you should buy him diapers."

Where was Goose, anyway? He seemed to be missing. The French bulldog mix had been a rescue from Greenville after the Dixie Fire burned through the town, and Olivia worried that he would take off one day in search of a home and a family that were no longer there.

Richard was trying to keep calm, but Olivia heard the stress in his voice. "A person's character can be easily measured by how she treats animals," he said.

"And a moron's character can be easily measured by how often he lets his dog crap in his neighbor's yard."

Olivia felt her body tense. The shouting reminded her too much of her parents toward the end. They'd died in a car accident a month before their divorce would've been final. Olivia was an adult living in another state, so she never knew what had brought them together that last time or why her father was drunk when he got behind the wheel. Had they planned one last scotch-fortified dinner to discuss the division of assets? Or had they celebrated a reconciliation with too much champagne?

Olivia hoped it wasn't the latter. She liked to picture her mom resolute at the end. She hoped her dad hadn't been able to sway her with one more lie about how his latest lover meant nothing to him.

Nari took a long drink from her tumbler of green juice. In the heat, condensation beaded the glass. She whispered, "Think she's got much more left in her?"

"Meredith always has more in her."

Nari rolled the cup between her palms, popping the tiny beads of liquid.

"At least Richard's handling it well enough." She took another long drink, finishing it. She looked down at her empty glass with obvious disappointment. "Got any kale?"

Nari had once run a juice and smoothie shop. That was after she'd tended bar and taught yoga but before she'd signed up for paralegal courses. Nari bored easily. After the twins were born, she'd settled into remote work as a medical transcriptionist, though she still checked the online job boards weekly. In the twenty years Olivia had known her, only three things had held her interest: her children, her shakes, and her decoupage. When she'd first knocked on new neighbor Olivia's door, Nari had carried a decoupaged basket nearly as big as she was, loaded with seasonal fruit, her greeting a breezy "Where's your blender?"

"I might have spinach," Olivia said now.

But neither left the porch. There were two kinds of people on the street: Those who'd moved in after the kids went missing—the Millers, the Silvestris—and those who were there that night. The latter Meredith had always blamed for not being able to change what happened and for siding with Olivia in their feud.

Richard had spent years trying to convince Olivia they should move. He'd come home with flyers from houses that were newer, bigger, and more elegantly appointed. "This neighborhood is toxic," he'd say, and

Olivia would accept the flyers and tell him she'd think about it. Then she would bury them in the garbage. When he pushed her on the subject, she would point to the ticks on the walls that marked Adam's height or the bedroom with the always-closed door, no furniture in it but boxes of stuffed animals, textbooks, and academic trophies crammed in the closet.

Richard would look at her with sympathy then, but at least it wasn't the pity he would've shown had she told him the truth.

If we leave, how will Adam find his way home?

But was this still home?

"We're taking the kids to Daniel's parents' house for the weekend," Nari said. "You got someplace to go?"

"We're fine here." In the twenty years she'd lived at Ridgepoint, a wildfire had come close only once, burning to the edge of the highway a mile to the south.

"You sure?"

"I'm sure."

With everyone's attention on Meredith and Richard, Olivia considered pulling Nari aside and telling her about Richard's cheating. But, like so many times before, she kept silent. She told herself it was to protect Thea, but really, Olivia didn't want Nari to look at her the way her childhood neighbors had looked at her own mother. She wouldn't let Richard cast her as a woman to be pitied.

"You want us to take Thea?" Nari asked.

When Olivia's gaze darted to the window, Thea ducked out of sight.

"She's been complaining of a sore throat. Probably nothing, but I'd like to keep an eye on it."

The lie was easier than telling Nari she didn't trust her to take care of Thea. It wasn't personal. She loved Nari, but she didn't trust anyone outside the family with her daughter.

"Consider it, at least. There's a dark energy around the neighborhood today."

Olivia didn't argue. She felt it too. Ellie Byrd's disappearance had set everyone on edge, her most of all.

Nari rolled her empty cup in her hands, expression unusually serious. "I feel like something bad is about to happen."

Olivia's friend had fancied herself a psychic ever since she found her stolen bike in a creek after having a "vision" of running water. The vision had involved a faucet emptying into a sink, but, Nari claimed, such things were often hard to interpret.

Olivia had never asked Nari the obvious question: If she was truly psychic, how had she not known Adam would disappear? And why had Nari never gotten a vision as to where he might be? Every time Nari mentioned that missing bike, Olivia wanted to stick a wadded sock in her mouth.

Still, Olivia scanned the tree line. Where was Rocky? And her dog?

When she pulled her gaze away, she caught Meredith staring. The other woman strode toward her, eyes chilly.

"Where's Leyna?"

"She's *your* daughter."

"She was with *your* son."

Grief swelled, anger too, and she was too exhausted to hold the words back. She fired, knowing she would draw blood. "Seems after what happened with Grace, you would've learned to keep a close eye on your remaining daughter."

Meredith's jaw tightened, but she didn't flinch—Meredith Clarke wasn't the type to show weakness like that. Beside Olivia, Nari sucked in a quick breath, then hissed her name in shocked accusation. Even Richard gaped, his forehead knitting in obvious surprise.

Though Olivia knew she shouldn't have spoken the words, she didn't regret them. Not a bit. She felt a loosening in her chest, as if their release had made more room there. Meredith *knew* something about Adam's disappearance that she had kept secret for sixteen years, and because of that, Olivia would never apologize to her for anything.

Never.

Meredith pulled her shoulders back, her posture rigid, and Olivia sensed her composure required great effort. She waited for the other woman to fire back her own retort, but her lips compressed into a thin line and she remained quiet. The wind keened and the heat clawed, and a minute more passed. Yet still Meredith said nothing.

Somehow, her silence was worse than anything she might've said. Just as she'd no doubt intended.

CHAPTER 15
LEYNA

Saturday, 10:47 a.m.

When Leyna emerged from the Miller house, laptop tucked under her arm, she saw her mom stomping toward home. On her way to catch up, she passed Frank and Serena Silvestri, who lingered in their driveway after whatever argument had clearly taken place. If they hadn't been in front of their house, she wouldn't have known who they were. They'd moved in long after she'd moved out. Frank was younger than she'd expected. Not much older than Dominic, she guessed, and nearly as attractive. His short curls faded into a close-cropped beard. Serena, lithe and golden, wore the relaxed elegance of someone who'd studied color charts and makeup tutorials with the attention of a scholar. Leyna's own T-shirt had a stain from that morning's coffee, and the wind had tugged a few strands from her ponytail.

Leyna hesitated—should she go after her mom or try to talk with the Silvestris about Ellie?

Only one of the conversations had a chance of being productive. She brushed a hand over her hair and backtracked to the Silvestris' driveway.

She held her laptop against her chest like a shield. When she introduced herself, Serena's lips thinned. The woman's judgment surprised her. She usually got such looks only from the neighbors who knew her.

"I recognize you from the photos in your mother's house, though of course you're older now, and you've put on weight."

Leyna couldn't decide which was the greater shock, the woman's casual rudeness or that her mom hadn't yet removed all of Leyna's childhood photos.

"Both of those things tend to happen when children become adults," Leyna said dryly. "I was hoping you'd answer a couple of questions about Ellie Byrd."

Frank's forehead creased as he looked from Leyna to his wife. "We've already talked about it with that deputy."

Serena rested a hand on her husband's arm. "I'll fill her in, sweetheart. Why don't you go inside and finish your workout."

When Frank was gone, Serena pursed her lips and folded her arms. "Why do you care about this girl? You're upsetting your mother by being here."

That's just a bonus. "Tell me what happened and I'll leave."

She meant leave the Silvestris' driveway, but if Serena misinterpreted the comment, Leyna wasn't going to correct her.

Serena's face relaxed. "I know the Durans will be happy to hear that too. Did you really accuse their son of murder?"

Several times. "I'm not here to talk about that."

"Seriously, though. You've got guts coming back here after what you said."

"We were talking about Ellie?" Leyna reminded Serena.

"She knocked on our door at a quarter after twelve. Interrupted our lunch. Frank forgot to turn off the stove, so our chicken barley burned."

A sixteen-year-old girl was missing, and Serena cared more about her ruined lunch.

"She introduced herself as Ellie. She didn't give her last name, or maybe she did and I don't remember. But yesterday, we recognized her when we saw her photo on the Plumas County Sheriff's site, and Frank called them immediately."

"What did Ellie say to you?"

"She was only at our door for a couple of minutes before the smoke detector went off. The chicken barley." She said the last part as if it were an important detail Leyna should commit to memory.

"Between the introduction and the smoke detector, I'm assuming she didn't stand on your doorstep mute."

Serena's eyes narrowed, long lashes nearly touching. Leyna wondered if she practiced that—getting the lines just right, with no unsightly pinching at the corners. "Your mom said you're a smart-ass." She unfolded her arms and waved a dismissive hand. "The girl showed us a photo of the four of you. She pointed to you and said she knew who you were, but she asked for help identifying Adam and Dominic."

Leyna drew back, confused. At the restaurant, Leyna had been sure Ellie recognized Adam's name. Shouldn't she have known his face too? And if the photo had been the one used in the news reports at the time, wouldn't Ellie have had the names that way?

Unless that wasn't where she'd gotten the photo.

"She didn't recognize Adam?" Then again, maybe Ellie *had* recognized him and only sought confirmation.

Serena shook her head. "She said she'd been to Portola, and someone at the post office recognized the neighborhood but didn't know anyone in the photo."

"Did she say anything about meeting me?"

Serena smirked. "Another thing your mother said. It's always all about you."

Leyna didn't point out that Serena was the one who'd brought up Leyna in connection with Ellie, and she didn't call her out on her lie—with as much practice as Leyna had at fading into the background, her mom wouldn't have said such a thing. But it didn't matter. As the youngest Clarke, she'd developed a thick skin.

Serena threw her a curious glance. "So how'd you and the girl meet?"

Leyna was tempted to lie—Serena nearly drooled at the possibility of a rumor to spread. But wasn't that the point? To get the word out about Ellie? "She came to the restaurant where I worked." Leyna immediately cursed herself for using the past tense, but Serena seemed to miss it, focused on the juicier details of the story.

"You talked to her?" At Leyna's quick nod, Serena's eyes widened. "What did she say?"

"She mentioned a friend, and I got the idea it might be someone she was seeing."

"I didn't hear that she had a boyfriend." Serena blinked rapidly, lashes flapping like bat wings. "Do you think the relationship ended badly? I heard about this attorney who waited in his ex-girlfriend's car, forced her to drive to the beach where they'd had their first date, then strangled her with his tie."

Leyna had no interest in talking true crime with her mom's neighbor unless it involved Ellie Byrd. "I hadn't heard about that," she said. "When Ellie showed you the photo, did you identify Grace, Adam, and Dominic?"

"I even told her where Dominic works. It was the neighborly thing to do, wasn't it?" At her own magnanimity, Serena offered a smug smile. "Then the smoke alarm went off, and I suggested she talk with your mother. She thanked me and left."

"Did you see her near the Millers' house?"

Serena looked confused. "Why would she go there? The house was empty that day."

Leyna considered whether to mention the bracelet but decided against it. Serena's confusion seemed genuine, and Leyna preferred to spread the word herself. The better to tell if someone was surprised by the news, or lying.

"What about my mom—do you know if Ellie talked to her?"

"Sounds like a question for your mother, but I don't think so," she said. "Have you talked with Rocky?"

"I thought he was gone most of that day?" At Serena's practiced shrug, Leyna said, "His place is off the road. How would Ellie even know to look for it?"

"Not much goes on around here without the king of Ridgepoint Ranch knowing about it." Even Serena's sneer was perfect, from its symmetry to the gloss of her lips. "Besides, that's where Ellie headed—toward the trail that leads into the woods."

Headed toward Rocky's, just as Grace had been the night she'd disappeared. Even if Leyna was the only one who knew that.

The wind blew a wave of hair across Serena's face, one strand sticking in her lip gloss, and Leyna was reminded of the bug strips the Millers used to hang on their porch during the summer before they'd turned their place into a vacation rental. Serena grimaced as she pulled the hair free.

"She should've listened to me and gone to your mother's house instead of heading into those woods." Serena shivered with a little too much drama, but Leyna understood the underlying dread. Though Leyna had always felt at home in those woods, she knew how good they were at keeping their secrets.

CHAPTER 16
MEREDITH

Saturday, 10:52 a.m.

Irritated by her fight with the Durans, Meredith considered making herself a mimosa or a Bloody Mary. Halfway to the refrigerator, she thought, *Screw the charade,* and went for a bottle of cabernet instead. After pouring herself a glass, she adjusted the air-conditioning and pulled a stool to the edge of the kitchen island. She glanced toward the clock on the stove. She drained half the glass of wine, then punched in the number she'd seen earlier on her caller ID.

The art broker answered immediately, greeting her with an overly enthusiastic "Meredith! How have you been?"

"I'm fine." She didn't ask him the same in return. The last time she'd made that mistake, Brian had launched into a ten-minute story about a trip to Florence.

Meredith was fairly sure the art broker's real first name wasn't Brian and absolutely certain the man's real last name wasn't Smith, making his initials oddly appropriate. She wouldn't have been surprised to learn he'd picked the name for that reason.

Meredith had met the broker only once in person, preferring to exchange paintings and contracts by courier. In his early forties then, the man who called himself Brian Smith had worn his hair long that day (she suspected as a testament to his stubborn hairline) and his dress shirt tight (likely to show off his obvious gym habit).

A failed artist, Brian had an ego that was second only to his greed, and he knew how to capitalize on these same qualities in others. He had an instinct for which dealer would overlook his forged record of provenance to lock in a great deal.

On the other end of the line, Brian cleared his throat. "I trust you're familiar with van Gogh's *Girl in White in the Woods*?"

What was she, a freshman not yet enrolled in her first art history class? Of course she knew the painting. She instantly pictured it—captured in shades of red, brown, and deep yellow, a girl stood alone among the trees. What she didn't know was why he was asking about a van Gogh instead of hounding her about the Georges Braque he'd put a deposit on.

She took another sip of cabernet, then another, but the wine lacked its usual effect.

"Of course I know it."

"Can you paint it?"

She found the request odd. Brian had never approached her about a van Gogh before. "I'm not accepting new commissions right now."

"He's willing to pay six figures."

The figure should have enticed her, but it was too generous. A trap of some kind? At that rate, it had to be. "Get someone else."

"He doesn't want someone else. He mentioned you by name."

"You shouldn't be discussing me with strangers." She heard the ice in her voice. She hoped he did too. Though what she did wasn't technically illegal, strict nondisclosure language was written into all of her contracts.

"He said the setting has always spoken to him. Made him feel like he was right there, watching the girl from behind a tree."

Meredith touched her wineglass, then pushed it away.

Brian continued. "Maybe you can add in the bits of leaves, since he seemed to really appreciate that aspect of the original."

Another image flashed: sodden leaves clinging to steel.

While van Gogh worked on the painting, bits of oak leaves became embedded in the wet paint. The artwork had been praised for its sense of place—when viewing it once in person, she'd imagined the scent of the woods near her own home, perhaps because van Gogh had knelt on the forest floor while painting it.

Though Meredith had once appreciated *Girl in White in the Woods* for these qualities, thinking of it now made her abruptly claustrophobic.

"With the leaves, it would fail authentication, naturally, but he's not looking to sell it," Brian said. "Told me the painting reminds him of his childhood. He wants to hang it on his living-room wall for the pleasure of all his guests."

Goose bumps raised on her arms. "What's this client's name?"

"You know I can't say. Confidentiality."

"Listen, Brian, I appreciate your commitment to confidentiality." She reached for her glass again and finished her wine in one long swallow. Her mouth puckered at the rush of tannins. "Though I'm also a little concerned that it obviously didn't apply to your conversation about me with this mystery client."

"It's not like that. He approached me, not the other way around. You know I would never violate our agreement."

The words sounded rehearsed, the placating-a-difficult-client speech he'd probably given dozens of times. Meredith pretended the phone she clutched was her art broker's neck. "So you've said."

"Which is why I can't share more than I already have."

She could picture him checking the time on his stainless-steel Bulgari, already mentally preparing for his next meeting. "I'll double your cut," she said.

He couldn't get the words out fast enough. "His name's Adam Duran."

As soon as the name entered the room, the oxygen left it. The air grew warmer still. Heat rose in her cheeks, and she started to sweat in her linen button-down.

"And how did you meet this Adam Duran?"

As Brian started babbling again about the importance of maintaining privacy amid assurances of his commitment to their partnership, Meredith moved to the closet. She pulled out the nearly finished copy of *Plate and Fruit Dish* and placed it on the easel.

When the art broker came up for air, she said, "About that Braque I owe you?"

"You're done?" Fully engaged again.

"Not quite."

She'd gotten the pears in the foreground exactly right, though the shadows on the plate were a little off still. Perhaps a few more strokes of a darker paint? She picked up a palette knife.

Brian sniffed, probably irritated she'd drawn him back into a conversation he'd been wrapping up. "So what, then?"

"It's not as complex as some of Braque's later works, but it's a lovely reproduction." She traced the plate in the painting with the tip of her knife.

"You always do amazing work," he said.

"Of course I do." Her turn to be impatient. "You said it's a gift?"

"For my sister's wedding."

"Unfortunate, because I'm rethinking the commission."

He gasped. "The wedding's in three weeks."

"I'll return the deposit, of course, as per the terms of our contract."

"But there's no time to get her another gift."

"The Meadowood Mall had tracksuits on sale. His and hers. They looked comfortable."

The more Meredith considered the painting, the more she warmed to the idea of slashing it. She'd been toying with the idea of retiring anyway, and Brian really was an ass.

"You can't..." His voice trailed off, as if he was now worried he'd offend her.

She paused, pretending to give the matter thought as she twirled the knife in her hand. "Or," she said, "if I worked through the weekend, I could have it done by Monday." She paused again. "You know—if I weren't distracted by this Adam Duran matter."

Brian sighed in what she hoped was a signal of defeat. That really would be best, for his bottom line as well as his betrothed sister's happiness.

But when he spoke, he remained reluctant. "I've told you everything I know."

Did he really value his sister's happiness so little?

She sighed loudly to be certain he heard it, though she hoped he didn't notice the tremor in it. "I believe there were several color options available on those tracksuits, though I'm partial to the one with burgundy piping."

"We didn't even meet in person," he said, the last of his hesitancy falling away.

"What do you mean?"

Meredith brushed the edge of the canvas with the palette knife, considering again the shading. Perhaps it was perfect after all. It would be a shame to have to shred it.

"I was out of town that week, and according to my staff, he didn't even come into the shop himself. He sent someone."

"An assistant?" That would be a place to start. It shouldn't be hard to track an assistant to the person who signed the paychecks.

"A courier. Just some young guy in a ponytail with a cross-body bag and a form."

"What courier service?"

Brian gave her the company's name and address, which she jotted on the refrigerator whiteboard. "But I followed up with the service myself as soon as I got back in town a few days ago," he said. "I rarely get commission requests that way, and never from someone who isn't already a client. So I went in, verified the courier was legit. And of course, I tried to find out who'd hired them. Dead end."

"Yet you took the commission."

"I didn't take it for the money, if that's what you're thinking. Not entirely, anyway. Whoever brought it to me knew things about you." His voice grew hushed, though as far as Meredith knew, he was alone. "Things even I didn't know, like the name of your daughter. I was sure he was legit."

Meredith set down the knife before she could do anything rash. Her hand tightened on the handset. "What did he say about my daughter?"

"Nothing, really." Reading her mood accurately, Brian was suddenly Mr. Cooperation. "In the note, he just mentioned he knew you and your daughter Grace." Meredith detested the casual way he said her daughter's name. If she'd been holding the knife, the canvas would've been ruined.

"You still have the note?"

He sniffed. "You think I'm an amateur?"

She had many words for him at the moment, but *amateur* wasn't one of them. "What else did the note say?"

Brian went quiet, and she hoped for his sake he needed the time to search his memory, not to construct a lie. "He introduced himself. Said the best forgers are often the best liars—it was meant as a compliment." The broker chuckled, likely imagining what he'd do with his cut. He didn't know the story he'd been sold was a lie. "Apparently, his father commissioned a painting of yours before he died. Paid six figures for it."

Six figures again. Her broker might not recognize it for what it was, but she did. Through this story he'd shared with Brian, the man claiming to be Adam Duran was suggesting it would take at least a hundred thousand dollars to buy his silence.

What did he know? What *could* he know?

Regardless, Meredith would pay it.

Brian said, "Then he mentioned wanting to commission the van Gogh, but he didn't know how to reach you. Guess his dead father didn't think to list you in his contacts under 'art forger.'" This time, his chuckle felt forced.

"What exactly did he write about why he wanted the painting?"

"I'm not sure I can remember word for word what—"

"Of course you can. You're always impressing clients with your recall of the most obscure bits of art history." Meredith aimed for flattery, but the sarcasm was unmistakable. She cringed every time Brian started a sentence with *Did you know*...

"We've been over this, and I have an appointment in less than ten—"

"Tell me, Brian."

His sigh had a hint of irritation again. "'It's a scene straight out of my own childhood.' That's what he wrote. 'I want to hang the painting over the mantel so everyone who comes into my home can see what she's done.' Like I said, he's a huge fan. He actually called today to make sure I'd gotten the note since he hadn't heard from me." His tone grew petulant. "You haven't been taking my calls."

That explained Brian's persistence. Nothing like an impatient client to motivate the broker. "What did he say?"

"He didn't talk to me. He talked to my assistant."

She started to wipe the sweat from her neck, but her hand froze mid-swipe. Since she'd entered the kitchen, the temperature had spiked. Had the air conditioner switched off?

Her gaze landed on the stove and its digital clock. It had been on when she'd entered the kitchen. Off now. The generator had stopped working.

Her mouth was dry. From the cabernet, she told herself. That would teach her to drink red wine before lunch. "And how am I supposed to get in touch with this Adam Duran?"

"He said you'd know how to find him," Brian said. "Now, when will you have that Braque you owe me?"

CHAPTER 17

LEYNA

Saturday, 11:05 a.m.

Leyna stashed her laptop in the car and, as she had so many times in the past, started on the trail that led to Rocky's cottage. It wasn't a direct route. There would be spots overgrown with brush, dense with trees. Spots someone might get hurt if she wasn't paying attention. But this was the path chosen by Grace and Ellie. It would be Leyna's path too.

Unlike the neighborhood she left behind, the forest had always felt like home. Streaks of sunlight pierced the swaying canopy, setting a nearby fir aglow. With branches close to the ground and unstable roots, the firs were often cleared by fire crews before they trimmed the branches from the pines. Here, the firs still grew, and the pines kept their branches. It had been a while since a crew had been through here. Overhead, the small patch of visible sky had paled, more white than blue. At dusk, purple shadows would fall. It would grow dark. The forest could be dangerous at night.

How had Grace navigated these woods without a light to guide her? If she'd left her cell phone behind, surely she wouldn't have thought to bring a flashlight? If she had, Leyna hadn't seen its beam. Had the moon been enough? It had been waxing gibbous, only four days from full. The temperature that night had been in the mid-forties. Warmer than average, but Grace must have been chilly in the thin black blouse she wore.

These were the details Leyna had memorized to torture herself.

She scanned the trees, reminding herself of the way forward. That was when she spotted Goose. The portly French bulldog mix's white fur stood out against the pile of leaves and dirt he'd chosen as a temporary bed.

This I can do, at least.

Leyna called to the dog in her most soothing voice—"Hey, Goose. Come here, Goose"—and he cocked his head, tongue unfurling as he panted. She took a step, two—and the dog jumped up and bounded deeper into the forest.

Despite his stocky frame and short snout that hampered breathing, Goose could run. He stopped suddenly, butt wriggling, attention focused on something Leyna couldn't see.

Someone?

In the space between distant pines, sunlight rippled into darkness, then back to light. The dog bounded into the trees, instantly swallowed by them.

Leyna followed, steps slowing as she left the path. She drew closer to the pines and their shifting shadows, but she could no longer see Goose or any sign of what had drawn his interest.

She moved between the trees, no different than the pines and junipers that grew elsewhere in that forest but still abruptly familiar. She anticipated the clearing before it appeared, and when she stepped into it, her heart plummeted into her stomach.

Ahead of her, a long crack divided the earth. On the other side of the crevice, the dog faced her. He stared with dark eyes, whining deep in his throat.

She hadn't been back there since the day Grace went missing. The day it had all come to the surface.

Leyna tried not to dwell on the hungry wind or the crack in the earth that separated her and the dog. She forced herself toward the ravine until she was close enough to peer over its edge. It was deep. When she was twelve, it seemed nearly bottomless. She could still feel the bite of the sugar pine roots against her palms as she'd tried to climb out. Feel the throb in her arm.

Her hand found the scar, and she smelled him then. The chemical tang of lavender and rotting fruit.

She switched to breathing through her mouth, but she could still taste it, bitter on her tongue.

Leyna pushed away the memory, but Adam's scent belonged to the present. The wind carried it to her, wrapping her in a cloud of cheap body spray.

Adam was here.

Where?

She stepped back and turned, abruptly afraid of being shoved from behind. When she looked over her shoulder, the dog was gone, and she saw what she'd missed before. Lodged in the sugar pine's trunk was an arrow, its vanes a vivid green. The arrow pinned something to the bark. At a gust, she caught its glimmering.

Leyna moved closer, intending to jump the ravine. She could make it. Her legs were long enough. Her body coiled, but common sense kicked in, and with a frustrated breath, she followed the ravine for several minutes until it narrowed, then stepped across.

As she approached the sugar pine on the other side, Adam's scent finally faded, then disappeared.

Rattled, she reached out and touched the trunk just beside the arrow, and when she brought her fingers beneath her nose, she smelled only the hint of pine.

Leyna pulled the arrow from the trunk and saw that its tip was blunted. An arrow used by beginners. The small sheet of folded plastic wrapping that it had pinned fluttered to the ground. She stooped to pick it up and unfolded it. It was the wrapper from the cream-filled cupcakes that were Adam's favorite. The kind he'd forced Grace to steal.

The kind Ellie had purchased on Thursday.

On the plastic, three words were written in thick black marker.

It's your fault.

CHAPTER 18
OLIVIA

Saturday, 11:15 a.m.

Richard rubbed the hard lump of tension that swelled between Olivia's shoulders.

Olivia counted to ten before pulling away from his probing fingers. When she turned to face him, she could just make out the gold flecks in his hazel irises, one of the first things she'd noticed about him and one of her favorite things still. Richard had a thoughtful face, if not a traditionally handsome one. In the past year, his dark hair had started to silver, and his smile lines had grown more pronounced. Until a week ago, she'd loved that he smiled enough to create such deep creases. She would trace them, enjoying the fit of her fingertip in the grooves. She and Richard had always fit like that before, even when she'd been broken.

After a moment, she said, "I'm sorry Meredith was so horrible to you."

"She wasn't that bad."

She caught the half grin that made clear he was joking. She tried to smile in return. A sign that everything was still okay between them.

"She was awful," Olivia said.

"What're you talking about? She told me I was brilliant." He puffed his chest in mock pride. "*Fucking brilliant,* she said."

"That was sarcasm."

"So I guess she didn't mean the part about me being handsome either?"

Olivia managed a laugh. "She didn't say that."

"She did. 'Olivia must've married you for your looks,' she said. You really don't remember that?"

"I believe she followed that by calling you a moron."

"Ah, yes. Apparently her new nickname for me. I think it means we're best friends now."

"You wouldn't want her as a friend." She stepped away from him, her attention sharpening on the woods. She wished she'd never come to Ridgepoint. Rocky had sold Richard on his dream, but with all that had happened, now Olivia could see only the neglect and rot.

Ringing the street where the Durans lived, lots cleared for houses had been left to the weeds; unfinished roads led nowhere. Roads became trails until they, too, ended, the land returned to rugged ground and dense canopy that threw dangers into shadow. In this wild, Adam had broken his ankle as a child, and even Leyna had gotten lost once or twice. Meredith had never kept a close enough eye on her daughters.

Then there were the squatters. A few years back, a family had holed up in a small A-frame cabin left over from the days when the property had been a working ranch. They'd trapped deer and other animals to eat and manufactured hash oil for cash until the cabin had grown too rotted to withstand winter.

There were also the occasional campers seeking refuge on their way to something better—if they were lucky. Once, after a particularly harsh winter, a body had been found only a mile into the forest. But this wasn't a city mile. This was a bring-your-compass-and-bottled-water mile. The last time Olivia had hiked that deep into the woods, her thighs had burned for a full day, and she'd gotten blisters despite wearing thick socks and her best boots.

They should never have moved there.

Olivia shook off the dread, though she knew it would return for her. It always did.

"You could've just told her you were putting the trimmer away," she said.

"We don't owe her an explanation."

"You're right. She's just..." She was surprised at the crack in her voice. She and Meredith had been friendly once. Not friends, exactly, but close enough that her neighbor had trusted her girls with Aunt Olivia, and Meredith hadn't felt the need to scream at her husband in front of their home.

"I know it's difficult, especially when she acts like she did today," he said, "but we should try to remember—she's lost a child too."

The knot between Olivia's shoulders tightened again. A hurricane gathered in her chest. "Are you saying I should forgive her?"

"Absolutely not," he said. "We should stay as far away as possible from that family. I just hate seeing you upset."

He bent to kiss her neck, his lips lingering near her ear as he whispered, "Have you been on my computer?"

Her body stiffened before she could stop it. She tried to cover with feigned worry. "Someone's been on your computer?"

He returned to working the knot. "It's fine if you have, you know." His breath was warm against her neck. "The cameras are to keep you and Thea safe. You're welcome to look at the footage anytime."

She leaned against his massaging fingers and moaned—the only useful thing she'd taken from her mother's disastrous attempt to make her into a beauty queen was learning how to fake it—but her whole body had turned to ice. "It wasn't me," she said. "Why would you think someone has been on your computer?"

He laughed. That close, the sound boomed and her eardrums throbbed. "Really, it's fine, Liv."

She played into the rigidity her body had used to betray her. "It wasn't me," she repeated, voice icy. *If in doubt, pick a fight.*

He leaned back and held up his hands in a gesture of surrender. "Okay, okay, I believe you. I must have deleted the files by accident."

Olivia shifted to better read his expression. She realized immediately that was a bad idea, since it meant he could read hers too, and he'd always been the better liar. Though he smiled, his eyes sparked. Would he forgive her if she came clean now? But she couldn't do that. They both had their secrets, and she was starting to be afraid of what he might do to protect his.

"What files are missing?" she asked, because that was the question he would expect of someone who'd done nothing wrong.

"Just the recordings from Thursday."

She should've erased the whole damn week. "That's too bad. The police might want those, since that's the day that girl went missing."

She watched his face for signs of guilt, but it lacked any trace of guile. He brushed her hair off her shoulder. "I'm sorry, Liv," he said, though she had no idea what he was apologizing for. Accusing her falsely? The affairs? Something worse?

Richard pulled her gently against his chest, and she could feel his heartbeat, steady and slow. "It doesn't really matter about the videos anyway," he said. "I back up everything."

CHAPTER 19
LEYNA

Saturday, 11:26 a.m.

It's your fault.

Though she'd imagined the scent, the note was real. When she held it in her hand, it crinkled.

She crumpled up the plastic, willing the logo to disappear, willing it to be a hallucination, like the body-spray scent she'd imagined. But when she opened her fist, the logo taunted. It brought back the pressure of Grace's palms on her shoulders. The warmth of Adam's breath as he whispered in her ear. She'd seen Adam's writing only a couple of times—on family holiday cards she'd immediately tossed in the garbage, on a note to Grace that her sister had left on her dresser. Still, Leyna was sure he'd used the same blocky script.

Had someone drawn her back on purpose?

Hand trembling, Leyna tossed the wrapper on the ground, then picked it up again and stuffed it in her pocket. The arrow would be too awkward to carry for long, so she left that on the ground and snapped photos of it with her phone.

After she'd crossed to the other side of the ravine, Leyna spotted Goose again. He wasn't alone. Blocking her path, a tall and broad-shouldered man with gray hair and a dense beard cradled him. In his arms, which were thick and bristling with silver hair, the dog seemed no bigger than a football.

The imagined scent of Adam's body spray burned her nose. Though she'd headed into the woods intent on talking with Rocky, she took a careful step to the side, away from him and the crack in the earth, her footing suddenly unsteady.

"Hey, Leyna."

An icy prickle traced her spine. She glanced over her shoulder, marking obstructions, considering her exit. She fought back a shiver, out of place in the heat.

His arms tightened around the dog. Though Goose seemed relaxed enough, Leyna didn't like the way Rocky held him.

She motioned to the ground. "I can take him back home—unless you're going that way?"

Rocky stared at her for several seconds, then slowly lowered the dog. "I'm not."

Leyna knelt beside Goose and patted his haunches, scratched behind his ears.

Rocky studied her for several beats, a dark amusement settling in his eyes, as if he enjoyed making her wait for his information.

"It's probably good we came along when we did," he said. "Some creatures aren't safe out here alone."

A blast of wind sent her ponytail swishing, and she patted the dog's head. She stood, reached into her pocket for the snack-cake wrapper, and held it up for his inspection.

"Recognize the writing?"

"What am I, a handwriting expert?"

She noticed he didn't ask where she'd gotten it. "It looks like Adam's," she said.

"You can't know it's his."

Leyna found his response curious. It wasn't a denial. "So you recognize it too."

He squinted at the words written on the plastic. " 'It's your fault'?"

Another nondenial. "I found it pinned to a tree with an arrow."

"Even if it is Adam's writing, who knows how long it's been there. Plastic takes a long time to degrade."

Those words felt like an admission. So he had recognized the writing.

"Be safe, Leyna," he said, voice low in his throat. Then he started walking away.

When the dog trotted a few steps in the opposite direction, Leyna bent at the knees and heaved him to her chest. She expected a struggle, but he seemed glad for the lift, leaning against her, drool dripping on her arm.

Before Rocky could disappear into the trees, she called after him. "Did you see that missing Sacramento girl on Thursday?"

He kept walking. Caution kept her rooted for several seconds, but she knew she would follow. She'd come here for answers, and if there was even a chance Rocky had information about Grace or Ellie, Leyna would follow him anywhere.

The wind pushed at Leyna's back as she trailed Rocky. He paid her no more mind than he did the chattering leaves. Leyna repeated her question—"Did you see that missing Sacramento girl?"—and again, it was met with silence. The dog grew heavier, and her thighs burned with the effort of navigating the slope. She stopped to catch her breath. If she put Goose down, would he follow her or try to run again? She loosened her grip, the lure of the ground getting stronger.

Finally, he said, "Why would you think that?"

"She was in the neighborhood, and Serena Silvestri saw her walking toward this trail. Which leads to your place."

"I know where I live."

"So did you see Ellie?"

He turned to face her. In the days following the incident and even now when someone heard her story, people looked at her a certain way. Their eyes softened, their mouths gaped, curiosity hiding in a show of horror.

Relief there, too, that it had happened to her and not them. Rocky's jaw remained tensed, his eyes hard. Leyna would've taken comfort in that if she hadn't believed he knew what happened to Grace. After a few seconds, he shook his head.

"She didn't knock on your door?"

His posture was relaxed, but his eyes went flat. "Even if she had, I wasn't there. From what I've heard, she was here around noon. I didn't get back from town until late afternoon."

She scanned his face for some sign of guilt. She'd seen it enough in her own face to recognize it in others, but Rocky's expression was nearly serene. "What were you doing in town?"

He started walking again. "I've already told the deputy who came asking. Some of the neighbors too. I'm not hiding anything."

"But you won't tell me?"

"You can understand why talking with you might give me pause."

"Because of Adam."

"Guess you're a smart girl after all, though obviously not smart enough to know when not to stir up shit. You pissed off a lot of people."

"I take it you're one of them?"

"I don't piss off easily, but yeah. Taking a shot at Adam's memory will do it. He's family."

"The suspects have always been limited. Adam—or you."

"Me?" He seemed taken aback, then laughed. "That's the thing about zealots. They fail to see the big picture."

"I'm not a zealot."

Rocky's expression was bland. Deliberately harmless? The truth of the situation hit her. She was alone in the woods with a man who might've hurt her sister. The forest had always been her safe place, and because of that she'd been reckless.

"I'm sick of this conversation," he said. "We've been having it for sixteen years. I've said everything I'm going to."

"But now another girl is missing. She was seen here. And I found her bracelet in the Miller house."

His face relaxed, eyes going flat again. Leyna was starting to recognize the expression. He was hiding something.

"Serena called you the king of Ridgepoint Ranch, and she's not wrong. You know everything that happens here."

"Maybe once." He gestured toward the land surrounding them. "This isn't mine anymore."

"You still own the land. You still live here. And seeing as you don't have a job, you must spend plenty of time in these woods."

"The land belongs to the banks and the lawyers, and I make a decent living fixing things. And where else would I go? My family's here."

Leyna knew he did projects around the county, but she wondered if there were other things Rocky *fixed*. "So you have no interest in finding a missing girl?"

Rocky's jaw tensed, his patience obviously waning. "Leave it alone, Leyna."

"You know I won't do that."

"Yeah. I know."

He turned and began walking, shouting over his shoulder, "See you in another ten years."

Dog clutched to her chest, she took deep breaths of air, warm and earthy, as she hurried to catch up to him.

"You're the one who brought it up by saying I didn't see the *big picture*. What did you mean by that?"

As if waiting for a response too, the wind ceased, and the forest grew quiet. The wrong kind of quiet. Goose whined, growing agitated.

Leyna looked around, less familiar with this part of the forest, before finding Rocky's back again. It was as broad as many of the tree trunks they passed. "What do you think happened—"

Rocky stopped suddenly, raising his hand to silence her. She bristled, but the surprise of the gesture and the fact that she'd nearly collided with his back had the desired effect. She stepped up next to him.

He stood as still as the immovable hillside and stared ahead. At what? At nothing.

Goose started wriggling in her arms. She feared he might leap to the ground and break a leg. But instead, he burrowed against her, head butting her chest as if he were trying to find a way inside, like that famous *Alien* scene played in reverse.

In front of them, the shadows shifted.

Someone watched them.

No—*something.*

A pair of yellow eyes locked with hers. The dog whimpered low in his throat.

Though Leyna had been told that a pack of gray wolves lived in the hills, she'd never seen one. As far as she knew, no one in the neighborhood had. Wolves generally avoided humans.

So why was this one so close to the houses?

Rocky whispered, "Wolves are crepuscular by nature. More active at dawn and dusk."

She understood what he was saying: It was an odd hour for a wolf to be roaming.

She kept her voice low. "Then why is this one here?"

Rocky said nothing, but his nostrils flared as he inhaled deeply. "Not sure," he said, but he looked worried.

In her arms, Goose grew more frantic, and she feared she'd misread his intentions and that he might jump to the ground and charge with unearned confidence or hobble away, spurring the wolf to give chase. While wolves usually left humans alone, they were also opportunists. And they were patient hunters.

The wolf assessed them too, as if deciding if these creatures that walked on two legs were a threat. Did holding Goose, now mewling, make her more of a target?

She held her breath and aggressively petted Goose's head, trying to quiet him, afraid any sound might convince the wolf to strike.

"Stand your ground," Rocky whispered. "Don't run. And shut that dog up."

After Dixie, Leyna heard stories of wolves turning up at nearby ranches to feast on dead cattle. She held the dog more tightly, and her legs tensed as she dug her sneakers into the earth. *Don't run* was worthless advice. She couldn't have outrun the wolf if she'd tried.

Rocky took another deep breath. For a man who spoke so calmly, his body vibrated with tension. If she could sense it, she was sure the wolf could too.

Her arms strained at the effort of containing the dog. She felt him slipping. She held tighter, but he fought her, and the hand that had been cradling his rump slid to his waist.

Rocky reached out and—slowly, carefully—extracted the dog from her arms. He took one small step and angled his body so it blocked more of hers. Secure in new hands, the dog stopped struggling but continued to whimper.

In front of them, the shadows shifted again, and several additional pairs of yellow almond-shaped eyes blinked into focus. The wolf's pack.

The wind blew, and with it came a hint of woodsmoke. *Fire.*

The reason for Rocky's tension. Likely the reason the wolves were here in the middle of the day. They'd have to move territories, wait the fire out somewhere. In the Sierra Nevadas, there were plenty of burn scars to offer them refuge.

How close was the fire they ran from?

A moment later, a gust scrubbed even that trace of smoke from the air, but Leyna remained on edge as several pairs of yellow eyes pinned hers. Reminding her: *The forest is ours.*

Then the alpha turned away and trotted with the pack deeper into the forest.

CHAPTER 20
MEREDITH

Saturday, 11:28 a.m.

As Meredith inspected the generator, Serena loomed over her.

"That was quite the show you put on earlier," Serena said. "Olivia's head nearly popped off." She leaned in, blocking Meredith's light. "Did it run out of gas?"

Meredith shooed the other woman out of her light and shot her a *You can't be serious* look. "Of course not. I filled it this morning."

She sniffed the air for gas, which might've indicated a fuel-line leak, a cracked exhaust pipe, or a malfunctioning pump. The scent was no stronger than it should've been, as it competed with the bite of hot pavement and pine.

Meredith leaned in to check the fuel gauge. Serena leaned in too. The tank remained a third full.

"Looks like there's gas," Serena said.

Because I can't read a gauge? "Looks that way."

Serena moved away and leaned against the house, crossing her arms.

"Your daughter paid me a visit. Asking questions about Ellie. Don't worry, I didn't say anything."

Meredith scowled. "There's nothing to say. I don't know anything about that missing girl."

"That seems to be everyone's story."

"It isn't a *story*." She gestured toward the siding Serena leaned against in her white blouse. "It's been a while since I pressure-washed the exterior."

Serena leaped away from the wall like a startled cat, moving back into Meredith's light. "That girl of yours is stubborn."

"Yes, she is."

"Nosy too. I can see why all the neighbors hate her."

Meredith bristled, but she kept her voice low: "Get the fuck out of my light."

Serena's eyes went wide, but she stepped back. After a few blissful moments of silence, her neighbor tilted her chin toward the generator. "You didn't use old fuel, did you? Frank says you shouldn't use old fuel because it can degrade."

Oh, for fuck's sake. "Yes, old fuel, and I topped it off with raccoon piss."

If Leyna were there, she would've said something like *Fresh raccoon piss, at least?*

A smile nearly slipped out before she was hit by an unexpected pang of worry, a result of all the talk of that missing girl. Where was her younger daughter? She'd gone next door chasing some shadow and never come back. Typical.

"What about the coolant?" Serena asked.

"Checked it this morning." Still, she knelt to check for leaks she might've missed. There were no dripping connectors. Nothing pooling on the ground.

Meredith kept her back to Serena as she set the key switch to the off position, then did the same with the battery.

A second later, she tensed. She leaned forward, studying the cable that snaked into the battery.

What's that?

Meredith touched the cable, bending it to confirm what had first caught her attention. A small tear, no larger than a thumbnail clipping but large enough.

"Someone cut the battery cable."

Meredith hadn't meant to say the words aloud, but Serena moved closer to study the tear.

"Sure it isn't just frayed from overuse?" she asked. "Frank says that can happen if you don't perform regular maintenance."

Meredith ignored her, studying the damaged cable. By itself, she might not have given it much thought. She would've taken it as the prank of one of the Durans or the work of a particularly crafty rat. One with a sharp knife to cut it so cleanly.

But when considered alongside the phone call with her art broker, she knew someone dangerous was messing with her.

Brian's words still echoed in her ears: *He said you'd know how to find him.*

Meredith hadn't seen Adam in sixteen years.

But though it had been that long, every moment of that night remained etched in her memory like acid in stone. It wasn't like she could forget that image of Adam's hands wrapped around her daughter's throat.

Adam Duran had been a quiet boy. Bookish, like Leyna, and if he and her younger daughter had been closer in age, they might've been the better match.

Not that anyone could steal someone's attention away from Grace once she'd claimed it.

Grace was spontaneous and dramatic, often in the most engaging ways. When Leyna slipped into one of her funks, Grace might throw together a scavenger hunt in the woods or perform a monologue from *A Midsummer Night's Dream* with her expressions exaggerated to make her sister laugh. If faced with an awkward silence, she might break into song. She had a passable voice, but her passion convinced others her talent went deeper.

Grace wasn't book-smart like Leyna or Adam, but she could read people better than anyone, and even those she'd just met were moved to please her. When they did, the smile or laugh she'd give in return intoxicated them. She was like champagne that way—bright, bubbly, and likely to give you a hell of a hangover if you had too much.

Because Meredith recognized that her older daughter had a mean streak.

The year he turned fifteen, Adam sprouted up a few inches, and his shoulders started to widen. Still a boy, but he bore a hint of the man he might become. Grace finally took notice, and the teens started dating.

It went well, for a while. But then Grace turned hostile. The expensive new shampoo she'd requested left her hair dull. The concert tickets Adam had given her as a gift ended up in the trash. The must-have suede boots had been worn once before being left in the rain to mold. She'd convinced her father to let her live with him, but he'd quickly kicked her out, and she'd come back even crankier. If Meredith had believed in that sort of thing, she might've googled How to tell if your teen is possessed by a demon.

As foul as Grace's mood had been that evening, she'd skulked back into the house with surprisingly little fanfare for a change. No slammed doors vibrated in their frames. No proclamations of *Worst day ever* bounced like bullets off the hallway walls. The demon seemed to be taking a smoke break.

Later, Meredith wished she'd seen Grace's mood as a warning, but she hadn't yet recognized the violence silence could hold. So instead of worrying, she'd taken advantage of the quiet to try to paint. Inspiration hadn't come, though, and she'd been packing away her supplies when Adam knocked on the door.

"Grace home?" he'd asked.

Meredith had never been the kind of mom who refused to let her daughter be alone in her room with a boy. Better there than in the living room with the TV blaring or in the kitchen making a mess they'd forget to clean.

So she'd pointed Adam toward the back of the house.

"She's in her room."

Meredith had actually experienced a pang of gratitude. Grace was his problem now, not hers. The younger Duran boy could usually lighten Grace's mood instantly. But not that night. The argument had started within minutes. Meredith had no interest in eavesdropping, but the harshest words carried.

From him: "You're acting crazy" and "Stop being a bitch."

From her: "I hate you" and "It's over."

After nearly two hours of that, an irritated Meredith had decided to self-soothe with a cocktail. She'd just wrapped the ice in a tea towel and picked up the mallet—a few tension-releasing strikes, and the rum would do the rest—when the fighting stopped as abruptly as a switch flicked.

At this new silence, Meredith stilled, cocktail forgotten.

They must've made up, she told herself. There could be no other reason for the argument ending like that.

But instinct as cold as the ice she'd been about to crush settled along her spine. Grace never calmed that quickly.

Never.

Meredith had already started toward Grace's room when something heavy thudded against a wall. A second later, a crash like glass shattering.

As luck would have it, the usually locked door had been unlatched. Though, in hindsight, it hadn't been *good* luck.

When Meredith shoved open the door, Grace was on the bed, Adam astride her. Her head was thrown back at an unnatural angle, her mouth set in a grimace. Both of them were breathing heavily. For several heartbeats, Meredith thought she'd interrupted an intimate moment.

Not the type to be embarrassed, she'd nevertheless felt the tingle of heat in her cheeks. Why hadn't they thought to lock the damn door?

But then she noted that they were fully clothed. The shards of a ruined desk lamp rested at the base of one wall. The shade of a floor lamp had been knocked askew, casting the couple in a dim, honeyed light.

And Adam's hands were wrapped around Grace's throat as she struggled to breathe.

Meredith's own hand clenched around the mallet she'd forgotten she was holding. The wood bit into her palm as she raised it, her shoulder coiling as her body reacted ahead of conscious thought, the rush to protect Grace so complete that she trembled with it.

Get off my daughter.

Only a thought, left unspoken.

Meredith swung, the fury behind the movement as cold as it was unexpected, and when the mallet connected with the side of Adam's head, she couldn't tell if the crack came from wood or bone.

Then Adam fell away from her daughter, onto the floor, and Meredith saw the mallet was intact.

So not wood, then.

Serena took a couple of steps away now, as if she finally meant to leave. "With the fire north of here, are you staying?"

"Of course," Meredith said. "We're as safe here as anywhere."

Which, really, wasn't safe at all.

If it had been anything to worry about, though, the county would be issuing evacuation orders and knocking on doors. Her thoughts were fully focused on the call from Brian.

He said you'd know how to find him, Brian had said.

The trouble was that Meredith did indeed know exactly where Adam Duran was. She just hadn't thought he'd wait so long to cause her trouble.

CHAPTER 21

LEYNA

Saturday, 11:35 a.m.

For several minutes, Leyna and Rocky stood in silence. Then Rocky set the dog down. Both of them watched to make sure Goose didn't intend to run off, but he instantly burrowed between Rocky's legs, his belly flat on the ground, resting his snout between his paws.

Rocky looked down at Leyna. "Smoke can travel hundreds of miles," he said as if to comfort her.

"So you don't think the fire's close?"

He scanned the sky, still a pale blue, and she was grateful for the thought he gave before answering.

"The wolves would've been heading away from the fire," he said. "So it's probably good that they're here."

But they're still on the move.

Leyna kept that comment to herself, eager to return to their previous conversation.

"Was Grace pregnant?"

Rocky's forehead creased and what looked to be genuine surprise flashed in his eyes. "What?"

"Grace left sixteen years ago. Ellie's sixteen."

He shook his head in apparent confusion. "Grace would've had to be near the end of her pregnancy when she left. Did she look nine months along to you?"

Though she'd thought the same, she sighed, frustrated. "There's a connection there. There has to be. Ellie showed up at the restaurant where I worked. Showed up here, asking about Adam."

Silence stretched, fed by the wind and the itch of instinct.

Finally, he said, "There might be a connection. Probably is. But not the one you're seeing."

Leyna didn't tell him that it wasn't her theory; it was Dominic's. He'd always been more sentimental than her. When she'd stalked him on social media, she saw that he still listed *The Purge* as one of his five favorite movies, and he'd once posted a photo of himself wearing that old T-shirt from the band they'd seen in San Francisco.

Leyna, in contrast, was a realist. Either Grace was dead or she'd chosen to cut Leyna out of her life forever. Both possibilities wounded, but she held to the second one more tightly—the one where Grace lived, happy without her sister.

"What is the connection, then?" she asked.

"No idea. I wish I could give you what you want. Give everyone what they want." He checked his watch. "Sorry. There's somewhere I need to be."

"I'll pay you." She calculated how much she had in her bank account. "A hundred and fifty-two dollars."

He grinned. "Very specific."

"It's all I have. But I can get you more later, I promise."

The pity he'd kept from his face earlier bloomed there now, and Leyna's cheeks flamed with the humiliation of it.

"I can get money from my mom, too, if you need it sooner."

When she mentioned her mother, his expression hardened. "I don't want anything from her."

"Please." She hated how desperate she sounded.

He looked abruptly uncomfortable too. "I already told you I don't know anything about Ellie Byrd. I stopped at the grill for a pastrami sandwich, then I picked up some parts to fix the Millers' shower."

"What about Grace and Adam?"

His expression was sympathetic. "Your sister's been gone a long time."

Five thousand, nine hundred, and ninety-two days.

"I'm aware," she said. "You've got to have a theory about what happened."

"Theories are just rumors. Spread by fools, believed by idiots."

Rocky shot her a pointed look, and she knew it was a reference to her public takedown of Adam's memory. If he expected an apology, he'd be waiting until every last leaf fell from the surrounding trees and the wolves' great-great-great-grand-cubs passed back that way.

If Adam hadn't killed Grace directly, he'd had a part in it. Leyna was sure of that.

True, Adam never left bruises or broken bones, the only scar from that final day not on Grace's arm but Leyna's.

I know you're not going to say anything, right, Leyna? That acrid smell of body spray when he'd moved in close. *We're friends.*

But how many times had Adam used his affection as a bludgeon to convince Grace to cancel plans with friends? And charmed her into believing she'd misunderstood a situation? He'd only been having fun, he'd say. He hadn't meant it that way at all.

Even Leyna had missed it for months, but Dominic leaving for college had emboldened Adam. Without his brother and with the adults around him either uninterested or deluded, who was there to act as witness? Only a twelve-year-old girl who kept silent because her sister convinced her she was imagining things.

It's nothing, Ley. You'll understand when you're older.

"Come on, Rocky. You've got to have a theory about what happened to them."

He exhaled, the weariest sound she'd ever heard. "I think they're both dead."

Heart thrumming, a rush of blood made her dizzy, and she could force out only a single word. "Why?"

"If they weren't, we would've heard from them."

Leyna shook her head aggressively. "I don't believe that."

"There's a difference between what we need to believe and what we actually do."

She squared her shoulders, her eyes daring him to doubt her conviction. "Grace is alive."

"Okay."

"Don't *okay* me. She might be alive." She immediately regretted the way she'd hedged her words and the slightest crack in her voice that brought back Rocky's look of pity.

He hesitated as if considering whether to share more. Then he said, "Olivia blew the family's savings on private detectives looking for Adam. In the first few months, there was that tip about the campground and a few other leads that didn't pan out, but we've heard nothing else in years. No one's that good at hiding. And there are too many ways it can go bad for kids out here on their own."

Maybe Rocky really doesn't know what happened to her, Leyna thought. Then, a second later, remembering the message in her pocket: *Maybe Grace really is dead. Not just because of Adam, but also because of me.*

"Did you know?" she asked.

"Know what?"

"That Adam was abusive."

"Let's not rehash all of that," he said, not unkindly. "I've already told you everything. I wasn't home when Ellie visited Ridgepoint, and I didn't see Grace or Adam the night they disappeared."

"You don't remember anything else?"

"Nothing that's any good to them. Some nights, I run through that day again, hoping I'll remember something new." His eyes lost focus. "I never do, but I can still see them as clearly as if they were standing in front of me. Both in black shirts and jeans. Both so damn young."

As he talked, the sky seemed to darken, but Leyna knew it was only a trick of her eyes. Stars pricked, black pressing in from the edges.

Rocky continued, apparently unaware of the shift in her mood. "Grace was cranky that day, I'll admit that, but they seemed... not quite happy, but comfortable, at least." His eyes sharpened as they locked with hers, and he scowled. "I never saw any abuse. You've got to know I wouldn't have stood for that."

Unable to speak, Leyna gave a quick nod.

He smiled, but it was as weary as his sigh had been. "If they were alive, this place would've drawn them back by now," he said. "It draws us all back eventually."

His pointed look let her know he was talking about her. Rocky started moving away again. With his longer legs, Leyna knew she wouldn't catch him, and even if she did, he wouldn't say more. But she wouldn't have followed even had she been able to keep pace, because he'd already said enough.

Both in black shirts.

If Rocky hadn't seen Grace that night, how did he know she'd changed her blouse?

CHAPTER 22

OLIVIA

Saturday, 11:55 a.m.

The conversation with Richard rattled Olivia, and she'd welcomed it when he'd left her to double-check the files on his computer. As soon as he was gone, Olivia powered up her own laptop, intending to search for a frittata recipe. Instead, she typed in the browser Missing Sacramento girl. She navigated to the video from that morning's press conference.

The kitchen had once been her favorite room. When Adam was home, the cabinets were cherrywood, there'd been a brick arch behind the oven, and copper pans dangled overhead. The last time they'd been together here, she'd somehow convinced him to make banana bread with her—he'd snuck in chocolate chips when Olivia turned to get the pan—and he'd been in such a hurry, he'd slopped batter over the side of the bowl onto the dark granite countertops veined red.

After he went missing, Olivia had remodeled. The countertops were now white marble, the walls white too. The glossy cabinets had been switched out for a natural dark wood. The air was thick with the scent of pine cleaner, the sink empty and dry. No fingerprints smudged the refrigerator. Olivia once loved to cook, but it now felt like a chore, the kitchen mostly a place for grabbing a snack or plating takeout. How long had it been since she'd baked banana bread here?

On the screen, a photo flashed. It was the one posted with all the earliest news reports. Ellie Byrd, brown hair secured in a ponytail, wearing a purple-and-white soccer uniform. She looked closer to twelve than sixteen. Olivia understood her parents' impulse—when the deputy had asked for a photo of Adam, she'd given him one of her favorites: Adam at thirteen during his floppy-haired phase, when she'd had to bribe him to get a haircut, with a grin so wide that Olivia's heart seized even thinking of it now. At that age, Adam had been more boy than man. In the photo, the collar of his T-shirt was stretched because he hadn't yet cared about those things, his cheek smudged because he still played in the dirt. It was the last photo Olivia had from the time before Grace.

The deputy had looked at her with sympathy and asked, "Do you have anything more current?"

On her laptop, new photos joined the first, and Olivia thought she might be wrong about the first picture being old. Maybe Ellie still looked that way. Innocent. Trusting.

Then a new photo flashed, and Olivia slammed the laptop shut.

My God, she looks just like Grace.

Chest suddenly tight, Olivia caught movement at the edge of her vision, and when she turned to the window, she spotted Rocky at the end of the driveway. He gave her a nod and gestured toward the empty house next door. He knew there were no private conversations inside the Duran house.

Thank God he'd gotten there so quickly.

She slipped away to the Miller house before her husband could return, the photo from the press seared on her retinas.

Oh, Richard, what have you done?

Olivia had first suspected Richard of having sex with other women a few years after Adam disappeared. As a sales rep for a medical-device company, Richard often traveled—a day in Reno, an overnighter in Sacramento, a couple of days in San Jose. But that tour of the Midwest had lasted three weeks, and in the background of one of his calls from Milwaukee, Olivia heard the shower running. When she asked him about it, he'd claimed the hotel room had a broken toilet—kept him up half the night thinking he needed to pee, he'd joked—and she pretended she believed him.

In her marriage, Olivia was willing to tolerate a lot. She'd never been the type to be irritated by empty toilet paper rolls, for example, or dishes left in the sink. When Richard put down the deposit on the house in Ridgepoint Ranch, she'd started shopping for a warmer jacket and hiking boots. If they'd lost all their money, she would've happily lived with Richard in a seedy one-bedroom apartment. If he'd needed nursing or forgiveness, she wouldn't have hesitated to offer either.

In most cases. But from the start, she'd made clear the exception: Richard wasn't to cheat. No months-long affairs. No onetime lapses of judgment. Not even one flirty text that might lead to something more. She and Richard were not going to become her parents.

But when the moment came that he did cheat, she froze. And she'd never stopped hating herself for that.

While Richard was away, Rocky trimmed the hedges and mowed the small patch of grass out back. When the Durans' garbage disposal stopped working, he'd replaced it. He'd also installed new security lights over the garage.

The day Richard called to extend his trip another week, Rocky had offered to make her dinner, and she'd asked if he knew how to make Bolognese sauce.

His answer: "Doesn't everyone?"

The sauce was watery and oversalted, and Olivia had been able to choke down only half. She'd blamed it on a large lunch, but he'd laughed.

"Yeah, it's pretty awful," he'd said.

She'd gratefully accepted a second glass of pinot to cleanse her tongue of its salty coating. The wine pairing he'd gotten exactly right. "Then why did you say you could make it?" she asked.

He'd responded: "I could never tell you no."

She nearly slept with him that night in retaliation. The only thing that stopped her was the thought of ceding the moral ground to her cheating husband. What would've happened had she made a different choice?

As Olivia let herself into the Millers' house, she forced air into her lungs and the tension out of her body. When she found Rocky in the kitchen, she said, "Richard knows we erased the recordings." She looked around, then lowered her voice even though there was no one but them to hear: "He says he has backups."

She knew she shouldn't have involved Rocky, but she'd panicked, certain she'd overlooked some files. And now it seemed she might have.

Rocky shook his head. "He doesn't have backups."

"How can you be sure?"

"Because I helped him install the system. He's testing you."

Thea had started getting curious about the cameras and the laptop her dad kept in his nightstand drawer. Olivia wished she shared Rocky's confidence that there was no longer anything for Thea to find.

"There's no way to recover the files, right?"

His face grew more serious. "What was on those recordings, Olivia?"

The morning before, Olivia's only concern had been to protect Thea, and Rocky hadn't asked questions. Apparently, that was over. "Richard's cheating again."

How had Richard been stupid enough to have sex with a sixteen-year-old girl? One who was now all over the news.

"Do you know with who?"

She nodded but couldn't bring herself to say the girl's name. Olivia and Rocky were close, but Richard and Rocky were family.

The silence grew heavy as he waited for her to give a name.

Finally, she said, "Ellie Byrd."

To Rocky's credit, the shift in his expression was subtle enough that someone else might have missed it, but Olivia recognized it for what it was. Doubt.

"I saw her, Rocky. In our bedroom."

Olivia's first thought had been *My husband's sleeping with a child,* which in her mind meant the girl was nineteen or twenty, and her second thought was that she looked vaguely like Grace Clarke.

Rocky looked confused, as if he thought he'd heard the words wrong. "She was in your house?" At Olivia's nod, his nostrils flared. "Where was Thea?"

"I don't know. With Richard, I think. I wasn't supposed to be home."

The damn radiator. If Olivia's car hadn't overheated, she would never have known about his infidelity.

No, not *infidelity. Crime.*

"What did he say when you confronted him?"

Her cheeks flushed with shame. "I didn't," she said. "He doesn't know I was there."

Unless he really did back up those video files.

Olivia thought of how easily he'd passed off the running shower as a broken toilet all those years before, and she imagined the excuses he might've tried this time.

I don't know that girl. I have no idea why she was in our room.

Oh, she called me by name? I meant I didn't know her well.

Why was she in our bedroom, then? Poor girl was exhausted. She asked if she could lie down.

Of course I didn't mean to keep it from you or the deputy who canvassed the neighborhood. I did *tell them I saw her.*

You're being ridiculous. You know I love you.

Maybe Richard wouldn't even have tried to make an excuse. Maybe he would've said, *I thought you were in Reno for the day.* Or maybe he would've blamed her: *You're so obsessed with finding Adam that you haven't really been there for me lately.*

At his sides, Rocky's hands balled into fists. "What if Thea . . ." His voice trailed off, but Olivia could guess at the direction his mind wandered. What if Thea had been the one to walk in on the young woman in their bedroom? What if she'd found the recordings before Rocky had helped Olivia erase them?

Expression as stony as his voice, he said, "We should go back further.

Check out the recordings of the past few weeks, the days you and Thea were both gone." He unclenched his fists, but she could still sense his frustration. "If we'd had more time…"

Even though she'd thought the same, she shook her head. "He would've erased anything incriminating. Especially now that he suspects I know something."

Still, her thoughts drifted to Richard's laptop in that unlocked drawer next to their bed.

After several beats of silence, Rocky said, "You don't think he had anything to do with her disappearance?"

"Of course not!" Olivia mustered as much conviction as she could.

She tried not to think of Ellie's vague resemblance to Grace and what that might mean. She went through the details of that night and, for the first time, asked herself: Could Richard have done something to Grace? He would never hurt Adam, of course, but he'd always had a soft spot for the elder Clarke daughter. Had Olivia been so lost in her grief that she'd missed something important?

She said, "If the police find out, though, this will look bad for him."

Rocky's brow knit, and she could read his thoughts as easily as if he'd spoken them: *That's exactly why we should tell them.*

He lifted his hand as if to reach for hers, but he quickly dropped it. "Don't do anything that puts you at risk, okay?"

Olivia noted the time on the clock in the kitchen. She'd been gone too long. Richard would be wondering where she was.

"I won't," she said, though by being there with Rocky and by sharing what she knew, she suspected she might already be in danger.

CHAPTER 23

LEYNA

Saturday, 12:06 p.m.

When Leyna got back to the neighborhood, she placed Goose on the Durans' doorstep before Olivia could come out to claim him. Then she retrieved her laptop from her car and retreated to her mom's back patio, the spot farthest from the house where she could still get a decent Wi-Fi signal.

She put her laptop on a patio table and checked her messages and the news. No response from Amaya. No updates on Ellie. Remembering the scent of smoke in the woods, Leyna checked the weather too. A small fire burned north of them, but so far Johnsville was the only area evacuated.

When her mom joined her, Leyna looked up. "I saw Rocky in the woods."

Her mom's lips compressed into a thin line. She made no move to sit. "The generator was sabotaged."

Leyna leaned back in her seat. "What?"

"Someone cut the battery cable."

"You're sure it was cut?"

"Of course I'm sure. Fortunately, I was able to fix it. But with everything that's going on..." Her voice trailed off.

"Did you hear something about Ellie?"

"No. Not Ellie."

"Then what?"

She waved off the question. "Just an issue with my art broker. I'm dealing with it."

Leyna closed her laptop. "Did something happen between you and Rocky?"

Her mom pulled her spine erect. A posture of defiance Leyna had witnessed many times. *I'm in control of this conversation.*

"Why are you asking about Rocky?"

"When I mentioned your name to him, I got the impression you two haven't been getting along."

"We get along as well as we ever have." Her tone dismissive.

Leyna hesitated, then pulled the folded plastic wrapper from her pocket. She placed it on the table for her mom to see. "I found this pinned to the sugar pine with an arrow."

Leyna didn't need to tell her mom which sugar pine she meant. Leyna had told her the story when everything about Grace was coming out. The part about falling, anyway.

Meredith picked up the folded piece of plastic but didn't seem to notice the writing. "Olivia still uses the range." She grimaced in displeasure. "Her damn dog dropped an arrow in my yard just last month."

"It wasn't one of hers."

"How can you be sure?"

Leyna pulled up the photo on her phone. "This one had a blunted tip. Like the practice arrows Adam used when he was learning to shoot."

Her mom returned her attention to the plastic wrapper, unfolded it. Her scowl deepened. " 'It's your fault.' What the hell does that mean?"

Leyna shrugged.

"Maybe it wasn't meant for you," her mom said.

"Maybe." She didn't believe that, of course. Who else could it have been intended for when it was pinned to *that* tree? But then she noticed her mom's expression. The compressed lips. The shuttered eyes. Those three words—*It's your fault*—had rattled her mom as much as they had her.

Leyna stood and exhaled, and a fresh blast of wind stirred the trees, as if she controlled the weather. If only. She would've liked to feel in control of something. She was preparing to broach the subject of Grace's final night again when she felt movement behind her just as her mom's lips puckered in disapproval.

Must be a Duran.

Leyna turned to find Dominic standing about ten feet back. With the past so fresh in her mind, she saw in him his brother's nose, thick brows, dark eyes. Those eyes, especially, made her breath catch.

She fell back on her mom's ploy—distraction. "The generator stopped working."

Dominic looked past Leyna. "Need help?"

Her mom shook her head. "Already fixed. And it didn't *stop working.* It was sabotaged."

After shooting Dominic a pointed look, her mom stalked off, heading inside. Once she was beyond hearing, Leyna said, "Did you call about the bracelet?"

"They took down our information and asked us to hold on to it." Dominic held out a plastic bag with the bracelet inside. She took it and put it in her pocket. Her twill joggers were loose enough that she couldn't feel the sharp edges of the petals. "With this weather, they're swamped now, but they'll contact us when they have the resources."

Leyna held out an offering of her own—the scrap of plastic she'd found stuck to the tree. Dominic raised an eyebrow and gestured toward it.

" 'It's your fault'?"

Whether or not the message was meant for her, it might as well have been. She forced the words out.

"We fought the night Grace disappeared. That's why she wasn't at home. It *is* my fault, at least partly."

After saying it aloud, she felt a loosening in her chest.

"Leyna—"

She stopped him with a look. She needed to get it out. Since Grace had gone missing, she'd told the same story: She was asleep. She'd been having some stupid dream that evaporated as soon as she opened her eyes, unaware the world had changed while she slept.

But that wasn't the truth. She'd seen Grace slip into that damp March darkness. And she'd done nothing to stop her. Worse than nothing.

The events of those last few weeks had played in her head on a near-constant loop every day for sixteen years. She wondered if it was the same for Dominic.

That last day, Grace wanted to be alone with Adam, but Leyna had followed Grace and Adam anyway, despite the soda that cramped in her bladder. She'd started to notice the way he held Grace's arm too tightly, and his flashes of irritation had grown more frequent. At twelve, she hadn't been able to put her finger on it, but that day felt different somehow. So when they began walking faster, Leyna jogged to keep up.

It had been raining for days, and that afternoon the air was clean, the earth wet, and foam slicked the base of some pine trees. She breathed in the memory, years removed from the scent of the nearby forest baking in the heat. As she shifted, the leaves on the ground crackled. Different than that day, but near the same trees, the same ground, she'd explored as a child.

Grace and Adam stopped in a familiar clearing—next to a sugar pine that had shed strips of bark after that winter's frost and a ravine wider than she was tall and deeper still. By then, Leyna was winded, and she really had to pee. Her T-shirt stuck to her skin, and sweat bloomed from her armpits, the cotton straining against her stomach because of a recent growth spurt.

At seeing Leyna—sweating, chest heaving in her too-small T-shirt—Grace laughed. It was a blunt sound, and the flash of her eyes warned that she intended to wound. Recognizing her sister's irritation, Leyna knew she should leave, but her legs were rubber, her heartbeat a violent knocking, the urgency of her bladder temporarily on pause.

Grace's perfect eyebrows shot together. "You shouldn't have come." Her lips thinned and her hands darted to Leyna's shoulders, and no matter what Leyna would later tell her mom, Grace meant to push her as hard as she did. It hadn't been an accident.

The force of that shove sent Leyna several steps back. Her right foot caught the root of the sugar pine, and when her arms shot out for balance, she overcorrected. Gravity tugged her backward, toward the crack in the earth, and she tumbled in and landed hard on her backside at the bottom of the crevasse on a mat of dried brush and bits of rock.

Leyna brushed the phantom needles and gravel from her palms. In her memory movie, she usually fast-forwarded through the next part of the story, but if she was feeling self-destructive, she played it on repeat. Currently, she was in a skipping kind of mood.

Leyna had told Dominic some of it ten years before. Now she told him the rest of it.

"I could've saved her."

Dominic seemed to be waiting for her to say more, so she added, "Mom and Grace were arguing. I didn't hear what it was about, but it was a night for that."

There were only two volumes in the Clarke house—maximum and full silence. That night, the volume had been turned all the way up. Too far away for Leyna to hear clearly but loud enough to make her reach for her earplugs and lock her door. Those days, she always locked her door when Adam visited.

After her mom retreated to her own bedroom and after Leyna was sure Adam wasn't coming back, she slipped out of bed and locked Grace out of the house.

"I didn't intend to," she said. "Not at first. I'd gone to the kitchen for something to eat."

She didn't tell him how her arm had started to throb and how the shame of what had happened brought heat to her cheeks. But he already knew that part of the story.

"I saw the door leading outside, and I locked it." In the moment, it felt like a small victory. "Then I locked all the doors and the windows. Grace never mastered how to pick a dead bolt."

Even now, Leyna could see Grace at the window later that night. She was still tormented by the tapping of her sister's fingernails on the glass, her voice as she begged to be let inside.

The cloud-cloaked moon had cast anemic light, but her sister's face had been only inches from the window. Even in the near darkness, Leyna couldn't pretend she didn't see.

She tried to pretend anyway, shifting in her bed so she faced the wall.

"Open up, Ley." Grace never pleaded, and the unfamiliar tone nearly pulled Leyna from her bed.

Grace raised her voice to a more urgent whisper. "The doors are all locked, and I don't have my key."

Leyna's legs tensed and she was considering going to the window even after what Grace had done earlier when the tapping became a pounding. Leyna didn't need to face her sister to know she was using her fist.

"Come on, Ley." Her voice hardened with impatience. "It's fucking freezing out here."

Leyna burrowed deeper into her comforter until her sister gave up and walked into the woods; Leyna went to the window to watch her go.

Leyna noticed her fingers circling her scar, and she pulled them into a fist. She couldn't look at Dominic, certain she would see his judgment.

"And you never saw her again?"

She offered a slow shake of her head, and, unable to stand his inevitable disappointment in her, she started walking to her car. He stopped her with a hand on her shoulder.

"You couldn't have known she'd never come back."

"It was still a shitty thing to do." Her voice cracked. She'd left her sister out in the cold, at the mercy of monsters. One monster in particular. But she'd never been able to convince Dominic of that, and she wasn't about to try again.

Dominic tried to reassure her. "If she'd come back, you would've let her in, right?"

He'd obviously forgotten how stubborn she could be. Then again, he'd always had more faith in her than she'd had in herself. When they'd been friends, then lovers, he'd encouraged her to write a mystery novel, explore a career with the forest service, become a baker—*Find the thing that makes you happiest,* he'd say.

She'd wanted that to be him, but of course it couldn't be. There were only two things that would ever make her happy, or at least assuage her guilt.

Finding Grace or punishing Adam.

Leyna's various jobs in retail or as a server—those were just ways to pay the rent. Her college classes, the friends she grabbed drinks with, the men she slept with who weren't Dominic—those were ways to pass the time between leads. Because for sixteen years, her life's purpose had been finding out what had happened that night.

Leyna turned to face him. "Of course I would've let her in." She paused. "Eventually." She wasn't sure that was true, but she couldn't bear to give him a different answer, one that might cause his faith in her to fade. Being back here reminded her how much she'd missed it.

"It's not your fault," he said, his face so earnest she almost believed him.

She believed what was written on that wrapper more.

"So—where are we going?" he asked.

Leyna started toward the car again. "To search Rocky's place."

"He's going to let you do that?"

She opened the driver-side door and got in. "He won't be home," she said. "He told me he had someplace to be."

"Hmm." Not yet fully convinced. "Assume you don't have a key?"

"Nope."

Dominic slid in beside her. He buckled his seat belt and slung his left arm on the console, careful to take only half the space. "So breaking and entering. Cool." He slipped on a pair of sunglasses. "Though this is definitely going to make the next Duran family dinner a little awkward."

CHAPTER 24
MEREDITH

Saturday, 12:08 p.m.

Meredith took the cordless phone into Grace's bedroom. It was where she liked to go when she was angry. She despised being threatened. The words from the man claiming to be Adam Duran came back to her.

I want to hang the painting over the mantel so everyone who comes into my home can see what she's done.

Meredith opened the closet that once held Grace's clothes. Not long after Grace went missing, Meredith had packed up her daughter's clothing and put the boxes in the garage. Despite everything, she still expected Grace to show up at the house demanding her things.

In the years that followed, she'd turned the closet into a different kind of shrine. This was where she stored her daughter's portraits.

Most of the time, all the portraits but that year's were wrapped in plastic and Styrofoam and sealed in boxes, but for the month of Grace's birthday, Meredith would pick a few to display in Grace's room. She should've packed them away a week ago, but she hadn't. It seemed wrong to put them back in storage when she hadn't yet finished the one that would mark Grace's thirty-third birthday.

Meredith sat on the edge of the bed facing the closet and the wall where three portraits had been hung. Grace at eighteen, twenty-five, and twenty-eight. She put her notepad and pen on the bed next to her and called the courier service first. As expected, they had nothing to tell her.

After she hung up, she checked her phone contacts for a number she'd called only twice before. While Meredith had threatened her art broker's Braque, Brian would sell his father's fake leg when it came to high-value commissions. His sweet assistant Katie, however, would be much easier to persuade.

Let's see if fake Adam's identity stands up to the same scrutiny my replicas get.

With three pairs of Grace's icy-blue eyes watching her, Meredith punched the number into the handset and offered a breezy greeting.

"Hi, Katie." As if they were old friends, the kind of friend you did favors for. She'd met Brian's assistant only in passing, but Katie had made an impression in her sunflower-yellow blouse, garish green eye shadow, and bright orange braids. Meredith figured she used color to compensate for falling just short of five feet, even in heels. It worked. People noticed her. Unfortunately for Katie, her personality wasn't nearly as bold. Meredith found herself comparing the assistant to Grace, as she always did with women of that age. The comparison wasn't favorable to Katie.

"I need some information about a client who approached Brian about a commission. *Girl in White in the Woods*. I heard you spoke with him today."

"I'm sorry, Ms. Clarke. Truly. But I'm not allowed to give out that information."

"Brian's already talked to me about it. It's my commission. I just need to confirm the identity, since I must've written the name down wrong."

The assistant paused, then lowered her voice. "What's the name you have?"

"Adam Duran."

Katie sighed in apparent relief. She really was a nervous young woman. "Yes, that's right. That's the name."

"But you see, it's not. I know this for certain."

"It's the only name I have."

"Like I said, it's the *wrong* name." An edge crept into her voice. "You must understand why I'd need to confirm the identity of someone asking about me, especially since they have such sensitive information about my work. About my family."

"I really am sorry. Would you like to speak to Brian? I can see if he's available."

So Katie had finally stolen a backbone from the gallery's lost and found. Meredith would've been impressed if it hadn't pissed her off.

"No, I don't want to speak to Brian. I've already spoken with Brian, and now I'm calling you. Brian mentioned that when the client called today, he seemed anxious that he hadn't heard from me."

"I can confirm he called, but I can't share the details. I'm sure you understand." Her voice was annoyingly chipper. "Is there anything else I can help you with, Ms. Clarke?"

"You haven't yet helped me, Katie."

The assistant went silent, but she didn't hang up. She wasn't the type to disconnect first.

Meredith released her breath and spoke to Brian's assistant as calmly as she was able. "Listen, Katie, the worst that idiot boss of yours will do is fire you, and you know I'm capable of worse than that. Plus he won't fire you. Then who would schedule his bathroom breaks?"

For focus, Meredith studied the three portraits of Grace. She'd selected the newer paintings at random, but the first portrait she'd hung because it remained her favorite. It was the truest to the Grace she remembered. Unlike the others, which were interpretations of what Grace might have looked like in later years, this one captured her as she was then. In this first portrait, Meredith hadn't yet perfected the pale blue of Grace's eyes, but her skin and hair were exactly right, the same as they'd been when she was sixteen. Meredith had taken artistic license with only a single detail: She'd given Grace a smile, although it had been lost long before she'd gone.

Meredith returned to her friendly voice but with enough of a threat to make Katie wonder at the undertone. "I won't tell Brian you told me anything. Unless you don't help me, in which case I'll tell him I'll no longer work with him because of you."

The young woman huffed. "That's not cool." Katie sounded a little angry. *Good for her.*

"I agree, it isn't cool at all. But neither is being threatened by someone hiding behind a fake name."

On the other end of the line, Meredith heard a faint *click-clack* that might've been heels on tile. When Katie spoke again, her voice echoed as if she'd moved to a smaller room. Meredith could hear paper shuffling. "That's the only name I have." She dropped her voice. "But I got the impression it was someone who knew you well." Brian had said the same thing, and an impatient Meredith began drumming her fingers on her leg. "There is one thing..."

As she waited for Katie to finish both her shuffling and her damn sentence, Meredith went through her list of suspects. She thought first of her ex-husband—John always sought the easiest route to a paycheck, which was part of what made him a crappy artist, and he'd been the one to connect her and Brian. But Meredith and John had divorced long before the teens disappeared. On the rare occasions they'd spoken since, John had shown little interest in Grace, let alone the young man she'd been dating. Besides, John wasn't exactly the mastermind type.

She'd just dismissed the idea when it hit her that she was wrong. Grace *herself* could've told John everything about that night. Their daughter had spent a few months with him not long before she disappeared, and when she left Plumas County for good, she might've returned to her father for help. He wouldn't have helped her financially, of course, but he might've provided a ride and kept her secret—if the price was right. And there was the added bonus of sticking it to Meredith.

John could be petty and mean. After Brian rejected John's fake Monets, John had keyed the broker's Range Rover. Her ex-husband wouldn't have hesitated to blackmail her and use Brian to do it, especially if it meant John came out of it six figures richer.

But John was far from the only suspect. The neighborhood was full of people who hated the Clarke family. No one more than the Durans—Olivia. Richard. Dominic. Even that damn dog, always crapping in her yard. She would've added Thea to the list if she'd thought the girl capable of such a complicated plan.

Rocky had never been her biggest fan either, and Meredith was pretty sure the Silvestris were deep in credit-card debt. Serena loved her Fendi bags and Garavani sandals.

The names of those who might have betrayed her buzzed in her head like a swarm of damn mosquitoes, trying to bleed her. Filling her lungs, Meredith tried a visualization technique Serena had taught her, picturing each annoying mosquito clenched in her fist, its wings and thorax broken. It did little to lighten her mood. Maybe because she'd done it wrong—Serena's version had involved watering flowers or some such crap.

On the phone, Meredith heard more paper shuffling, then a sharp intake of breath. When Katie spoke again, her voice was a whisper. "Found it. Got something to write with?"

Meredith grabbed her pen and notepad. "Go ahead."

"When the courier dropped off the note, he mentioned the client had promised to promote his band—'Creatives should support creatives' is what Mr. Duran said, according to the courier. So they exchanged social media handles." She paused. "You won't say you got it from me?"

"Of course not." Meredith knew that if Adam Duran had let slip that information, he'd intended it to find its way back to Meredith, and it was only Brian's incompetence that had kept it from her for this long.

Katie released a breath, her relief obvious even across the phone line. Meredith thought it was sweet that the girl trusted her so easily. Stupid, but sweet.

"I can't believe I didn't remember it," she said. "It's adamduranlives. Hope that helps."

Then Katie hung up.

CHAPTER 25
LEYNA

Saturday, 12:12 p.m.

A minute into the drive, Dominic turned to study Leyna's profile, sun glinting off his lenses. "So why are we breaking into Rocky's place, again?"

"You're welcome to stay in the car."

"Not what I asked."

Dominic shifted to better assess her, the heat of his attention making her uncomfortable, more so because she couldn't see his eyes behind the sunglasses. She was surprised to find her mouth dry when she answered. "I'm hoping he'll have information about Ellie."

"You have anything to go on?"

His skepticism was nearly as oppressive as the heat. "He was evasive. He denies seeing her."

Damning. She waited for his retort: *So does your mom, but Rocky has an alibi.* When he kept silent, she added, "Serena saw Ellie headed toward the trail."

Dominic's silence grew heavy, and she risked another quick glance away from the road. "What?" she asked.

"There are more than a million acres in that forest."

She pulled her attention to the road again. "I'm not talking about searching the whole forest. Only one small part of it."

"So thousands of acres, then," he said.

"Ellie wasn't traveling thousands of acres on foot." She paused, then: "Rocky told me I need to accept that Grace is dead."

The air in the car grew suddenly charged as Dominic faced forward again. She could guess what connections he was making: If Rocky had suggested Grace was dead, he likely believed the same about Adam.

"He needs to keep his opinions to himself," he said.

"There's something else." When he shifted to look at her again, she said, "Rocky also mentioned Grace had been wearing a black shirt when all the reports at the time said she'd been wearing a blue one."

"So he got it wrong."

"That's just it. He didn't. She changed right before she left." In the beginning, Leyna had kept that detail to herself because she didn't want anyone asking why Grace had changed and then how blood had ended up on Grace's sleeve. But then the fake sighting of Grace at the campground had been called in, and the detail became a way for Leyna to separate the truth from the lies. Apparently, she'd been right to hold back. "He's always claimed he didn't see her that night, but she was headed toward his house, and he knew about the color of the blouse. So obviously he's been lying."

Leyna glanced at Dominic, but his only reaction was a tensing in his jaw. She forced her eyes back on the road, but she could feel him thinking. "What?"

"I want to find Ellie, and of course I want to find the connection to Adam and Grace."

"But?"

"Rocky is family. He's the one who taught me how to build my first birdhouse. He taught me the difference between a crankbait and a jig."

"Assume that's a good thing?"

She felt him smile. "Types of fishing lures," he said.

"Of course."

"I'm always willing to commit a felony for you, but let's reserve judgment until we see what's actually inside his place."

Dominic was right, but Leyna found herself unable to admit that. They rode the last couple of minutes in silence.

Rocky's place was easy to find. There was only one structure at the end of the gravel road—a simple gray cottage with a red door.

Leyna said, "Does Rocky have a car?"

There was no garage. If Rocky was home and had a car, it should've been parked here.

Dominic nodded. "A newer Chevy Colorado."

Wherever Rocky had gone, he'd taken his truck. Dominic got out of the car and crossed his arms, studying the house.

"What's your take on Rocky?" she asked cautiously, not wanting to restart their argument.

He hesitated, adjusting his sunglasses. "Like I said, he's a good guy. Loyal, and he's been there for us." He uncrossed his arms. "You're sure he's not here? I would hate to walk in and find him cleaning his rifle."

Leyna nodded. "I'm sure." She wasn't. "Besides, if he was, you wouldn't be the one he aimed at."

Dominic rubbed his hands together in exaggerated pleasure. "So let's go commit our first felony."

The red door was flanked by two single-paned windows, a large one looking into the living room and a smaller one revealing the kitchen. He glanced at the windows, then faced her. When she caught her reflection in his sunglasses, Leyna reflexively smoothed her hair.

"You picking the lock?" he asked.

She shook her head. Well beyond her abilities. "We're breaking a window. Unless it's unlocked?"

Dominic tried the knob. "It's not."

She sighed, disappointed but not surprised. "A rock it is."

He left her on the porch, she guessed to find a rock, and returned a moment later with a shovel. The handle was splintered, the blade bent, but the tool was more than adequate for breaking a window. He held it out to her.

"You want to do the honors or should I?"

Seized by an urge to break something, she grabbed the shovel. "Better I do it. Wouldn't want your parents mad at you."

He touched her arm. "Wait." He removed his sunglasses and handed them to her. When their fingertips brushed, she flinched like a middle-schooler. She put the sunglasses on, grateful for something to hide behind.

"Thank you," she said, tone deliberately brusque.

After he stepped back, Leyna smacked the window with the edge of the blade, shattering the glass. She continued striking, pausing only to remove the screen, until all that remained was a border of jagged teeth.

She dropped the shovel, and Dominic stripped off his shirt to knock away the last shards. He draped his shirt over the now-empty frame and pulled himself up into the opening. Leyna tried to ignore the way his shoulders and upper back strained and the scent of sweat the wind pushed in her direction.

Once inside, Dominic unlocked the front door, T-shirt in hand.

"Good news. He's not inside cleaning his rifle. So—what're we looking for?"

She shrugged, avoiding any glances at his chest. That only forced her attention to his smile and those damn dimples. "Why don't you start in the bedroom? I'm sure Rocky has a shirt you can borrow if that one's ruined."

He grinned, then shook out his T-shirt, inspected it for any bits of glass, and slipped it back over his head. "Sorry. I didn't realize me being shirtless bothered you."

"Not at all. It's just not safe."

"Really?" He seemed amused.

"I'm serious. What if you were cut or burned?"

"I wasn't aware cotton was fire-resistant."

"I meant, like, what if you're splashed by something caustic."

"Caustic?"

"Like battery acid or drain cleaner."

He laughed. "Hmm. Didn't realize we were here to unclog his drains. But it's good to be safe again."

Aware of how ridiculous she sounded, Leyna grew impatient; she took off his sunglasses and handed them back. "You start in the bedroom. I've got the front of the house."

Grin still firmly in place, Dominic headed in that direction but paused in the doorway. Without turning, he said, "For the record—you're a distraction too."

Leyna was glad he didn't wait to see her reaction.

The cottage was small, not more than eight hundred square feet, but still larger than Leyna's apartment. Plain, but cozy enough. It smelled of pine and beer. Her mom would've hated it.

Leyna popped her head in the bathroom, which also housed a stackable washer and dryer, but decided to leave that for Dominic. She started her own search in a kitchen that was frozen in the past—tile in shades of mustard and brown, cabinets and a small table made of fake oak, and a refrigerator and ceiling fan in well-scrubbed white. One of the cabinets had been removed, and half the floor tiles were gone. The subfloor showed the early signs of rot.

She flashed to her earlier search of the Miller house. That had felt like a different kind of intrusion—entering a place where she wasn't invited that was not quite a home. But a man lived here. She found traces of him everywhere, pieces of himself he hadn't intended others to see.

A drawer stuffed with loose nails, batteries, and takeout menus, mainly Italian and steak houses but also one for a "globally influenced" vegan restaurant in Reno.

A prescription for heartburn medication on the kitchen counter.

A book of poetry by Gary Snyder on the table. When she riffled through its pages, an old photograph slipped to the floor—a faded image of Rocky and a woman Leyna guessed was his wife. She bent to pick it up, recognizing the terrain behind them even if the houses hadn't yet been built. The groundbreaking for Ridgepoint Ranch. Within a couple of years, that smiling couple would be broke and divorced.

She slipped the photo back into the book, glad she'd left the bedroom to Dominic.

She checked the refrigerator last, but it held no secrets. Only bottled beer, foil-wrapped plates, and a produce bin filled with apples, zucchini, and tomatoes that had started to soften.

Done with the kitchen, Leyna moved to the living room. Decorated in cabin chic, there was even an elk head mounted to the wood-paneled wall, watching her transgression with dead eyes. A plaid throw had been draped over the corduroy sofa. After thoroughly searching the sofa, she shook out the throw, then carefully folded it and put it back in place.

She repeated the routine with the matching chair, its ribbing worn to smoothness on the seat cushion. On the coffee table were more books of poetry as well as memoirs, science fiction, and mysteries. She picked up one by Agatha Christie—*The Murder of Roger Ackroyd*—and traced its spine with her fingertips. She'd read it half a dozen times, though Rocky's copy was older, its pages yellowed. She imagined him turning the pages, careful that they didn't tear, and wondered if her favorite parts were also his.

She checked each book in turn, but there was nothing hidden in the pages.

Dominic walked in the room just as Leyna moved on to a set of drawers against the wall.

"Leyna..." he said, his voice tentative.

She pulled open the drawer. "Did you find something?" She had not yet looked up, transfixed by what the drawer held. Drawings and maps of Ridgepoint Ranch. Or, rather, of the project as Rocky originally envisioned it. Only the first phase had ever been completed, and that left Leyna with a surprising melancholy.

Things never work out the way we hope, do they?

There were drawings of the original buildings, including the sprawling ranch house—two stories, a wine cellar, and a wraparound porch—that had been razed to make room for the unfinished clubhouse. She'd always wished she'd seen the home before it was destroyed, and its outline here brought an unexpected wave of sadness. For generations, a family lived there. Raised children who had explored the woods just as she and Grace had. Livestock had been tended in the nearby fields. Now, in its place was the unfinished clubhouse and a fairway overtaken by crabgrass and thistle. It didn't seem like an improvement.

Leyna snapped a few photos with her phone before she realized Dominic hadn't answered her. She could feel him hovering, and she looked up, intending to ask again.

She didn't need to. Dominic was holding something in his hand.

"I found these," he said, "in an envelope taped to the bottom of one of his dresser drawers."

Face far more serious than when he'd left her, Dominic held a small stack of photos by the edges, as if worried he might smudge them.

Her breath caught in her throat. "Ellie?"

He shook his head, then carefully fanned out the photos so Leyna could see.

They were all of Grace.

THE FIRE

The fire moves slowly, but the ground is starting its upward slope. Heat rises and the narrow walls of the canyon act as a chimney. Soon, the flames will run up the hillside.

In other parts of the forest, fire crews have cleared the fir trees and the lower branches of the pines—the ladder fuels that can push a fire upward. But there are more than a million acres in the Plumas National Forest alone. Far too many for crews to maintain. Here, the firs and lower pine branches remain intact. This fire will be well fed.

At the Plumas County Sheriff's Office, the dispatcher is unaware of the threat. Since taking the job earlier that year, she has lived on energy drinks, melatonin, and Advil, and what occupies her now isn't the fire she knows nothing about but a back that's throbbing from sitting too long in her chair.

Later, the transcripts from that day will be shared in the media, dissected by the incident team, but in those initial moments, the dispatcher's voice and pulse are steady.

She doesn't yet know how close the fire is or how quickly it will spread.

Dispatcher: 911, state your emergency.

Caller: There's smoke. There might be a fire.

Dispatcher: What's on fire? A structure? Vegetation?

Caller: I don't know. Maybe a house?

Dispatcher: Where's the smoke coming from?

Caller: Near Collins Road.

Dispatcher: Do you see flames?

Caller: (*Pause.*) No. No flames.

Dispatcher: Fire units are on the way.

Even when fully staffed, the sheriff's office has only about thirty people to address a critical response. But, unconcerned, the dispatcher isn't yet thinking about that.

Then, ten minutes later, the second call comes.

Dispatcher: 911, state your emergency.

Caller: I think there's a fire. Near our house. I smell smoke.

Dispatcher: We've received a report of a possible structure fire outside of Johnsville.

Caller: We're on Juniper Court. (*Muffled conversation.*) My neighbor says the fire's on the other side of the highway.

Dispatcher: How far away is the fire on the other side of the highway?

Caller: I don't know. A couple hundred feet, maybe.

Dispatcher: And how large is the fire?

Caller: Big. Like, a dozen acres at least. You need to send someone. My mom—she's in a wheelchair.

Dispatcher: I've alerted fire and rescue crews. You need to get out of there, okay? If you're seeing flames, you need to leave. Don't bother with your belongings.

The dispatcher's training kicks in, and familiar questions start to needle. How many roads in and out of the area? How heavily populated? Are there livestock to evacuate? Getting farm animals to safety can take hours.

All these questions lead to the most important ones: How much time will the residents of Collins Road and Juniper Court need to evacuate?

And do they have that much time?

It's only a dozen acres, according to the caller. The dispatcher believes there is time. Those first pencil-thin wisps that rise in the sky stoke caution, not panic.

But heavy with soot, ash, and branches, the column of smoke rises ever higher until it hits a layer of cooler air and collapses like a bowling ball dropped in water. The smoke spreads across the sky. Stretches across the ridgeline.

The calls grow more frequent, and more alarming.

Dispatcher: 911, state your emergency.

Caller: (*Frantic.*) The hill is on fire.

Dispatcher: Where are you calling from?

Caller: It's getting really bad out here.

Dispatcher: We have reports of fires on Collins Road and Juniper Court. Are either of those near you?

Caller: No. I'm on Beaumont.

This doesn't make sense to the dispatcher. Beaumont is a mile south of the other locations. She wonders if more than one fire is burning. Or if it's larger than initial reports suggested.

Dispatcher: Where is the hill from where you are?

Caller: (*Voice shaky.*) It's close. A quarter mile?

Dispatcher: Are you able to evacuate?

The caller's next words are unintelligible; then, panicked, he begins to shout so loudly that the dispatcher's ears thrum for several seconds.

Caller: My God, it's all burning! It's all fucking burning!

The man's location puts him seven miles northeast of Ridgepoint Ranch. In two hours, the fire has burned five miles.

And now, having reached the hill, it's starting to climb.

CHAPTER 26

OLIVIA

Saturday, 12:30 p.m.

Olivia was in the side yard with Goose when a white SUV pulled up to the house. Its door was emblazoned with a familiar green-and-gold logo, and Olivia felt the flush of adrenaline. She held her breath, and her body stilled, as if hope were a small bird she might startle away.

Adam?

Her son's name in her head brought the rest of him with it—the too-big glasses that slipped down his nose when he read, the peanut-butter-and-raisin sandwiches she'd find moldering in his backpack, the fullness of his smile, the emptiness of his bedroom, the downy stubble that would never grow into a beard, the lanky limbs that would never fill in with muscle.

The bird she imagined wasn't hope at all, but fear. She felt the grip of its talons, the slice of its beak.

The deputy approached, his face grim, and a new thought pricked.

Is this about Ellie Byrd?

The deputy was young—late twenties, she guessed—with tight curls cropped close to his head and a cleft chin. He spoke before he'd made it fully up the driveway.

"Olivia Duran?" His tone and expression were matter-of-fact. A man with a job to do.

Whether that job involved her son or the missing girl, Olivia knew that men in uniforms rarely brought good news.

Please don't ask to come in. Olivia inhaled, lungs swelling to fill her chest. *Please don't ask if there's someplace we can sit.*

The worst news always followed being asked to take a seat. When the police came to talk about Adam, that was one of their first requests.

She'd led them to the living-room couch, choosing the spot where Adam had fought off a recent virus and remembering how she'd brought him tea and soup and brushed the hair from his forehead while he slept. Remembering, too, how she'd done the same when he was a toddler, his head in her lap, the entirety of him fitting in the crook of her arm.

Olivia had picked at the leather on the armrest and waited for the lead detective to share whatever update was so horrible that they'd requested her to sit first.

"I'm sorry, Ms. Duran. There's no sign of where your son's gone."

Where your son's gone. As if he'd left voluntarily. She'd never believed that, no matter what Meredith claimed.

Her nails, already bitten to nubs, scraped the armrest. She'd willed herself to hold the detective's gaze even as it scalded with its sympathy.

"We'll share any news as it comes in."

Updates that were frequent at first fell off as the trail ran cold.

"And of course, feel free to reach out. Anytime."

Her calls were returned quickly until new cases demanded their attention. She tried not to blame them. She'd been the one who'd failed to protect Adam, not them. They'd only failed to find his body.

Out of reflex, she'd thanked them—*Always be polite, Olivia*—even as her fingers throbbed from gouging a hole in the leather. After they'd gone, she'd called a local nonprofit to arrange a donation of the couch. She could no longer stand to look at it.

Now Olivia nodded, waiting for whatever it was the deputy had come to tell her and resentful that it always seemed to be that way.

Though the silence lasted only a few seconds, Olivia considered saying, *My husband might be involved in that girl's disappearance.* If she told the deputy about Richard and Ellie before he could pose the question, she and the kids would be safe, at least.

Unless...

She bit the inside of her cheek to keep from saying anything stupid.

The deputy said, "A wildfire is burning near Johnsville."

A wildfire. She released her tension in a shallow hiss. If he noticed the change in her breathing, he gave no sign.

"System flagged your address as a nonresponse. You signed up for the emergency alerts?"

"Cell service is out, but we have a landline." A landline she'd ignored when it rang because she had larger concerns than a wildfire a dozen miles away. "Are we being evacuated?"

"It's voluntary for now, but with the wind, this fire could be a bad one. Be ready to evacuate." On cue, the wind shuddered. "How many people in the house?"

"Four." She lowered her pitch and tried not to smile in relief. "Me, my husband, and our ten-year-old daughter live here, and our adult son is visiting."

"Anyone require special assistance?" At the shake of her head, he said, "Any animals?"

"Just a dog."

He pulled out a neon-pink ribbon. "Stay safe," he said. "And please pay attention to those alerts."

"I will."

The deputy stopped at the edge of her property and tied the pink ribbon around the trunk of a small tree. Then he walked across the road to where the Kims lived.

CHAPTER 27
LEYNA

Saturday, 12:32 p.m.

Seated on the sofa next to Dominic, Leyna studied the three Polaroids laid out in a row on Rocky's coffee table.

She'd seen them before, but only at a glance, clipped to twine strung across Grace's bedroom wall. Until Dominic had handed them to her, she'd remembered only the blank spaces on that wall. She'd spent years trying to fill in those blanks through countless searches of cardboard boxes, dresser drawers, and her own faulty memories. Now here they were, laid out in front of her, the images she'd tried unsuccessfully to conjure. Unremarkable but also everything.

Leyna studied the row of photos, each one feeling like an attack.

The photos were lightly damaged, as if folded and smoothed again, and smudged by fingertips.

The first showed a group shot taken at a neighborhood potluck the fall before Grace disappeared. Leyna was in this one too, standing next to her sister, both of them in sweaters because the weather had already turned crisp.

The second was a close-up of Grace in a pale blue cap-sleeved blouse, the tiny fake sapphire pendant she always wore with it resting in the hollow of her throat, Grace nearly smiling, strawberry-blond hair fanned by an invisible wind. *The blouse makes my eyes pop, don't you think?* she'd said more than once. The necklace was never recovered.

Leyna plucked the third and final Polaroid from the coffee table. It showed Grace on the patio behind the Clarke house, the angle and Grace's outstretched arm suggesting she'd taken the photo herself. Smiling again, back when Grace smiling had been a thing. Two others were in the photo: Rocky, stone-faced and in profile, his attention wholly on Grace at the other edge of the frame, and, wedged between the two of them, a third person with a guarded expression.

Her mother.

The air in the living room was stale and too warm. Meredith Clarke had claimed not to know Rocky well, yet here she was standing next to him and her missing daughter.

These were three of the Polaroids that Grace had taken down before she disappeared, Leyna was certain. So what were they doing tucked inside an envelope in Rocky Hamlin's bedroom? And where was the one still missing?

Something else about the photos bothered her in a way she couldn't yet identify. Something other than how Rocky looked at Grace.

The photo of the Duran brothers and Clarke sisters that Ellie had shown around town wasn't among the Polaroids. There was no proof the girl had ever been there.

Suddenly aware they were in the house uninvited, Leyna picked up the photos and slipped them in her pocket. Dominic moved closer to her on the couch, the heat of his thigh burning into her own. Reading her body language, he said, "We should go."

"He'll notice the photos are gone."

"He'll notice the broken window first."

Despite the risk, neither of them moved. "How do you think he got these?" she asked.

"Either she gave them to him or he took them."

"Looks like it's time to talk to Mom." After several minutes of preoccupied silence, she said, "Judging by the photos, they were friendly."

"Were they?" He sounded doubtful. At his tone, she could guess he was remembering the photo of Rocky staring at Grace, Meredith between them.

"That one creeps me out too," she said. She wondered what he was thinking. Was he disappointed that there were no clues about what happened to his brother or to Ellie Byrd? For a moment, she'd let herself forget that he grieved his own loss.

"She looked happy enough," he said. In the pause that followed, she felt the qualifier coming. A second later, it did. "But if they'd been close, wouldn't you have known that?"

Leyna sorted through her memories as she had earlier, but she still found none that included Rocky.

"They were close enough for Grace to have taken this photo and hung it on her wall," she said, trying on the argument even as it struck her as false. She'd felt the hint of connection when she found his battered copy of Christie's *The Murder of Roger Ackroyd*. And yet, after finding the photos of Grace, doubt reemerged, more insistent now.

If they were friendly, what kind of man befriended a teenage girl?

"I need to talk to Thea too."

Beside her, she felt Dominic stiffen.

"Why would you need to talk with my sister?"

"Because when I asked her about him earlier, she was evasive. She was hiding something."

"Of course she has secrets. She's ten. And she was born six years after Adam and Grace went missing. What could she possibly know?"

"Probably nothing." Leyna patted the pocket that held the photos. "But shouldn't we at least ask again now that we have these?"

Dominic closed his eyes, rubbing his face with enough vigor that she worried he'd do damage to his skin. When he opened his eyes, he exhaled.

"I'll talk to Thea," he said. "You talk to your mom. More efficient that way anyway."

"How about you talk to my mom, and I talk to Thea?"

He laughed, and her heart thudded at his smile.

"That's a hard pass," he said.

"I've shown you mine, now it's your turn."

"I like the sound of that."

She felt herself flush. "I meant that now I've told you everything about that night. So what do you remember? Anything you haven't told me?"

"That's decidedly less fun."

"Come on, Dom."

His eyebrows knit; the premature grooves in his forehead deepened. "You know I wasn't here."

She felt confusion slip onto her own face. "You weren't?"

"I had a midterm the next morning and left after lunch."

"I could've sworn you were home for at least part of that evening."

He shook his head, and his expression grew wistful. "I wish I were, but I was back in my dorm room by five. I didn't get the call from my mom until the next morning."

"You're sure?"

The grooves cut deeper still. "Of course I'm sure." Tone suddenly defensive. Too defensive? "You think I'd be able to forget the night my brother disappeared?"

Of course he wouldn't. It had been a foolish question.

"Are you ever going to let go of your obsession with Adam?" Dominic sounded as weary as he had when it had ended with them.

Even after Leyna's very public argument with his parents, her relationship with Dominic had limped along for a couple of weeks. Dying, even if they were unaware of how mortally it had been wounded.

In their last conversation as a couple, Leyna had shared the story of how she'd gotten the scar. He'd traced the patch of skin gently, as if it were a fresh injury. He'd touched his forehead to hers, and though it wasn't his apology to make, he told her how sorry he was.

Each of his attempts at comfort only made her angrier.

"You've got to know I'm right about him."

She figured if Dominic could see Adam as she did, he would join her side of the fight.

But by then Dominic had grown weary of fighting. “Can we talk about something else, just for today?”

“What else do we have to talk about? They’re all we have.”

She saw in his expression that her words had found their mark. Still, he didn’t leave. After sharing her story about the scar, Leyna suspected he lingered to make sure she was okay. Even years later, she remembered the force of his exhalation as much as his words.

“Sometimes, I think you’d rather be right than happy.”

That concern for her happiness again. If only he’d left then, twenty seconds earlier. But of course he hadn’t. Dominic always stayed.

“I could never be happy with you.” Each word a dagger. “You’re his brother.”

Dominic’s jaw had tensed, but all he managed was a quick “I’m sorry you feel that way.”

Then Dominic, the man who always stayed, left without looking back.

Now, he waited for her answer.

“I’m trying to let it go,” she said, even though she knew she wasn’t. That she couldn’t until she knew what had happened to Grace.

For the first time since Leyna had returned to Ridgepoint, the silence that settled between her and Dominic lacked comfort, their shared history rising between them like a concrete wall.

CHAPTER 28

MEREDITH

Saturday, 12:36 p.m.

Like Meredith's social media account, which she rarely checked, adamduranlives was set to private. After approving a follow request, Meredith had to wait a torturous twenty minutes for her blackmailer to do the same.

While she'd waited, she'd scanned the profile. The photo, a man in sunglasses, was too small to see clearly. Meredith took a screenshot of the profile photo and ran a reverse image search. It brought up multiple versions, all on retail sites advertising sunglasses. As she'd suspected, a stock photo.

The account had been started three months earlier, and there were five posts. Once approved, she became the account's only follower, but adamduranlives was following three accounts.

Three?

She clicked for details. The second account was the Plumas County Sheriff's Office.

Adamduranlives had never engaged with the sheriff's office account, and if anyone there had requested to follow back, it hadn't been approved.

But the threat was clear. Meredith was one tag or follow-back away from being exposed.

The third account was Ellie Byrd's.

Another taunt. Meredith felt an unreasonable impulse to give the screen the middle finger. Instead, she clicked on the most recent post, a video that showed a time stamp of only a few minutes before.

The video was short, less than thirty seconds. It opened on a close-up of a small bunch of blue wildflowers, paired with twigs and sprigs of icy-green leaves. It zoomed out slowly, capturing the ground around it, until it reached the edge of a patio.

Her patio.

Then it faded to an inspirational quote.

Live every day as if it's your last.

The flowers had been arranged on the barren ground where, earlier in the year, she'd harvested her Red Russian kale. At the edge of the frame, two small weeds sprouted. The lighting suggested the video had been shot in early morning, but she'd picked those weeds a few days earlier. With that timing, it could've been anyone filming.

She quickly read the caption on the video.

There's a fire in Plumas County. Hope all my friends up there are safe. #thoughtsandprayers.

Heart thudding, she scrolled through the rest of the posts.

Five days ago, a photo of the arrow Leyna had found in the tree. So the message *had* been meant for Meredith. The caption contained only hashtags: #bullseye, #waiting, #watching, #whereareyou, and, in all caps, #ITSYOURFAULT.

A month before, clip art of stacks of cash next to a bottle of champagne.

Not to brag but . . . about to come into a quarter mil. Time to quit my crappy job? #livingthegoodlife #lifegoals.

Six weeks before, a photo of van Gogh's *Girl in White in the Woods.*

Isn't it cool how you feel like you're actually in the painting with the woman? This one brings back memories. #likeiwasthere.

That left the last photo, the first posted, from the same day the account was opened, and when she saw it, she stopped breathing. She stared into the faces of her daughters and the Duran boys. Meredith was sure this photo had once hung on Grace's bedroom wall, but there had been so many photos of the four of them taken back then, she couldn't be certain.

Family is everything, isn't it? #whathappenedtograce #stillmissing.

Forcing herself to breathe again, Meredith realized she'd gotten an alert that adamduranlives had sent her a private message. She opened it.

> Glad you finally got the message. I was starting to worry you didn't want to be friends.
>
> Today. Wouldn't want any evidence to burn before I get my money.
>
> $250,000

Below that, an email address had been included for the online transfer. Meredith was sure it was a disposable email and that the banking information attached to the account would be untraceable. But did that even matter? While blackmail was a crime, there were worse ones. If there weren't, Meredith wouldn't have been targeted for blackmail.

She stared at the screen, considering her next step. The truth was, Meredith could scrape together a quarter of a million, but just. It would clean her out. She'd need to sell the house, and she couldn't do that. She could never do that.

A moment later, the account's story was updated with a countdown. White letters on a black background. Repeated six times across the top was the same emoji—the face with the green tongue and dollar signs for eyes.

In caps above the countdown, adamduranlives had typed: TELL THE TRUTH.

According to the countdown, Meredith had zero days, two hours, and fifty-nine minutes to comply.

CHAPTER 29

LEYNA

Saturday, 12:50 p.m.

Though the candles had been snuffed hours before, the scent of spiced vanilla hit Leyna as soon as she entered the house. She intended to confront her mom with the Polaroids, but she wasn't in the house. Maybe she was in the backyard? Leyna looked out the window and saw her at the edge of their property line. Before heading out, Leyna stole a quick glance at her laptop. What she saw stopped her in her tracks.

She'd gotten a message from Ellie's friend Amaya—Call me, with a phone number.

Leyna immediately located the cordless handset and punched in the number. Amaya picked up on the first ring. "You found Ellie's bracelet?" She sounded guarded, as if she'd responded to many messages like Leyna's that had turned out to be nothing.

"In an Airbnb in our neighborhood."

"And where's that?"

"Plumas County."

"Describe it."

"Open gold cuff with a hinge. A pair of red roses." Amaya's silence confirmed what Leyna already knew—the bracelet was Ellie's. "Do you know if she was wearing it Thursday?"

"She wears it every day." Leyna noted the use of the present tense, even though Leyna had the bracelet and Ellie was gone. "It was a gift from her parents."

"What about a boyfriend—does she date?"

"Casually, sure. But Ellie plans to go to college in a year if things work out. She's not looking to start anything serious."

"Maybe she didn't tell you."

"She tells me everything."

Leyna felt Amaya slipping away, so she tried a more neutral tone. "Any chance she just met someone? Someone she felt she had to keep a secret, even from you?" she asked.

She heard the hiss of breath that suggested Amaya had relaxed. "Ellie's been into theater ever since she was cast in the role of Molly in our middle-school production of *Annie*. She should've gotten the lead, she was that good." She paused, and Leyna could feel her weighing her allegiance to Ellie against the possibility that Leyna might be able to help find her. "Ellie's always been good at reading people. At knowing what it takes to get them to open up."

"Why would she lie to me?"

"Why wouldn't she? She doesn't know you."

"She had a photo of me, my sister, and a couple of childhood friends," Leyna said. "She was showing it around. Asking questions."

Amaya went quiet. Finding her words or constructing a lie?

"Did she know a guy named Adam Duran?" Leyna asked.

The silence stretched, and Leyna gave Amaya time to think before she nudged. "She seemed spooked when I mentioned him, and she'd been asking around about him too."

"We didn't talk about anyone named Adam." Even though Leyna was just hearing it on the phone, it sounded like a lie. "She might've known him from social media or whatever, but he wasn't someone who was important to her."

"Then why did she come to Plumas County?"

Amaya sighed. "Because at the restaurant, you told her that's where you're from."

This time, it was Leyna who fell silent. Finally, she said, "But like you pointed out, I don't know her." She felt the sudden sting of intuition. "Was our meeting at the restaurant random?"

Amaya laughed. "Nothing Ellie does is random. She's had a five-year plan since she was twelve."

"So she tracked me down because—"

"She came across you on some forum or something. She's into true crime."

So that's what it was after all—a murderino or podcaster interested in dredging up an old missing-persons case. But why? There was no body. No real clues. Most people still believed the teens had run away.

But maybe that was the point. With the case so cold that the file might as well have been stored in a freezer, there would be less competition for a young podcaster or journalist looking to break the story.

Young love turned deadly?

By adding the question mark, Ellie could make the angle whatever she wanted.

Did Adam kill Grace?

Did Grace kill Adam?

Did the teens join a cult, go on a murder spree, buy a bookstore in Poughkeepsie?

"Was this for a podcast?"

When Amaya went quiet again, Leyna said, "The video you posted, this call... you must care about Ellie."

"Of course I care about her," she said, halfway between indignant and bone-weary. "She's my closest friend."

"Then why aren't you being straight with me?"

Amaya sighed. "I don't know as much as you think. If I did, I'd know where to find her."

"You must know why she was up here. You loaned her your car for the day." When she was met with more silence, she went on the attack. "Unless that video was just a way for you to get views."

"Fuck you."

"Then tell me why she was up here showing that photo."

Leyna could feel Amaya distancing herself from the conversation. Leyna wished she were with Amaya so she could read her expressions. When did she look away? When did she smile? When did her face twist in an obvious lie? It would've been harder for Amaya to disguise the weak parts of her story if they'd been sitting across from each other.

"I'm not sure," Amaya said. "It was spur of the moment. She was going to tell me everything when she got back but..."

"Okay, then, so why'd she dye her hair that shade of strawberry blond?"

"For a part, I think." She paused. "I almost didn't tell my parents. When she wasn't home by ten, I thought it was just Ellie being dramatic. Making us worry."

"Is Ellie close to her parents?"

"She'd been fighting with them a lot lately, but they're cool."

"What were they fighting about?"

Amaya paused, as if choosing her words. "That's another reason I almost didn't tell my parents she was late," she said. "I knew her mom would go batshit and lock her in her room for life."

Leyna wasn't sure whether to take Amaya's comment as hyperbole or a warning sign. "How's the Byrds' marriage?" she asked.

Amaya made a confused sound. "Uh—why?"

"Just curious."

"It's okay, I guess. I mean, they're parents. It's not like I've ever asked them about it. 'Hey, Mr. and Mrs. Byrd—still keeping the fire alive?' Not my business, and... gross."

"Is Ellie adopted?"

"Why would you ask that?" Her surprise sounded genuine.

"Was she?"

"No." Confused again.

"She doesn't look like her parents."

"Do you look like your parents?"

Leyna looked like her father, or so her mom used to tell her every time they argued. "Unfortunately."

"Well, not everyone does."

"You're sure?"

When Amaya answered, she was adamant. "Being adopted isn't something she would hide from me. It's not like it's a big deal. Plus you know how moms are, especially Sarah—talking about how long labor lasted and how she'd had an emergency C-section. She even showed me the scar. I think it's our moms' way of making us remember how much we owe them."

Though Amaya aimed for nonchalance, Leyna heard the affection there.

"What did you mean when you said Ellie plans to go to college if things work out?"

"Her family's broke, and NYU isn't cheap."

Money. The most violent crimes often came down to that, didn't they? Leyna considered greed as a possible motive, but it didn't feel right. "What do you think happened to Ellie?"

Amaya had probably spent every moment since Thursday night considering that question because she didn't hesitate.

"The car was dumped, obviously," she said confidently. "Did you hear about the bumper?"

"News stories said it was dented."

"They're pretty sure the car was dumped somewhere with the keys in it and then someone took it for a joyride," Amaya said. "The police found blue paint on a tree not far from where my car was found. Which is what I thought all along. Ellie wouldn't have stopped to use a port-a-potty, especially after dark."

Amaya stopped short of voicing what that meant: Ellie was taken.

Though she'd run out of questions, Leyna was hesitant to break the connection. Amaya seemed hesitant to hang up too, and as they settled into the awkward pause before goodbye, Leyna again looked out the window at her mom.

What is she doing out there in this heat?

Amaya broke the silence by taking a breath. Leyna expected a quick *Goodbye.* Maybe a *Text me if you hear anything.* Instead, Ellie's friend said, "I know you're looking for a connection, because she has that photo and she's been asking about this guy you knew. Adam. But I've got to ask—did you give her Adam's name?"

In the yard, her mom stopped what she was doing and trekked back to the house. She held something in her hands. Had she been weeding?

"Leyna?"

"Sorry. Yes, I mentioned him. Why?"

"I told you Ellie was into theater, right?" At Leyna's mumble of acknowledgment, Amaya said, "Some might describe her as a method actress. Like, she really gets into it. Especially with the tragic stories."

Like Grace's.

Amaya continued, "I wasn't lying when I said she dyed her hair for a part. For her senior project, she's writing and acting in a play."

"About what?"

"She wouldn't say." She must've sensed Leyna's disbelief, because she quickly added, "She tells me everything, like I said, but with her art, it's different. With that, she's all about the big reveal. As far as I know, the police haven't even found any of her notes on her laptop." She paused, and Leyna could feel her thinking. Amaya sucked in a breath, then said, "But if I had to guess? It probably has to do with you and this Adam Duran. I know she was interested in you before she made that trip to Reno. It wouldn't surprise me if she went to that restaurant to get a reaction. Original material for her play."

"And the photo?" Leyna waited for her to confirm that the photo Ellie had been flashing around town was the fourth Polaroid missing from Grace's wall, that it belonged with the other three that Dominic had found at Rocky's place.

Leyna heard the back door click shut as her mom entered the house.

"Ellie got that photo online, I think. Social media, maybe?" Amaya said. "Ellie digs deep when she's researching a role."

Leyna couldn't help but notice the two qualifiers—*I think* and *maybe.* So Amaya didn't know or she wasn't saying. Either way, yet one more dead end.

CHAPTER 30
OLIVIA

Saturday, 1:00 p.m.

With Richard helping Thea pack—*just in case*—Olivia retreated to the master bedroom to do the same. The air there was ten degrees colder than anywhere else in the house. Richard couldn't sleep if it was warmer than sixty-four degrees. Even then, he splayed out across his special-ordered cooling sheets, feet and arms untucked.

She closed the door, fighting an urge to lock it—if he met with resistance when he turned the knob, it would give her away as surely as the deleted files had.

She moved quickly to her husband's nightstand. That was where he stored his laptop. When he was deep in a project for work, he would relocate to the office, with its ergonomic chair and standing desk, but for casual use, he sat on the bed, propped against pillows, the laptop resting where its name suggested.

After their earlier conversation, she thought the drawer might be empty, but she found the laptop waiting for her. Probably a test. Didn't matter. This might be the last time she'd get the chance.

Olivia pulled out the laptop and logged on. It was password-protected, but he'd given her the password long ago. The one to his phone too.

I have no secrets from you, he'd told her.

Olivia suspected he'd installed spyware on the laptop and that he kept a second phone.

Their security system included a control panel in the entryway, sensors on all the doors and windows, and cameras and security lights mounted outside.

The video could be accessed on their phones too. For her, it had been about security, but Richard had always been more concerned about the cameras inside the house.

Her husband liked to watch. He always had, and Olivia had used that when he'd balked at the expense of the new night-vision cameras or questioned why they needed the facial-recognition software. She wished she'd pushed for audio.

The daily video files were viewed and purged regularly. She didn't know how often, though she suspected he did it every day, especially since he'd already noticed Thursday's files were missing.

Not all the files were deleted. Some he kept in a folder for repeated viewing. Olivia clicked on that folder first even though she dreaded what she'd find.

There were dozens of videos of Olivia getting undressed, and Richard and Olivia having sex. Watching them, she understood why Richard preferred that she be on top. She got better lighting that way.

There were also dozens of videos of Olivia showering. Even without the date stamp, she could tell which were from the earlier days, before she'd perfected her performance. In these early recordings, she slouched when she shaved her legs. She was rougher with her skin and hair, picking at blemishes and squatting to inspect ingrown toenails. Occasionally, she masturbated.

Later, her pageant training had kicked in, and she'd grown more focused on the arch of her back and her angles. If there'd been awards given for Best Shower Performance, Olivia would've swept the category.

She didn't mind Richard watching, especially if it kept him distracted or kept him coming home. The only videos he'd ever saved had been of her, but now she worried that she hadn't checked the footage often enough. That worry made her lean into the screen until she'd watched every video. By the time she'd finished, she'd grown sick of seeing her own naked body.

There were no videos of Ellie. No videos that featured anyone other than Olivia. If he'd made any, he'd stored them elsewhere or deleted them.

She switched from the folder marked KEEP to the more recent videos. There were no videos featuring Ellie here either, though there was another one of her showering. She stabbed the Delete key, then glanced at the door. She'd already taken too much time, but she had only a few more hours of video to get through. She had to be sure.

When she was done, Olivia returned to the KEEP folder and emptied it. She closed the laptop—and immediately froze at the soft click of the door opening. She looked up to find Richard watching her from the doorway. He smiled, eyes bright, and she couldn't tell if he was angry or aroused.

"I knew you'd been on my computer," he said softly. He held out his hand, indicating he wanted the laptop. "You didn't need to lie, Liv."

CHAPTER 31
LEYNA

Saturday, 1:04 p.m.

Whatever Leyna's mom had been doing in her garden, it had been dirty work. Her bare arms bore the smudges of her labor. In her hand, she held a small bunch of dried blue flowers and sprigs of leaves. She tossed it in the kitchen garbage.

Upon seeing Leyna, she grimaced. "You're back," her mom said with as much enthusiasm as she'd earlier shown the bag of Goose's crap. "I thought perhaps you'd taken my advice and headed home."

Leyna pointed to the trash can. "An odd time to be gardening."

Her mom crossed to the sink and washed her arms until they were clean if slightly red from her scrubbing.

"Not really," she said. "We got an alert that the wildfire near Johnsville is spreading. I figured it couldn't hurt to prune some of the dead vegetation."

Leyna raised an eyebrow. Trimming a few wildflowers and leaves would do little against a wildfire that close to the house, but she had other arguments to start.

Behind her mom, the canvas was propped on an easel, facing away so she couldn't see what was on it. She was considering asking about it when she felt suddenly dizzy; she quickly sat on one of the stools at the island.

She looked up to see her mom hovering, wearing an expression she hadn't expected. If she hadn't known her mom better, Leyna would've labeled it *concern*.

"You need to eat something."

That was the last thing she needed, yet when her mom pushed the yogurt and spoon in her direction, Leyna ate it all in a few bites. She finished with a couple sips of water from a glass that had appeared as quickly as the yogurt.

Her mom pulled up a stool across the island from her and studied Leyna with a sharpness that made her feel exposed. As if Leyna were the one with the secrets.

I guess that's fair.

Leyna's hands shook as she took the three Polaroids from her pocket. She fanned them out as if asking her mom to pick a card for a magic trick.

Was your card a queen of spades?

Her mom took them from her hands and set them one at a time on the counter. Leyna was surprised to see her mom's hands trembled too.

"Are these from Grace's wall?"

"They're from Rocky's house."

"Why were you in Rocky's house?"

Leyna ignored the question. She pointed at the Polaroid that featured her mom, Rocky, and Grace. "I thought you weren't close."

The last of the concern in her mom's expression evaporated, replaced by a more familiar irritation. "Really, Leyna. How many people live on this street? A dozen? There are photos of all of us together at one time or another, especially before it happened."

Leyna didn't ask for clarification. She knew what *it* meant.

The photo of the three of them seemed to have been taken the year before Grace went missing. If Rocky had been a visitor to their home during that time, shouldn't Leyna have some memory of that?

"I don't remember him visiting the house," she said.

Her mom's gaze challenged. When Leyna was younger, the hard edge of that stare would've made her look away. Even now, her eyes watered with the effort of holding eye contact.

"You were close enough to have him at our home," she said, "and for Grace to keep his photo on her wall."

Until she'd taken it down.

Why had she taken it down?

"If you found these photos at Rocky's, how do you know they're your sister's?" Her mother tried for a casual tone but there was a slight softening in her expression when she said Rocky's name. "Grace wasn't the only person who had an instant camera. The Duran boys owned one too." Her mom's face hardened again, if it had ever gone soft in the first place. "Those damn Durans."

That was one of her mother's signature moves—deflect and confuse—but Leyna wouldn't allow herself to be distracted. She was sure the photos had once hung on Grace's wall among the others, but she shook her head. Her way of saying, *I'm not letting you off the hook this time, Mom.* "Doesn't matter if they're Grace's. They're *of* Grace."

"They're just a few old photos, Leyna. Not a smoking gun."

The photos faced her mom on the island, upside down to her but every detail still clear. The first time Leyna had touched the Polaroid of Grace alone back at Rocky's place, Grace had seemed so happy, so alive, in the picture that an imagined spark made her palms tingle. "Where was I when that one of you three was taken?"

Meredith shrugged, her shoulders too stiff to pull off the gesture. "Wherever you always were. Reading. Climbing a tree." Her tone dismissive. "What does it matter where you were?"

"If these photos aren't significant, why were they in an envelope taped to the underside of a drawer?"

"You went through the man's things?" She shook her head in exaggerated disappointment. "You never said—why did you break into his house in the first place?"

"Who says we broke in?"

Her mom's eyes flashed. "We?"

"Dominic's the one who found the photos."

The admission was a challenge, and as Leyna had expected, the corners of her mom's mouth twitched. "I bet he did."

The suggestion buried in her tone brought Leyna to her feet too quickly, and she had to hold on to the island to steady herself. She sat down again. "What's that supposed to mean?"

"That family has always known more about what happened that night than they've said. I wouldn't be surprised if Dominic was involved in some way. Did you actually see him find the photos?"

The urge to defend Dominic rose swiftly, fueled by her own earlier doubts, which she still stubbornly shoved aside. "Dominic wasn't even here that night."

"Hmm." A lot of doubt was packed into that simple interjection, and Leyna realized her mom had done it again—made the conversation about something else.

She tried to steer it back on topic. "How did these three photos go from Grace's wall to an envelope in Rocky's cottage?" Leyna asked. "And where's the fourth one?"

In the silence that followed, Leyna fought an urge to climb the stairs to Grace's room. That was part of why she was here, wasn't it? To get the other photos and take them back to her apartment? If she saw them again, maybe she'd be able to name the doubt that wriggled just out of reach.

"I have no idea."

"Well, what *do* you know about Rocky?"

Her mom huffed. "Really, Leyna, this is starting to feel like an interrogation."

From the countertop, Leyna plucked the close-up photo of Grace—in her pale blue shirt and fake sapphire pendant—and held it inches from her mom's face. She let the image of a smiling Grace be her only response.

After several moments of silence, her mom tilted her chin, signaling she would answer, if reluctantly. "He commissioned a painting."

Leyna couldn't help the knitting of her brow. "A forgery?" Rocky didn't seem the type. Then again, she didn't really know him, did she? That was kind of the point.

Her mom nearly smiled at that. "God, no. A landscape to hang in the clubhouse when it was finished. I knew the project was dead, but that poor man didn't, so I figured what the hell—do the guy a favor."

Leyna swallowed a burst of sarcastic laughter. That was her mom. Always quick with the acts of kindness.

"What was the painting he wanted?"

She waved her hand dismissively. "What always hangs on the wall in places like that?" she said. "A landscape of the local scenery. The foothills at sunset. Trite, I know, but he seemed to appreciate it."

And no doubt he paid you well for it.

Her mom pushed away from the island and stood. A clear signal: *We're done with this conversation.*

"Other than that and seeing him around here, I barely know the man," her mom said.

Leyna stayed seated and crossed her arms. "And what about Grace? Why would he have these photos of her?"

Meredith's face clouded, and Leyna suspected whatever came next would be a lie.

"I'm not sure about that." To Leyna's surprise, it sounded like the truth. "Grace was good at keeping secrets, especially toward the end."

Wonder where she got that from.

"Grace wasn't the saint you think she was," her mother said at last.

CHAPTER 32

OLIVIA

Saturday, 1:10 p.m.

As they went about securing the house and gathering the items they would take with them, it was Olivia who became the watcher: Was Richard holding tension in his temples as he did when he was angry? Was he speaking in a monotone, suggesting indifference toward her? When he helped pack their things, did he take less care with hers? But he gave nothing away.

Olivia wondered if she hid her emotions as well as he did.

Though the evacuation was still classified as voluntary for their area, the Kims had gone half an hour earlier. In the short time the Durans had spent packing, the Silvestris had left too, and Rocky, after helping Richard secure the house, headed back to his place to grab his things with a promise to return so they could follow him out. Rocky knew the area better than any of them. If the smoke grew too thick to see, he would be able to lead them to safety. Of that, at least, Olivia was certain.

Only two families remained in the neighborhood: the Durans and the Clarkes.

In the kitchen, Richard grabbed his keys from the dish and stashed his laptop in his overnight bag.

"I think we're good to go with the house," he said. She knew why he was worried—once the evacuation was mandatory, the authorities were responsible for protecting the neighborhood from looters. Until then, the responsibility was theirs.

"You ready?" he asked. When she nodded, he squeezed her shoulder. "I've got a few last things to grab, and then I'll get Thea. We'll be on the highway in five minutes."

She nodded again, pulling away from him. After fighting him all day on leaving, five minutes seemed suddenly too long to stay in that house. She took her bag and waited on the porch with Goose next to the open front door.

A moment later, Dominic joined her.

Olivia could always tell when her elder son was troubled by the deepening grooves in his forehead and the way his eyes seemed to shutter. When he thrust his hands in his pockets, his body curled in on itself as if in protection.

"Where's Leyna?" she asked, and she saw from his expression that something had gone wrong there. She tried not to take joy in that.

He ignored the question. "Is everything okay with you and Dad?"

She winced. "Why would you ask that?"

"So—no."

Apparently, he could read her as easily as she read him. "Dominic—"

"It's fine, Mom. Everyone is entitled to their secrets."

"Oh, really? You have secrets?"

"A few." Dominic pulled his hands from his pockets and straightened his shoulders. He was nearly as tall as Rocky, though with his frequent slouch and leaner build, Olivia sometimes forgot that. She had the sudden urge to hug him as she had when he'd been younger, back when the top of his head grazed her nose. How old had he been then? Nine? No older than ten. Even though that was decades in the past, Olivia could still feel the weight of him as he'd jumped into her arms, no embarrassment in it, the force nearly knocking her off her feet.

Now, there was a reserve in him. He squinted into the distance. "Do you remember when Adam was five and he decided to build a campfire in the backyard?"

She nodded. "He lit a paper towel on fire on the stove, but it burned too quickly. He dropped it on the rug by the door in the kitchen."

"It's my fault that rug was ruined."

That couldn't be true. Even as a child, Dominic hadn't lied—at least, not well. His inability to maintain eye contact when he wasn't telling the truth always betrayed him.

"I found Adam foraging through the kitchen drawers looking for matches." He looked at her again, his lips curling in a half smile. "He'd already assembled all the ingredients for s'mores. Marshmallows. Chocolate. Only instead of graham crackers, he'd gotten out a box of those flat multigrain crackers, the baked kind with the flaxseeds." The smile widened. "We spent ten minutes looking for a lighter or a pack of matches, and Adam got that look on his face. Like he was about to cry. He wanted that campfire so badly. So I grabbed a paper towel and turned on the burner."

She laughed. "Not your best idea."

"Unfortunately, not my worst either."

"So you're the one who dropped the paper towel?"

He shook his head. "It was Adam. But the idea was mine, and when he insisted on carrying it, I should've told him no." The smile faded. "But he insisted—he wanted to be the torchbearer."

"The torch . . . oh. That was during the Summer Olympics." Adam had been obsessed with the opening ceremonies, and the archery, of course. Tennis, too, for some reason, though he'd never shown an interest in the sport.

"When the paper towel got close to his fingers, he let out this little yelp and dropped it," Dominic said. "Right on that ugly rug."

"It was attractive enough until someone dropped a burning paper towel on it."

He lifted an eyebrow. "It looked like it had been woven from barfed unicorn fur," he said.

A pastel shag, the rug had been a chore to keep clean. In hindsight, she realized Dominic wasn't wrong. It really had been an ugly rug.

His gaze drifted again, deeper into his memory. "I should've kept him safe."

"You were seven," she said. "But, again, it was a really stupid idea."

Goose wheezed at the thickening smoke, and Olivia cast a worried glance toward the door. She would give Richard another minute. No more.

Dominic exhaled so sharply, at first she mistook the sound for the wind. When he looked at her, his eyes had grown troubled again.

"Adam liked to shoot birds out of trees with his bow and arrow."

"I remember. He brought home a pheasant and insisted I cook it for dinner." She'd had no idea how to prepare a wild bird, so she'd thrown it away and cubed and heavily seasoned some chicken. "He said he didn't want it to have died for no reason."

"A year before he disappeared, he spent half the spring out in the woods." Dominic hesitated as if reluctant to finish his story. Inside, Olivia heard Richard calling for their daughter.

She'd taken a reflexive step toward the door when Dominic said, "I caught him shooting at a nest in the woods. When it fell from the tree, he picked up one of the baby birds and held it in his palm. Watched until it stopped breathing."

Adam was likely saddened that the bird had gotten hurt or angry at himself that his aim had been off. He'd no doubt been shooting for a larger bird, though if Richard had caught him, Adam would have been grounded, his bow taken. He wasn't practiced enough to take such reckless shots.

"When he noticed me watching, he made this show of burying it," Dominic said. "I asked him about it, and he said it was no big deal. Most birds don't make it to adulthood anyway, he said, what with predators and the weather and parasites."

Olivia shook her head. "It was obviously a mistake. Your brother was gentle and kind."

"He was, sometimes. But people are more than one thing."

She stiffened. "Why are you telling me this?"

"I've been thinking."

"Don't say it."

"I'm not saying Leyna is right," Dominic said. "Adam would never hurt anyone, especially Grace. Not on purpose, anyway."

"He wouldn't hurt anyone *period*."

But even as she said it, she thought of how she'd silently defended him a moment earlier—in her mind, the shooting down of the nest had been a mistake. The ruined rug too.

"What if he did something stupid?" Dominic asked. "Not out of malice but out of curiosity or because he was upset. Adam could be impulsive."

Inside, Richard called again for their daughter. She cut the conversation short by opening the front door and yelling inside that they needed to get going.

"Is your stuff in the car?" she asked Dominic, swiveling back.

"I'll follow you out."

"You're coming with us."

"I'll be right behind you," he said, "after I make sure the Clarkes get out too."

"You mean Leyna."

"I mean the Clarkes."

Olivia tried not to think about what might happen to those left behind. Richard had once made her watch a documentary on Pompeii, and she could still picture the remains, bodies flexed and preserved in ash. It wouldn't be like that for the victims of this wildfire. Most likely, it would be the smoke that got them. As the fire consumed much of the oxygen around them, they would grow disoriented. Lose consciousness. Die.

But such thoughts weren't healthy.

Where was Richard?

As if on cue, her husband called their daughter's name again. And again.

By the fifth time he called, Olivia was in the house too, no longer preoccupied by thoughts of ruined rugs or dead birds or even the wildfire to the north. She was focused wholly on why their daughter wasn't responding.

CHAPTER 33
MEREDITH

Saturday, 1:10 p.m.

That damn adamduranlives countdown and the bouquet left at the edge of her property had gotten to Meredith. What other excuse did she have for telling Leyna that Grace wasn't a saint?

Meredith turned her back to Leyna, eager to hide her mistake. She fought to keep her eyes off the back of the canvas of Grace.

Behind her, Leyna sighed deeply, but Meredith had no intention of turning toward her. For the conversation she knew was coming, it was better if Leyna couldn't read her expression.

"What do you mean, Grace wasn't a saint?"

"I shouldn't have said that about your sister."

"Actually, you should've said more."

Meredith sighed. "Let it go, Leyna."

Her daughter's resolute silence told her that wasn't happening.

Although she'd urged Leyna to drop it, Meredith found herself struggling to do the same. The memories insisted, and Meredith was again in

Grace's bedroom sixteen years earlier. Adam on the floor. Grace angry. Back then, she'd always been angry.

After Meredith struck Adam in the head with the mallet, Grace rubbed the side of her neck where it met her shoulder, the spot occupied seconds earlier by his hands.

She'd slurred, "Why'd you do that?" The words ran together, her confusion amplified by whatever drink she'd imbibed or pill she'd popped.

"He was choking you," Meredith reminded her. Her indignation faded quickly as she realized she'd misread the situation. Adam had been holding Grace down, not throttling her. Still not okay, of course, especially with her daughter visibly impaired. But she couldn't stop herself from wondering about that fight and what might've led to it.

The mallet grew abruptly too heavy, and Meredith dropped it on the rug. Its handle landed against Adam's leg, as if, even though he was unconscious, he was holding it for her.

Meredith's gaze darted to Adam's head. If he was bleeding, she couldn't tell in the shadows of the bedroom floor. The only light, from the lamp with its crooked shade, fell on Grace. The spotlight was always on Grace.

Now Leyna moved to the other side of the counter, locking her eyes on Meredith's, arms crossed as she awaited answers. She seemed to be feeling much better now. Meredith shouldn't have given her that yogurt.

"I only meant that Grace was in a foul mood the night she ran away."

It was more than Meredith had ever offered Leyna, but her daughter appeared dissatisfied. "Why do you assume she left on her own?"

"Like I said, she was in a bad mood that day." She motioned to Leyna's scar. "As you know. She'd been talking about leaving for months, and I always assumed that's why she left."

Meredith declined to mention all that had happened with Adam after she'd thwacked him with the mallet.

Grace's question that night came back to her but in Adam's voice: *Why'd you do that?*

Meredith almost told Leyna what she'd realized when her daughter started suspecting Adam in Grace's death: *If Adam killed her, it might have been in self-defense.*

Meredith was girding herself for whatever question came next when Leyna said, "I don't believe she ran away, though maybe she intended to."

Leyna let her statement settle, a challenge—she was offering her own memories, but they came at a cost. One Meredith couldn't afford to pay, for Leyna's sake. And for Grace's memory.

But perhaps she could give enough that it felt at least a little like the closure her daughter had been seeking for far too long.

"Tell me," Meredith said.

Leyna nodded once, confirmation of their unspoken contract—a secret for a secret.

"I saw Grace leave that night. She'd changed from the blue blouse to a black one. There'd been . . . a fight, and there was blood on her sleeve."

Meredith struggled to keep her expression masked, even as her thoughts churned. Was it possible Leyna knew about Meredith hitting Adam with the mallet? There had been so much blood—head wounds were like that—and some of it had indeed landed on Grace. Meredith hadn't realized Grace had changed her shirt, but of course she had. She must've been a real mess by the end of the night.

But she quickly realized that wasn't the blood Leyna referenced. She'd meant the fight between her daughters that had left Leyna with a wound on her arm. Meredith didn't know all of what had happened—Leyna had always been stubborn with her secrets—but she knew enough to understand the fight had been Grace's fault. It was always Grace's fault.

Leyna stared at her before she finally said, "That's the problem with the anonymous tip about Grace being seen at that campground after she went missing—the caller said she was still wearing her blue shirt. She wasn't."

A cold dread seeped into Meredith's bones. So from the beginning, Leyna had known the tip was fake.

Did she also suspect Meredith had been the one who called it in?

Meredith composed her expression but didn't trust herself to speak.

Leyna's gaze was sharp, her smart green eyes assessing. But she would never see the guilt there. Meredith was a master of deceit.

"I think she might've meant to run away but something happened," Leyna said. "Someone stopped her. And even if she did leave on her own, I don't think—" She paused for a quick breath. "I don't think she would've been in good shape."

Meredith fought a tic at her right eye. *Why can't she ever let things go?* "Why would you think that?"

"She wouldn't have left for good without taking some things with her."

"What would she have taken?" Meredith said dismissively. "Not her phone, because that could be tracked. She didn't have credit cards. So cash, her ID. Or, even better, a fake ID. A photo or two. All of that could fit in her pockets."

Leyna's expression didn't waver. "She would've taken her camera, at least."

Meredith had nothing to say to that, because Leyna was right.

"She was heading into the forest, not toward the road," Leyna said. "She didn't have access to a car, and how far is it to town? She couldn't have gone on foot. She wouldn't have."

Another truth. Grace loved to run, to dance, to move. But in spurts. She bored easily, and a long walk into town or even to the main highway wouldn't have appealed to her.

Leyna continued. "Besides, she was alone. Wasn't your theory that she and Adam left together?"

"It wasn't just my theory. They'd talked about going to Chicago, and remember that woman, Charlotte something, who owned the house before the Millers? She saw them walking toward the road holding hands."

"Charlotte lied," Leyna said. "I know what I saw."

"Perhaps she decided to go it alone. She and Adam were fighting. It could've been because she wanted him to leave with her, and he didn't want to go."

Leyna's eyes became lasers. "Like I said, she would've taken—"

Her expression faltered, and her breaths came quicker. Whatever had occurred to her, she kept it to herself. But a moment later, Meredith got there too. The three Polaroids from Rocky's place. Creased. Smudged.

Voice shaky, Leyna said, "If she'd taken photos with her, she would've had to fold them so they fit in her pockets."

And yet, all these years later, the photos had found their way back into this house.

Leyna looked away. Unfortunate, since that brought her gaze to the hidden canvas at the end of the room. Her thick brows shot together and she canted her head. Meredith sensed her intention before she took a step. She slipped between her daughter and the easel.

"Why're you painting in the kitchen?"

Meredith never painted in the kitchen.

"I'm not," she said. "I just wanted to see it in this light."

"The lighting's too warm in here." Her eyes narrowed suspiciously. "Or so you've always told me."

Not for the first time, Meredith wished her daughter were more obtuse. "For painting, that's true, but it's perfect for viewing this particular work," she said, hoping the authority with which she spoke would kill her daughter's curiosity.

It didn't. "What're you painting?"

"It's for a client." *That should do it,* she thought. Leyna avoided extended conversations about Meredith's work. Her profession wasn't illegal—not exactly—but the grayer areas of life had always made her younger daughter uncomfortable. That was Leyna—driven to do the *right thing,* as if it were ever as clear as that.

"Let me see." There was an unexpected challenge in Leyna's voice.

"It's not finished."

"That's fine."

"Not my best work either."

"I'm sure that isn't true. Let me offer you a second opinion."

Leyna had once said a cow sculpted of butter was the most amazing work of art she'd ever seen. "We should think about evacuating before the roads are blocked," Meredith said.

"Deflect and confuse."

"What?"

"What're you hiding?"

Meredith opened a closet and quickly stowed the painting. She hardened the planes of her face.

"Leave it."

Irritation flashed in her daughter's eyes, but when she spoke, her voice was weary. "Do you think Grace is dead?"

Meredith wanted to reassure her as she had so many times before, but she knew any attempt would ring false. For the past sixteen years, she'd been protecting her elder daughter, but if Leyna was right—if Grace had walked into the forest alone that night—maybe Meredith was wrong about everything else too.

CHAPTER 34

LEYNA

Saturday, 1:18 p.m.

Someone pounded at the door. There was an urgency behind it—or was it anger?—and she pictured the visitor outside wielding a side fist like a hammer. Leyna's first thought was Dominic, her second the fire. She hesitated, anxious about an update on either of those topics.

Her mom yanked open the door, stance wide, as if ready for a fight. On the porch, Rocky met her mother's scowl with an even deeper one before his eyes found Leyna's.

Yeah, definitely anger there.

"You broke my window," he said. Clearly, their visitor wasn't looking for confirmation.

"I did." She offered no apology, plucked a photo from the counter. It was the one of Rocky with Grace and their mom.

He crossed to her, and she waited for him to snatch the photo from her hands. Instead, his arms remained pinned to his sides as he squinted at the Polaroid. "Yeah. So?"

Rocky took a step into her personal space, his body radiating heat, and she was reminded of the foot or so he had on her. In height and width.

"What were you doing in my house?" It wasn't quite a growl, but the threat was clear.

Leyna tilted her chin to better see his face but kept her feet planted. She wouldn't be the one to retreat. She raised the photo to keep it in his line of sight. "Finding this." She gestured toward the counter. "And those."

This set him back a step. Eyes narrowing, he spent several seconds assessing her. Then he went to the counter and stood over the photos. He didn't touch these either. After a moment, he turned back to Leyna. "What are these?"

"Obviously, they're photos. From your cottage."

"I can see they're photos, but they're not mine." He pointed a meaty finger toward the picture she held. "I've never seen any of these."

"They were in an envelope—"

He interrupted. "Envelope?"

"These were in an envelope taped to the bottom of a dresser drawer."

"What're you playing at here?" His face darkened, and she felt abruptly more afraid of him than she had at any time during their walk in the forest. "You're not going to make me the villain in this story like you tried to do with Adam."

Her mom surprised her by coming to her side. "She found these in your cottage. You must've known they were there, considering your place is only slightly larger than my downstairs bath."

Leyna shot her a look. "You've been to his place?"

"Jesus, Leyna, you act like I just admitted we're sleeping together." She rolled her eyes. "I told you I did a commission for him. He invited me in for a beer."

"You drink beer?"

Rocky stepped back from the island, as if disavowing ownership. "Not mine," Rocky said again, more emphatically.

"Your cottage," her mom repeated.

"When's the last time you checked underneath your dresser drawers?"

"Why would I? There's nothing there."

"Five minutes ago, I would've said the same." He turned to Leyna, scowling. "You owe me a window. Hopefully it won't cost more than a hundred and fifty-two dollars."

Leyna gathered the three Polaroids, returned them to her pocket, and threw a sideways glance at Rocky, who seemed to be the only one who wasn't looking for answers about what had happened to Grace.

Maybe because he already knew.

"You got the fourth one?" Leyna asked. "Because it's still missing."

"I didn't even have those."

Leyna closed the small gap he'd created between them. "She wasn't going to meet Adam that night," she said. "She was headed to your place. Did she get there?"

Rocky's silence was answer enough.

"That's how you knew she'd changed her shirt."

Rocky's eyes narrowed in warning. *Drop it.* "Someone probably mentioned it."

"No one else knew." She turned to her mom. "Did you know?"

"No. I didn't."

Leyna locked eyes with Rocky again. "See. Only me and, apparently, you. She wanted a ride, didn't she?" It was a guess—if Grace had run away, she would've needed a lift into town—but Rocky's deepening scowl confirmed she was right.

"Did you give her one?"

This time, he shook his head and directed his response to her mom. "I told her to go home, and if she still needed a ride in the morning, I would give her one."

His expression hardened as it had back in the forest when she'd mentioned her mother. Leyna studied his face for any sign that he'd lied, that there was something he was afraid to say. He didn't look like he was lying or afraid. Still, she suspected he held something back. And the way he stared at her mom made her think her mom knew whatever it was he kept from her. "Why did she want a ride?"

"She didn't say."

There. A twitch at his right eye. A lie. Leyna pushed. "She must've said something."

"I told her to go home," he repeated.

Leyna thought she saw a flash of regret, but he buried it quickly. If he was telling the truth, she understood. For sixteen years, she'd lived with her own guilt after watching Grace walk away.

But again—*if* he was telling the truth.

"A girl comes to you in distress asking for a ride and says nothing about why she needs it." Leyna made her sarcasm as thick as she was able. Which was pretty damn thick. She'd learned from the best of them.

Rocky turned to her mom again, as if she were the one Leyna had addressed and they were both awaiting her response. She felt her mother stiffen beside her, but neither she nor Rocky spoke. In the silence, his breathing grew heavier. Her mom's too.

Rocky looked at Leyna. "We'll settle up on the window later. I'll mail you an invoice."

He started to leave, then paused in the doorway. "I'm sorry for your loss, Leyna, but if you come near my house again, I might have to shoot you."

CHAPTER 35

OLIVIA

Saturday, 1:20 p.m.

With Goose's help, Olivia found Thea under the bed in the room that had once been Adam's, noise-canceling headphones over her ears. Olivia lay down on her side on the floor, and Goose wriggled between them.

"We need to go," Olivia said. "You got your bag?"

Thea, lying on her back, took off the headphones but continued staring at the bottom of the bed.

"We'll find a hotel," Olivia said, "and then we can go out for pizza. You must be hungry."

"We were supposed to have brunch," Thea said. "We were going to have frittatas and invite Leyna over."

Frittatas, yes. Leyna, no. "I'm sorry, sweetheart. Things just got… complicated. Next weekend."

Olivia felt a surge of guilt at disappointing her daughter the same way her parents had disappointed her so many times. She vowed to herself that the following Saturday, she would make Thea a brunch with waffles, pancakes, *and* French toast.

She reached under the bed, but her fingertips fell short of Thea's. "Tonight, though, there will be pizza," she said. "Whatever toppings you want."

Thea stretched out and rested her palm on Goose's back. The dog squirmed against her hand, self-petting. "Where's Dominic?"

"He was looking for you," Olivia said. "We all were."

"I don't want to go. They said we didn't have to yet."

She considered getting Dominic. He'd always been better at reading Thea. When Thea's closest friend had moved away, he'd drawn monkeys in dry-erase marker on a glass pie plate and added water to make them dance. When she'd gotten a C minus on a science project, he'd recited the names of famous scientists who did poorly in school and made her laugh when he added cartoon characters to the list: *No, really, Rick Sanchez and Professor Farnsworth both failed fifth-grade science.*

Dominic listened and responded with whatever it was Thea needed, whether that be a thoughtful word, a silly joke, or silence and cake-batter ice cream.

Olivia tried to channel her son—what did Thea want in that moment?

But of course it was obvious. She wanted to stay, and Olivia couldn't give her that. So she gave her the truth instead.

"It's voluntary for now, but the fire's getting closer, and we don't want to wait too long. You remember what happened the last time. It's not safe to stay."

Thea remained on her back but turned her head toward Olivia. "Can I go with Dominic?"

"Dominic's coming with us." No matter what he'd said, Olivia wasn't leaving without her son in the back seat of the Audi.

Olivia reached out to brush the hair from Thea's forehead, but her daughter retreated farther under the bed.

"What about his car?" Thea asked.

"He can leave it." Olivia felt the last of her patience draining away. She reached to where Thea's hand rested on Goose's back and grabbed it tightly so she couldn't pull away. "We need to go, Thea. Now."

When she felt Thea strain, Olivia released her hold. Her daughter rolled over so she could scratch Goose's rump. His hind legs kicked in appreciation. Watching them jerk, Thea grew agitated. "Can I sit in the back seat with Dominic?"

"Of course." Olivia patted the floor to get the dog's attention. "Come," she said to Goose. She glanced at Thea. "Both of you."

The girl wriggled away and emerged a second later on the other side of the bed. Olivia could tell something was bothering Thea, but she'd explore that later, when they'd made it to the hotel. She wondered if they would have to drive all the way to Reno to find a room. Were any roads closed?

Whatever. They'd figure it out.

In the hall, Olivia slowed as they passed the wall where she had marked the kids' heights, Adam's and Dominic's lines faded, Thea's bolder.

They walked past the bathroom the brothers had shared, then Dominic's bedroom, still arranged as it had been when he'd left for college.

In her head, she rewound the years to a time both of her sons had been alive and happy in this house, and her grip tightened on her daughter's hand.

Then she remembered the woman her husband had screwed in their bedroom, and maybe it wasn't enough to replace the sheets. Maybe it would be best if the whole neighborhood burned to ash.

But not just yet.

From her spot in the hallway, Olivia watched Richard in the living room. Her husband was still unaware that she knew what he'd done, and she worried she wouldn't have time to fix his mistake. For their children, she owed him that, at least.

CHAPTER 36

LEYNA

Saturday, 1:32 p.m.

There was only one thing Leyna cared about bringing with her. She headed upstairs to her sister's bedroom.

As much as Leyna wanted answers about Grace, she suspected she'd missed her chance to know more. As time passed, her own memories grew fuzzier—she was nearly certain Grace had been wearing jeans with her blouse, but she couldn't remember if her hair had been loose or in a ponytail. And how sure was she that Grace's hands had been empty? Earlier, she'd *known* that her sister carried nothing with her, but in her experience, there was nothing more unreliable than unwavering certainty. Outside her sister's door, she closed her eyes and tried to reconstruct Grace as she'd been that night, but a thousand other images competed, and the only thing she could be sure of was that Grace was gone and that Leyna could've prevented it.

She hadn't been able to help Ellie either, but maybe her story would end differently. Amaya said Ellie liked to force reactions from others, that she was fully committed to her craft. Maybe this was what Amaya meant, and

Ellie had immersed herself in the role of Missing Girl and was now on her way back home to scavenge the emotions of her loved ones for her play.

Screwing her eyes more tightly shut, Leyna tried to picture it—Ellie walking through her parents' front door with an awkward apology: *Sorry I made you worry, but it wouldn't have been the same if you'd known.*

Yeah, that felt like bullshit.

Either way, Leyna hoped the girl was safe. The wildfire wouldn't reach Sierraville or Sacramento, but Leyna knew there were other dangers even more deadly and unpredictable.

She left the hall light on and pushed open the door—and inhaled sharply when she saw Grace's face. Three of them, actually, staring back at her from the bedroom wall.

My God, she was beautiful.

She moved slowly closer, stopping a couple of feet from the portraits. She resisted the urge to reach out and touch them, brush the blush of Grace's cheek with her fingertips, afraid the sweat from her hands might stain them or start the process of corrosion.

She must've lingered over her memories longer than she'd realized, because she heard the door close and then her mom coming up behind her.

"You did a great job with these," Leyna said, her voice husky.

"Thank you." Her mother's voice was surprisingly reverent. She pointed to the one where Grace looked youngest and wore her pale blue blouse. "I painted that the year she turned eighteen. Seventeen months after she disappeared."

Carefully, she took down the portrait. Then she went to the closet and selected what Leyna guessed was a second portrait, this one secured in a cardboard box.

She counted the boxes. Twenty-one. She'd assumed her mom painted Grace once a year, but it looked like it was more often than that. She was overcome by the urge to go in the closet and rip open all the boxes to see as many versions of Grace as existed in the world.

Leyna gestured toward the one her mom held. "Can I see?"

"We should be going."

"Please."

Her mom hesitated, then unwrapped the box, taking care to keep the packaging intact. When she was done, she propped it up on the bed, against the wall, beside the portraits of Grace.

It was a portrait of Leyna. Leyna's hair was shorter—just above her shoulders, tucked behind her ears. She always tucked her hair behind her ears when she wore her hair that short. She had on a white collared shirt and wore a gold medallion necklace. She'd once owned that shirt, and she still owned that necklace.

"I might've stopped by the restaurant a few times." Her mom cleared her throat and looked away.

"I never saw you."

"I never went in," her mom said, as if this were the most obvious and natural thing in the world, stalking her daughter. And yet—Leyna felt a moment of unexpected warmth.

Meredith fidgeted. "Do you need a minute?" she asked, as if she needed one herself.

Leyna shook her head. "You're right. We need to leave. I just have to do one thing first."

Leyna snapped a photo of each of the remaining portraits with her phone, then moved on to the Polaroids still hanging on Grace's wall. There were dozens of them, clipped onto twine. She considered taking them down and throwing them all in a shoebox, but it suddenly felt right leaving them there, and what most interested her wouldn't fit in one anyway. There was no way to store that blank space where the fourth missing Polaroid had once been clipped.

She followed her mom to the bedroom door, stealing one last glance over her shoulder at the portraits. On the wall of Grace's bedroom, at least, the sisters had been reunited.

CHAPTER 37
MEREDITH

Saturday, 1:41 p.m.

When she'd entered Grace's bedroom, Meredith had closed the door behind her out of habit. Too many ghosts lived in that room; best to keep them contained. Now Meredith opened the door to semidarkness. Though it was only midday, the room-darkening blinds were drawn to help fight the heat, but Meredith would've bet her Winsor and Newton brush set that she'd switched on the light when she'd come up the stairs.

Leyna moved closer to her, steps tentative, as if she, too, was surprised by the gloom. They remained still as their eyes adjusted. Meredith listened intently for sounds beyond her daughter's breathing.

Leyna glanced at her mom, brows raised, and mouthed: *Is someone here?*

Meredith shook her head, more wish than answer. Even in the dim light, she felt seen in a way that raised goose bumps on her arms.

Leyna's fingers grazed the wall next to the light switch, the one Meredith was now certain had been toggled on before she'd entered Grace's room. An inch to the right, followed by one soft tap, and the hallway would be cast in full LED light. Leyna hesitated before dropping her hand. Was she thinking, like Meredith, that it might be safer to remain in the dark?

Downstairs, a door clicked shut.

Someone leaving? Or someone entering?

Earlier, the severed battery cable had seemed a nuisance, a message not much worse than others delivered before, like the mail thrown in Meredith's garbage or her recycling can "accidentally" upended. A message like the bag of dog crap Meredith had once tossed in the open window of the Durans' Audi.

Now Meredith's heart drummed at that click of the door. She waited for the generator to fall quiet again or for the sound of glass shattering, drawers opening, footsteps ascending the stairs.

The hall was quiet but she couldn't shake the sensation of being watched. Someone had threatened her through Brian. Someone had sabotaged her generator. Someone had left a warning for her in the woods. And now, someone was in her house.

Her house.

She clenched her fists to stop their shaking.

How dare they.

Leyna lifted her foot as if to take a step, then set it down again, likely afraid a creak of the floorboards would give them away. She glanced at her mom, mouthed another word: *Who?*

There was only one way to get that answer.

Meredith thought of the knives in the kitchen, the tools in the garage, and the Taser locked in the box downstairs. All useless to her. At the moment, she would've settled for a turpentine-soaked rag and a match.

Meredith's eyes locked with Leyna's, which were wide and bright. This was the expression her daughter had worn as a child when climbing trees or trailing, unwanted, after her sister.

It was also the expression she'd worn at eighteen when she'd announced loudly to the neighborhood that Adam had killed Grace, and anyone who didn't believe that had their head firmly lodged somewhere dark and unpleasant.

Meredith had forgotten how fearless her daughter could be.

Leyna marched down the stairs, flipping light switches as she went, each spotlight a challenge. She'd spent more than half her life looking for her sister. Why would Meredith expect her to hide now that she'd gotten that close to the truth? Her daughter had never been built for half measures.

In the kitchen, a canvas was on the easel, facing away from them. She'd stowed the half-finished portrait during her argument with Leyna, before they'd headed upstairs. So who had brought it out again and stuck it on that easel for her to find?

Meredith crossed the room to the easel. A sudden chill shot up her spine. When Leyna stepped around her to view the portrait too, she gasped.

"Is it—was it—another portrait of Grace?"

That she had to ask spoke to the violence with which the painting had been defaced. The eyes had been removed, the mouth gouged, the cheeks slashed to ribbons. The palette knife that had been used still jutted from Grace's throat.

Leyna stared at the painting with open revulsion that quickly gave way to anger. "Why?"

Meredith knew it was because of what had happened to Grace and Adam. But the question occurred to her again—who could know about that?

Whoever had done this had likely entered with the intention of sending a message—*I know what you did*. If the person hadn't stumbled across the painting, Meredith might've found the same message written on her refrigerator whiteboard that Leyna had found on the snack-cake wrapper pinned to the sugar pine.

As Meredith stared at the angry slashes that crossed Grace's painted face, the dull anger inside her chest sharpened into something far more dangerous.

Meredith grabbed her designer duffel, two portraits—one of each of her daughters, now hastily wrapped in paper pads—and the locked metal box that contained her Taser. "You can drive." Meredith handed the bag to Leyna and excused herself. A minute later, she came back with a bottle of wine. She tipped it in Leyna's direction.

Two paintings, a bottle of wine, and a Taser. The necessities.

"If I'm going to spend the night in that tiny apartment of yours, I'll need a good cabernet."

The wine would also dull the anger that continued to eat at her, allowing her to focus on finding out the identity of the person fucking with her family—and fuck with them right back.

CHAPTER 38

LEYNA

Saturday, 1:49 p.m.

Outside, the sky was smokier than Leyna had expected. After she loaded the bag and two canvases in the back of her Ford Focus, she propped her phone in the closest cupholder. She wanted to be ready when she caught a signal.

When Meredith approached the passenger seat, she wrinkled her nose. "I should've brought my sheets. I'm guessing yours aren't linen."

"Actually, Mom, I sleep on a burlap sack."

Her mom slid in beside her. "I'm so sick of this crap," Meredith said. "I'm not even going to complain if it snows all damn winter."

A memory floated, no more substantial than a fleck of ash. When Leyna reached for it, it dissolved as easily.

Leyna had always loved Plumas County winters—the earthy scent of petrichor after the first rain, trees and mountains frosted with fresh snow, puffs of breath hanging in the air like tiny clouds. Everything green and white and quiet. But Grace and her mom both hated the cold. All winter,

Grace would complain about the short days and the hideous sweaters and bulky boots she was forced to wear.

Why can't we move to San Diego so I can wear sandals all year?

Grace would stay in her sundresses and blouses well into autumn, until her exposed skin grew too numb and she packed them away in defeat. Winter always won.

Around them, the ash swirled like flakes of snow.

Her mom spoke then—"Forgotten how to drive?"—but Leyna was so absorbed in her memory that the voice seemed to come from a great distance. Heartbeat spiking, she pulled out the Polaroids. She flipped through them, stopped on the one of the potluck. Her eyes burned, but she forced them wider. She couldn't be sure.

She grabbed her phone and quickly scrolled through the photos. She zoomed in on one she'd taken of the collage on Grace's wall.

In her left hand, Leyna held the Polaroids. In her right, the phone. For several seconds, her eyes darted between them. Then, nearly breathless, she turned to her mom.

"I need to talk to Dominic."

Her mother's eyebrows shot up and she folded her arms across her chest. She stared for a beat, then said, "Why the hell would you need to do that?"

The Durans were gathered in the driveway preparing for their own evacuation when Leyna approached. When he noticed her, Dominic walked toward her, which earned him a disapproving look from Olivia. Rocky didn't seem happy to see her again either.

Olivia scowled at her son. "We need to leave," she said.

Dominic gave his mom a quick hug. "I'll meet you in town," he said, and returned his attention to Leyna. "What's going on, Ley?"

Olivia seemed unsure what to do. She stood halfway down the driveway. "I'm not leaving without you."

At her obvious panic, Leyna felt a pang of guilt. She was about to wave off his help—*Never mind. I can do this alone*—when Dominic called over his shoulder, "I'll be right behind you, Mom." When Olivia still didn't move, he added, "Get Thea out of here."

That did it. Olivia lifted Goose into the back seat next to Thea.

Once Dominic and Leyna had moved out of earshot of his parents, she held up the Polaroid taken at the neighborhood potluck. He squinted at the photo; the groove between his eyebrows deepened.

"Do you remember what month this was?" she asked.

"Late September, early October."

"You're sure?"

He nodded. "It was my first trip home after I started college."

On her phone, Leyna zoomed in on a second photo of the potluck, this one part of the collage that still hung on Grace's wall. Enlarged to that scale, the image blurred slightly, but it was clear enough that her pulse quickened as it had minutes earlier when she'd made the connection.

Leyna stabbed the screen. "I've been focused on the photos we found in Rocky's cottage when I should've paid more attention to the ones still on her wall."

Dominic leaned closer, staring over her shoulder. Her heartbeat grew more erratic. She blamed the thickening smoke.

In the printed Polaroid, Grace was standing, partially obscured by Leyna on one side, Adam on the other. Grace had always known how to find her best angle. But in the second photo of the potluck, Grace sat in a folding chair, hands folded on her stomach.

Did Leyna imagine the extra bulk there? Though it was only early autumn, Grace already wore one of the sweaters she hated.

Leyna lifted her phone closer to Dominic's face. "We know Grace couldn't have been pregnant when she went missing—"

"So you've said."

"But what about earlier?"

He took the phone from her and studied the screen. After a moment, he handed it back. "The potluck was right before she went to stay with your dad for a few months," he said, slowly but with contained excitement.

Spoken aloud, the theory didn't sound as crazy as it had in her head.

"It was four months, I think," she said. "*That* math works perfectly."

"So even if Grace—"

He stopped abruptly, but she knew what he'd intended to say: Even if Grace died the night she disappeared, Ellie might still be Leyna's niece—and, if Adam was the father, Dominic's too.

Leyna forced herself to finish the sentence Dominic couldn't. "If Grace is dead, the Byrds could've adopted her." She hesitated, working through her conversation with Ellie's friend and the doubt that still intruded. "But Amaya insists she's seen Sarah Byrd's C-section scar."

"You talked to Ellie's friend?" At Leyna's nod, he asked, "What else did she say?"

Aware they didn't have much time, she recapped the call quickly. Less than a foot separated them, and though she knew she imagined it, she felt the heat of him against her skin. The familiar cedar scent he always carried with him mingled with the pines and junipers and oaks. He'd always smelled like home to her. He moved closer suddenly, now only inches away, and she thought he'd noticed something she missed. But then he turned to her, his face serious, his eyes so dark they appeared black. Dominic touched her cheek, and she was transported back to his tiny apartment ten years before, fighting him for the last pot sticker. When he kissed her now, his tongue tasted of ash. She was sure hers did too.

He stepped back, and as he stared, she saw that he breathed as heavily as she did. Probably not smart, considering all the smoke.

His expression held a hint of regret, as if the kiss was a preemptive goodbye. She turned away before he could translate that expression into words. She couldn't survive another goodbye from him.

The silence grew charged. Awkward.

Dominic spoke; his voice was huskier than before. "What if Ellie came back here?"

"After Quincy?"

"Yeah."

Leyna had considered that. She'd run through the timeline over and over, but each time, she'd dismissed it because the math didn't work.

Just as she had with the pregnancy.

So she ran through the timeline again.

At about ten thirty a.m. Thursday, Ellie stopped at the market in Sierraville for gas and snacks. She'd asked the two workers if they were familiar with Plumas County. When they'd said no, she left without showing them the photo.

She'd then gone to Portola where, according to Serena Silvestri, someone at the post office recognized Ridgepoint Ranch from Ellie's photo. Later, Serena helped Ellie out by verifying Adam's and Dominic's identities and pointing her toward the youth center where Dominic worked.

So Ellie headed to Quincy. Dominic wasn't there, but she asked around about him and about Adam. She left the youth center by one thirty p.m.

That was the last place Ellie had been seen—but it hadn't been her last known location. She'd continued to update Amaya, who also tracked her on her phone. The last text from Ellie had been delivered Thursday afternoon.

But there had always been a major flaw in that timeline. A phone could be taken, and texts could be faked.

"Can I see that video from the security cameras at the youth center?"

He looked confused, but he pulled out his phone and found the video. As it played, she zoomed in as much as she could. She had missed it the first time because she hadn't been looking for it.

A small flash of gold. Even enlarged, it was no more than a sliver poking out from the sleeve of her hoodie.

The bracelet. In Quincy, Ellie had still been wearing it.

Which meant she'd come back here. The Miller house was the last place any trace of Ellie had been found.

In a blink, it all disappeared—the kiss, the fire, even her questions about what happened to Grace. Leyna's heart seized.

"She's here."

Of course Ellie returned to Ridgepoint after she'd gone to Quincy.

From the moment Ellie had arrived in Plumas County, her quest had been focused on Adam and Dominic. When she'd asked around, they were the subjects of her search. She hadn't asked about Grace. Serena had identified Leyna's sister in the photo, but Ellie hadn't seemed interested in her. No. She'd only asked for help identifying the Duran brothers.

Leyna tried not to think of the implication—that Ellie didn't ask about Grace because she'd already learned from her parents that Grace was dead and that was the reason they'd adopted her. That must be where Ellie had gotten the photo—from the Byrds.

Leyna paused the video and tapped the screen. He saw it immediately.

Dominic whispered, "Told you that you were the smartest of us."

"But if Ellie's still here, where is she?"

Between Dominic and the deputies who'd come through the day before, they'd checked all the houses, all the buildings, even the abandoned clubhouse.

Leyna scrolled through her phone, stopping on a photo of the blueprints she'd taken in Rocky's cottage. This one showed the location of the original ranch house, long since torn down, and a cabin near the northern edge of the property. Leyna remembered the stories about that cabin—a family had squatted there before a brutal winter had driven them away—but she hadn't gone that far into the woods.

But Grace had been more reckless. She had a Polaroid of that cabin. Leyna was sure of it. Fingers shaking, she quickly found the photo on her phone. It showed a small cabin in disrepair, with a sagging roof and walls that gaped.

Leyna felt Dominic's gaze, likely curious at her sudden inability to take a full breath.

Leyna poked the screen. "Where is this?"

"That cabin was abandoned years ago."

"You sure?"

As she waited for his response, she tried to ignore the bit of ash that clung to her eyelash and the smoke growing thicker around them. She forced from her mind an image of the wildfire burning closer.

What if Ellie hadn't knocked on Meredith's door because she'd never made it that far? Someone had taken her, maybe at the Miller house. And if that was the case... that cabin was the perfect place to torture someone or dump a body.

Leyna tried not to think about that or that the wildfire was even closer to the cabin than it was to them.

"We need to find her," Leyna said, too softly for him to hear. Leyna yelled to her mom that they would be right back, and when she turned, Dominic was already jogging toward the forest.

As they moved quickly through the trees, Leyna let the arid wind wash over her until her eyes burned. After a few minutes, Leyna paused to look around. She was pretty sure they were lost. A hot wind whined, rattling branches. The smoke made it harder to see, and at some point, they'd veered off the trail. Where the hell were they?

She was just about to ask Dominic if he knew where they were when she saw a tree formation she thought she recognized. Relieved, she pointed. Neither of them wasted their breath on words.

Dominic jogged ahead. Or maybe she held back. Either way, the gap between them widened. She was still deciding whether she really had seen that stand of trees before when the world exploded, and Dominic collapsed onto the forest floor.

THE FIRE

The McRae Fire grows increasingly ravenous, many times hungrier than any since Dixie.

If the wind pulled it to the east, the blaze might die at the scar of the Moonlight Fire. To the west, the Dixie scar would stop it. But in the space between, its appetite swells.

Feed me, it seems to scream.

At the edge of the fire, a bank of flames slams against a boulder, but its maw stretches wide. The wind pushes it toward dry and rotting timber, and it chews through trees a hundred feet high as if they were matchsticks. The wind pulls it along an open field of grass. Flames sheet across the ground like rushing water.

The fire spans a thousand acres. Completely uncontained.

Many trees, long threatened by drought, don't produce sap, but inside the ones that do, the sap boils. In spots, the fire nears a lung-blistering three thousand degrees. A fire tornado whirls, sending a column of flames hundreds of feet into the sky. Winds exceed a hundred miles an hour. They uproot trees and scatter bits of bark, starting new spot fires.

One of the spot fires cuts off a section of Highway 89—the highway leading away from Ridgepoint Ranch. Before the residents can be ordered to evacuate, it is already too late.

Near the blaze's perimeter, timber barons create their own fire breaks. It will be fruitless. Billions in timber will be lost, though firefighters will save the nearby town.

Residents in more remote areas won't be as lucky. Especially those who choose to stay behind.

One man, realizing he's trapped, seeks refuge in a spot already burned by this fire. He believes he will be safe there. But the man sinks into an ash pit, and his skin blisters to his knees.

A mile away, a daughter and her elderly mother trying to save their house with a garden hose jump into their pool to avoid quick-moving flames. They huddle together, but falling debris burns them both.

And to the south, a young woman's eyes sting with smoke.

She claws at the straps on her hands and feet, but two days without food and not enough water has weakened her, and the duct tape might as well be concrete. When she cries, she is too dehydrated to produce tears. When she screams, the tape stifles it, and the fire screams louder.

The fire doesn't care that it isn't her choice to stay. It cares only that the structure is made of old wood and that it stands near a forest dense with dying trees.

Like it has for the others, the fire will come for Ellie Byrd too.

CHAPTER 39

OLIVIA

Saturday, 2:00 p.m.

Richard put the Audi in drive and started down the street, following Rocky's Chevy. Thea had insisted on riding with Goose in Rocky's truck. Olivia had protested at first, but it was probably better that way. Olivia planned on coming back to take care of the last-minute things she'd had no time or privacy for, but mainly for Dominic. Richard insisted their son would be fine—the evacuation wasn't even mandatory yet, he'd said—and Olivia had been too weary to argue. But once Thea was safe, she would return for him.

Ahead of them, Rocky hit the brakes hard, and Richard did the same a second later. Olivia's neck snapped forward. The car lurched to a stop in front of the Kims' empty driveway.

"Damn it, Richard."

Her husband ignored her, so focused was he on Rocky, who had gotten out of his truck to study the space between the Kims' privacy hedges.

Curious, Olivia tracked her husband's gaze. "Do you see something?"

Again, she was greeted with silence. He threw the car in park, released his seat belt, and jumped out of the car, headed for his cousin. She followed him to the hedges, hoping that whatever had caught the men's attention wasn't serious.

"I thought I saw—" Rocky stopped, craning his neck to see between the hedges.

Richard did the same. "Me too," he said.

All Olivia saw was a sliver of murky sky.

Rocky let out a long breath, visibly relieved.

"Thank God," he said. "For a second, I thought I saw flames."

Then Rocky's body went rigid. In the distance, the sky flashed orange. Far, but not nearly far enough. Olivia grabbed Rocky's arm for support.

How did it get this bad so quickly?

But Olivia knew. The Tubbs Fire traveled twelve miles in three hours. With the Camp Fire, the first evacuations were ordered just over an hour after ignition. Like many people in Plumas County, Olivia had memorized such facts.

Memorized and yet ignored.

The road to the highway impassable, Richard backed up down the street and ran inside their house to call 911. A moment later, Rocky parked alongside. His presence comforted her. Rocky would keep them safe until emergency services arrived.

But when Richard came out a few seconds later, Olivia saw it on his face: The landlines were down. Help wasn't coming.

CHAPTER 40

LEYNA

Saturday, 2:04 p.m.

Dominic's lower leg twisted unnaturally, pinned in the steel jaws of a bear trap. He groaned, nearly a growl.

"Fuuuuck."

The trap was large, the pan that had triggered it nearly the size of a dinner plate, the steel thick and obviously heavy. The teeth looked sharper than they should've. Had the trap been modified? Was it a relic from a time when trappers meant to kill, not capture?

Leyna fell to her knees beside Dominic. She touched his forehead. He was pale, clammy, but conscious. "You okay?"

His attempt at a reassuring smile became a grimace. "Pretty fucking far from it, actually." His chest heaved with his effort to talk. "We need to find Ellie."

He shifted and his face contorted with fresh pain.

"We'll find her, Dom." Leyna hoped he missed the edge of panic in her voice. She leaned toward the trap. Springs jutted from either side of the circular pan. She struggled to compress them, but the springs wouldn't give. Too stiff. She couldn't manage alone.

"Are you able to help with this?"

"Yeah, I think I can just—" Dominic twisted to reach and instantly fell back to the ground with a new stream of curses.

Desperate to free him, Leyna followed the chain to where the trap was staked into the ground. She tugged until it jerked loose. A gesture that solved nothing.

Leyna knelt beside him again. His leg bulged above the ankle, crooked and bent. Obviously broken.

Dominic's eyes swam in and out of focus. "How bad?"

Pretty fucking bad. "Not great." Her hand fell gently to his sneaker, his foot already swelling around it. Should she remove it? Or were there bones and ligaments being held in place by the rubber and mesh? Was pressure being applied to an unseen wound, stanching the bleeding?

Or would Dominic lose his foot because she'd failed to remove a shoe that restricted blood flow?

Forcing her hand to stop shaking, Leyna touched the exposed skin near his ankle. "Can you feel that?"

Dominic shook his head. His brow beaded with sweat. The way the blood flowed from his leg, she wasn't sure how much longer he would be alert.

The wound needed to be irrigated, right? The broken bone splinted. He needed pills for the pain. A transfusion of blood. He was losing so much of it.

Mouth drier than the summer wind, she noted that the metal was rusted. She flaked off bits of it. He might need a tetanus shot too.

But the threat of tetanus was nothing compared to the more certain danger of the approaching wildfire. How was she supposed to get him out of there?

Hands trembling, Leyna was afraid to touch Dominic. Afraid not to.

As someone who'd once spent a lot of time alone in the woods, she'd taken first aid classes, but it had been years, and she was far from that Red Cross training room. Of course she'd practiced making splints. It was why she'd taken the class. To make a splint, she needed something to keep the leg immobile.

Like a tree branch. Leyna desperately scanned the forest floor.

But even if she found the perfect stick, she had nothing to wrap his leg with. Could she use his shirt? Tear it into strips? Would using a tree branch and dirty T-shirt lead to infection? A warning from her instructor echoed in memory: *Be careful not to introduce bacteria.*

That was about all Leyna remembered. She hadn't done particularly well in the class. If she'd missed two more questions on the written test, she would've had to retake the course.

On the ground, Dominic gasped as blood continued to seep into his pants.

"Hurts like a motherfucker." He seemed dangerously close to passing out.

Please don't pass out on me.

Leyna steadied her breathing and studied the damage more closely. Blood still flowed, but not as heavily as she'd thought. No major vessels had been damaged, apparently, so Dominic stood a chance, especially if she could get him to a hospital.

Dominic's eyes opened to slits; his breathing grew labored.

"I'll get you out of here." She whispered the promise, afraid if she said it louder, it would sound like a lie.

"You need to go, Ley." He struggled to speak each word. "Find her."

"I'm not leaving you."

She studied the trees, trying to find the main trail, but they'd stepped off it at some point. She didn't know how close they were to the cabin—she'd been counting on Dominic to show her the way, and he wasn't walking out of these woods. If she had a cart or a tarp to drag him . . . which was a ridiculous thought, because she didn't have a cart or a tarp, just like she didn't have bandages or a pocketful of painkillers.

Just like I can't open the damn trap, she thought. *Any splint will be useless if I can't get him free.*

Dominic grabbed her arm, but his grip was even weaker than his voice. "The fire—not safe. You can... come back... for me. After."

"Not. Leaving. You."

Leyna's gaze darted around as she considered trying to move him, trap and all, out of sight of predators—animal or human. But unseen wasn't the same as safe. Even had Leyna been able to drag him a few feet, the most she could manage, there was nowhere a predator couldn't track him or the fire couldn't reach him.

His eyes fluttered, and she thought she heard him whisper, *Please.* Or maybe it was his wheezing as he struggled to breathe. At least he was still conscious, but he was fading quickly.

Desperate, she checked her phone. No bars, and at least two minutes wasted while she'd always had only a single option. Help wasn't in that forest. It was at Ridgepoint Ranch.

Leyna scanned his body, trying to pretend he was a felled tree and not a man. Not Dominic. *Her* Dominic. She watched his chest to make sure he still breathed, then quickly looked away.

Leyna stood up and ran, adrenaline coursing, grateful when the forest started to look familiar again.

Grace would've been proud of how she sprinted, clumsy but somehow remaining upright. When they'd come into the woods as kids, her sister would fly across the uneven forest floor, hopping over felled trees or inconvenient bushes, not once scuffing her Nikes. Leyna would labor behind her, sweating in her old track pants and sneakers and breathing like her lungs held water. Grace would laugh—*Oh, Leyna*—as if her younger sister's lack of agility was a trick performed just for her. On these treks, Grace never slowed when Leyna fell behind, expecting she would catch up. Leyna had loved her for that, for thinking that she could. Until they'd grown apart, no one had believed in her as much as Grace had.

The belief weighed on Leyna, even as she fought to keep moving. As she ran toward home, she pretended Grace was with her, yelling over her shoulder for Leyna to catch up. She pictured Dominic, who for some reason believed in her too and had been caught in a trap because of it. His only hope was that she would get help fast enough.

Saving Dominic was her only hope too. Leyna wouldn't lose him again.

CHAPTER 41

OLIVIA

Saturday, 2:09 p.m.

Rocky had returned to his cottage to stock up on supplies, since their mission had changed—now the goal was to find someplace safe to wait it out. The sky reflected the flames coming for them, and the wind rumbled in warning. Olivia took a step forward and stopped at the edge of the back patio, her gaze fixed on the tree line. "What do we do now?" she asked Richard.

She kept her voice low so Thea wouldn't hear. About twenty feet in front of them, their daughter watched the forest as intently as Olivia did, Goose a lump at her feet. From the way the dog's chest heaved, she could tell the heat and thick air were getting to him.

Richard moved closer so his arm brushed hers. Even with the smoke, she could smell him—musk and breath mints. A week ago, she would've found comfort in the scent.

"We need to get to Hermann Creek," he said.

With the lack of rain that winter, Olivia worried the creek would be dry. "What about the golf course? It's flat. Open, with not many trees."

"Rocky should be here any minute," he said. "We'll all go in his truck since it's equipped for off-road driving. If the usual roads are closed, we can make our own. Follow the creek away from Ridgepoint."

The creek wouldn't save them. Years of pretending kept Olivia's face neutral, but she knew there was no way out, and beneath the mask, guilt pricked. If something happened to her children, the blame would be hers. She shouldn't have stayed. As soon as the deputy delivered his warning about the fire, she should've taken her kids and gone. But even that would have guaranteed only survival, not salvation. To truly save her family, she should have left long before the fire started.

When Olivia pictured Richard with those other women, she flashed to an image of herself at fourteen, her mom beside her at the bathroom mirror teaching her how to contour her cheeks.

So many men are going to love you, Livvy, her mom had whispered. *Be sure and pick one who doesn't fuck around.*

"It's too late."

Olivia thought the words existed only in her head until Richard said, "It's not too late. We just need to find a safe place, like the creek."

Safe? Such a place didn't exist here. Had never existed here.

"Even if there's water in the creek, it won't protect us from the smoke." Her voice was sharp, her calm starting to crack.

"Rocky knows this place better than anyone. If he believes the creek will work, it will."

Richard's voice had risen too, and Thea shot them a look over her shoulder. His smile, meant to be reassuring, was more a grimace. Olivia hoped their daughter didn't see it.

"Come closer, Thea," Olivia said.

Thea took only a single step before she knelt to pet the dog, but Olivia was too tired to start another argument with her daughter.

Richard dropped his voice again. "When Rocky gets here, he should take you, Thea, and the dog. Dominic and I can take his SUV when he gets back."

Olivia looked at her daughter and the wheezing dog. Her heartbeat seemed nearly as loud as the wind. Richard leaned in, his breath warm on her neck. "Do you want me to go look for him?"

Olivia shook her head and scoured the shadows between the pines for movement. Dominic was an adult. She couldn't justify waiting much longer.

She said, "Rocky and Dominic will both be back soon, and then we'll all leave together."

He'll be okay out there. He will.

Why had Dominic gone with Leyna in the first place? Olivia should've tried harder to stop him.

Olivia carried a mental picture with her always: Adam learning to walk, Dominic, two years older, by his side all summer. Adam's legs still slightly bowed; Dominic's face earnest as his hand wrapped around Adam's, helping to keep his younger brother steady.

Sometimes, though, they'd stumble, hands unclasping the moment Adam hit the ground. Even as a toddler, Adam hated to fail, and at the indignity of a butt-plant, he would usually howl until his cheeks flushed red. But not if Dominic was next to him. Those times, Adam's pudgy hands would shoot into the air, waiting for Dominic to help him get back on his feet.

That was the image Olivia held to fiercely. Her boys, hand in hand. Stronger together. Happy.

But there was another image that sometimes snuck in at two in the morning, when she was groggy and too slow at erecting her walls, of Dominic and Adam toward the end. They'd been fighting over Grace. In the weeks before Grace's disappearance, her moods had darkened, and she'd grown more mercurial. That along with Adam's blind crush had finally shattered the trio's childhood friendship.

The last time Dominic was home from college, he'd tried to warn Adam away from Grace.

Be careful, he'd said.

We're in love had been the reply.

I'm not sure she knows how to love. At least, not anymore.

And those had been the last words exchanged between the brothers before Dominic headed back to the University of Nevada, and Adam headed back to Grace. The last time Adam had fallen—for a girl who demanded love but was incapable of giving any in return—Dominic hadn't been there with an outstretched hand. He'd been a state away, and then Adam was gone, and there was no taking any of it back.

"I've changed my mind," Olivia said. "Maybe you should go look for Dominic."

Too tentative, she decided, as usual. So she said more firmly, "Find our son."

CHAPTER 42

LEYNA

Saturday, 2:17 p.m.

So focused was Leyna on making it home without twisting an ankle that she nearly missed the man waiting at the edge of the woods. When she finally picked him out of the thickening smoke and swirling ash, she thought of Adam and tensed. If he meant to finish the job of the failed trap, there would be no avoiding it. He would kill her, and there would be no one to save Dominic.

But it was Richard who broke into the clearing, and she knew what question he would ask. *Where's my son?*

Leyna couldn't bear to hear the words spoken casually. As soon as he drew close enough, she shouted, "Dominic's hurt." Her tongue felt swollen, as if she might choke on it, and she had to swallow several times before she could continue. "He triggered a bear trap."

Richard's face grew nearly as pale as his son's had been. "How bad?"

She shook her head, unable to answer.

Voice breaking, Richard said, "Show me."

Leyna took the lead. Around them, smoke billowed and ash whirled.

Though she'd passed that way only minutes before, her lungs were forced to work harder now.

She wheezed, which triggered a series of phlegmy coughs. Beside her, Richard seemed to have no problem breathing, despite the haze.

Leyna slowed, taking in her surroundings. Though she'd traveled the path twice in the past hour, details grew suddenly jumbled in her head, the trees and boulders that had once seemed unforgettable landmarks blurring to patches of green and gray.

When she picked up her pace again, so did Richard.

"Was he conscious when you left him?" Grief made his tone gruff.

When you left him. Leyna knew Richard hadn't meant the words as an accusation, but guilt soured her stomach nonetheless.

She managed a quick "Yes" between breaths, then: "There was a lot of blood." She pictured the bloom of red below his knee and felt a sudden urge to explain her decision to abandon him. "He was too heavy to move."

A minute later, they found him.

Winded more from emotion than the jog back through the forest, Leyna forced in a breath and knelt beside Dominic. He was so very still, the only movement the wind tugging at strands of his dark hair. Blood now claimed more of his pants. Wind brought the metallic scent of it to Leyna, searing her nostrils. So thick she could nearly taste it.

"He's going to be okay," she said, mainly to herself.

At the sharpening metallic tang on her tongue, a wave of nausea left Leyna suddenly unsteady. She shifted to make room for Richard.

Richard pulled out a pocketknife and gently cut through Dominic's pants, exposing pale skin and matted leg hair. "You okay, son?"

Dominic managed a nod.

To Leyna, Richard said, "The bleeding's stopped, and it doesn't look like anything major was cut." To Dominic, he said, "Your leg should be okay to splint once we remove the trap."

Leyna allowed herself a few moments of solace at Richard's certainty and at how quickly they were able to pry the trap apart and free Dominic's leg. They used a stick and Dominic's T-shirt to fashion a makeshift splint, and with her help, Richard lifted Dominic upright so that he stood on his good leg. He wrapped his arm around Dominic's waist, supporting his weight.

"Usually, I would leave you here until help came, but looks like that's us today." He paired a reassuring tone with a smile, but Leyna noticed the overbright sheen to his eyes.

She also noticed the implication of what he'd said. *Looks like that's us today.* While the gusts made a helicopter rescue impossible, an ambulance should get there nearly as quickly.

Richard met her gaze and gave a quick shake of his head. "Phones are down," he said. "The main road is closed too."

The weight of that information knocked Leyna back a step, but she tried to keep it from her face. She didn't want Dominic's fear to feed off her own.

With his free hand, Richard brushed the hair from his son's face.

"Not going to lie," Richard said, voice low. "This is going to be rough. But I've got you."

Leyna moved to Dominic's other side, but Richard took most of the burden. He gave no sign he struggled. Leyna was reminded of the day he'd helped a thirteen-year-old Dominic from the soccer field after he'd sprained his ankle, though this injury was so much worse, and there was no medic waiting a few yards away.

As they made their way slowly back to the trail, Leyna trying to disguise her own labored breathing, she scanned the tree line. Usually this was the place she felt most at home; now, the rustling pines and shadows between them seemed to warn of coming danger. But she felt numb to it. The worst had already happened. Dominic was hurt, and they hadn't been able to find Ellie.

CHAPTER 43

MEREDITH

Saturday, 2:20 p.m.

Still irritated that Leyna had left her like that—*dismissed her,* really—Meredith was forced to find a way to buy them both more time. Fortunately, the idea had occurred to her quickly.

Would some people deem it too extreme? Of course. The world was full of passive handwringers. But would it work? Probably. And if it didn't, at least her house would be the one still standing.

Meredith headed to the corner of the garage where she stored old art supplies. A few years earlier, she'd experimented with encaustic painting, a form of art that used pigmented and heated wax. She'd hated it. The medium offered too little control, and her attempts turned out nothing like she'd intended. She'd thrown out the wax immediately.

But she'd kept the blowtorch.

The fire was coming for them. There was no getting around that. But she could create a defensible space. She grabbed the torch and screwed on the canister of butane. How much time did she have until Leyna came looking for her? Another sixty seconds? She hoped that would be enough.

She carried the torch to the edge of her property. The wind gusted southwest, toward Ridgepoint Ranch. Toward her home. The taste of smoke sharp on her tongue, she considered the path the fire would likely take. The hardscaping around the house was fire-resistant—concrete, river rock, flagstone pavers. But beyond that, nothing but trees with crisp leaves or brown needles, trunks stressed by drought, and acres of wild grasses that would burn quickly.

She looked at those grasses, flattened by the wind. She could do nothing about the trees, but if the flames met a field already scarred by fire, they might be forced onto a different path. True, carried by the wind, the flames might jump that dead space and consume her home anyway. But she couldn't dwell on that. In any case, the fire was coming her way.

She eyed the patch of dirt to her left, grown hard after so many dry summers. She couldn't risk firefighters digging on her property or water from their hoses eroding the ground.

She turned the knob on the blowtorch until she heard the hissing of the gas, then stabbed the ignition button. She turned up the blue flame to its highest setting. She touched the flame to a patch of dry grass, praying the wind didn't turn on her.

That night in Grace's bedroom, Adam hadn't been unconscious for long. After a few tense minutes, he'd opened his eyes and stumbled to his feet, the mallet that had rested against his leg landing with a soft thud on the carpet. He touched his head, and his fingers came away tipped in red.

Just as Grace had, he asked, "Why'd you do that?"

Meredith offered him the same explanation she had her daughter. "I thought you were hurting her."

This set his eyes blinking, quick and rhythmic, like the lights at a rail crossing. He dropped on the bed, and Meredith got the impression it hadn't been by choice. More urgently, he said, "I feel kinda sick." His fingers rose to his head again and he winced.

Not good.

"Let me get you some ice." Meredith moved to leave, but he stopped her with a hand on her wrist. She was surprised by his strength. When he lowered his hand, Meredith noticed on her wrist a smear of Adam's blood, nearly black in the dim light.

In horror, she thought, *I did that.* She swiped her wrist on the leg of her pants. *Olivia is going to kill me.*

Adam seemed unconcerned with his wound now, was focused wholly on Grace. Her mouth thinned, and she crossed her arms. Her eyes were feverish and slick, and Meredith couldn't tell if she'd been crying or if she was about to.

Meredith knew she needed to get Adam help. She was fairly certain he had a concussion, and she recalled a story about a high-school athlete who'd died recently during a scrimmage. In her head, she heard again that sickening sound of bone cracking. A mallet strike would've done at least as much damage as a tackle on the football field. Adam's lack of consciousness, no matter how brief, worried her too.

Not good at all.

Meredith left to get Adam a clean towel and some naproxen. When she got back, Adam was gone.

She clutched a phone she hadn't yet dialed. "Where's Adam?" she asked her daughter.

The sound coming from Grace's throat was growl-like, and she vibrated with obvious rage. At Adam? Or at her mom?

Meredith was deciding which it was when Grace exploded. She upended her mattress with little effort, and it slid to the floor. She swept everything off her dresser. She yanked the lamp off her nightstand, throwing the room into darkness, and shattered it against the far wall.

"We need to help Adam," Meredith said emphatically, but her daughter sank deeper into her fury.

Grace had always been quick to anger, but it had never been that bad. Meredith remembered the insults Grace had hurled at Adam earlier. The way her eyes had flashed when Meredith had interrupted—what, exactly? She still wasn't sure.

After several minutes, Grace burned herself out and fell onto the box springs of her now mattress-less bed. She stared at the ceiling, and somehow this sudden silence marked only by her daughter's labored breathing was worse than the anger that had come before.

In the quiet, Meredith glanced at the phone she clutched. Had Adam gone home? She waited for Olivia's inevitable call. The accusations she knew would follow: *What have you done to my son? What kind of monster hits a boy in the head with a mallet?*

Meredith would have preferred to make sure Adam was okay before sending him back to Olivia, but if he was already on his way home, perhaps it was for the best. His mother could take him to the hospital. She wondered if Olivia would report her to the police. If she had already reported her. Would she wake up in the morning to flashing lights in her driveway?

Staring at the ceiling, Grace whispered, "Get out."

Meredith had been happy to oblige. She picked up the mallet and left Grace's bedroom.

Though it had been burning for only seconds, the small fire Meredith had started zipped along the grass. Toward the Millers' house. Toward the Durans'. But, thankfully, away from her home. Just as she'd intended.

The wind pulled the flames away from her, and in a couple of minutes, when enough of the grass had burned, she would extinguish them with a hearty blast from her garden hose.

A gust picked up several glowing leaves and dropped them on the roof next door. Not hot enough to do damage, and even if they did, it wasn't her house.

Meredith felt a stillness settle in her chest. She'd been waiting for this day for sixteen years. She would burn down the whole neighborhood if it meant protecting her daughter.

Meredith had to protect the grave, because bones didn't burn.

CHAPTER 44

OLIVIA

Saturday, 2:32 p.m.

If not for Goose's interest in Meredith's garden, it would've taken longer for Olivia to realize what Meredith had done. But when she and Thea rounded the corner chasing after Goose, who had sprinted in the direction of the Clarke house—again—it was hard to miss.

Meredith aimed a hose at the flames that shot along the grasses that separated their houses. She'd actually started a small fire to protect her own house at the risk of everyone else's. It appeared to be under control, but with the wind, Olivia knew there were no guarantees that would last.

A dull anger gathered, but before she could shout at her neighbor, Olivia caught sight of Goose digging just beyond Meredith's garden.

Olivia dropped Thea at the Clarke patio. She ran back to the car for Thea's noise-canceling headphones and her iPad, then turned Thea's chair toward the house. Thea had already witnessed one blowup between her mom and Meredith that day. No reason for her to witness round two.

It wasn't hard to convince Thea to stay. She'd been avoiding her parents all day, and truthfully, Olivia was tired of her daughter's attitude.

Olivia strode toward Meredith and stopped about twenty feet away. She felt her eyes widen in incredulity.

"Are you trying to set my house on fire?"

This wasn't how the day was supposed to go. This should've been a moment of triumph, or at least of closure. She checked the time and released a long breath. An hour left on the countdown, but she thought, *Screw it.*

"Well, Meredith, it looks like in addition to the two hundred and fifty thousand, you're going to pay me whatever the insurance doesn't cover if you burn down my house."

Meredith's eyes narrowed. "I knew it was you."

Olivia laughed, the harshness of it burning her throat. "You didn't or you would've set your little fire closer to my house."

It had been such an elegant plan that Olivia was disappointed it hadn't occurred to her sooner: Rattle Meredith. Force her to make a mistake. Get her to admit that she knew what had happened to Adam. But Olivia hadn't yet gotten the money or the answers she was owed.

When Meredith spoke, her voice trembled with poorly concealed fury: "At first, I thought it might be my ex-husband, but when I saw what you'd done to the painting of Grace—" Her voice cracked.

Olivia was genuinely confused. Painting? What painting?

"John would never do that. No one else would either," Meredith said. "The only person who hates Grace enough to do that is you."

Olivia shook her head. "I have no clue what painting you're talking about, but if it bothers you this much, I'll take the credit."

Meredith cocked her head as if trying to understand. "If you were bent on revenge, on making me suffer, why not turn my broker in instead? That would've ruined me."

This woman. She still didn't get it. She was still making it about her, as she always did. Olivia thought of how many times Leyna had come to her home as a child, the need in her eyes so transparent that Olivia's heart broke, and she'd tried to fix it by frosting cupcakes or brewing tea. But mostly, she thought about Adam.

"I've never cared about *your* suffering," she said.

The dog whined as he scratched at the ground, and Olivia moved closer to the garden. What was Goose doing? Why was he so interested in—

Olivia froze as a terrible understanding dawned. Goose's unflagging interest. The careful way the ground was maintained. Even the shape of it.

This wasn't a garden. This was a grave.

Olivia grasped at reasons for why it wasn't Adam—garbage left to compost, or the large pet of a friend buried there as a favor. Or Grace. Olivia's stomach heaved at the thought, but she clung to it with everything in her.

Oh God, let it be Grace.

Olivia tried to pull her eyes away from that horrible plot of earth, but she was transfixed. If she'd planted the bouquet of wildflowers closer, she would've seen the grave days ago.

"That's why you're always so angry when Goose is in your garden, isn't it?" Her voice was quiet because that was all she could manage with her limited breath, in limbo between knowing and not knowing; her chest burned. "Who's buried here, Meredith?"

She waited for her neighbor to tell her she was wrong, that it wasn't a grave at all. She waited for the inevitable and snarky comment about Olivia's dog defecating in the yard or how grief had made her stupid.

Goose waddled back to her, tired of digging. With his flat face and narrow nostrils, he often had trouble breathing, and the smoke and heat didn't help. Olivia glanced at Thea, still curled up in one of Meredith's patio chairs, headphones on. The smoke and heat weren't great for her daughter either.

She looked at Meredith again. The other woman's face was a mask. "I don't know what you mean," she said. But Olivia noted the way her shoulders had started to sag.

Olivia covered the distance between them in seconds, stopping just a few feet short of her. Near her ankles, Goose wheezed.

Olivia's body shook with the effort of containing a hundred different memories, a thousand different kinds of pain. Adam's first smile, all gums and drool. His first day of school, his tentative steps as he trudged forward in his oversize Green Arrow T-shirt. The pain of all the lasts, too, grieved only in hindsight.

Adam. Had he really been this close to her for the past sixteen years? She wanted to be wrong. Her stomach roiled with the longing, so fiercely she feared she might vomit. Stars pricked her vision, which had started to go black.

Meredith cocked her head, and her mask slipped, revealing—guilt? "I think you need to sit for a second."

Fuck this woman's fake concern.

Olivia retreated to Meredith's garage, then returned with a shovel. She fought an urge to swing it at the other woman's head.

"What did you do?" Her voice held unexpected steel.

"Really, Olivia, you don't look well."

Olivia stamped toward the grave and began digging. The first layer was soft as if recently overturned, but the ground below was hard, and the dirt she dug up was meager. For a few minutes, Goose pawed at the ground too, then collapsed, exhausted, to watch.

After ten minutes, the shovel struck bone. When Olivia uncovered the top of the skull, she released the shovel and dropped beside the grave. She brushed dirt from the yellowed bone, her gestures frantic, until the jaw was clear—she was seized by the irrational thought that he needed to breathe. When she was able to see the skull and several of the ribs, Olivia pressed her palm tenderly on the frontal bone where once she'd placed wet washcloths to help with fever.

It was Adam. It had to be.

Olivia looked up at Meredith, who watched from a spot several feet away. She stole a glance at Thea, and then, in a voice as low as she could make it and still be heard, she asked, "Is it him?"

Tears of frustration stung her eyes. She should've recognized her own son's bones. She hated that she had to ask Meredith for confirmation.

Meredith didn't answer, her attention drifting, concern obvious on her face. Olivia turned to see what had her neighbor worried. What could be more important than this?

Leyna had emerged from the forest, half jogging, half stumbling. Olivia straightened, steeling herself to tell Dominic and Richard about Adam. Thea, too, if she hadn't already figured it out. Olivia glanced toward the patio, reassured when she saw her daughter's head still bent over her iPad.

But that didn't mean she hadn't seen or heard something.

Olivia turned back toward the tree line and waited for Dominic to break through, winded but voice strong. Steady, as he'd been the summer he'd taught Adam to walk.

She waited for him to call to her: *I'm here, Mom. I'm okay.*

Instead, Leyna drew close enough that the wind and distance wouldn't swallow her words and stopped. There was blood on her shirt.

Why was there blood on Leyna's shirt?

"Richard says you have a wagon in the garage?"

Olivia knew which wagon she meant: the heavy-duty one with the all-terrain wheels they took camping. She shook her head—they no longer had it—but why was Leyna asking about the damn wagon?

But then she knew. All that blood on Leyna's shirt that obviously wasn't her own.

Olivia's knees turned to rubber, and her hands flew to her ears. Whatever Leyna had to say, she didn't want to hear it. Because she recognized the expression on the young woman's face. She'd seen it before. She closed her eyes to keep from seeing it now.

But the image had already been seared into her memory, and several minutes later when Olivia opened her eyes again, Richard had broken through the tree line too, his body bowed with the weight of what he carried.

Who he carried.

Shock kept Olivia's hands pinned to her ears, but Richard's words found her anyway.

"Dominic's hurt."

Leyna moved back toward Dominic but stopped when Olivia called, "Stay the hell away from my son."

A few minutes later, Rocky returned to the Duran house with his truck. Taking immediate stock of the situation, he ran to help Richard. He scooped a semiconscious Dominic into his arms and loaded him into the bed of his Chevy. Rocky retrieved a first aid kit and a couple of bottles of water from his go bag and took out a packet of ibuprofen. He helped Dominic swallow the pills and used the rest of the water to quickly rinse the skin broken by the steel jaws.

Richard was saying something about a bear trap near the old squatters' cabin. She knew she should be paying attention, but she couldn't focus on anything beyond her son. She placed a hand on his neck. The skin was clammy, his pulse thready. His skin had gone several shades paler. How much blood had her son lost?

Dominic's face went slack, his body limp, his breathing shallow. Olivia felt powerless. She'd insisted on installing thousands of dollars of surveillance equipment to protect their children, yet now she could do nothing for her son.

Rocky closed the tailgate of his truck. "I've got some first aid supplies at my place. Some stronger painkillers too." He got in front of Olivia so his face was only inches from hers. "I'll grab them and get him somewhere safe," he said. "Promise."

He forced something into her hands, then got in his truck and drove away.

Olivia realized she was kneeling only when her thighs began to cramp. Gravel bit into her knees. She welcomed the cramping and she ground her kneecaps into the tiny bits of rocks, but the pain remained dull, distant. Not nearly substantial enough to distract her from the other, larger hurt.

Another son lost. Another worst-ever pain.

No, not lost, she reminded herself. Certainly no one died from getting his leg caught in a bear trap? He would be stitched up at the hospital. Rocky would find a way.

Aware of a stabbing sensation in her clenched hand, Olivia opened it to see what Rocky had given her. Dominic's keys. He must've taken them from Dominic's pocket. Her son's Toyota 4Runner was a better choice than their Audi.

The fire. For a moment, she'd forgotten about the fire.

Olivia felt abruptly woozy. She leaned forward to catch her breath, palms planted on her thighs for support, knees peppered with gravel.

Richard squeezed her shoulder but said nothing. What was there to say? *He'll be okay*? A lie. *He's not conscious, so he's probably not suffering*? She would've slapped him.

How much had Thea seen? How was she going to tell her all of it? She couldn't find the words to get it straight in her own head. How was she going to break the news to her ten-year-old daughter? Thea hadn't known Adam, so his loss had never seemed real to her. But she adored Dominic, as he did her.

Olivia looked around but saw no sign of Thea. She must've left her daughter on Meredith's patio. Goose too. Her head throbbed. She didn't know how much she had left in her.

"I'll tell her," Richard said as if reading her thoughts, which maybe he had. About their daughter, at least, they'd always been in sync.

While she'd expected the grief, a new swell of anger caught her off guard. Unlike the pain in her gravel-pocked knees, this sensation was substantial enough to eclipse all else.

"She's still at Meredith's. I'll get her." She couldn't bring herself to tell him about Adam. Not yet.

As she approached the edge of the Clarkes' property, she spotted them in the middle of their backyard. Meredith's arm was around Leyna, a gesture of comfort. Even from that distance, she could tell that Leyna cried.

How dare they grieve *her* loss?

The anger gave her weight and tethered her so she no longer felt like she might float away. She was firmly in the world again, with all its horror and injustice.

Olivia caught the woodsy smell of smoke. Her nostrils flared as she inhaled. The fire tempted her with its promise of permanent release.

She felt an irrational urge to walk toward the unseen flames as a tingling in her feet. She took one small step. Then another. She imagined the fire burning along some not-too-distant hillside. If she set out in that direction, how long would it take for her to meet the fire? And when she caught it, how long would it take before she burned to bones?

But, Olivia realized, she wasn't the one who deserved to be destroyed by fire. She imagined the flames erasing the Clarkes from her life forever.

CHAPTER 45

LEYNA

Saturday, 2:58 p.m.

Dazed, Leyna left her mom's embrace and wandered to the spot where she'd seen Olivia digging, her movements nearly feral. She peered at the patch of earth. Though Olivia had lost interest in the grave when she'd seen Dominic injured, she'd cleared a significant amount of dirt. In the process, she'd uncovered bones. A skull and a few ribs. Enough for Leyna to guess whose they were. Grace had been wearing a synthetic blouse. Leyna thought of the woman's body unearthed in Los Angeles after two decades, the polyester dress found with her bones. Grace's blouse wouldn't have decomposed as quickly as Adam's cotton T-shirt.

"Are these Adam's?" Horrified.

The smoke coated her throat, making her cough, but her mom seemed unaffected by it. "For years, I kept waiting for her to return. She had to know I'd keep her secret. I *did* keep her secret." She tilted her chin in a gesture of defiance but a tremor was in her voice. "I called in that tip about Grace and Adam being spotted at that campground. Better they look along the banks of the Feather River than near Adam's grave and better for everyone to believe Grace was a runaway rather than a—" She left the last word unspoken.

Leyna swayed, but her disbelief kept her upright. "Grace isn't a killer."

Her mom looked at her with something close to sympathy. "The night they disappeared, I found Adam with his hands around Grace's throat. Or at least, that's what I thought at first. Then I realized he was holding her down to protect himself." Leyna fought an impulse to touch her scar. "I thought—I thought he was hurting her. I hit him. In the head, with a mallet. Just once."

There was no apology in her voice, as if hitting Adam a single time made it somehow okay. *A misunderstanding. One thwack of the mallet. An accident.* She half expected her mom to shrug.

"He left the house suddenly, and at first I thought he'd gone home. But when Olivia didn't call to ask what had happened, I started to worry he'd never made it." Her voice broke, the slightest of cracks but deafening in its unfamiliarity. Meredith Clarke never showed weakness. Her eyes grew weary too, and when she exhaled, her torso curled in on itself, as if protecting its most vulnerable parts. "I went looking for him. First in our house, then in the neighborhood. And, finally, in the forest." Her gaze softened as it settled on the spot where she'd buried Adam. "When I found Adam, his skull was crushed on one side." When her mother saw Leyna's look, her lips thinned. "It wasn't from me hitting him, if that's what you're about to ask. It was on the wrong side of his head, for one thing, and also—it was brutal. That's all I'll say."

"What about Grace?"

Her mom straightened slightly, though her shoulders still slouched under the weight of the truth. Or was this a performance meant to gain her daughter's trust? Leyna sensed her preparing excuses, but instead Meredith went still, her eyes growing large and dark.

"Curious how you're going to answer this one, Mom," a voice said behind them both.

The voice was raspier than it had been all those years before. Deeper too. But Leyna's breath caught in her throat even before she turned. She'd been chasing a ghost for sixteen years, always knowing none of the young women she passed on Virginia Street or heading north on the highway or in the aisles of Sprouts would ever actually be Grace.

Until, now, it was.

Grace emerged from the far side of their mom's house. At first, she seemed an apparition, but she took firmer form as she drew nearer. Grace was here. Grace was really home.

But this wasn't the Grace that Leyna had been chasing. This Grace had shorter hair, glued to her forehead with sweat. Lines etched the skin around her mouth. The girl who favored cap-sleeved blouses wore dirty khaki shorts and a blue T-shirt with stains ringing its collar.

What had she been up to these past few hours? Where had she been?

Elation filled Leyna's chest until the stab of long-carried hurt pushed it out of the way. Her legs felt wooden and too heavy to lift. Her vision doubled, and she thought she might pass out. Cautiously, she started moving toward her sister, stopping when only a few feet separated them. Her thoughts grew muddled.

How was Grace alive?

And why had she let Leyna believe she was dead?

Leyna extended her fingers, reaching, but she pulled back at the last instant, afraid stress and the thick haze had made her hallucinate. If she'd covered those last few inches, would she have grazed skin or would she have grabbed smoke?

The smile Grace offered was as guarded as her eyes. "Hi, Ley."

After sixteen years, the casual greeting seemed an insult. Even an illusion could be expected to do better.

Hi, Ley. Really? That was all she got?

How about an apology? *I'm sorry I left you, Ley.*

Or, better, an explanation: *I had to go away because…*

She'd been hunting for an end to that sentence for more than half her life, and Grace appeared at the exact moment they had no time for it.

Typical Grace.

Leyna sensed movement near the patio. Had Olivia finally come to get

Thea and Goose? She kept her eyes on her sister, afraid if she turned to check, Grace would disappear again.

"You're here," Leyna said, tone reverent.

From the corner of her eye, she saw Olivia closing in with hurried strides, Thea pulled alongside. Goose waddled at their heels. Olivia stopped abruptly a few feet from Grace, her arm a vise on her daughter's shoulder.

"It *is* you," Olivia said, tone and stance hostile. "What did you do to my son?"

With great effort, Meredith pulled her attention away from Grace to look at Olivia. "Leave us," she said, cool but not unkind. Shock softened the planes of her face. "This is a family matter."

A strangled sound escaped Olivia's throat, too much grief and rage in it to be called a laugh. "*You* talk to *me* about family."

Grace took a small step backward. "We've *all* got to go," she said, frantic. Her eyes locked with Leyna's. "I'm not sure how much more time we have to find her." Grace's chest heaved, though Leyna couldn't say whether emotion or exertion caused it. "Ley, I'm sorry—"

When Grace moved toward her, Leyna retreated. She wanted to embrace her sister. She wanted to rail against her, apologize, ask all the questions she'd gathered like priceless treasures since she was twelve. But there was only one thing she wanted more than finally getting her answers—to save the niece she'd never gotten the chance to know.

"You're right," Leyna said. "We need to find Ellie." Without taking her eyes from Grace, she said, "We'll meet you at the creek, Mom. After we find Ellie. That'll be the safest place."

Her mom and Olivia both acted as if they hadn't heard her. Olivia took a step forward, nearly tripping over Goose. "That girl isn't anywhere near here," she said. "Why do you care so much about her anyway?"

Meredith sniffed loudly. "Because they're not sociopaths."

"Because she's my daughter," Grace said.

At once, the group fell silent. Meredith stiffened, and her mouth gaped. Olivia clutched Thea so tightly that the girl winced.

"She's what?" Olivia shook her head. "How?" Thea tried to shrug off Olivia's grip, but that only made her mom hold on more tightly. A second later, Olivia's eyes grew large. "Is she Adam's?"

Grace ignored her, eyes pinned to Leyna's. "I've looked everywhere. The forest. The old maintenance building. The clubhouse." She paused. "Mom's house."

Leyna flashed to the painting of Grace they'd found in the kitchen, face shredded, canvas attacked with obvious hostility. How hurt had Grace been to do that?

Beside her, she felt her mom shift.

Olivia released Thea and moved closer still.

"Is she Adam's?" Olivia asked again, more insistent now that the initial shock had worn off.

Grace sighed, her body trembling with impatience. She spat the words: "She's his."

Her eyes bored into Leyna's, wearing the same pleading expression she had that night at the window but several times more desperate. "You're coming, right, Ley?"

"Of course I'll come," she said, voice heavy with years of pent-up emotion.

Meredith moved closer. "I'll come with—"

Grace cut her off with a quick shake of her head. "I don't want your help, Mom, and I don't want those creepy portraits you've painted to memorialize your guilt," she said, voice low, more sad than angry. "All I want is for you to leave me the fuck alone."

As if driven by the force of Grace's pain, the fire their mom had started with her blowtorch took hold on the Durans' roof, suddenly ablaze in a flash of embers.

CHAPTER 46
OLIVIA

Saturday, 3:11 p.m.

As the house burned, the air grew smokier. Bits of ash landed on Olivia's skin. When she brushed them away, they dissolved like dirty snowflakes.

Richard was in front of their house with a garden hose, battling the fire Meredith had started. It looked like he might even be able to save the house, or at least part of it. The fire had begun in the back of the house, so the kitchen might survive. Adam's room, though, would be a total loss. Dominic's too.

Screw the house.

Adam had a daughter.

Inside Olivia, grief raged stronger than any fire. Her fingers and feet tingled with it. She wondered if, after burning for so many years, it might finally consume her. She realized she didn't care whether she survived any more than she cared about the damn house.

All she cared about was making sure Thea was safe and finally doing the right thing. She could still save Ellie. Then she'd make the Clarkes pay. Not with cash. The blackmail had never been about the $250,000. It had been about forcing the truth. Now, the Clarkes owed a far greater debt.

Olivia cast a sideways glance at Dominic's SUV.

She nudged Thea toward the vehicle. "Take Goose and wait there," she said. When her daughter had gone, she turned back to Richard.

"It's not worth saving," she called to him. She wasn't sure whether she meant the house or their marriage. "Adam won't be coming home."

Richard dropped the garden hose and stood stone-still, watching her.

Olivia moved closer so she wouldn't have to shout. "Apparently, he's been buried on Meredith's property for sixteen years." Inappropriate laughter threatened to bubble up, but she choked it down.

Shock flashed across Richard's face, despair too, but before he could speak, Olivia said, "I know you've had affairs. For the past couple of days, I've been sure you were cheating again."

"What happened to him?" Richard's voice broke, and Olivia felt an unexpected pang of regret. She quickly quashed it.

"Sounds like Grace killed him." She instantly caught the tentative phrasing and squared her shoulders. "She definitely killed him." And then she'd taken the last piece of him with her when she left.

He shook his head. "I've never cheated on you." He sounded so damn sincere that if she hadn't known better, she might've believed him. "Everything I've done—even the horrible things I can't take back—I've done to protect you."

She squared her shoulders again, making it clear she was done—with his lies, with him. "I don't believe you." Though she spoke softly, the sharp edge of her words sliced through the wind.

Richard slouched under the weight of his emotions, and had it been earlier in their marriage, she would've gone to him. Held him. Taken on some of his grief. But she had no room in her for forgiveness.

His next words were nearly a sigh, forlorn but resigned. "I'm not your father. I've never cheated. For me, you've always been enough."

There was a kindness in his voice, but to her it felt like judgment. Even now, he still believed her too weak to handle the truth. Because she couldn't be wrong about his cheating. He would never be able to convince her of that.

Richard looked around, probably for their daughter.

"She's fine," Olivia said. "She can't hear."

For several seconds, the only movement came from the shivering branches and thrashing leaves. Then he said, "I watched the backups. The ones you deleted."

The wind moaned, a sound that seemed to rise from Olivia's own throat.

It was her turn for shock. "You knew, but you didn't save her?"

"You didn't either, Liv." That fake kindness was back. How dare he.

"I didn't know who she was then."

"That shouldn't have made a difference."

An unexpected calmness settled within her, a pause in a gathering storm. He was right. About that, anyway. "I'll meet you and Thea at the creek. Don't forget Goose."

Richard kicked the hose aside and turned off the water. "Liv, we need to—"

But Olivia shut him out. There was no *we* anymore, and she was done listening to what he wanted from her. She trusted him to take care of Thea—he'd always been a good father, at least. Because Olivia was the only one who could still save Ellie.

She started running and didn't look back, even when Richard called for her to stop, to listen. Even when he shouted, "She's gone."

But maybe that wasn't what he'd shouted after her at all. The howl of the wind and the distance between them swallowed whatever apology he'd intended to make.

For a moment, Olivia wondered whether, if she'd stolen one last glance at Richard, he would have appeared surprised that, finally, she'd left. She'd always stayed before, even when he'd had his affairs. Even when he'd looked on her with pity because she grieved too slowly. Why wouldn't Richard believe she'd stay and listen to him now?

Olivia ran toward the forest, toward the spot where Dominic had nearly died. Toward the abandoned cabin where it might already be too late for her granddaughter.

CHAPTER 47

LEYNA

Saturday, 3:15 p.m.

As soon as Grace was seated in the car, Leyna reached into her pants pocket. Her hand coiled around metal warmed from being held near her skin. She offered the bracelet to her sister, whose eyes welled as she took it.

"For luck," Leyna said.

Then she laid on the gas. When they approached the highway, the acrid scent of smoke grew stronger, and she could see it now—a gray haze pushing against the car, trying to get in. While the speedometer ticked upward, she closed the windows and vents, but the odor had already seeped into the upholstery.

"She'll be there, right?" Grace's voice shook, the desperation as thick as the air around them.

Leyna nodded but didn't dare answer, afraid her sister might hear her doubt. Grace's search had been thorough, but she remained as convinced as Leyna that Ellie had returned to the neighborhood. Where else would

Ellie go? Rocky had been right. Eventually, Ridgepoint Ranch drew them all back.

"I've already checked the clubhouse. Twice."

Leyna had run through all the possibilities in her head. Then she'd remembered the blueprints. It had seemed obvious in the moment, but if she was wrong...

She couldn't allow the horror of that thought to take root.

As Leyna drove, she caught Grace stealing glances at her arm. They both held back their apologies. Ellie first, then they'd have time to talk. But still, having her sister that close, Leyna felt her scar burn with memory.

After her sister had shoved her into the ravine, Leyna tested her feet and arms—nothing broken, nothing sprained. She clenched against her unrelenting bladder. She needed to get out of there.

Above her, she heard the scrape of footsteps. Then a deep chuckle. When she glanced up, Adam and Grace stared down at her. Adam carried a bow over his shoulder, and at his hip was a quiver with several arrows. Grace, looking surprised, had been wearing her blue blouse.

"I only meant—" Grace glanced at Adam and her face hardened. She put a hand on his arm. "Let's get out of here."

Adam shook off her hand, squatted, and stared at Leyna with eyes that made it clear he didn't intend to help her. The look alone nearly made her wet herself.

"I heard you told your mom about our little shopping trip." His voice echoed off the sides of packed earth. "Why would you do that?"

He sounded hurt more than angry, but his expression betrayed him. Leyna scurried away from them. Standing on tiptoes, she tried to reach the ground above her, but the crevasse seemed nearly bottomless. Where she reached, the dirt was loose, the leaves slippery.

"We're friends." He seemed irritated that she hadn't immediately apologized. "Your sister and I let you come with us to that market, and you snitched."

She looked up to find that Adam had tracked her. She hadn't snitched.

Not really. But when their mom found the stolen snacks and beer in Grace's room, Leyna had laid the blame where it belonged—on Adam.

Leyna leaned against the dirt wall, the crack of sunlight above her seeming to retreat the longer she stared into it. She scratched at the dirt, the flesh beneath her nails instantly raw. The urge to pee grew more insistent.

Adam shrugged his bow from his shoulder. He wasn't really going to *shoot* her, was he? And Grace wasn't going to *let* him?

Leyna blinked to clear the panic and studied her prison with fresh eyes. There. A spot where the roots of a sugar pine jutted from the earthen wall like broken fingers.

"Not cool, Leyna."

She sidestepped toward the clump of roots. If she could climb it, she would be on the opposite side of the ravine, and she could run, but would the roots hold? The pine's trunk remained brown, and needles clung to its branches. But it might be infested with beetles or weakened by fungus.

She forced a breath, grasped the roots, and pulled herself upward, trying to clamber up the compacted earth.

The roots slipped in her hand. She held tighter. Pulled harder. Planted her feet more firmly against the earthen wall.

She fell to the ground. At least on her feet this time. She realized it didn't matter what she did. With his long legs, Adam would have no problem making the jump across the ravine.

Adam chuckled, but he looked irritated by her attempts to get away. The snake watching the helpless hamster in the maze.

"Stop it, Adam," Grace said. "You're acting just like your mom."

If he was offended by the comment, Leyna couldn't tell. He pulled out an arrow and touched the tip.

"I was looking to shoot some rabbits or squirrels, so these are blunt tips." He nocked the arrow on his bowstring. "Don't get me wrong. It'll still sting like a bitch."

Grace grabbed his arm. "I said stop."

Whether it was the jolt of Grace's touch or his own intention, the arrow found its mark so quickly, it took a second for Leyna to realize it had grazed her arm. Her bladder released as the blood welled.

Adam instantly feigned concern—a performance for Grace, but Leyna wasn't fooled. Especially when he smiled at the wet spot that bloomed on her pants.

After he and Grace helped her from the ravine, he'd pulled her close; Leyna gagged on the rotting-fruit scent of his body spray and her own urine. He'd whispered, too quietly for Grace to hear, "The next one goes in your fucking eye, snitch."

When Grace came in to change her shirt, before Leyna had locked her out, her sister insisted that Adam's hand had slipped on the string because she'd touched his arm. He'd shot the arrow without intending to. When Leyna told her what he'd said, Grace said he must've been joking and accused her of exaggerating. "It's those books you read, Ley."

Even at twelve, Leyna recognized her sister didn't believe what she herself had said.

It hadn't been such a bad cut, really. If Leyna had cleaned it, it probably wouldn't have scarred. But part of her thought she deserved that reminder of Adam etched into her skin after leaving Grace out in the cold.

The bleating of the fasten-seat-belt warning snapped Leyna back to the driver's seat of the car. She ignored it; the thought of being pinned to her seat raised bile in Leyna's throat. Ash fluttered. Here, the hellish blizzard, lit by sparks, grew so thick that the road blurred. She squinted at a thickening layer of ash coating the windshield.

Leyna flipped the wiper switch, and the blades smeared ash across the glass. She felt the *bump-bump-bump* of the car as it veered onto gravel. She slowed down and cracked open the window, coughed on a blast of smoke. She forced herself to take smaller breaths.

Stretching her neck out the window, she found the road again. Leaves skittered across the asphalt, their edges glowing. The smoke and shallow breathing left her lightheaded. She blinked rapidly to clear smoke from her eyes.

On the hillside to their left, the flames she'd first believed were imaginary rippled. It was hotter here too, and panic seized her. Any closer to the highway and her car would catch fire.

"We just passed the service road. It'll save a few minutes." Grace, who had always spoken confidently about everything, didn't sound confident about that. Her voice wavered.

Leyna backtracked and, a quarter mile up the road, she slowed beside the old maintenance building, enclosed by wire fencing. The posted sign warned against trespassing. On the other side of the road, an old Chevy rusted not far from a pile of dumped junk, including a sofa and a dining-room set with three broken chairs. They'd been there long enough to mold and stain. Leyna knew they'd be gone by nightfall.

Grace pointed. "I already checked," she said. "Once we have her, we could snip the fence, or drive through it..."

Her voice trailed off as they both scanned the perimeter for an opening. The squat building blocked a small field that might've provided egress, the back of the property ringed by trees and heavy equipment. Leyna clutched the wheel and blinked against the gathering smoke.

No way out here either. At least not by car. And if they attempted it on foot, they would be dead.

That understanding sparked between them even as Leyna tried to reassure Grace. "The fire might not make it here."

"I'm not an idiot, Leyna," she said. "Drive."

Abruptly, the car slowed, the engine overheating because of the smoke and decreased oxygen intake. Then it stalled, two blocks from the clubhouse.

CHAPTER 48

OLIVIA

Saturday, 3:25 p.m.

The thinning trail felt familiar, but in the dense smoke, everything looked different. She started left, then froze. That was wrong.

She scanned the trees for a landmark to guide her. To the right, the trail disappeared into a stand of pines.

This is near where Dominic was hurt.

Olivia started running, her eyes laser-focused on the path, searching for trip wires or tree roots that might make her stumble. When her breathing grew labored, she slowed and broke into a fit of phlegmy coughing.

The fire might cost her everything after all, and it would be her own damn fault.

She felt the pull of the cabin even thought the forest around her was shrouded in a thick haze. She began moving again but almost immediately froze mid-step, right foot on tiptoe, irrationally afraid that placing her foot flat on the ground would trigger another trap or shatter the illusion. Was it an illusion? In the hellscape of the approaching fire, the cabin that stood in this remote corner of the forest was closer than she'd thought. Thankfully not yet destroyed by fire.

She moved ahead slowly, eager to open the door but also aware that someone had once planted a trap a quarter mile back to protect this property. What deadly relics might be waiting this close to the cabin?

Olivia thought—*hoped*—she heard a scuffling sound from inside and she forgot to breathe for several seconds. The trees around her were awash in apocalyptic light. It formed a spotlight on the door, and dread unspooled inside her. The lock next to the handle was overkill for this old and rotting structure, and in her haste, she'd forgotten the key.

Olivia looked around for something to pound the door with but quickly gave up and started kicking. The rotting wood began to splinter. The planks fell away, chunk by chunk, until the inside of the cabin stood exposed. Olivia could hear the fire now, behind her. How close?

Some of the light sliced into the darkness of the living space, enough so that Olivia's heart squeezed. She checked the bathroom with its chipped sink and water-stained toilet, and the bedroom, bare except for the wagon spotted with Ellie's blood.

The cabin was empty.

Shocked, Olivia stumbled backward, away from the cabin. Her eyes darted around, searching for Ellie but also for a way out. The world surrounding her blazed.

The fire made the choice for her. There was only one path not overtaken by flames.

As Olivia ran, her nose clogged with woodsmoke and ash, her lungs too, and she prayed the cabin had been empty because Ellie escaped. She took comfort in that—Olivia might die, but maybe her granddaughter had made it out. She held to that hope as tightly as her mother once clung to her worry beads.

CHAPTER 49
LEYNA

Saturday, 3:36 p.m.

The original ranch house had been torn down for the clubhouse and golf course. Grace once told her how Rocky had maintained the greens those first few years, waiting in vain for an end to his financial struggles, until he'd finally been forced to sell his riding reel mower. But in Leyna's memory, the fairway had always been as it was now—prickly weeds and dead grass, the cart paths cracked as nature worked to reclaim them. The concrete was strong, but nature was patient. Leyna had long grasped for meaning in that—if she kept pushing, answers would eventually come—but most days she'd felt more like the busted-up concrete.

A chunk of fence was missing and other sections listed, one good kick away from toppling. The fence shuddered in the wind, and Leyna wondered if that was what would finally take it down or if it would wait for the flames.

If they couldn't make the creek, the golf course might work. A wide-open space and breaks in the tree canopy. There was the pool, too, now an empty basin. A basin constructed of inflammable concrete.

The clubhouse, with its simple gable roof and timber details, had been abandoned halfway through construction. Leyna had expected to find it decaying like everything else, but the wood had been stained in the past few years. She even detected the hum of a generator out back.

Leyna froze and cast a quick look at her sister. Why would a place like this need a generator?

The glass door was locked, but one large pane remained empty, even after all those years. On a dare from Adam, Grace had shattered it with a hammer, and the four of them had used the space as their clubhouse. Plastic sheeting had been stapled to the window frame and a plywood sheet secured over the doorway with screws. Both easy to remove.

The building had originally been intended to include a restaurant and pro shop, but as Grace and Leyna hastily moved through it, they couldn't tell one space from another. Concrete stretched in every direction, bordered by walls of exposed two-by-sixes.

Deeper in the clubhouse, the construction had been further along. Drywall was marked by graffiti and holes at the height of fists and feet. Though it looked like Rocky had tried to maintain the clubhouse's facade, less effort had been made inside. Despite the attempt to secure the doorway, small animals had found their way in, piles of pellets and scat left behind.

At the room that might've been intended as the pro shop—it was small and closest to the greens—they found their first door. The knob turned freely. In the half-finished building, any attempt at security would've been pointless.

Grace insisted on entering first, and she immediately cursed in frustration. But Leyna moved toward a stack of wood piled in the corner. Unlike the planks elsewhere, these were newer. Not yet rotted.

According to Rocky's blueprints, that was where the entrance to the old wine cellar would've been. Where a basement for storage had been planned for the clubhouse.

Leyna pushed the planks aside, and Grace was instantly beside her, yanking open the door that the stacked wood had been hiding. Grace pulled out a flashlight and started down the stairs.

Leyna's first clue was the stiffening of her sister's back, then the moan that came from deep in her throat. Leyna didn't want to see what had caused her sister to make such a horrible sound, but she couldn't allow herself to look away.

In the beam of Grace's flashlight, Ellie lay on the floor, wrists and ankles bound with tape, a strip of it covering her mouth. Her shorts were torn and her tank top stained, her hoodie a lump on the ground next to an old, soiled pillow. She was chained to the wall, but the way she winced when she heard their footsteps suggested that the threats and infliction of pain she'd suffered would've been enough to keep her there.

The churn of emotions—joy, revulsion, pity, anger—nearly knocked Leyna off her feet.

Grace's face went ashen as Ellie squinted at their sudden appearance.

"My God..." Her sister swallowed a sob.

When Grace dropped beside her daughter, Ellie curled into herself, a wounded animal bracing for another kick. Grace's eyes flashed and she cupped Ellie's cheek. She made small circles on her daughter's skin with her thumb, then pulled out the bracelet—a simple cuff of gold that had helped lead them there. "I'll always find you, Ellie Bean," she said, her gaze landing for a moment on Leyna. "*We'll* always find you."

Through her nose, the girl's inhalations were desperate whistles. Mucus or swollen nasal passages made it hard for her to breathe. Her chest jerked, each rise and fall growing more desperate as she struggled for air. The spark in Grace's eyes became an inferno.

Leyna pulled the tape from Ellie's mouth. The girl's eyes widened as she filled her lungs with smoky air. Leyna tugged at the tape that bound her limbs, but it was too strong. Grace handed Leyna her flashlight and gingerly slipped the bracelet in her daughter's pocket. Then Grace began yanking at the chain that secured Ellie to the wall, but the wood here was solid, and the anchoring deep.

CHAPTER 50
MEREDITH

Saturday, 3:36 p.m.

As Meredith threw the emergency radio and pallet of water in the BMW, a familiar wheezing drew her attention to the ground. When she glanced down, she saw the Durans' dog lumbering toward her. Reflexively, she bristled—he'd better not be headed to take a crap in her garden again—but weariness quickly replaced her outrage. Her garden was unlikely to last the hour.

Have at it, Goose.

A few seconds later, the child appeared. She stared at Meredith, anxious but also with obvious expectation. What could the girl possibly want with her? And what was she supposed to do about the dog?

Thea glanced over her shoulder several times, then stopped a few feet away. "Can we come with you?"

Meredith recoiled in surprise. Of course the girl couldn't go with her. Meredith needed to get to her own family. She didn't have time to babysit this child and her dog.

She studied Thea's face more closely and realized she'd misread her expression. It wasn't anxiety but fear. Maybe even terror.

Meredith scowled. "Where are your parents?"

Thea shrugged but averted her gaze.

Meredith looked toward the Duran house. She shouted for Olivia, then for Richard, but she didn't know where either of them had gone. She'd been too distracted by Grace, by the fact that her elder daughter was alive.

And that, apparently, Meredith had a granddaughter.

The first few years, Meredith had waited for Grace to reach out, reasoning she would eventually need money or she'd want to talk to her sister. Meredith had looked for Grace at Leyna's first few birthdays, her graduation, all the major holidays. And instead, she'd shown up in the middle of a wildfire, so angry that she'd destroyed the portrait Meredith had painted.

Seeing Grace again, Meredith suddenly understood why she'd been unable to finish the latest portrait of her daughter. She'd gotten it all wrong. The eyes she'd believed she'd perfected weren't the right shade of blue at all. They were colder now. Muted. The portrait also lacked the faint lines etched near Grace's lips and the skin grown ashen. On the canvas, her hair held a deeper luster too.

The portrait hadn't done her daughter justice.

Meredith recognized that age alone wasn't to blame for all the changes in Grace—the loss of Ellie marked her as surely as it had Meredith when it had been Grace who disappeared. But unlike Meredith, Grace didn't hide behind a carefully constructed mask or erect posture. The intensity of her daughter's loss blazed—more fury than grief—and even Meredith had struggled to hold eye contact.

She'd felt a flash of pride—*How strong she is now. How strong she's always been*. But Meredith quickly recognized that it wasn't her victory to claim. By protecting Grace, had she also failed her? The idea caused Meredith unexpected discomfort. She rarely failed at anything.

She turned that truth over in her head—she'd failed her daughter. Both of her daughters, actually. Her heart seized, and yet—Grace was safe. Not okay—she wouldn't fool herself about that—but safe. For the moment, at least. That knowledge was a salve, and motivation. Her daughters didn't want her to follow them. Fuck them. Since when had she ever let someone tell her what to do?

But there was the small problem of the Duran girl.

"Let's find your parents."

Meredith started marching in the direction of the Durans' house. She squinted against the smoke, and this time she caught sight of Richard, his back to her, moving quickly toward the Kims' house.

"I know you hate my family," Thea said.

"I don't hate your family."

"It's okay. They hate you too." Thea moved away from Meredith and out of her father's line of sight. "I don't, though. I think you're okay. And Leyna's going to teach me how to pick a lock."

Meredith considered calling after Richard, but the girl's expression made her hesitate. Thea seemed afraid of her father. Which made no sense. While Olivia had always been tightly wound, even Meredith could admit that Richard wasn't a half-bad father. A moron, yes—he would've had to be to stay married to Olivia—but he had seemed more weak than frightening.

Down the street, Richard stopped. Though he was too far to hear Thea, the girl whispered, frantic, "Tell him I went with Rocky. Please."

Meredith was about to say she would *not* be doing that when the girl streaked toward the trees. She lingered at the edge of the forest, watching.

Meredith exhaled sharply, coughing, and advanced in the direction Thea had fled.

"Come back!" she shouted. "You're going to get yourself killed."

The girl's not my problem, she thought.

Goose battered Meredith's ankle. How the hell had she gotten stuck with the damn dog?

Though it was midday, in places where the smoke and trees were densest, it could've passed for midnight. Meredith watched as Thea slipped deeper into the trees. If not for her lavender T-shirt and the flash of her calves as she ran, she would've been absorbed by that darkness instantly. Soon, even her pale shirt and skin wouldn't give her away.

Richard turned then. His movements were hurried, as agitated as Thea's had been, likely looking for his daughter. When Thea spotted him, she faded into the trees, invisible now.

Meredith took several steps forward, blocking the dog from view, as Richard advanced. He stopped at the edge of her property. "Were you shouting for me?"

"Thea—" She hesitated. Why the hell did she hesitate? Thea should go with her father. But when Meredith raised her hand to point to the woods, she remembered Thea's wide eyes and the way her chin had trembled, and she dropped it. "I wanted to tell you that I saw Thea climb in Rocky's truck earlier. Probably wanted to be with that damn brother of hers. I figured I should say something, in case you missed it." It wasn't hard to slip the hint of judgment in her voice.

"You're sure?"

"I'm sure."

"Which direction?"

She pointed forward, toward the road Rocky had taken and in the opposite direction of where Thea hid among the trees.

Richard nodded, relieved, but didn't move. His face grew suddenly weary, his sadness as palpable as the heat, and she could tell in that instant that he knew about Adam.

A second later, he confirmed it. "I know what your daughter did," he said, voice cracking. "When my family's safe—when we're all out of here—Adam needs to come home."

Visibly broken, Richard loped toward his Audi. Would his grief turn to rage when he discovered she'd also lied to him about Thea being somewhere safe with Rocky?

After Richard left, Meredith picked up the dog and went after Thea. She found the girl in a stand of trees sitting on a pile of needles with her back against the trunk of a dead juniper.

Perfect kindling.

She set down the dog. "We need to get out of here," Meredith said impatiently, even as she thought: *And go where?* The roads were blocked, and they wouldn't make it far. Even the creek that had been her original plan seemed impossibly distant.

A warning she'd often heard echoed in her head: *In a wildfire, if you're near timber, you're dead.* Any place would be safer than where they were, surrounded by trees and dry brush.

The girl peered up at her, the fear Meredith remembered widening her eyes. She wasn't moving, though, so whatever frightened her, it wasn't the fire.

"Why'd you come?" Thea asked.

Because apparently I'm just as much of a moron as your father.

"My dad's gone, right?" Thea's voice was faraway. Meredith didn't like how it sounded. At Meredith's nod, the girl relaxed. "Thanks for lying for me."

What a fantastic example I'm setting.

Meredith tugged gently on the girl's arm. "If we stay here much longer, we're going to burn to death," she said. "Then how will my daughter teach you how to pick a damn lock?"

Thea stood, but she hesitated. "We have cameras in the house," she said. "Rocky helped my dad put them in, but he doesn't think it's healthy. I've heard him fighting about it with my dad." Her voice dipped; she was obviously bothered by something but taking the scenic route to telling Meredith what that something was.

We don't have time for this. "Thea, we have to—"

"Rocky says my dad's using Adam as an excuse to control my mom, but it was her idea." Her eyes went soft again, and Meredith debated whether she could carry the girl. How much did she weigh? She supposed she could manage it without the dog.

"My mom says she needs to keep me safe so what happened to my brother doesn't happen to me."

The girl's expression made Meredith shiver despite the heat. "Is that why you're hiding from your dad—because you're mad about the cameras?"

Thea shook her head.

"Then why?"

"Because I think he did a really bad thing," she said. "The deputy asked about cameras, but my dad only gave her the video from the ones facing the street. He didn't mention the others." She paused and started petting Goose, the strokes growing increasingly urgent. "I think he lied because he hurt that girl. The one who's missing."

For a moment, Meredith forgot about the fire. "Why do you say that?"

"I was playing in the woods even though my dad told me not to and—I saw him with a body." Thea's lip trembled, but her chin jutted out, as if she were daring Meredith to doubt her story. "I was pretty far away, but it had to be him."

Meredith's mouth tasted of ash, but she was sure that ash wasn't the cause. "Why would you think that?"

"Because he's strong," she said. "And my dad and Rocky are the only ones with a key to the cabin."

CHAPTER 51

LEYNA

Saturday, 3:45 p.m.

In the beam of the flashlight, Grace tugged on the chain lock before turning to Leyna. "Do you have something I can pick this with?"

Leyna considered the flashlight but then shook her head. "In the car, maybe." She definitely had a ballpoint pen and some bobby pins in the glove box. "I'm not sure what Mom brought besides the wine, the paintings, and her Taser, but I can check her bag too."

Leyna stood, assuming Grace would want to stay with her daughter, but Grace shook her head. "I'm faster."

Behind her, Leyna heard footsteps, and she turned the flashlight in that direction. Richard had stopped halfway down the stairs. He brought up his arm to block the light, and with his free hand flipped a switch on the wall. Fluorescent light flickered overhead.

"I heard voices and thought you might be Olivia," he said. "She ran off, and I've been looking for her but—she's not anywhere."

His voice broke on the last few words. When Leyna lowered the flashlight, he caught sight of Ellie for the first time. He stilled, face going pale.

"My God. Is that—" His voice trembled. "I have a first aid kit in the car. It stalled a couple of blocks up, halfway between here and the house, but it's not too far." He made a move to leave, but Leyna shook her head.

"It's okay, Grace can grab it. Stay." Leyna looked at her sister. "Check Mom's stuff. There's got to be something there that can help us."

She didn't add: *Run.* They didn't have much time—minutes, maybe—but her sister would know that. Grace had to be asking herself the same question: How had Richard, temporarily blinded, known about that switch?

Leyna shot a glance at Richard as Grace brushed past. He remained on the stairs, frozen at the midpoint, as if undecided which direction he should go. He screwed his eyes closed and breathed deeply. When he opened his eyes again, they welled with sorrow, and Leyna noticed the shadows beneath them. But there was no surprise in his expression, and Leyna knew—Richard had played a part in the violence against his granddaughter. Leyna tried to keep the horror from her face, but she could tell she failed.

Richard backed up a step. "I've got more water in my car."

Unless he had tankers full of it, water wasn't their most pressing need. She was torn between wanting him to leave and wanting him to pay.

"No. Stay." Her tone icy.

He backed up another step. "I really need to get going. Look for Olivia. She's out there somewhere..."

Leyna shifted so she faced the doorway and could keep an eye on him. She scanned the ground for some forgotten tool that might help. Near an old roll of insulation, she spotted a rat carcass. Only that.

On the floor, Ellie whimpered and scooted away from Leyna.

She fought for the words that might reassure the girl, but what could she say—*You'll be okay*? That promise wasn't one Leyna could make. A bruise mottled the girl's skin at the side of her face, near where blood matted her hair. Leyna saw that at least there were a few empty bottles of water nearby. Not nearly enough. In that heat, it wouldn't have taken long for her to get dangerously dehydrated.

Leyna switched the flashlight from her right hand to her left as she tested the duct tape that bound the girl. The girl's whimpering became a keening.

"Almost there," she said.

She had just managed a small tear in the tape binding her ankles when she heard movement on the stairs. She glanced over her shoulder at Richard, who'd retreated several more steps.

"I'm sorry," he said.

The tear in the tape must've been larger than Leyna initially thought, because Ellie's frantic scrambling toward the corner ripped it the rest of the way.

Ellie wasn't trying to get away from Leyna. She was terrified of Richard.

Leyna positioned herself between the girl and him. In the moment, she was grateful that she hadn't promised Ellie she'd be okay. She understood now that they weren't getting out of there, not without Grace.

"You would do anything for your sister, right?" Richard's gaze was beseeching. "Think of what you've sacrificed for her. Your life..."

His voice trailed off when he realized his words weren't gaining traction. It had been Leyna's sacrifice to make, and she'd been the only casualty of her single-minded pursuit.

But maybe that wasn't right. She'd hurt others too, including the man standing in front of her now. Still, she had no sympathy for Richard and no patience for his excuses.

He slumped under the weight of—what? Guilt? Regret that he'd been found out? Or anguish over what he felt forced to do next?

"What you'd do for your sister, I'd do for my wife." He had the tone of a zealot, willing Leyna to believe. "That's what I vowed—to make all of it all right for her, always." His voice swelled on a surge of whatever emotion darkened his face. He looked at Ellie. "I didn't know. Who you were. But even if I had—"

He didn't need to finish the sentence. Leyna understood. If given the chance, to protect Olivia, he would do it again.

"I found her, and I brought her here. Gave her water." He gestured toward the pillow. "Tried to make her comfortable."

"She would've been more comfortable if she'd been at home in her own bed."

His sigh was filled with anguish. "Drop the flashlight, Leyna. It's useless anyway."

She clutched the flashlight, feeling the weight of it against her palm. Richard took another step, approaching now, and when she dropped the flashlight and kicked it away, his eyes tracked where it landed.

See, Richard, not useless after all.

The staircase creaked again, and Richard stiffened, but her distraction gave Grace the seconds she needed to return with the item she'd retrieved from the car—the Taser in their mom's locked box, the one she'd left in the car along with her bottle of wine and portraits of them. The box had been solid. Hard to break quickly. But the lock would've been easy for her sister to pick.

"I didn't do this," he said.

Leyna thought he might be telling the truth, but they couldn't take that chance—especially since he'd admitted to dumping her there with a dirty pillow and a dead rat as her only company. No matter his claims of altruism, nothing he'd given her would've protected her against a wildfire.

At Leyna's nod, Grace pulled the Taser's trigger; the barbs embedded just above his groin, and he tumbled down the last few stairs.

CHAPTER 52

MEREDITH

Saturday, 3:48 p.m.

The fire had reached the forest behind them. Meredith had no plan, but she pulled Thea along, the dog at their heels, deeper into the forest because that was now the only path left to them.

In their haste, Thea stumbled, and Meredith's own foot caught the same fir tree root. Her body slammed against the trunk. She traced her fingertips along the bark.

Meredith looked around and realized that they'd run farther than she'd believed. She flashed to Leyna's story about falling into the ravine the day Grace disappeared. Leyna had pointed out the ravine once. Wasn't it near here? Lightheaded, Meredith struggled to remember its location and how deep Leyna had said it was, but Meredith's memory was muddled by exhaustion and, dangerously, smoke. Plus she'd never paid close enough attention to what her daughters told her.

Meredith made a fist around the imagined roots of the sugar pine Leyna had described, nearly feeling the bite against her palm. If the tree was still there and healthy—if its roots were still exposed—they could climb down into the embankment that way.

She couldn't help worrying, though, that the tree would be dead like so many others, its roots decaying and ready to snap, like a secret carried too long.

Other concerns pressed too. Was the sugar pine surrounded by grass that would burn quickly or by dead trees that would soon become torches? Would the ravine be littered with the large cones of the pine, tacky with flammable sap?

Would they even make it that far?

She shook her head in an attempt to clear her thoughts. She couldn't risk a bad choice. It would doom them both. But even more dangerous would be making no choice at all. Unless she left Thea behind, she couldn't outrun the fire. There was no creek, lake, or pool near enough. No roads or meadows with their hidden reserves of groundwater. Their only shot was the ravine and the hope that the wildfire would jump it in its hunt for fuel.

Snot dripped from her nose. Her skin felt both scorched and sticky.

She spotted the sugar pine first. Then the ravine appeared, as wide as she'd hoped. She prayed it was as deep too. Meredith risked a quick glance over her shoulder, relieved that they would likely beat the flames.

Meredith pushed Thea toward the ravine, less than twenty feet away now. The dog dropped to the ground, refusing to go any farther.

To Thea, Meredith said, breathless, "Go," and she knelt to pick up the dog. He seemed heavier than he had before, and her back ached. When Thea separated from Meredith, she fell to the ground. Meredith picked her up too.

We'll make it, Meredith thought. *We have to make it.*

Heat on her back near blistering, dog clutched to her chest, Meredith pulled Thea to the edge of the ravine, even deeper than Leyna had described.

The sugar pine was on the wrong side.

Holding the dog and Thea's hand, Meredith thought of her own daughters. Whatever happened here, Leyna and Grace had each other, at least.

Meredith nudged the girl, and they both jumped into the ravine.

CHAPTER 53

LEYNA

Saturday, 3:53 p.m.

Grace hadn't needed to pick the lock to free her daughter from the chain. She found the key in Richard's pocket right after she hit him with the Taser a second time.

Leyna sent Grace and Ellie ahead to the creek, Grace supporting Ellie's weight as the pair stumbled across the golf course toward rougher terrain. She intended to go back to the neighborhood, make sure their mom had gotten out. Now that Ellie had been found, she couldn't leave—

Leyna froze as the road came into view. The flames licked the sky, nearly at the car Grace had visited minutes before, now covered in ash. The fire howled a warning: *I'm coming for you.* But she knew it wasn't actually capable of malice. It wanted the branches, the grass, the leaves. That it would consume her too, leaving her bones on that road if given a chance, would be only a consequence of its hunger.

There would be no returning to Ridgepoint Ranch for any of them.

Heart and lungs near exploding, Leyna raced to catch up with her sister and niece. The fire crashed toward them. The smaller pines swayed as if they too were trying to escape. Through eyes stinging with smoke, Leyna scanned the tree line marching toward the sky to her left and right. In front of them too. Behind them, the ground sloped downward, toward the fire and the clubhouse where a temporarily incapacitated Richard might already be stumbling up the stairs.

She and Grace bore Ellie's weight between them and accommodated her bound wrists, and she thought of Dominic and how she and Richard had carried him between them in much the same way.

But she had no time for mourning or regret. That would come later. In that moment, the three of them existed in that most dangerous of places—uphill and downwind—and her niece was weak. Dragging her feet, she stumbled often, and each time Leyna kept her from falling, her back strained with the effort. Still, they had no choice but to climb, even knowing the fire would sprint up the hill many times faster than they could.

Winded, they stopped halfway up the hill, leaning against each other and a large pine, needles dancing far overhead.

She took a breath and she and Grace urged Ellie forward again. They banked a hard right, dodged a manzanita, then began scaling a hillside slippery with fallen leaves and loose dirt, their steps growing sluggish. In one spot, the trees grew so dense they were forced to turn sideways to squeeze through the opening, and even then, Leyna held her breath to allow extra clearance. Ellie and Grace slipped through easily. Bark scraped Leyna's stomach, and her lungs burned when she finally exhaled.

Wheezing, the collar of her shirt soaked with sweat, Leyna kept climbing.

Remembering the wolves, she pulled Ellie toward the burn scar of a past blaze, calculating its distance, even as it dawned on her that they would not make it. Hermann Creek was their only option. How far? A couple of minutes? They had that much time. She hoped.

But a second, more important question mocked. How deep? What if they spent their final minutes stumbling toward a creek that had gone dry? And even if water still ran, it might not be enough to protect them.

It might be just enough to give an illusion of safety in the moments before they boiled in it.

"Stop." Her chest heaved as she halted behind a boulder to catch her breath. She listened, then started moving again. As they ran, her lungs burned, and her share of Ellie's weight grew heavier. How much farther could the girl go before she collapsed? She had a head injury and likely hadn't eaten in days.

If they had any chance of surviving, they needed to remain upright. She hitched Ellie's arm higher up on her shoulder and she and Grace pulled her forward up the hillside.

Flames swallowed the timber. Flecks of burning grass churned around them. The sky grew livid. Reflex forced a labored breath into her lungs, and she sucked in ash. Her head throbbed, and a wave of dizziness made her sway. She glanced behind at a wall of flames. Her eardrums pulsed as the fire howled.

A crack split the air, loud even over the keening fire. She jumped back, nearly dropping Ellie, her reflexes warning her an instant before the tree fell in front of her. On impact, sparks danced, and the ground vibrated.

Up ahead, a tree flared and exploded. Nearby trees ignited, and it was daylight again, the sky an angry orange.

Behind her, the flames chased.

The heated air seared her lungs, and her heart dropped. They wouldn't make it. Though she'd spent more hours in this forest than nearly anywhere, somehow she'd miscalculated the distance. When it mattered most, her superpower had failed her. She didn't know these woods at all.

But a second later, they crested the small hill, and Leyna pulled her focus away from the girl and toward the creek below.

Too exhausted to talk, she pointed and dropped her head, and the three of them launched themselves down the hill together, toward a creek gone nearly dry in the drought.

CHAPTER 54

OLIVIA

Saturday, 3:59 p.m.

Olivia had been on her way to meet a potential client in Reno on Thursday when her car started to overheat. She'd canceled her meeting, dropped her car off at a shop in Portola, and gotten a ride home.

"You can leave me at the end of the road," she'd told the driver, whose car apparently needed a new muffler; the one he had sounded like a can of pennies being shaken. Later, she wished she'd asked him to take her all the way home, announcing their arrival with his car's rattling.

She'd arrived at the house in silence around two o'clock—several hours earlier than expected. Normally, she would have called out for Thea or Richard, but she'd seen them walking with Goose toward the forest.

When she crossed into the living room, her body registered the intrusion first. The hairs on her arms pricked upright, and she felt a chill at the back of her neck. A heartbeat later, she heard it. Movement in the back of the house.

Someone who was not her husband or daughter was in the master bedroom.

Her heart raced as it conjured a familiar wish: Had Adam come home?

But her son would've greeted her outside the house or in the living room, loud and happy, and Thea and Richard wouldn't have left him here alone to take the dog for a walk.

Rocky fixing the loose tile in the master bathroom? Dominic home two days early? But no, there was something stealthy in the movements, as if whoever made them wasn't supposed to be here.

Phone in hand, Olivia punched in 911, though she waited to hit Send. She pushed open the door, startling the young woman who stood there holding one of Richard's T-shirts.

Ellie Byrd. Her granddaughter, she knew now. But on Thursday afternoon, she'd seen only an anonymous young woman in her bedroom, comfortably helping herself to her husband's clothing while Olivia was supposed to be an hour away in Reno.

Olivia clutched her phone, still deciding. Call 911? But at the time, the young woman didn't seem a threat to her. Only to her marriage.

She hit Cancel and stowed her phone. "Who are you?"

The young woman she now knew was Ellie Byrd balled up Richard's shirt.

"I'm waiting for Richard."

"Why?"

"Because he asked me to."

After viewing all those videos, Olivia now suspected that Ellie had lied—that Richard didn't know she was in their home, much less their bedroom. Olivia was sure no one even knew Ellie had returned to the neighborhood a couple of hours after her initial visit. She was also sure Ellie had planned it that way. In her walk up the road, Olivia hadn't seen the girl's borrowed car.

But that afternoon, Ellie had seemed so sure of herself that Olivia had thought *of course* her husband would be attracted to a young woman so pretty and so much less tentative than Olivia had become.

"Please leave," she'd said. Even then being polite.

Ellie had lifted her chin, defiant. "Not until I see Richard."

Olivia now recognized that Ellie was angry that day. When Ellie had come to their door, Richard had lied to her, claimed not to recognize Adam or Dominic. He'd thought she was another podcaster or another true-crime junkie.

So Ellie had come back and walked in through the unlocked door.

Olivia didn't know any of that then. She only saw Ellie kneading Richard's shirt, something possessive in the gesture. Until she'd learned Ellie was her granddaughter, Olivia was certain *that* was why Ellie Byrd was at their house—to hook up with Richard.

The photo she'd been showing around made no sense until Olivia decided that it was likely only a story Ellie had told the Silvestris, a reason for her to be spotted in the neighborhood. A reason other than sleeping with her older, married boyfriend.

Olivia grabbed the shirt that Ellie held, but the girl wouldn't let it go. Angry, Olivia released the shirt suddenly. Ellie slipped and hit her head on the nightstand. An accident.

But when she watched the struggle later on video, Olivia was shocked by the rage she'd worn on her face. Shocked, too, when she saw the small shove she'd given as she'd released the shirt. She hadn't realized she'd done that. When Ellie fell, Olivia noticed that Ellie held on to the shirt so tightly because it had snagged on her bracelet.

Ellie was small, only about thirty pounds heavier than Thea, and a very motivated Olivia had little trouble carrying her to the Millers' empty house, where, according to Dominic, he and Leyna had found the girl's bracelet. It had likely slipped off when she'd tried to escape. Olivia should've been more careful but she was distracted.

Olivia had coaxed sleeping pills down Ellie's throat and wrapped her wrists and ankles in duct tape. She'd hesitated before covering Ellie's mouth.

"I'll be back," she promised the unconscious girl. "When I figure out how to spin this."

Olivia had spent years in corporate communications putting a positive spin on even the worst crises. She could figure this out. She just needed a little time.

She found the car Ellie had been driving and dumped it in a Truckee shopping center. She left the keys in the ignition, tempting potential car thieves. (That went better than expected: piecing together the police reports afterward, she learned that someone not only stole the car but even thought to clear the GPS history.) Then Olivia called an Uber. She arrived home a second time, asking this driver to take her all the way up the road. She wanted people to notice her return.

After the Silvestris left and with the Kims not yet home, she'd sent Richard and Thea into Portola for burrito bowls she promised but neglected to order ahead. Every minute counted.

Olivia used the wagon to move the girl to the cabin and left it in the bedroom. She'd intended to return before too long.

But the next morning, Richard had watched her too closely, and then she'd seen the news. The young woman in her cabin was no longer a stranger sleeping with her husband but a sixteen-year-old girl reported missing.

How was she supposed to spin that?

Looking back, Olivia found it most tragic that when she'd sealed her granddaughter's mouth with duct tape, it wasn't Adam she'd recognized in her face. It was Grace.

Now, dizzy, Olivia squinted toward the horizon. She could just make out the shape of the clubhouse and the golf course beyond, but she'd grown so damn sluggish, and it seemed impossibly far away. The tightness in her chest made only the shallowest of breaths possible. Olivia was fairly sure she wouldn't make it to the fairway, though she didn't know which would take her down, the flames or the smoke.

She kept running, though her gait became more lumber than sprint. Behind her, the fire seethed, close enough she could hear it chewing up the trees. Her eyes burned with its heat and the furnace blast of the wind at her back.

Her most urgent problem: That the wind pushed her forward meant the flames were headed that way too.

Winded, legs numb, Olivia hesitated outside the clubhouse. She thought she heard Richard shouting.

What would Richard be doing here? He and Thea were supposed to be waiting for her at the creek.

Olivia hurried inside. She found the basement room where Ellie had obviously been kept. In the corner, she saw a small camera, and she understood. Ellie hadn't escaped from the cabin. She'd been moved. After Richard had watched the backups, he'd searched for Ellie and brought her here.

Then she saw Richard, curled in a fetal position. He was having trouble breathing, but when he saw her, his face relaxed.

"You're here." He let out a breath, a slight smile coming with it. "You're okay."

She moved closer, stopped a couple of feet from him, looked around. There were bottles of water and a dirty pillow on the floor. He'd tried to make his captive—*her* captive—comfortable, but Olivia was no longer focused on Ellie.

"Where's Thea?"

"She's with Rocky—" He winced as he struggled to a sitting position. "Meredith saw her get in his truck."

Olivia's throat, already raw from the smoke, burned from a surge of bile. "Thea didn't go with Rocky. She was waiting for you in the car." She fought to keep it together. "You were supposed to keep our daughter safe."

Alarm replaced relief on Richard's face, and he struggled to stand, but his legs wouldn't hold him. His gaze darted over her shoulder. He scanned the space as Olivia had a moment earlier, as if expecting to see their daughter in the doorway at the top of the stairs or in the shadows behind her mom.

"Why would Meredith lie about that?"

Olivia laughed harshly. Why *wouldn't* she? She'd lied about their son's death for years.

Richard gestured with his head toward the stairs. "Leyna and Grace have Ellie." Each word seemed to cause him pain. "She's safe."

He said this as if Ellie's freedom had always been part of his plan. As if he'd been waiting for Olivia to find a way to spin what she'd done so he could let her go.

What would happen to Olivia now that he had? Ellie was her granddaughter. Surely the girl could forgive her. It had been an accident. A misunderstanding.

But Olivia didn't care about that. She'd trusted Richard to take care of their daughter, but he'd been so fixated on protecting Olivia that he'd failed to protect the person who mattered most. If he'd just left Ellie where she was in the cabin and taken Thea to the creek as she'd asked, their daughter would be safe. They would all be safe.

Richard managed to stand, legs shaking but holding him. "You go to the creek. Find the others." His breathing grew steadier but still required effort. "I'll go back to the house. Get Thea."

She laughed again, and even she heard the ugliness in it. What was Richard thinking? The others wouldn't welcome her at the creek, not now that they knew about Ellie, and their home had been consumed by flames. Besides, Richard could barely stand. He wouldn't have been able to make it back to Thea even if their world had not been on fire.

Olivia watched him, his balance unsteady, and a thought seized her: Her freedom had always been hers to take. She moved forward, leaned in, and kissed him on the cheek.

Goodbye, Richard.

Her eyes were too dry, too hot, for tears, but the ache in her chest took her by surprise.

When Richard touched her arm tenderly, she pushed him away. Just as she had with Ellie, Olivia shoved harder than she'd intended. He fell backward, expression equal parts hurt and confusion.

Olivia turned and left the clubhouse. On her way out, she thought she heard Richard on the stairs, but she knew he wouldn't make it, and she had no energy left to help him. Outside, she saw that the fire had made it to Ridgepoint Ranch. In that instant, she experienced it all. She felt the hard labor of Dominic's birth. Heard the echo of the empty house the day Adam disappeared. Saw the grave near the edge of the forest, dirt still crusted under her nails from the digging. All the worst-ever pains joined together—swirling, consuming—in the advancing wall of flames.

If Thea was behind that wall, she was gone.

Olivia had been wrong. The worst-ever pain wasn't a single moment but her whole fucking life.

Olivia shuffled toward the center of the golf course, each step a labor. Around her, embers fluttered and dark clouds churned, and the fire's rage had grown deafening, a mirror of her own. Rage made a sturdier handhold than blame.

As near to the center as she could drag herself, she stopped.

Not the fire or the smoke, she decided. *It will be the grief that kills me.*

Olivia released a rattling breath and collapsed onto the fairway.

THE FIRE

The wildfire has created its own weather, the superheated plumes mixing with cooler air, forming fire clouds. These ice-containing clouds can cause thunderstorms and more dry lightning strikes, like the one that had hit the dying pine thirty-six hours before.

It is Sunday morning, but though the sun dawned an hour earlier, the sky remains midnight dark. In the branches, embers glow, but they are fading. A stand of green trees remains untouched next to stumps that smolder on blackened earth. There are on average seven thousand wildfires a year in California. Soon, the McRae Fire will die, and another will ignite somewhere else in the state.

Deeper in this forest, near the abandoned golf course, firefighters will eventually find bones that they will identify as belonging to Ridgepoint Ranch resident Richard Duran.

While tissue and other organic matter burn quickly, the bones and teeth remain intact. Temperatures exceeding two thousand degrees are needed to break down the minerals, and though other spots exceed that, this is the spot where the fire died. It will be assumed that, disoriented by smoke, Richard Duran fell while attempting to follow his wife up the stairs to safety.

Investigators will comfort the victim's family, including his imprisoned widow, with the news that Richard was unconscious when the flames consumed him. *He went quickly,* they'll say. They won't be certain of this, of course, since only the bones remain to tell the story. But they won't want the family to know he might have suffered, especially since he burned not far from the fairway where rescuers found his widow alive. They won't tell her that her husband might have survived had he not followed her up the stairs. Even if she is guilty of other crimes, these half-truths are intended to spare her additional guilt. After all, they think, it's not like there was anything Olivia Duran could've done to prevent her husband's death.

Among themselves, though, they will talk about how horrible it would have been if he was alive when the fire came for him.

CHAPTER 55

LEYNA

Sunday morning

The flames had whined like a jet's engine, the heat so intense Leyna imagined blisters erupting on her skin, but eventually, the fire raced past them. Rescuers found Leyna, Grace, and Ellie in the nearly dry creek, where enough water flowed to allow them to wet their shirts, to cover their mouths. But what had saved them wasn't the water but the brush, too sparse to keep the fire's interest. The flames had flashed across the ground toward the trees on the ridge, leaving behind ash, a scorched field, and the three of them somehow alive. When Ellie was lifted up and wrapped in a fire blanket, she held tightly to her mom's hand, and Grace held to Leyna's just as fiercely.

What the economic crisis and Rocky's poor judgment had started decades before, the wildfire finished. Nothing remained of Ridgepoint Ranch except Adam's bones. Those were still there, buried at the edge of the burn scar. For a while longer, anyway. Leyna doubted Olivia would wait until the land inevitably hit the market and some new developer brought in bulldozers and excavators. She'd waited sixteen years to bury her son properly. She wouldn't wait much longer, especially since she'd been arrested; she'd want to see Meredith punished too, despite how she'd saved Thea. The habit of hating each other was too deeply ingrained.

Everyone but Richard had survived, though with Meredith concealing Adam's death and Olivia kidnapping Ellie, prison looked likely for both of them. Olivia had already talked with Dominic about getting custody of Thea, and the girl had Rocky too. Meredith had volunteered to watch Goose until everyone got settled. *The damn dog needs some stability,* she'd said. Leyna's apartment was going to feel much smaller for a while.

It was Dominic's tibia, the larger of the lower-leg bones, that had been broken. Above the ankle and below the knee, according to the orthopedic surgeon who'd put in the screws that would keep the pieces aligned while he healed. Dom's leg would be immobilized in a cast for a few weeks, but the worst of his injuries couldn't be fixed with screws or fiberglass.

In the dim lighting of the hospital room, Leyna rested her hand on his. He tried to smile, but the pain corrupted it.

"Thanks for saving me." He slurred the words, as if his tongue were wrapped in the same cast as his leg.

"Richard helped."

His face clouded at the mention of his father. "I'm not just talking about the leg."

He looked at her through a haze of painkillers, but Leyna saw herself more clearly. She'd been stuck in her vendetta against Adam. Before she'd left at eighteen, how many times had she walked past his grave, hating him?

"I'm sorry about your dad," she said. "And about Adam."

"I am too." His voice broke, and she could feel him fading.

"I'll be here when you wake up." *I won't screw it up this time.*

"Stalker." Then, his eyes hooded and slipping out of focus, he said, "I think I might love you, Leyna Clarke."

It was probably the painkillers talking, but she leaned in and kissed his forehead.

"I think I might love you too." When she pulled away, he was already asleep. She hoped the medication prevented dreams. Dominic had lost so much, she couldn't imagine that any dreams would offer him comfort.

Or maybe she was wrong. In sleep, the strain of his grief and physical pain faded from his face, and she imagined him lost in a happier time. Adam on that skateboard in the minutes before he fell—beaming, free, *alive*—or the four of them exploring the woods before it all burned.

Leyna found Grace in the hospital cafeteria. The youth center where Dominic worked had dropped off new clothes that morning after they'd both been discharged, and Leyna smiled. She wasn't sure she'd ever seen Grace in a pair of sweatpants.

Grace gestured at a paper cup on the table in front of her. "I was going to order a coffee for you too, but I didn't know how you took it."

Of course she didn't. This version of Grace didn't know this Leyna at all.

"I'm fine," she said.

"How about raspberry tea, then? You used to love that."

Tears pricked her eyes that Grace remembered, but she shook her head.

"Something to eat? They had some cinnamon walnut croissants in the case."

Leyna realized Grace needed to do this, so she nodded. "That would be great. Thanks."

She watched Grace as she moved to the counter and ordered the pastry. When she bent her head to get her card from her purse, Leyna felt a pang at the slope of her neck. She swiped at her eyes and dropped her gaze to the tabletop, studied the speckles in the plastic as intently as if she were reading one of her favorite books.

Back at the table, Grace set two croissants and a cup of tea between them, and the silence grew heavy until Leyna asked, "How's Ellie?"

"Not good—not yet—but she's alive. Thank you." She paused. "How's Dom?"

"He won't be home for at least another couple of days," Leyna said, "but he's improving."

Leyna tore off a piece of the croissant, searching for a way to start the harder part of the conversation. Grace beat her to it.

"I found out I was pregnant at the start of summer break," she said. "I didn't tell anyone, not even Adam. I couldn't. Could you imagine Mom's reaction? Things were always complicated between us, and that"—she shook her head—"Mom wouldn't have understood. Too much shit had happened between us."

You're too much alike, Leyna thought but didn't dare say. She didn't know if Grace and their mom would ever find their way back to each other, but maybe one day they'd recognize what had driven them apart. Leyna dropped the piece of croissant she'd been holding and pushed the pastry away. She wasn't hungry, and she'd spent far too many years feeding her grief.

"It was hard. That year... I couldn't sleep. I was afraid to eat because when I ate I threw up, and what if Mom suspected the reason for that? Besides, I couldn't allow myself to gain weight. Then Mom would *definitely* know. If there was one thing she always noticed, it was when one of us put on a few pounds."

Grace picked at her own croissant, taking a moment to gather her thoughts before resuming her story. Had she practiced it as often as Leyna had practiced her own questions?

"As soon as the weather started to turn, I broke out the layered tops, oversize coats, loose sweaters. Stopped using the bathroom when you or Mom were around. I started wearing more makeup, hats, large earrings. Anything to distract from my stomach." She paused, glancing down. "Until I couldn't. One morning I woke up and it was just"—she made a gesture indicating a baby bump—"there. I know it didn't really happen overnight, but I swear it felt like one day I went from not being able to button my jeans to not being able to *zip* them."

When Dominic had shared the theory, Leyna was certain Grace

couldn't have been pregnant because they'd shared a bathroom, and she'd seen Grace undress in the days leading up to her disappearance. But she'd never noticed how Grace hid from her when her belly started to swell the previous fall.

"I had already stopped having sex with Adam, of course—too busy, not feeling well. I ran through all the excuses. But I couldn't hold him off forever. So I manufactured a fight, and I used that as an excuse when Mom asked why I wanted to live with Dad. Her exact words: *Why the hell would you want to live with that deadbeat?* But as much as she hates Dad, she didn't put up much of an argument, because she hated being a mother more."

Her gaze grew distant. "But maybe I was wrong about that."

Leyna wondered if she was thinking of the paintings, one of which had survived in the back of the Ford Focus. It was funny, the things that remained after everything else was destroyed.

"Dad knew about the baby?"

"Dad?" Grace laughed harshly. "Of course not. I didn't spend a day in that apartment with him and his horrible wife. I told him I was running off with my boyfriend, and he agreed to cover for me if I convinced Mom to pay him child support. Two of his favorite things—lying to Mom and free money."

"So where were you?"

"I found a young woman who needed a roommate, and I lied about my age. She knew I was lying, but she could also see I was in trouble. Melanie isn't the kind of woman who's going to turn away a pregnant teenager." She nearly smiled. "You'll like her."

Grace took a sip of her coffee, and her nose wrinkled the way it had as a kid when her tea was too hot. Then she set the cup back on the table and folded her hands in front of her, the gesture surprisingly tentative. In her sister's eyes, Leyna saw her own loss reflected.

"But I couldn't pretend I was staying at Dad's forever, especially since Mom was paying him the child support," Grace said. "I always knew I'd come back." Her voice grew apologetic. "But not to stay. Melanie would've watched Ellie as long as I needed her to, but those weeks I was back at Ridgepoint without Ellie, I was bursting out of my skin with missing her. My breasts ached too, and it's not like I could ask Mom to buy me a pump. But the milk dried up quickly because I wasn't eating."

Even if Grace had lost the baby weight, her stomach must've been soft, but Leyna didn't remember it that way. That was the thing about a child's memory—it was unreliable, suggestible. How many of Leyna's memories hadn't been of the real Grace at all but of her Polaroids come to life?

"We found your Polaroids at Rocky's place."

She nodded. "He's a good guy. Gave me a ride that night and didn't ask questions." She smiled. "Though, really, I think part of that was to get back at Mom. I gave him those photos, but I kept that one of the four of us. I almost wish I hadn't. Then Ellie would never have—" She stopped, likely realizing that if Ellie hadn't found out about her family, Leyna and Grace wouldn't be sitting across from each other now.

Dominic in the hospital, Richard dead, Ellie traumatized—too large a price had been paid for their reunion.

"I worked at restaurants off the books for a while," Grace said. "I avoided social media. Started using a new name. But none of that would've worked without Melanie. The lease, utilities, even my first car... all in her name. I planned on leaving California once I'd saved some money. I was going to move across the country, do an even better job of getting lost." She smiled. "But then Melanie introduced me to her brother—Paul Byrd."

Grace tore off a piece of the pastry, considered it, tossed it back on the plate. "I assume you saw the press conference?" At Leyna's nod, Grace said, "That was Melanie behind Paul."

"At the time, I thought she was Ellie's mom."

Grace winced. Leyna felt a stab of satisfaction, then remorse at her own pettiness.

"You can't really stay a ghost if you're on camera at a press conference," Grace said.

"Paul knows?"

She nodded, then swiped her phone and pushed it across the table. On the screen, a pink-cheeked toddler nibbled on a sun hat, tufts of blond hair and eyes so blue there was no doubting whose he was.

"I have a son. Kyle. Two years old. Paul thinks he looks like me because of his eyes, but I know he looks like you."

Leyna reached out and tapped the screen before it could go dark.

"I almost called you when he was born," Grace said.

"Why didn't you?" The edge of accusation slipped in no matter how hard she'd tried to keep it out.

Grace sat up in her chair, as if bracing for what came next. "I'm sorry."

Leyna waited for her to say more. There was a lot for both of them to apologize for, and Leyna wanted to know what sins Grace counted on her list.

"Mostly for leaving you so early. I'd always planned on leaving the day I graduated."

Leyna nodded, remembering the calendar pages Grace left on her pillow, counting down the days to graduation.

"I had to go earlier, for Ellie, but later—it felt like too much time had passed, but really, I was a coward. Growing up a Clarke, I'd learned to avoid the difficult conversations. But I kept up with what you've been up to."

Leyna put it together. "Your son's name—Kyle. Are you Kyle's Mom from the message board?"

Grace shrugged. "It's where you spent most of your time, but I admit, it was heartbreaking."

Yeah, for me too. Leyna wished she'd known. She would've saved all those exchanges, meaningless at the time but priceless in hindsight.

Grace buried her attention in her paper cup before she looked up again. Her expression softened.

"I'm also sorry about asking Amaya to lie to you," she said. The corner of her mouth quirked up. "Ellie *can* be dramatic—she's going to study theater at NYU—and she did find you through the message boards." She paused, studying Leyna's face. Trying to gauge whether Leyna judged her?

"But she found the Polaroid of the four of us first. I asked Amaya to exaggerate so you wouldn't connect Ellie to me, but if you hadn't been so stubborn..." Her eyes sparked. "We would've lost her. So thank you for being stubborn."

Being a Clarke too, Leyna had learned her own lessons.

"You were right about Adam," Grace said. "We were all wonderful friends, the four of us. Your heart. Adam's wit. My—flair. And Dom—he was always the best of us."

Always. Leyna tried to picture him as he'd been before the fire. That grin that always set her off balance. But she couldn't erase the image of the bear trap snapping on his leg or the knowledge of how much he'd lost.

Grace finished her coffee, then crumpled the cup. She squeezed the wadded paper in her hand until her knuckles turned white. "But all that changed when it became something more between Adam and me. He changed too. He became more like his mom. Controlling. Jealous. I had to protect Ellie from him."

"Is that why you two fought that night?"

Grace shook her head. "He never knew about her." Relief in her voice. "That night, we were fighting about you. About what he'd done." Her gaze fell to the spot on Leyna's arm where her scar had once been visible; now it was covered by a patch of burned skin, pink and inflamed. "About what I'd done, too, by not stopping him. If Mom hadn't interrupted us that night—"

"She thinks you started that fight. That he was holding you down so you wouldn't hurt him or yourself."

She shrugged. "I'm okay with her believing that. And honestly? Maybe I would have hurt one of us that night. Like I said, it was a rough year."

"Did you kill him?" Leyna had already guessed the truth, but she wanted to see if Grace trusted her enough to confirm it.

Grace's face scrunched, another expression familiar enough to cause Leyna's chest to constrict.

"Why do you ask that?" *Deflect and confuse.* Their mom would've been proud.

"Because Mom's right. You're one of only two options that make sense."

Grace took another deep breath and met Leyna's eyes. "Just between us?"

"I'm done with secrets."

Her sister's lips thinned. "Then I can't tell you."

"Mom said his skull was crushed," Leyna said. "That's how he died. According to Mom, at least."

"I struck Adam with a rock when I found his body, but he was already dead," she said. "I figured if Mom saw that damage, she'd assume Adam fought with someone after leaving our house that night."

She didn't need to say the rest of it, maybe because she couldn't. Leyna's heart broke for her sister. How horrible that must have been—for Grace to feel like she had to do that to someone she'd once loved.

"So it was Mom who killed Adam," Leyna said. "With that strike to his head." She pictured it clearly: Adam stumbling toward the forest before succumbing to that injury. Grace had covered their mom's act, just as their mom believed she'd covered for Grace.

At Leyna's expression, Grace said, "You aren't surprised."

Leyna shrugged. "Adam was a big guy. Stronger than you or Mom." At the end, the only two suspects Leyna had been left with. "Someone crushed his skull, and he didn't try to defend himself?"

Grace tilted her head, assessing. "It was dark. He could've been surprised." She wasn't arguing, just seeing what Leyna would say.

Leyna shook her head. The forest was never quiet, especially at night. Leaves crunched. Sticks cracked. Stones shifted. It had been at least a thousand feet from the back door of the Clarke home to where their mom found Adam's body. Too great a distance for an attacker to disguise her approach.

"So if you knew, why—" Her eyes flashed as understanding dawned. "You were seeing if I'd tell you the truth."

A current passed between them, and Leyna wanted to reach for her sister's hand. But it was too soon, or too late. She couldn't decide which.

"So, I was thinking..." Leyna started, mouth dry. "Maybe you want to come with me to visit Dominic again when he wakes up?"

Grace's eyes shuttered, and Leyna could feel her preparing to say no. Beg off because she had to get back to her children and husband. To a better version of family that she'd built.

Grace crossed her arms. "I want to help prepare the house for Ellie's homecoming today," she said. But then she added, "Tomorrow?"

Leyna gave a quick nod, not trusting herself to speak.

Tomorrow. After sixteen years, Leyna had started to believe they might never have that.

"I almost forgot." Grace pulled a small square of paper from her purse. She slid the paper to Leyna. It was a page torn from a desk calendar. Written there: *One day since I've been back.* On it, she'd taped a Polaroid of herself and Leyna as kids, lying on the forest floor near a rock that looked like a hedgehog.

"That one never reached the wall," she said. "I kept it with me."

This time, Leyna's hand made it across the table. She rested it on top of Grace's.

"Thank you. And I'm sorry too. I shouldn't have locked you out that night."

"I would've left anyway, but yeah—that was a pretty crappy thing to do." But she laughed as she said it.

Leyna knew it would be a while before she trusted Grace again—if she ever could—but she had her sister and Ellie and a nephew who apparently looked like her. And Dominic.

"Ellie would love to see you once she's settled, and you can meet Paul and Kyle." At Leyna's hesitation, she added quickly, "I mean, if you aren't busy."

Leyna smiled. "I'd love that."

Grace returned the smile—as brilliant as Leyna remembered it.

Her sister, one day back.

Since the wildfire, Leyna had been thinking even more than usual about what it meant to be a Clarke. In a wildfire, small grasses burned first. They didn't generate much heat, but grasses ignited trees, and a small fire became a larger one. That was what it had been like with their family.

A hundred small things that grew into an inferno and became nearly unendurable.

Leyna thought of how quickly the weather had turned the night before. The wind died. Temperatures dropped. Humidity rose. And then there was the burn scar of a previous blaze, which stopped the McRae Fire on its most dangerous flank. A fire needed fuel. And eventually, even a burn scar would heal.

Maybe their scars could heal too, in time. For now, knowing their healing had begun was enough.

ACKNOWLEDGMENTS

Around two a.m. on October 9, 2017, my husband and I were awakened when our phones began buzzing on the headboard—texts from his brother and my friend. Both were variations of the same message: *Are you okay?* We looked outside at our Santa Rosa neighborhood to find orange skies and drifting ash. Our family had minutes to evacuate. We grabbed our cats and dog and whatever else seemed important in the moment. For me, a box of photos. For my husband, his basket of laundry. For my daughter, her favorite jeans and her older brother's football jersey.

We were lucky; though we were temporarily displaced, our home was spared. But others weren't as fortunate. At least twenty-two people died, and thousands of homes were lost.

It took six years before I felt ready to tell a story loosely inspired by my experience that day. In researching this book, I was fortunate to be able to draw on the experiences of others, including first responders and survivors of some of the state's worst natural disasters. Where I've strayed from fact should be attributed to artistic license. Thank you to everyone who helped me tell this story, including Jeremey Pierce, Thonie Hevron, Danny Hevron, Karen Liebowitz, Katie Kerrer, Josh Codding, and Chad Hermann.

Thank you, too, to the book community—the booksellers and libraries, the readers and reviewers who've given their time to these pages. I know what a precious gift those hours are, and I appreciate it more than you know.

Profound gratitude also goes to the generous authors who've commiserated, celebrated, advised, or endorsed; there are far too many to list here, but special thanks to Elle Marr, Samantha Downing, Margarita Montimore, Jan M. Flynn, Vanessa Lillie, Jaime Lynn Hendricks, Megan Collins, Anika Scott, Robyn Harding, and Dawn Ius. If I've inadvertently left anyone out, I apologize. Feel free to kill me off in your next book.

Thank you to my wonderful agent, Peter Steinberg!!! (Three exclamation points for you.) And thank you to the stellar United Talent Agency team, including Addison Duffy, Yona Levin, and Harry Sherer. I'm also deeply grateful to the dedicated team at Little, Brown and Mulholland: Judy Clain, Bruce Nichols, Craig Young, Terry Adams, Josh Kendall, Karen Landry, Gregg Kulick, Taylor Navis, Tracy Roe, and the #bestteamever super-trio—Anna Brill, Gabrielle Leporati, and Liv Ryan. (There should be capes, or at least really cool T-shirts.) It's an honor to work with every one of you.

A deeply heartfelt shout-out must go to my editor, Helen O'Hare, a truly brilliant and insightful collaborator and an incredible human being who I suspect has either cloned herself or has evolved to function without sleep. (If she's a clone, the publishing world is lucky to have more than one of her.) Thank you, Helen, for the countless hours you spent honing this story and for all you do to make me a better writer.

As always, I couldn't have done any of this without my family. To my parents, thank you for your ceaseless support. Jacob and Maya, you're my joy and the inspiration for my fiercest, kindest characters. And, finally, Alex—you're forever my rock. There's no one I would rather have beside me on this journey.

ABOUT THE AUTHOR

Heather Chavez is a graduate of the University of California, Berkeley, English literature program and has worked as a newspaper reporter, editor, and contributor to mystery and television blogs. She lives with her family in Santa Rosa, California. She's the author of the thrillers *Before She Finds Me, No Bad Deed,* and *Blood Will Tell.*